I0639038

G. Fraipont

The Masterpieces of Charles=Paul de Kock *NOW FOR THE FIRST TIME COMPLETELY TRANSLATED INTO ENGLISH* Paul and His Dog *BY GEORGE BURNHAM IVES*

WITH ONE WATER-COLOR FACSIMILE AND FIVE PHOTOGRAVURES AFTER PAINTINGS BY LUISA CHATROUSSE AND GUSTAVE FRAIPONT

IN TWO VOLUMES
VOL. I

Philadelphia
PRINTED FOR SUBSCRIBERS ONLY BY GEORGE BARRIE & SONS

PAUL AND HIS DOG

I

A MASQUERADE AT THE OPÉRA

What a crowd! how eager all these people are to make their way into the ball-room! they begin to push and elbow one another even in the street, in front of the entrance to the theatre; the carriages move too slowly to suit the persons inside or the police officers whose duty it is to keep all vehicles in motion.

See those maskers; those dominos have hardly time to alight from their coupé, for the coachman must move on instantly to make room for the confrère behind him; many persons even alight before they are in front of the theatre, hoping to reach their destination more quickly.

It is evident therefore that they must be afraid of not finding room, of not being able to crowd their way into that sanctuary of pleasure, of folly, rather; and yet one can always get in, at any hour. Though the hall be overflowing with people, though the foyer be full to suffocation, though it be impossible to move in the corridor,—

it makes no difference: one can always find a way to slip into the vast throng.

People push you, bump against you, tread on your feet, force you to go to the right when you want to go to the left. You do not find the person you are seeking, you are separated from your companion; if you have arranged yourself with great care and elegance, in a few minutes your clothes are rumpled, torn, stained.— But what does it matter! you are at the Opéra masquerade.

You are speedily bewildered by the noise made by the multitude that surrounds you; the heat becomes stifling; add to this the odor of the bouquets and of the perfumery used by the ladies, and lastly the strains of the enormous orchestra playing galops, waltzes, polkas, mazurkas, with a swing, a precision, a vigor which makes your legs twitch; and do not be surprised if you begin to feel like a different man, if your brain whirls, if your heart beats more rapidly, if you suddenly become inclined to play pranks, to enjoy yourself—no matter how.

But you do not intend to have come to the Opéra ball for nothing. You aspire to an intrigue, a conquest, an unexpected meeting. You seek pleasure, no matter under what form it presents itself, and you often pass several hours in the quest, or rather, in quest of the unknown.

Ah! it is so provoking when a domino with a graceful figure, a tiny hand and a well-arched foot takes your arm, saying:

" I know you! "

I know you! those three words, uttered by an unfamiliar voice, but by a woman who takes your arm, clings to it familiarly, leans toward you and looks into your eyes in a very alluring way—those three words disturb you, excite you, toss you at once into the field of conjecture. No matter how many times you may hear them during the night, they always produce their effect, and especially, as I said just now, if the masker who says them to you has a pretty figure, a pretty hand, pretty eyes— all of which make one desire or hope for a charming face.

First of all, you try to identify the person who speaks to you ; you examine her eyes, the lower part of her chin, which the mask imperfectly conceals ; you pass in review the feet, the arms, the figure, the hair. You listen attentively to the tone of the voice, which is never perfectly disguised to a very sharp ear.

But when all these have failed to give you any information ; when you abandon the idea of recognizing your companion, then you proceed to imagine a woman to match your ideal. Behind the mask that covers her face, you place lovely, intellectual features of the sort that you most affect ; your imagination takes fire—you have met the woman of your dreams, you are beginning to fall in love ; a few seconds more, and you will have a full-fledged passion on your hands. But no ; it will not go so far as that. You will restrain yourself, for there is always a reverse side to the medallion ; and that reverse side the sirens themselves are blundering enough to show to you. You have not had your lady on your arm ten minutes, when she says to you:

"Aren't you going to ask me to take something?"

Ah! what a tumble your imagination takes at that! how suddenly your dreams of a woman of fashion, distinguished, mysterious, passionate, are transformed into humble flower-makers, corset-makers, waistcoat-makers, and sometimes something even humbler!

"Aren't you going to ask me to take something?"— can it be that a woman of breeding, a woman of the *beau monde,* or even of the *beau demi-monde,* would ask that question?

No, that has the savor of a grisette, or a *fillette,* a league away! I am aware that Carnival has its license, and that, with the face masked, one may venture to say things that one would not say with the face exposed. But it is none the less certain that that unlucky phrase is almost equivalent to the unmasking of your conquest, and brings you down at once from the fertile land of illusions to the much more arid regions of reality. And then, as if they instantly divined the wishes of your fair companion, the dealers in bonbons and oranges always arrive at the moment the question is asked. You are too gallant to refuse, moreover, you probably know that, if you should refuse, your conquest would at once drop your arm, saying:

"Bah! what a skinflint! Thanks! I've had enough of your acquaintance; it ain't worth the cost of a stick of sugar candy!"

Plume yourself then, if you can, upon having been that damsel's escort, upon having felt her arm lean upon yours and her hand respond to the pressure of your hand; alas! there is no excuse for pride.

But, you will tell me, there are exceptions; ladies of the best society, pretty bourgeoises, even women of honorable name, indulge in the pleasure of the masquerade; there is no danger of their unmasking, you may be sure! on the contrary, they disguise themselves with the greatest care, in such wise as to turn aside all suspicions and to deceive everybody who knows them. But those things which they never succeed in concealing are their elegant manners, their distinguished bearing, their refined language.

Yes, there are, doubtless, some of those ladies at the Opéra; they have longed to satisfy their curiosity by a glimpse of one of these orgies.

Sometimes a more powerful motive leads them thither; they desire to surprise a disloyal lover, to confound him, to unmask his treachery; or,—and this is much more agreeable—they have consented to come secretly into this crowd, because they know that they will meet here someone whom it is impossible for them to see elsewhere; and perhaps, under cover of the mask, they will consent to let fall from their lips a sweet confession which you would never have obtained otherwise.

It is true that there are these exceptions, and that you have a chance of falling in with one of these ladies. Indeed, it would distress me to rob you of the many

illusions in which the charm of a masquerade consists;
but I must remind you that these *comme il faut* ladies
are not at the ball to enter into an intrigue; it is always
an intrigue already begun that brings them there. And
then, what probability is there that one of them will
come to you, take your arm, and say: " I know you!"
when she does not know you and has not come to the
ball on your account? Are you not convinced now that
you will not intrigue with one of these ladies?

No, you are not, because in your heart you consider
yourself a sufficiently attractive youth to take the eye
of a nobly-born dame, who may not have come on your
account, but who would be very glad to make your acquaintance. That is your idea; it is very pleasant to
you to believe that! Very well, believe it! If it makes
you happy, you are wise. Cradle yourself in the sweetest
illusions, let your imagination run riot, though you have
nothing to show for your stick of candy.

On a certain night, in the year eighteen hundred and
fifty-six—it was Mi-Carême, and consequently the last
day of license permitted after the Carnival. It was therefore the last Opéra masquerade, and so it was magnificent in respect to numbers, uproar and eccentric costumes. There were, as always, numbers of pretty little
women dressed as *débardeurs,** that is to say, in high-

* The *Débardeurs* formerly constituted one of the Parisian trade
guilds. Their occupation was the handling and discharging of the
lumber rafts that were floated down to Paris. Their dress was a dis-
tinctive one, persistently adhered to, and became a favorite one with
masqueraders.

necked shirts, velvet or satin breeches with broad bands of brilliant colors, sash tied behind, and on their heads a sort of foraging-cap covered with flowers and worn over the ear in the true swaggering style.

There were Pierrots of all colors and sizes, a few ladies dressed à la Pompadour, many gypsies, and some of those young men who are determined to attract notice at any cost, and for that purpose adopt a costume to which it is difficult to give a name. One, dressed in knee-breeches of spangled satin, wore high postilion's boots and a Turkish jacket; on his back he had a quiver, on his head a saucepan by way of helmet, and fastened to the saucepan, a plume of enormous size. This plume, which waved in the air three feet above the crowd, could be seen from one end of the hall to the other. It must have been fatiguing to have that immense thing on one's head; but what do not people do at a masquerade, to attract attention?

Another represented a savage or a bear, it was hard to tell which. He had made himself a sort of crown with those little brooms which are sold for three sous. He carried an umbrella in one hand and a fan in the other. The more extravagant one's costume, the more trouble one takes to be seen by the multitude.

But the orchestra gave the signal for a quadrille. As a general rule, all those maskers who are costumed in character dance, for they aim to display as much extravagance in their dancing as in their costumes. Unluckily for them, there are officials whose duty it is to

moderate their enthusiasm and to call them to order
when they put too much *laissez-aller* into their steps.
In heaven's name, what would they do if they were not
watched!

The quadrille almost always ends in a general galop.
Thereupon everyone joins in and is whirled away in the
vortex. The innumerable sets are confounded in a resist-
less torrent of gallopers which roars around the ball-
room, in five, six, sometimes seven rows at once; all
galloping and jumping and running! Woe to the unlucky wight who stumbles! the torrent stops only with
the music, and he would inevitably be trampled under the
feet of the dancers.

But do not be alarmed, nobody falls; they all are sure-
footed and agile performers; and those pretty little
female *débardeurs,* who seemed to you but now so slender
and delicate, are often the most intrepid of all in that
mad galop in which one must not pause.

Toward the end, the orchestra quickens the time; then
it ceases to be a dance; it is a genuine delirium, a frenzy;
shouts and singing blend with the music, and the whirl-
ing mass passes before you like a railroad train. At
that moment, the sight is truly miraculous, truly interesting to watch; and we know many people who go to the
Opéra ball solely to sit in a box and watch the galop at
their ease. In truth, I doubt whether anything similar
can be seen elsewhere.

Two dominos had just entered one of the proscenium
boxes. The first, pearl-gray, trimmed with rich lace,

was worn by a tall, slender woman whose well-developed figure it outlined sharply. Despite her disguise, one could divine that the costume covered a person well accustomed to the noisy demonstrations of the maskers and to the eccentricities of the dancers. There was something bold and determined in her manner, and, as she watched the galop which was then at its height, the gray domino seemed neither surprised nor fascinated; she gazed at that rushing torrent, not like a person enjoying an entertaining spectacle, but like a person at the theatre who pays no attention to the play that is in progress, but is solely occupied in looking for someone among the audience.

The second domino was black; it was worn by a person of medium height and decent demeanor, in whose appearance there was nothing to attract attention. She, however, seemed to take much pleasure in watching the galop, and from time to time uttered exclamations eloquent of the surprise which that frenzied dance caused her.

The two ladies had seated themselves at the front of the box, where, in all probability, their seats had been engaged. The gray domino, whose eyes were fastened on the dancing throng, was certainly looking for someone; the black domino, who was looking for no one, cried from time to time:

"Oh! look there, my dear! how they push one another! See! that tall Pierrot has taken his partner in his arms and away he dances with her! Mon Dieu!

suppose he should fall! And see that Marquise Pompadour with her wig half off; she's going to lose·her wig! look, Thélénie!"

"Yes, yes, I see; but I beg you, my dear Héloïse, not to make so many exclamations; anyone would think you had never seen anything."

"But I haven't ever seen the Opéra ball. I've been to Valentino, Sainte-Cécile, and the Salle Barthélemy."

"Enough, enough! for heaven's sake, keep quiet, and above all things, remember not to call me by name when you speak to me. You must see that it isn't worth while for me to disguise myself carefully if you are going to shout my name in the ears of everybody who passes."

"I only mentioned your given name."

"And that's just the one that people know best; and as it isn't so common as yours, anybody would know it was I."

"That's so; your name's a very pretty one—like a name in a novel; did your parents give it to you, or did you take it?"

The gray domino did not think it best to answer this question except by a slight shrug, which clearly signified: "Mon Dieu! how stupid you are!"

But the black domino, who perhaps did not understand pantomime, went on talking none the less.

"For my part, I'd rather be named Thélénie than Héloïse: Héloïse is very common, and then it seems there's some story about a Héloïse and her lover, a

Monsieur Abelard. I don't know it myself, it must be an old story, for I've never read it in the papers. But it seems that it's laughable, for the men who make love to me say: ' O lovely Héloïse, I'd like to be your lover, but not your Abelard! '—I always pretend to understand, for I don't want to seem ignorant; I wouldn't dare ask them to tell me about the adventures of those two, so I just laugh and say: ' Tell me, why don't you want to be my Abelard? you're very hard to suit! ' Then they laugh harder than ever.—I say, Thélénie, you know such a lot of things, you've had an education—tell me that story, won't you? "

Tall Thélénie, for we know now the pearl-gray domino's name, thanks to her companion's prattle, suddenly placed her hand on the black domino's and said:

" Hush! I think I see him—that young man dressed as a postilion, at the left, with a dairymaid on his arm; look, I say! "

" That postilion—Monsieur Edmond! oh, no! his nose is much longer."

" No, no, you are right; it isn't he! "

" Is Monsieur Edmond to be disguised as a postilion? "

" How do you suppose I know how he's disguised, or if he is disguised? I am not even certain that he's at the ball; and yet I have a shrewd idea that he'll come; it's the last masquerade, and he's so fond of sport."

" Bless me! it's natural at his age! how old is he? "

" Oh! how you pester me with your continued questioning, Héloïse! "

"Mon Dieu! how touchy you are to-night! Is it my fault, I should like to know, that you've quarrelled with your lover, that he plays tricks on you! When that happens to me, I console myself very quickly; I take another, and very often that brings back the old one, who is angry because I do as he does, and becomes much more in love than before! But you must know that method—all women employ it and it invariably succeeds."

"Yes, I know it, and I used to make use of it; but now—I can't act like that with Edmond."

"It seems that you are really caught, my dear! An experienced woman like you! I'm amazed!"

"You're amazed at everything to-night!"

"That proves that I am not *blasé,* and that's something."

"Do you say that to insult me?"

"Hoity-toity! now I'm insulting her! On my word, you're in a murderous mood! If I had known, I wouldn't have come to the ball with you. To be sure, you paid for my domino; but I could have found someone else to pay me that attention. I came to the ball for fun, not to quarrel."

"Come, come, Héloïse, don't lose your temper. I am in an ugly mood to-night, that's true; my nerves are all on edge, for I don't know where he is, the traitor, and I want to know. I still love him; I love him; and remember, he is the first man who ever introduced me to that sentiment."

"Indeed? If you said that to him, I should believe it was humbug, as we always say to our last lover: 'Ah! my dear! you are the first man who ever taught me what love is!' but you've no reason for lying to me; I don't dare to say again that you astonish me; you might tell me again that I am astonished too much."

"My dear Héloïse, my life has been decidedly agitated, I admit; I don't set myself up to you as a pattern of virtue!"

"You are quite right, for I shouldn't believe you."

"I will even tell you honestly how old I am,—a thing that women do not often admit to each other. I am thirty-two; as you see, I should have had some experience."

"Thirty-two! Well, without flattery, you may lie fearlessly on that subject, for no one would think you more than twenty-eight at most."

"At thirty-two, with my face and figure, I thought that I might still fascinate a young man of twenty-six."

"That you might! I should say so! Why not, I should like to know? Is a woman old at thirty-two? For my part, I hope to make conquests at forty-five; but I have plenty of time before me, thank God! I am in my twenty-third year."

"I have had more than one liaison, it is true, but I tell you again, Edmond is the first man I ever loved— with love; and when a woman feels that sentiment so late in life—why, it's very violent, so violent that it makes her capable of anything!"

"Oh! mon Dieu! you frighten me, my dear! But don't get excited; it will pass away."

"I wish it might, but I have no hope of it."

"If he loved you, and you were sure of it, in a little while you would cease to love him; it has always worked that way with me."

"Hush! hush! here comes someone I know; above all, don't turn."

The door of the box was open, and a gentleman had entered. He was a man of about forty, but still very handsome; tall, with a fine figure, regular features, a distinguished face, and a piercing, ironical glance; in his brown eyes, which were rather too heavily shadowed by his lashes, there was almost always a mocking look, which, however, was quite in accord with his always mocking speech.

An extremely yellow and bilious complexion detracted somewhat from the advantages which this gentleman would naturally have owed to his physique; but there are ladies who prefer yellow skins to white ones, and whose preference does not stop short of the mulatto.

This personage, as he entered the box, toyed with a beautiful gold-rimmed eyeglass, which was suspended about his neck by a light hair chain. He remained on his feet for some time, closely watching the pearl-gray domino. But, since his arrival, the two ladies at the front of the box pretended to be gazing with interest at the ball, where the galop had just come to an end; and neither of them turned.

Annoyed by the persistence with which the two dominos showed him only their backs, the newcomer stepped over a bench and seated himself behind them. Then he tapped the gray domino's shoulder lightly and said to her in an undertone:

" My fair friend, it's of no use for you to persist in not turning, and to force your companion to follow suit, which seems to be very distasteful to her; it doesn't prevent my recognizing you. I watched you just now from below; your black eyes shone like carbuncles; those eyes betray you, my love; when you don't wish to be recognized, assume the costume of Fortune, and wear a bandage over them."

" I don't know what you want with me," said Mademoiselle Héloïse's companion, carefully disguising her voice; " my eyes shine, you say? so much the better; I am delighted. I have no reason to hide them. If I don't turn round, you may be sure that it's not on account of you, whom I don't know, and whom I have no desire to know! "

" Ah! my dear Thélénie! If I hadn't recognized you already, your last words would have left me in no doubt as to your identity! A person may disguise her face and figure, or change her voice,—that's all very well; but she must remember also to change her mental habit and her mode of speech. You have always had a considerable leaning toward impertinence; and you yielded to it again just now when you said that you had no desire to know me. Tell me, am I not right? Take my word for it,

and profit by this advice—if you want to puzzle anybody and to avoid being identified, be good-natured,
indulgent, and don't speak unkindly of anyone; then I
promise you that people won't recognize you."

The tall Thélénie with difficulty repressed an angry
exclamation; however, she forced herself to laugh as she
replied:

"Ha! ha! ha! that is all very pretty! Well, why
aren't you disguised as a magician, since you pretend to
be able to tell everyone so exactly what sort of person
she is?"

"Oh! I don't disguise myself any more; my time
for that has passed."

"True; you are too old for that."

"There are many older than I who continue to disguise themselves. It is not age that prevents a man
from making a fool of himself, it's the degree of pleasure he finds in doing it. See, look at that tall Polichinelle just passing you, with two Swiss women on his
arms; that is old Simoulin, the lorettes' banker. He is
more than fifty years old, but that doesn't prevent him
from disguising himself still; he must have intrigues,
love-affairs, mistresses; he imagines that he still makes
conquests—an old idiot who doesn't understand yet that
his money is the only thing that attracts the women. He
has done many foolish things for them; he has already
consumed three-fourths of his fortune, and the rest will
probably go the same way. Then all these beauties, for
whom he will have ruined himself, will turn their backs

on him and order their maids to shut the door in his face if he has the audacity to call on his former mistresses. —Isn't that true? But I am telling you nothing new. You know it all better than I do, for you have been intimately acquainted with that beggarly Polichinelle.— And that tall young man yonder, dressed to represent Gille.* His costume is well chosen, at all events. Poor fellow! what a haggard face, what hollow cheeks, what a dull, brutish expression! Ah! he was once a good-looking fellow. He's a Hungarian; why in the deuce did he leave his country with such a well-filled wallet? He wanted to know Paris, to enjoy himself here! I don't know if he has enjoyed himself very much—I trust so. But to run through a hundred and fifty thousand francs in six months—that is rather a rapid pace; nothing less than a princely fortune will stand that sort of thing. Now this young Hungarian is obliged to borrow until his worthy father chooses to send him some money. But the father keeps his pockets buttoned; he thinks that his son has been rather too magnificent. You know this young foreigner also, my dear—know him very well, in fact. But it isn't he whom you are looking for in this throng; it's little Edmond Didier—your latest passion! I say your latest—I think so, but I wouldn't swear to it. You have had so many! Have you made a memorandum of them all, with a view to writing your memoirs some day? If you have not, you are making a

---

* The name of the conventional simpleton in the old plays given by strolling players at country fairs and markets.

mistake, for I assure you they would have a good sale. I will engage a copy in advance."

The gray domino made no reply, but one could see from her nervous movements that she could hardly restrain her wrath. The black domino, who was tired of keeping silent, thought that she was doing an excellent thing in suddenly observing to the gentleman who was talking to her friend:

"Mon Dieu! my dear man, you must see that you bore us to death. For heaven's sake, leave us in peace! We didn't come to the Opéra to listen to your *ragots*— silly backbiting."

The gentleman laughed heartily.

"Ha! ha! *ragots!* not a very refined expression! My little Héloïse, your friend ought to give you lessons in refined speech, otherwise you might compromise her; and she didn't bring you here for that."

"I say! do you know me, too?"

"Bah! you little bungler! you give yourself away at once; really you are not shrewd enough to accompany Thélénie; but you are not pretty, that is why she gives you the preference!"

"I am not pretty! well, upon my word! this long yellow-face is very polite!"

"Ha! ha! ha! I see, mesdames, that you are really going to be angry; I will leave you."

"That will give us great pleasure."

"I forgive Héloïse her ill-humor; she simply obeys the orders that are given her. But I am very sorry that Madame de Sainte-Suzanne does not act differently. When one has been on very intimate terms with a person, and when one is aware that that person knows exactly what one's worth is, one should always be affable with that person; it is not clever to adopt a different course. Good-evening, mesdames. My dear Thélénie, if I see young Edmond, I shall not fail to tell him that you are looking for him, and to describe your costume, so that he may recognize you."

Thélénie turned suddenly, and seizing the gentleman's arm as he was about to leave the box, said to him, no longer seeking to disguise her voice:

"Oh! don't do that, Beauregard; I beg you not to do that; for I don't want Edmond to know that I am here."

"Well, well! so you know me now! Ha! ha! this is amusing; I was beginning to think I had made a mistake myself."

"Come, Beauregard, don't be so spiteful! don't betray me! What motive can you have for injuring me? Have I ever done anything to you?"

"You? oh! you certainly have done no more to me than to other men. And yet—there is a certain matter —But let us not talk of that here; this place would be ill chosen for a serious conversation. I will see you again, and then, I hope, you will answer my questions frankly. I will leave you now, and if I see young Edmond, I will tell him nothing."

"Do you promise?"

"Do you want me to swear?"

"No, that is not necessary."

"You are right; between ourselves, you and I know what to think of oaths."

And the gentleman, with a very slight inclination of the head, left the box in which the two dominos were.

II

EDMOND AND FRELUCHON

In a pleasant little bachelor apartment, on the fourth floor, but in a house occupied by most excellent tenants, on Rue de Provence, a young man hardly twenty-six years of age was impatiently pacing the floor of a bedroom which was used also as a salon. He glanced constantly at a small clock on the mantel, and muttered:

"Almost ten o'clock, and Freluchon doesn't come! Does he expect me to pass my whole evening waiting for him? Oh! these people who are never on time ought to be fined! I'll give him five minutes more, and then, if he hasn't come, so much the worse for him—I shall go! After all, he won't have any difficulty in finding me."

The young man who said all this to himself was named Edmond Didier. I have told you his age; I will add that he was a very comely fellow, well-built, above middle height; that he had blue eyes shaped a little like

those of the Chinese, but with a sweet and tender expression to which the young man owed many conquests.
His nose was well-shaped, although it was not aquiline—
there are some very pretty noses which are not aquiline;
his mouth was intellectual, his teeth suited to the mouth,
his forehead broad and open, his chestnut hair very fine
and silky, and always arranged simply and without that
horrible parting which imparts to the heads of the most
dandified men the aspect of those wax models which you
see in hair-dressers' windows.

Young Edmond, as you will see, was a very good-
looking fellow, especially if we add that all these features
combined to form a whole in which there was much
character; for you might bring together a pair of large
eyes, a pretty mouth, a Greek nose, and handsome hair,
and therewith form a whole which would have no expression at all. We often observe this in women, and
say as we look at them: "There's a beautiful statue!"

Do not you consider that that which has animation is
to be preferred, even though it be less beautiful?

Young Edmond, whose parents had retired to the
provinces with a moderate fortune, had received from
his uncle some sixty thousand francs, which he had invested in a business house where he was supposed to
work, but where he did not work, because he had none
too much time to amuse himself, and because he hoped
that the thirty-six hundred francs which he received as
interest on his investment would suffice for his amusements.

Edmond was good-natured and clever; nature had
endowed him with a delightful voice, because of which
he was very popular in salons. He sang ballads with
almost as much soul and taste as poor Achard, who sang
so beautifully and who required so little urging; and
who died so prematurely, when he was still in the heyday
of his talent, leaving behind him so much love, so many
friendships, and such deep and lasting regret!

Edmond Didier had a warm heart and rather an un-
reliable head; he was easily moved and generous, but
forgetful, changeable and careless. He lost his temper
quickly and recovered it as quickly; he was naturally
light-hearted, but had fits of melancholy when he dreamed
of a *Sleeping Beauty in the Wood,* whom he would have
liked to awaken.

Every day he resolved to turn his mind to something,
to work, to try to become a capable man, a man qualified
to fill an important post or to manage a business house;
but the current of pleasure whirled him along; he always
had some new song which an attractive woman had
begged him to sing at her next reception; and how can
one refuse a woman who tells you that it is her greatest
joy to hear you sing? So that he had to study the
song instead of going to the merchant who had his
funds, to study bookkeeping.

Ah! if the ladies knew how seriously they interfere
with a young man's duties! especially with those of a
young man who asks nothing better than to have them
interfered with!

Now you know young Edmond Didier, who, after trying to be content with the income of his sixty thousand
francs, had begun to encroach upon his principal.

At last the bell rang and Edmond hastened to open
his door. Another young man, very short and very
slender, with a long, peaked face, a long, pointed nose,
shrewd eyes, something of the marten in his face and
much *abandon* in his bearing, entered the room, with his
hands in his pockets, crying:

" Sapristi! how cold it is! "

The newcomer's name was Freluchon; he had inherited money from his mother and from his uncle, and
his pockets were always full. He spent it freely, but he
did not throw it out of the window; he devoted much
time to pleasure, but he occasionally took a turn in business or speculated a little on the Bourse. He was generally very fortunate in what he undertook, and often
succeeded in making more than he spent. He was three
years older than Didier, whose intimate friend he was.

He was a good fellow, that is to say, he was always
ready to do what anyone wanted him to do, so long as
it was not a bore to him. Beneath a frail and sickly appearance, he was blessed with the strength of a Hercules,
and could kill an ox with a blow of his fist. Men of
that type as a general rule never seek a quarrel with
anybody.

" Here you are at last! " cried Edmond as his friend
entered. " It's very lucky. I was just going away.
You're a full half-hour behindhand."

"First of all, have you a fire? On my word of honor, I am frozen!"

"Oh! we can warm ourselves at the young ladies' room, as they're waiting for us; it's not worth while to settle down here."

"But I say it is; the order of the day and the line of march are changed.—Ah! good! there is a fire; with a little blowing and another stick, it will go all right."

"What is there new? Why aren't we going to Henriette's, where Amélia was to join us? That was all arranged this morning."

"Yes, but since this morning, many things have happened.—Where in the devil do you keep your bellows?"

"There, in that corner.—Come, Freluchon, I should be very glad to know what all this means."

"Just a moment,—when the fire's well kindled; good! now it's blazing up. A fine invention is fire; it must have been the sun that suggested the idea. The Peruvians worship the sun, and I believe I am descended from them. I too worship the sun—especially in winter; in summer I would gladly do without it."

"When you've finished, perhaps you'll answer me."

"How impatient he is! Let us go softly—*piano,* as the Italians say.—My dear fellow, this is what has happened: we went much too fast with those young women —so-called flower-makers! We made love to them, they listened to us; they are very pretty. Now, that is all very well, but we undertook to dazzle them by our generosity—there's the foolish blunder! Not content with

treating them to superfine dinners, set off with iced
wines which they poured down like Prussians, we began
at once to give them presents. You gave your Amélia
a beautiful opera glass which you used at the theatre,
and I handed over a dainty gold-rimmed eyeglass which
I had lent to Henriette, who assured me that it was perfectly adapted to her sight. When those damsels saw
that they had only to wish in order to obtain, they said
to themselves: ' We must wish for something else.'—
They took us for great nobles or for gulls—perhaps for
both—and determined to hold us to ransom."

" You always think that somebody is trying to cheat
you. Why think that of those young flower-makers,
who seem to be fond of work and to lead orderly lives?
I have been to Amélia's only three times, but I have
always found them at work making flowers."

" So have I; but I have noticed that it was always
the same flower that was under way. It seems that it's
a difficult one to make! "

" They don't seem to be hard up; they have some very
pretty mahogany furniture, which they pay for by pleasure."

" Yes; as for that, I have never doubted it. Indeed,
Henriette told me, in the beginning of our intimacy, when
I complimented her on her lodgings, that she had paid
for it all by her work and by the way she passed her
nights; but as they lie constantly, they forget one day
what they told you the day before. Here's a proof of it
—look."

"What is this letter?"

"A billet-doux that I received from Henriette this morning; she doesn't write badly, I must do her that justice; and not a mistake in spelling! That's very nice for a flower-maker, but it's all the more dangerous. Take it and read it."

Edmond took the letter that his friend handed him and read as follows:

"My dear Freluchon:

"A terrible catastrophe has befallen me; my furniture, which I thought was paid for, is not. The upholsterer is going to compel me to leave my apartment instantly, if I do not pay four hundred francs on account. Be kind enough to lend me that amount, which I will pay you very soon. Otherwise you will not find me at my rooms, as I shall be turned out, and I have no idea where Amélia and I will go. You may hand the money to the woman who brings this letter; but be sure to seal it.

"Your loving and faithful friend,

"HENRIETTE."

"Well! what do you say to that?"

"Why! I say—but what reply did you make? did you send the money?"

"I'm not so foolish, I tell you! In the first place, this letter is altogether too much! What does she mean by 'her furniture, that she thought was paid for, but is not?' And this upholsterer who will have her turned out of her apartments if she doesn't pay him? An upholsterer may take back his furniture, but he doesn't turn you into the street by that. The trick was too plain; and in order to write such stuff to a man, one must take him for a goose. As I don't care to be likened to that bird, I instantly informed the messenger that I was terribly distressed, that I was in despair, but that I was unable to hand her anything for Mademoiselle Henriette, and she went away with that answer.—*Bigre!* four hundred francs at one slap, for a flower-maker—that's too magnificent! You aim too high, my love!"

" Well! what next? "

" Why, there is no next."

" Didn't Henriette send to you again? "

" Not at all! she made the best of it, like a brave heart. She said to herself: ' There's a young buck who isn't such an ass as I thought.'—And I am sure that I have gained greatly in her esteem; that pleases me."

" I can see nothing in all this to interfere with our going now to call for the young ladies and taking them to the Opéra ball, as we agreed."

" Ah! you can't, eh? Well, when I went out for a stroll before dinner, I thought I would find out if the catastrophe had had any results, and I walked as far as Rue de Saintonge, where our turtle-doves had their perch. I asked the concierge: ' Is Mademoiselle Henriette in? '—Thereupon that counterfeit Swiss looked at me with rather a bantering expression, and replied:

" ' No, monsieur, those young women have gone away.'

" ' Will they return soon? '

" ' Return! oh! I fancy they won't return here; they carried off their belongings very cunningly in little bundles, and then they skipped. The landlord came and made a row with me about it, and said that I didn't ought to let anything go out of the house. But what can you expect? the women nowadays wear skirts puffed out like balloons, so, you see, those girls could have stuffed their whole wardrobe underneath. Ah! those skirts are very deceitful; they'll be the cause of many *poufs.' * *

" ' But,' I said to the man, ' what is the landlord afraid of? Those young women had some very nice furniture, and I don't suppose they put their mattresses and their wardrobes with glass doors under their skirts, did they? And this isn't a furnished lodging-house; they had their own furniture, didn't they? '

" ' That is to say, they had their own furniture to pay for; the upholsterer wanted to carry it away this morning; but not much—the landlord must be paid first and they owed him for three quarters. For all that, it's mighty unpleasant; it always ends in a row! When the upholsterer found that he couldn't carry away his furniture, he was crazy. " You ought not to have let those women go! " he said; " I'd have had them put in prison." And so on and so forth. Have I any right to keep tenants from going out, I'd like to know? '

---

* *Faire des poufs* is said of a person who runs into debt, knowing that he will be unable to pay, then suddenly decamps.

" ' No, certainly you haven't any such right; a concierge's authority doesn't go so far as that; perhaps it may come, though, I shouldn't be surprised! They do some pretty rough things already, but they haven't got to the point of imprisoning tenants.'

" ' Never mind; when we let rooms to two girls together again, it will be hotter than it is now!'

" ' Do you think there's less danger when they are alone?'

" ' Certainly, one can keep a closer watch on them then; but when there's two of 'em, why, they do nothing else besides going back and forth before one's eyes, and it's impossible to know who goes in and out—so one gets totally bewildered.'

" That, my dear fellow, is the conversation I had with the concierge of those damsels, who strike me as being decidedly a bad lot. You see that it's no use for us to go to their last lodgings to look for them."

" I see that the letter wasn't so far from the truth, when it said that they would be turned out if they did not pay."

" They succeeded in escaping unaided. I asked how much the upholsterer claimed: it was eight or nine hundred francs, I believe; but if I had turned in four hundred francs, do you imagine for a moment that they would have given it to their creditor? Ah! how little you know of that breed! They would have vanished with my money, that's all!"

" Do you think so?"

"In other words, I am sure of it. 'Brought up in
the harem, I know all its devious ways.' These girls
pass their lives making *poufs;* then they make a trip to
England, to try to make the conquest of some *lord;* and
when they don't succeed in that, they are obliged to sell
everything, even to their chemises, to pay for their return trip to Paris. I tell you that I know the whole business, step by step."

"It's a pity! I regret Amélia, for she was very
pretty!"

"There are others! Paris swarms with pretty women.
Henriette was very attractive, too; pink and white,
Watteau style."

"I am terribly annoyed."

"But you're not unprovided for; you must fall back
on your beautiful brunette, whom I christened the Andalusian—your Madame de Sainte-Suzanne, a woman
almost *comme il faut;* at all events, she is pleased now
to affect the manners of one."

"I told you that I had broken with that lady; she
insisted on having me always at her side, and questioned
me about every step I took; I had to render her an
account of my most trivial acts, and it was downright
slavery! A little more and she would have confined me
to my room. You can understand that that sort of thing
didn't suit me!"

"Bless me! not unless you're an absolute idiot. Still,
there are men stupid enough to allow their mistresses to
lead them by the nose. There's Dutaillis, for example;

he can't take a step for fear of a row! When he goes out, it's: 'Where are you going?' When he comes in: 'Where have you been? what makes you so red? why are you so pale? why is your collar so rumpled? where did you pick up all that mud?'—There's no end to it. And the jackass takes a world of pains to prove that he's no redder than usual, and that his collar rumpled of itself because it wasn't well starched! And the prettiest part of it all is that he'll end by marrying his Virginette! What a grovelling future I foresee for the poor wretch! —Your chimney is in bad order, it doesn't draw."

"I don't know whether Madame de Sainte-Suzanne flattered herself that I would marry her; I don't think she went so far as that; but she was atrociously jealous."

"Did she carry a dagger in her garter?"

"No, but she had several in her room, and very beautiful ones, encrusted with jewels."

"They were gifts."

"However, I must do her justice: people told me she was a very covetous woman and had ruined several of her adorers; but when I attempted to give her rather a handsome present, she refused it; she would accept, or rather take, nothing from me except a big lock of hair."

"The devil! that's much more dangerous; she'll probably make some kind of a spell with your hair, some charm that will force you to love her. For my part, I never give away any hair; I sell it, especially as I shall be bald very early in life. Ah! then I'll make them pay dear for it."

"Thélénie has beautiful black hair, very long and thick."

"Ah! that makes a lovely ornament for a woman! When I have a mistress with handsome hair, I lose no time in removing her comb and arranging her hair like a Bacchante's. But you must be careful; several times, when I have supposed that I was dealing with real hair, upon removing the comb suddenly—without asking permission—I have seen the whole business fall: bands, curls and chignon! And then they flew into a rage with me.—I am more prudent now and always ask if I may touch."

"Thélénie has jet-black eyes, too; you rarely see eyes of such a pure black."

"Why, it seems to me you're still in love with her!"

"Oh, no! not at all. I made her acquaintance, as one makes many acquaintances, by chance. She is a beautiful woman, always dressed with no less taste than style. Such a conquest is always flattering to a young man; but I soon saw that there was not the slightest sympathy between that woman's temperament and mine; she is imperious and exacting, and, as I said, very jealous."

"And you have broken with her?"

"I haven't set foot inside her door for a week."

"That's not very long. Hasn't she written to you?"

"Indeed she has, letter after letter; but I don't answer them."

"Very good! but take my advice and wear a coat of mail when you are out late at night."

"Bah! what nonsense! Tell me, what motive for revenge can that woman have? I didn't take her away from anybody else, I made her no promise of marriage; I never swore that I would pass my life at her feet."

"It would have made your knees ache."

"I am sure that it's simply her self-esteem that makes her anxious to renew our intimacy; she is vexed because I was unfaithful first."

"She isn't used to that."

"Never mind—I regret Amélia; I have only known her a week."

"And you haven't had time to tire of her yet, eh? Well, console yourself; I'll bet you something that we shall find those two young women at the Opéra ball."

"You think so? It isn't probable, they've no money."

"A grisette may have no money to pay her rent, but she always has enough to go to the ball. I thought that you were farther advanced in such matters, Edmond; you still have much to learn, my son."

"Very well! if they're at the ball, so much the better; no matter how much they may be disguised, I am very sure that I can recognize Amélia; she has a funny little accent that she can't lay aside."

"And what about me! how shall I recognize Henriette? She has a very distinct mark, a raspberry; to be sure, I doubt if she'll let me look at the place where it is, in the ball-room."

"Let us start; we'll go into the Café du Passage for a little while."

"One moment! Chamoureau is coming. We can't go without him."

"What's that! Chamoureau coming? What on earth induced you to ask that donkey? If he were amusing, or unpretentious, I wouldn't say a word; a man may be stupid and a good fellow; but he isn't that sort. And then, since he lost his wife, he pulls out his handkerchief as soon as she's mentioned! He is forever lamenting and weeping for his Eléonore!—Great God! let him weep for his wife, let him regret her—I wouldn't prevent him; but I have no inclination to share his grief. That you should sigh with him—that's all right, I can understand that; for his wife was very nice. You were always at their house; you took madame to the theatre and to drive."

"It was Chamoureau's wish."

"And that suited you very well. I am not blaming anybody. Indeed, Chamoureau has the head of a fellow to whom that sort of thing is sure to happen. But frankly, why do you want him to come and groan in our ears? Surely he won't go to the masquerade with us."

"You think so, my dear fellow, but you don't know Chamoureau at all; he is infinitely more amusing than you think. He's a man to be studied; I propose this evening to put you in a position to judge him. But hush! I hear someone blowing his nose on the stairs; it must be he."

III

A WIDOWER

The doorknob did, in fact, turn at that moment, and the person of whom they were speaking entered Edmond's room.

Monsieur Chamoureau was a man of about thirty-five years of age, who appeared fully forty; not that his face was lined or his features altered; on the contrary, his ears were red and his complexion ruddy. But he was already blessed with a protruding paunch and had only a bunch of light hair on the top of his head, quite separate from that which still adorned his ears and the base of his skull. The good man's features were not repellent: his eyes were of the blue seen in faïence; his nose, which was a little too long, was very straight; his mouth was small and delicate, his teeth were very handsome, his chin was well-rounded and embellished by a little dimple that would have made a chubby-cheeked angel envious, and his light whiskers were very unkempt. He was of medium height, but not well-built; his calves were conspicuous by their absence, and his knees often met when he walked. All this, however, did not prevent Monsieur Chamoureau from considering himself a very handsome man.

"Well! here's Chamoureau at last!" said Freluchon, offering the newcomer his hand. "I knew he would come, for he promised."

"Good-evening, messieurs. Monsieur Edmond, it is very presumptuous of me to come to your apartment like this, but Monsieur Freluchon asked me to; I don't quite know why, for you two are going to enjoy yourselves, you think of nothing but ending your Carnival in good style, while I—Ah! God!——"

Here Monsieur Chamoureau drew his handkerchief and blew his nose at great length.

"You did very well to come, Monsieur Chamoureau. Come to the fire and warm yourself."

"Sapristi! how fine you are, Chamoureau! You have a brand-new coat, I do believe, and trousers too, eh?"

"Yes; one must dress decently."

"We think of amusing ourselves, Monsieur Cha-moureau, that is true; but it's not a crime. And you yourself, if you could divert your thoughts in our company, where would be the harm?"

"I, divert my thoughts! Ah! Monsieur Edmond, when a man has met with such a loss as mine, there is no possible distraction. It is all over; I must bid pleasure adieu forever."

"Forever! that's a terribly long time. It's two months already since you lost your wife."

"Two months and four days, monsieur; and it seems to me as if it were yesterday. Ask Freluchon if I didn't tell him so when I dined with him to-day."

" You did; you said it while we were eating that lobster with Marengo sauce, that was so good."

" A little too much garlic, my friend, a little too much garlic; it was pretty well seasoned, but you can get it even better at Javault's on Rue de Rivoli, opposite the Hôtel de Ville."

" You think that it's better there? "

" Oh! I am sure of it, my dear fellow! that's an excellent restaurant. And when you happen to want a truffled snipe *à la provençale,* just order it in the morning when you go out to walk; it will be all ready for you at six o'clock, and you can tell me what you think of it."

" You seem to know the good places, Monsieur Chamoureau."

" What would you have? my knowledge goes back to the time of my marriage; Eléonore liked good things to eat and we often dined at restaurants—with Freluchon. He always went with us; my wife liked to have him because he knew all about wines and I knew very little. My wife would say: ' If Freluchon doesn't come with us, we shall have some wretched madeira.'—But he never refused to come, the dear fellow."

" It was a pleasure to me."

" To be sure, where my wife was, one could never be bored; she had so much wit! "

" Ah! she was agreeable, was she? "

" Agreeable! Eléonore! Why, monsieur, she was a very superior woman—a regular bluestocking! She could have written her own memoirs if she had wanted to; but she wouldn't do it, she was too bright for that. She just sparkled with fun, with imagination. I shall never find another woman like her, never! never! What a loss I have sustained! I can never be consoled; when I lost her, I lost all!"

Monsieur Chamoureau drew his handkerchief again and began to weep.

"Come, come, Monsieur Chamoureau," said Edmond, "you must be reasonable!"

"It's too much for me, my dear friend. I feel that I am no longer of any account on earth, bereft of my Eléonore!"

Freluchon seized the tongs and began to stir the fire, saying:

"Chamoureau, do you remember the trick she played on an old lady one day?"

"Ah, yes! at Saint-Cloud!"

"At Saint-Cloud, just so; it was at a restaurant, one very hot day in summer."

"Yes, yes; there was only one small salon with two tables vacant."

"That's right. Eléonore—I mean your wife——"

"Mon Dieu! that makes no difference, it wasn't worth while to correct yourself. You were intimate enough with us to call her Eléonore.—Go on."

"When we entered the small salon, your wife noticed the grimace and the disdainful expression which our appearance called forth from an old lady covered with jewels and laces, who occupied the other table."

"Yes, yes, she noticed everything, Eléonore did! What an eye!—Go on."

"Your wife asked the waiter in an undertone who that person was who put on so many airs, and the waiter replied:

"'She's a very rich lady, who has a carriage below. Sometimes she comes here to dine all alone, and she usually has a private room; but as they were all taken to-day, they put her in here, where she wanted to be alone just the same. She's very angry because we put somebody in with her; although we assured her that they were very nice people. She said to me: "Serve them as quickly as you can, so that they won't stay long." —But you mustn't disturb yourselves; stay as long as you choose.'

"'Never you fear,' said Eléonore—your wife; 'I'll wager that we will stay longer than she will. Oho! indeed! so we offend that lady, do we? that's a great pity! In that case, I propose to make myself at home.'

"With that, she took off her hat and shawl, and, at a sign from her, we removed our coats. The old lady muttered between her teeth. After the soup, Eléonore said to us: 'You are still too warm; pray take off your waistcoats and cravats; we don't come into the country to be uncomfortable.'"

"Yes, yes, I remember; we took off all those things. The old woman with the jewels rapped angrily on the table with her fork. Ah! how amusing it was!"

" Finally, at a sign from your wife, I put my hand
to my belt, saying: ' Faith, my trousers are too tight!
With your permission?'

"At that the old woman jumped from her chair as
if she were moved by a spring, upsetting her plate and
glass and smashing everything on the table, and rushed
from the room, crying: 'What an outrage! they're
going to make savages of themselves! It is shocking!
it is frightful!'"

"And meanwhile, we three—Ha! ha! ha! we nearly
died laughing."

"Your wife was almost helpless!"

"With good reason. When I think of it—Ha! ha!
what a joke! Ha! ha! ha! I can still see that old
woman when she thought Freluchon was going to appear in his shirt! Ha! ha! ha!"

When he saw Chamoureau laughing with all his
might, Edmond began to believe that the widower's grief
was less incurable than he had hitherto supposed.

But Eléonore's husband soon ceased to laugh and
began to sigh once more, saying:

"You can understand, Monsieur Edmond, that one
couldn't be bored in the company of so clever a woman."

"Yes, I can understand it."

" The fact is, that with her there was a constant fire of
bons mots, sallies and repartees, eh, Freluchon?"

"That's so; in conversation she had the knack of
forcing one to be agreeable; she imparted her own wit
to others."

"Exactly! So that now there's a void in my life, which I shall never succeed in filling, alas!"

"I beg your pardon, but with time, the greatest griefs are allayed."

"Time won't have any effect on mine. Oh, no! I can feel it in the depths of my soul. Dear Eléonore! O God! O God! hi! hi! hi!"

And Monsieur Chamoureau produced his handkerchief again and put it to his eyes.

"Your wife had many agreeable social accomplishments, also," said Freluchon.

"I should say so! she had them all!"

"She sang very well."

"That is to say, she had a ravishing voice, a voice which would not have been out of place at the Opéra-Comique."

"There was one song in particular that she used to sing so sweetly. It was——"

"Oh! I know what you mean! it was the song from *La Fanchonnette.*"

And Monsieur Chamoureau began to sing:

"La! la! la Fanchonnette
Vous chantera landerirette;
La! la! la Fanchonnette
Vous chantera landerira!
Ah! ah! ah! ah!"

"Oh! she used to sing that roulade differently from that," said Freluchon; "she marked her notes. Listen! like this:

"Ah!—ah!—éh!—éh!
Oh!—oh! oh!—éh! éh!—ah! ah!"

"That's so. But that last roulade—Listen! I will
sing it as she did:

"Oh!————oh!—"

"Exactly! it was just like that."

"And then her air from *Les Fraises*—how she could
sing that! Listen, Freluchon:

"Ah! qu'il fait donc bon,
Qu'il fait donc bon
Cueillir la fraise
Au bois de Bagneux,
Quand on est deux,
Quand on est deux!"

"Excellent! I imagine I am listening to your wife!"
Chamoureau continued:

"Mais quand on est trois,
Quand on est trois,
Mamzelle Thérèse!
C'est bien ennuyeux,
On est bien mieux
Quand on est deux!"

"Perhaps I haven't the words just right, but I'll
swear to the tune."

"Ah! qu'il fait donc bon,
Qu'il fait donc bon
Cueillir la fraise—"

"Yes, yes, we know that," said Edmond, who was
beginning to have enough of Chamoureau's singing; but
he immediately resumed:

"And the air from *Galathée,* which Madame Ugalde sang so beautifully—how well Eléonore sang it!

> '' Déja dans la coupe profonde
> Tout s'éclaire d'un nouveau jour
> J'y vois les caprices du monde—''

" Sapristi! is he never going to stop singing?" said Edmond in an undertone to his friend, who had turned his head away to laugh. " For heaven's sake, make him keep quiet a moment!"

" Ah! that will be hard, my boy. When a man who has lost his wife begins to sing, there's no reason why he should stop—I say, Chamoureau, we know that tune, too!"

But Chamoureau did not hear; he was shouting at the top of his voice:

> '' Verse encore!
> Verse encore!''

The two young men were compelled to listen to the whole of the selection, to which Monsieur Chamoureau added some impossible roulades. When he finally ceased, Freluchon said to him:

" Do you know, Chamoureau, you have a most surprising voice for a widower!"

" Oh! I sang much better when my wife was alive. We often sang duets together; there was one she was especially fond of."

" Great heaven!" muttered Edmond, " does he propose now to sing duets all by himself?" And to change

the subject, he said: "Monsieur Chamoureau, have you
been to any of the balls during this Carnival?"

"To balls! I!" exclaimed the widower, resuming his
grief-stricken expression. "Oh! my dear friend, you
forget my sad plight, my misfortune! Is it possible for
me to think of amusing myself when my heart is still
full of my grief? when my eyes are always looking for
Eléonore—for I do look for her all the time, and there
are moments when I forget that I have lost her; then,
when I hear a woman cry, or speak rather loud—Eléonore always spoke loud—I turn round, thinking that it's
she; and then I realize that it was only a delusion and
I have to go back to the ghastly reality!—Ah! then, you
see, I fall into such utter prostration—the suffering is
terrible! You do not suspect how I suffer!"

Chamoureau took out his handkerchief and put it to
his eyes.

"Yes, yes," said Edmond, "I see that you are quite
inconsolable."

"Yes, monsieur, inconsolable is just the word; you
could not express it better!—O Eléonore! you may flatter yourself that you were dearly loved—may she not,
Freluchon?"

"Parbleu! of whom do you ask the question?"

"Ah! I do you justice, my dear friend; you regret
her almost as keenly as I do! But we will weep for her
together—that affords some relief."

"I say, Chamoureau, how lovely your wife was at a
ball! How well she danced!"

"Why, my dear fellow, she was Terpsichore in person! she was so light——"

"Yes, your wife was extremely light." *

"And so graceful! She didn't dance like other people; she had her own peculiar way of dancing; many women tried to imitate her and failed."

"That is so; she had a way of doing the *avant deux*. I don't know what the steps were, but it was fascinating."

"I know, I remember perfectly; look, Freluchon, I'll show you."

And Monsieur Chamoureau rose, assumed the third position, hummed a dance tune and began to take steps and go through evolutions, saying:

"Wasn't it like this, eh? How's this for her little swagger, her free-and-easy way?"

"Yes, yes, that's it."

"And the *poule*—I'll just show you. Come and be my vis-à-vis, Freluchon—I can do it better. Forward, give the right hand. Tra la la la—tra la la la—la la la. Cross over! balancez! salute your partners!—Monsieur Edmond, come, be the lady—in the pastourelle figure. —Tra la la—tra la la."

But Edmond was unable to comply; he was laughing too heartily at Chamoureau's dancing.

The latter stopped at last, after a pirouette which he came very near ending on his nose, and, seeing that Edmond was roaring with laughter, he said:

---

* There is a play on words here, *légère* meaning inconstant and frail —wanton—, as well as light of foot.

" What on earth makes you laugh like that? Do you think I dance badly? "

" No, no! on the contrary, you leap like a chamois! But it occurred to me as I watched you going through your steps, that you might imitate your wife much better by going to the Opéra ball with us."

" Oh! upon my word!—you surely don't mean it, Monsieur Edmond! I, go to the Opéra ball—with the burden of grief that I have on my heart!"

" Why, that is an additional reason: it will dissipate your grief."

" Oh! never! on the contrary, nothing can dissipate it, and——"

Freluchon planted himself in front of Chamoureau and said, assuming a very solemn expression:

" Look you, my dear fellow, do you expect to fool us much longer with your inconsolable grief?"

The widower stood thunderstruck and stammered:

" What's that! fool you! What does this mean? For what reason do you ask me that, Freluchon?"

" For the reason that, when a man really has a great sorrow in his heart, he doesn't laugh and sing and dance as you have just been doing; nor does he know where one should go to eat snipe *à la provençale.*"

" All that was in memory of Eléonore, and——"

" You regret your wife, I don't doubt that, and she was well worth the trouble. But I tell you again that you ask nothing better now than to be consoled, and above all to make new conquests."

"Little devil of a Freluchon! What an astonishing creature!—Do you really think that I might make conquests?"

"I will go so far as to promise you some to-night, if you come to the Opéra with us."

"To the Opéra ball with you, my boys! Far be it from me to say that it would be distasteful to me, because, after all, one might as well listen to reason; a man always ends by being consoled, a little sooner or later; but the world is what I dread! What will the world say if I am seen at the masquerade, so short a time after—my calamity? The world is so unkind!"

"Parbleu! if you're afraid to be seen at the ball, there's one very simple means of avoiding it—disguise yourself."

"True, that is an idea. But men don't wear masks, I believe."

"No, but with a fancy costume, a wig, a little rouge and a false nose, I'll undertake to make you unrecognizable."

"Oh! if you'll answer for that, it's all right, I'll run the risk and go with you. By the way, do you disguise yourselves?"

"Oh, no! it isn't worth while; we are not afraid to be recognized!"

"And where shall I find a costume?"

"I know a costumer where you will find a lot to choose from."

"You see, Freluchon, from the moment that I make up my mind to disguise myself, I insist upon being well

costumed; I want something that will favor me, something—er—original."

"Let us go softly, Chamoureau, softly! Just now,
you were afraid of being recognized, and now you want
to attract attention!"

"One may attract attention without being recognized.
Suppose I should dress as a woman?"

"The devil fly away with you! As a woman? Why,
a man can't make conquests in a woman's clothes; the
fair sex dislikes us when we assume its skirts, and it is
quite right; when a man rigs himself up in that way he
is good for nothing but to arouse laughter or contempt."

"Yes, that's true; I won't dress as a woman; but
how shall I dress, then?"

"You can decide at the costumer's and dress there;
it's within a few steps of the Opéra."

"All right. But my clothes?"

"The costumer will send them to your concierge."

"Deuce take it! no; I can't have that; I have no
desire to go home in a Carnival costume, so that every
one may know that I've been to the ball in disguise. A
business agent—and sometimes clients call very early
in the morning!—A Carnival costume would not inspire
confidence."

"Well then, as I live very near the costumer's, let
him send your clothes to my apartment; then you can
go there and put them on when you please."

"Bravo! in that way, all the proprieties will be observed!"

" Come, messieurs, I trust that we may start now. It is nearly twelve o'clock, and before Chamoureau is dressed——"

" Yes, yes! let us start. Forward, and *vive la gaieté!* "

" Faith, yes! one must divert one's thoughts; it's an excellent thing."

And the widower went dancing after the two young men.

IV

SCENES AT THE MASQUERADE

A few moments after the tall gentleman named Beauregard had left the box where the pearl-gray domino and her friend were seated, a Spaniard entered the ball-room, arm-in-arm with a short young man with a long, thin nose. The reader will at once recognize Chamoureau and Freluchon. The widower wore a costume resplendent with spangles and gold braid. His cherry-colored doublet was heavily trimmed with very rich embroidery, his white satin shortclothes, slashed with red, were decorated with spangles and bows; a gold-fringed sash confined his waist; the flaps of his huge yellow top-boots fell a little too near his ankles, his leg being too deficient in calf to hold them in place. A large ruff about his neck did duty as a cravat; over his shoulder was thrown a small light-blue cloak, lined with white satin; and lastly,

he wore on his head a little velvet cap, also blue, covered
with false jewels, and surmounted by two enormous white
plumes which drooped over the cavalier's left shoulder.
To complete his disguise, Chamoureau had donned a
brown wig with long curls falling over his neck. He had
covered his face with rouge, and, in addition, he wore a
false nose to which a pair of moustaches was attached,
reaching from ear to ear.

All this formed such a unique whole that everyone in
the room turned or stopped short, in order to have a
longer look at the Spaniard; and Chamoureau, overjoyed by the effect he produced, and convinced that
everybody considered him magnificent, said in Freluchon's
ear:

"How they stare at me! eh? I am very glad I chose
this costume. I must be superb; I read admiration in
every eye! Say, Freluchon, am I not superb?"

"It is a fact that you are well worth looking at; if
you should make them pay ten sous each, it would be
none too much."

"Oh! you are always joking! But I don't see so
rich a costume as mine in the whole place; I am covered
with spangles."

"It's enough to make one's eyes ache to look at you;
you produce the same effect as the sun!"

"Do my plumes float gracefully?"

"Like a swan on a lake."

"Is my cap well placed?"

"Like a vane on a steeple."

"There's nothing wrong but these infernal boots, which keep falling; they are too big."

"It may be that your legs are too much like spindles."

"What a pity to be obliged to wear a false nose with all this!"

"Why is it a pity?"

"Dear me! it's easy to see that. As I am the possessor of rather an attractive face, if I hadn't this false nose, I should be even more fascinating in this costume, and I am sure that I should make conquests in swarms."

"By Jove! that's true; I entirely forgot that you were a handsome man!"

"Still, my wife used to repeat it often enough: 'Ah! how handsome he is, my Chamoureau!'"

"Yes, to the tune of the *Postilion de Longjumeau.*— But after all, you know, you're under no compulsion to keep your false nose on, if you want to take it off."

"Oh, no! the deuce! someone might recognize me then, and I should be compromised!"

"Try to make a conquest with your nose."

"That's quite possible—Damn these boots!"

And Chamoureau halted to raise the flaps.

"So you are inclined to make a little acquaintance, my inconsolable widower?" asked Edmond, who was walking beside Freluchon and had overheard the Spaniard's last words.

"Oh! my dear Monsieur Edmond," he replied, after adjusting his boots, "you will understand that my heart, my poor heart, will have no part in it! Henceforth

nothing will ever touch that; it is dead to love. Eléonore
has carried with her all the sentiment it could possibly
contain—dear Eléonore!"

"Are you going to shed tears, Chamoureau? they will
spoil your rouge."

" No, no, I said that just as I would have said anything else."

At that moment a man dressed as a Swiss woman,
with long locks hanging down his back and a number
of little brooms in his hand, halted in front of Chamoureau, crying:

"Ah! my hearties! what do I see? A sunbeam disguised as a Spaniard! How brilliant it is! how it
gleams! Are you just from Peru, my ducky? It is at
the very least *Le Cidre* or Gusman with a sheep's foot,
who knows no obstacle! Isn't he fine, the *coco!* But
while you had the cash, Gringalet, you should have
bought some calves, for you lack 'em altogether! and
your parapetted boots will fall on the floor!"

The crowd had stopped and formed a circle to listen
to the Swiss woman who had attacked the Spaniard.

Chamoureau, being rather disconcerted, began by making sure that his false nose was secure, then muttered:

"If I have no calves, it's fair to presume that I don't
care for them."

"How now! is that all you've got to say for yourself, you poor thing? Did you spend all your wit to
buy your costume? What a simple air the great clown
has! He must be some keeper of turkeys who's been

dismissed, and is entirely out of his element when he's no longer surrounded by his flock."

Chamoureau, sorely vexed to be called a keeper of turkeys, retorted sourly:

"Since when have the Swiss been fishwomen, and presumed to insult people like this?"

"Bravo, Chamoureau!" said Freluchon, "that's not bad; go on; drive the nail home!"

"Since they have sold little brooms for flies. Ah! so you're getting angry, Rodrique!—Come, Rodrique, have you any pluck? We'll fight a duel, I with my broom and you with your nose; is it a bargain? You'll have the advantage, as your nose is longer than my broom."

The roars of laughter from the crowd increased Chamoureau's vexation; he hastily dropped Freluchon's arm, for he was laughing louder than the rest, and gliding into a throng of masks, tried to overtake Edmond, who was hurrying after a little *débardeur* in whom he fancied that he recognized his grisette Amélia. As he was not at all desirous to have Chamoureau always hanging on his arm, he said to him:

"Why did you leave Freluchon?"

"Because he laughed like a fool at the absurd nonsense that a man dressed as a Swiss woman has been spouting at me for the last few minutes; he is a low creature and said the coarsest things to me. The blood was beginning to go to my head, and I left the place, because I might have allowed my anger to carry me beyond bounds."

" For heaven's sake, my dear Monsieur Chamoureau, do you think it necessary to take offence at all the nonsense maskers say to you? If you do, you ought not to come to the ball, and above all things you shouldn't disguise yourself."

" That's so, of course; you are quite right. I was wrong to attach any importance to that foolish talk, it's a Carnival scene and nothing more. Still, I have an idea that Freluchon knew that Swiss woman.—My nose makes me terribly warm, especially because of the moustaches."

" Take them off."

" No, I'm afraid of being recognized.—Drat these boots!—there are some very pretty women here—they're too large, they'll fall down over my heels, and I shall end by walking on them."

" Take them off."

" What's that? you want me to take off my boots, and walk about in my stockings? "

" Why, yes, rather than be discommoded."

" I am not discommoded, for I dance in them."

" What are you complaining about, then? "

" My dear Monsieur Edmond, it seems to me that you don't listen very closely to what I say; you're not interested in our conversation; are you looking for someone here? "

" Parbleu! at a masked ball one should always be looking for someone."

" Ah! indeed! well, that is an idea; but who in the devil is there for me to look for? "

"I thought that I recognized Amélia in a pretty little *débardeur* who ran away from me. Yes, it must have been she."

"Who's Amélia?"

"A very pretty flower-maker; an animated, saucy face, eyes full of fire, a charming figure, and nineteen years at most."

"Fichtre! how exactly that would meet my views—longing to love, as I do; for at my age, you understand, it makes no difference how much a man may suffer from grief and regret, nature, powerful, fruitful nature always cries out within us and makes us understand that we are not on earth to give all our thoughts to the dead. —Ah! there goes a domino who looked into the very whites of my eyes. What a look! there were a great many things in that look.—We were saying that your Amélia is very attractive, and only nineteen; is she free?"

"Yes, since she left me."

"How long since you parted?"

"This morning."

"That's not long; so it's to be hoped that she hasn't replaced you yet."

"I wouldn't swear to it."

"If she is still free, and we find her, will you permit me to apply for the vacancy?"

"I permit you to do whatever you choose, absolutely."

"Ah! you're very good, on my word! you're not like Freluchon, who will never turn his ex-mistresses over to me; and yet it seems to me that he owes me that much.

—A little *débardeur*, you say? what color? what sort of head-dress?"

Edmond, who was tired of Chamoureau's company and had been trying for several minutes to devise some way of getting rid of him, suddenly exclaimed:

"Did you hear that pink domino who just passed us?"

"No; what did she say?"

"She said to the shepherdess on her arm: 'That Spaniard yonder has turned my head. I tell you, my dear, I'd like to catch him!'"

"Really! you heard that?"

"And the shepherdess replied: 'Very well! speak to him, puzzle him.'"

"'Oh! I don't dare, my dear.'"

"She said she didn't dare, eh? Well, I will dare. Where is this pink domino?"

"Look—over yonder, near the Polichinelle. Go quickly, or you'll lose her."

Chamoureau voluntarily dropped Edmond's arm, to run after the person in a pink domino whom he had pointed out.

Having thus rid himself of the widower, young Edmond thought of nothing but finding his last mistress, with whom he was still in love, probably because she had ceased to run after him. Only that morning he had seen Amélia, and they had been on the best possible terms; so that if she avoided him now, it could only be because Freluchon had refused her friend Henriette the money she asked him to lend her.

Why should she espouse Henriette's quarrel? Still, as she lived with her friend, when the latter was obliged to quit her domicile, Mademoiselle Amélia also was turned into the street.

Edmond said all this to himself as he glided through the crowd, running after every woman he saw in a *débardeur's* costume. He caught one by the arm, but saw that she was not the person he sought, just as she said to him:

"If you'll treat me to supper, I'll stay with you—if not—no, thanks!"

"I would gladly invite you to supper, if I were not looking for someone, whom I took you for at first; but as I hope to find her, I shall sup with her."

"Bah! let her go! She'll sup with three other men perhaps; don't run after her. You're good-looking, I like you; come, dance with me."

"I am sorry to refuse you, but I don't want to dance now; later, I don't say that——"

"Oh, yes! with the other; good-night, little donkey!"

The little *débardeur* ran away from Edmond, to join the dance; and almost at the same moment the young man's arm was taken by a little blue domino, who said to him:

"She's not the one you are looking for; whom are you looking for, Edmond Didier?"

"Ah! you know me, do you?"

"Yes, I know you very well; also your friend Freluchon with whom you came to the ball. But I don't know the tall greenhorn disguised as a Spaniard, who came with you two, and who was on your arm just now. Mon Dieu! what a stupid-looking creature! and how wretchedly he carries his costume! Such a figure too! Who on earth is that scarecrow?"

"Do you know that you are very inquisitive? you ask such a lot of questions one on top of another!"

"It's because I like to know about things. Won't you answer me?"

"Oh, yes: the Spaniard is a friend of Freluchon, very well-to-do, a business agent, who has just lost his wife and is now trying to find a place for his heart."

"For life?"

"Oh, no! just for a term of years. If you desire to form an agreeable connection, I commend him to you."

"Thanks; he's too clumsy; he does nothing but pull up his boot-flaps, and I am tempted to offer him a pair. of garters to keep them in place."

"You would do him a great service."

"Is he better looking without his nose?"

"He's not at all bad-looking."

"What is the idiot's name?"

"It is perfectly evident that you aspire to make a victim of him."

"Oh, no! you are mistaken; but perhaps I might like to have a little fun with him. What's his name?"

"What I am going to do is rather indiscreet perhaps, but as he will be delighted to be mystified, I will tell you his name: Chamoureau."

"Cha——"

" Moureau."

." Oh! how well the name suits the man! Chalumeau would be even better, for he looks like a stick; but never mind, Chamoureau is not bad. Ha! ha!"

" And now tell me how you happen to know me? "

" Well; try to guess."

" Faith! I confess that I haven't the faintest idea."

" You have answered only one of my questions. Won't you tell me now what woman you are looking for? "

" Oh, no; such things aren't to be mentioned! As to the Spaniard's name, that's all right! but I won't tell you the name of the person I would like to meet; guess it, if you can."

" It should be the fair Thélénie—Madame de Sainte-Suzanne, if you prefer."

" Ah! you also know——"

" That you have been her lover. Who doesn't know that? But are you so no longer? have you ceased to love her? "

" You are becoming too inquisitive again; I shall not answer that."

" You are unfaithful to her, I see; who in the world has succeeded in captivating you? Come, my little Edmond, take me for your confidante; that's a very modest rôle for me to assume."

At that moment Freluchon rushed up to them, seized Edmond's arm and led him away, saying:

" They're right over there, both of them—dancing. I recognized their Andalusian steps. Henriette is dressed as a Folly; come at once; they don't propose to be recognized, but we'll bring them to it."

Edmond instantly threw off the little blue domino's arm and hurried away with Freluchon.

Two women, each wearing a small mask of velvet, without a barb, and dressed, one as a sort of *débardeur,* that is to say, in a high shirt, velvet trousers with broad satin bands, a fringed sash and a round hat covered with flowers; the other as Folly, with a fool's bauble in her hand, bells on her arm and legs and cap, around her waist, everywhere, in short,—were dancing with two men whose costumes were eccentric to the last degree.

One, in a Greek tunic, with deerskin breeches and riding-boots, wore a Roman helmet. The other, dressed as a Cupid, with quiver and arrows, had on his head the sort of head-covering usually assigned to Don Quixote, that is to say, a dish turned upside down.

The dancing of these gentlemen was in keeping with their costumes; it was very daring. The man in the helmet whirled his arms about like the wings of a windmill, with terrifying rapidity. The Cupid kicked up his heels almost in the face of his vis-à-vis, and from time to time, when he was doing the *cavalier seul,* threw himself flat on his stomach and executed the evolution known as the *spider.* As yet, the two little women had ventured upon nothing more than permissible cancan steps.

" The devil!" said Freluchon, planting himself behind the Folly; "those bucks have a style of dancing that's rather risky for their partners. Look out, Henriette;

that Cupid will land his foot in your eye, and that's more dangerous, I assure you, than a kick somewhere else!"

The Folly pretended not to hear and went on dancing.

Edmond meanwhile, standing behind the little *débardeur,* said to her:

"My dear Amélia, I am very much afraid that your Roman will carry away your nose while he imitates a windmill with his arms; that would be a pity!"

The *débardeur,* like the Folly, made no reply; but a slight movement of the shoulders betrayed her, and seemed to say:

"Oh! let me alone; you bore me!"

A moment later Freluchon called loudly to his friend:

"I say, Edmond, they turned me out of my lodgings this morning, because I hadn't paid my rent or for my furniture! Did you ever hear such nonsense? Just imagine that my furniture, which I thought was paid for, wasn't!—Well! it didn't take away my spirits; on the contrary, it put me just in the mood to dance and enjoy myself!"

"But I, who lived with you—where am I to sleep?" rejoined Edmond with a laugh; "here am I too without a home!"

"Never fear! we'll find some Roman or some Cupid to give us shelter!—And to think that for lack of four hundred francs I missed the finest match!"

"Nonsense! really?"

"Yes, my dear fellow, a superb match! a flower-maker, thoroughbred, who would have brought me as her dowry, in addition to her virtue, of which I will say nothing, the most agreeable disposition to have me shut up at Clichy,—with or without an eye-glass—in a very short time."

The little woman disguised as a Folly suddenly walked up to Freluchon and said to him under her breath, but in a voice that trembled with anger:

"Monsieur Freluchon, if you don't stop your spiteful remarks, I'll see that you're punished by my partner."

"Ha! ha! ha! so you recognize me now, O fickle Henriette!"

"Yes, I recognize you, but I no longer know you; when a man treats a woman as you treated me this morning, and leaves her in a horrible plight without coming to her assistance, he's a rat! yes, he's worse than a *rat*, he's a *toad!* * and I don't have anything to do with toads!"

"Ha! ha! very pretty! that word, in your mouth, has a wide meaning—inasmuch as your mouth is not small. Is it because you are covered with bells that you put on so many airs to-night? Bless my soul! if you had asked me for nothing more than bells, I'd have given them to you. I didn't know that you were so fond of them as all this! But really, seeing how enthusiastically you dance, and especially these innumerable bells with which you are loaded down, I confess that I can hardly

---

* *Rat* and *crapaud*—rat and toad—as used here, signify a skinflint and an ugly little creature.

G. FRAIPONT

mourn over your terrible plight of this morning.—Come, leave your Don Quixote, who looks to me amazingly like a vender of theatre tickets, and come to supper with us. I'll give you as many kisses as you have bells; isn't that a seductive prospect?"

Meanwhile Edmond was saying to the *débardeur:*

"Look you, my dear Amélia, after the quadrille, leave your Roman, who looks to me too much like a *claquer,* and take my arm. We were not at odds this morning, why should we be now? You are wrong to espouse your friend's quarrel. Henriette will make you do all sorts of foolish things; you are too nice a girl to dance with such fellows!"

The young grisette seemed to hesitate; but every time that her friend passed her, she said earnestly:

"Don't speak to these fellows! You know what I told you; it's all over between us if you go back to Edmond. My dear girl, women must stand by each other, or else these men will make fools of us."

"Ah! the pretty bells! Mon Dieu! what a lot of bells!" cried Freluchon, still laughing as he watched Mademoiselle Henriette. "I have seen many Follies, but none that approached this one in the matter of bells! I say, Edmond, if a poodle wore as many bells as this, he'd be mistaken for a mule. Oh! how tickled I should be to have bells on all my clothes instead of buttons!"

The Folly was beside herself with rage; she whispered in her Cupid's ear. The Cupid—Don Quixote was a tall, solidly-built fellow, who had every appearance of being a formidable athlete. He walked up to Freluchon, planted himself directly in front of him, and said in a voice that seemed to issue from a cavern:

"I say, counter-jumper, ain't you about through bothering my partner? Understand that if you don't leave her in peace, her and her bells, I'll knock off your hat with the top of my boot and send it up to the gallery."

"Oho! my handsome Cupid, that's a trick I should be delighted to see," retorted Freluchon in a mocking tone. "Really, it would please me immensely if you should succeed."

"Ah! you want to see it, do you? well, look!"

As he spoke, the Cupid suddenly threw up his leg, expecting to kick Freluchon in the face. But he, by a gesture as quick as thought, seized the leg in its passage, and grasping the ankle in his right hand, squeezed it so hard that the Cupid made a horrible grimace and cried:

"Ten thousand million milliards! Let me go, you hurt me, you squeeze too hard! Let me go, I say!"

"If you had struck my face with your foot, wouldn't you have hurt me, you second-hand Cupid?"

"Look here! just let him go this minute, will you!" observed the gentleman dressed as a Roman, approaching Freluchon with uplifted arm, while the latter still held the Cupid by the leg.

But the little fellow, with his left hand, struck his new adversary a blow that sent him reeling backward; there the Roman fell in with Edmond, who gave him an additional push, while Freluchon suddenly released the

Cupid's leg with a violent jerk, so that he fell on his back among the dancers.

Thereupon there was a great outcry on all sides, and, as usually happens, the police appeared on the scene and ordered the combatants to leave the ball-room with them, to explain their conduct elsewhere.

Mesdemoiselles Henriette and Amélia took advantage of the moment when the young men were surrounded to glide among the dancers and disappear.

This scene had taken place almost in front of the box in which the pearl-gray domino and her friend Mademoiselle Héloïse were seated.

A few moments earlier, a little blue domino, the same who had questioned and mystified Edmond, had come to report to the fair Thélénie the result of her conversation with the young man. But when she saw the man she was looking for talking with the little *débardeur,* and observed the quarrel that followed their conversation, Thélénie at once divined that the woman disguised as a *débardeur* was the woman for whose sake the man she loved had come to the ball.

Having watched with some anxiety the brief scrimmage which took place during the quadrille, she rose hurriedly and left the box, muttering:

" I will find that woman, and I will see to whom he sacrifices me! "

A few moments later, Edmond and Freluchon returned in triumph to the ball-room. Their adversaries, whose too delirious style of dancing had already been remarked,

had been turned out, and when Freluchon offered them
his card, they had declined it, saying:

"Thanks! it isn't worth while; we've had enough."

"And now," said Edmond to his friend, as they returned to the ball-room, "let us try to find those girls
again."

"Thanks," said Freluchon; "you can look for your
Amélia, if it amuses you, but from this moment I no
longer know Henriette! I can forgive a woman her in-
fidelities, her lies, her tricks, her humbug! But when a
woman tries to make two men fight, I see nothing more
in her than an evil-minded wretch whom I despise, and
I never speak to her again."

V

CHAMOUREAU'S STICKS OF CANDY

Chamoureau had hastily left Edmond, to run after a
pink domino whom Edmond had pointed out to him as
having expressed a desire, as she passed them, to make a
conquest of the Spaniard.

Our widower pushed and elbowed his way through
the crowd, jostled by this one and tossed aside by that
one; but at last he succeeded in overtaking the domino
who had been pointed out to him, and who had on her
arm a poorly dressed shepherdess, without a mask, whose

common face suggested a fruit woman enjoying the Carnival.

Chamoureau took his stand in front of the domino and gazed amorously at her. She seemed to pay no heed to him, but pushed him aside so that she could pass. The two women left the dancing enclosure and walked toward the foyer.

But our Spaniard followed them, and they were no sooner in the foyer than he once more placed himself in front of them.

" Well, well! are we bound to find this tall Spaniard in front of us all the time? " said the pink domino to the shepherdess. " Is he chasing us? What on earth does he want of us? "

" My dear, you or me must have made a conquest! "

" Do you think so? Then it must be you, as you are not masked."

" But he seems to be looking at you."

" He looks to me like a big simpleton."

"We might as well have some fun with him while we're waiting for our men to join us."

" We must make him treat us to something."

Notice that this is the constant refrain of the ladies whom one meets at public balls.

While the two women whispered to each other, Chamoureau, with one hand on his hip, assumed a seductive smile and kept his eyes fixed on the pink domino, who finally said to him in a voice that seemed in the habit of crying fish for sale:

" What makes you look in my eyes like that, my handsome Spaniard? Do you know me? If you do, say something to prove it, instead of standing there staring at me like a porcelain dog! "

" I do not know whether I know you, fascinating domino," replied Chamoureau, still smiling, " but I certainly should be most happy to make your acquaintance; and if you have no objection, why then—it seems to me —you understand——"

" Pardi! it isn't hard to understand. You want to make a conquest; you're a seducer—anyone can see that at once! "

" And what about me, do you mean to seduce me too, Spaniard? " inquired the shepherdess, showing an assortment of teeth of different sizes; " you'd find it hard work, for d'ye see, I've vowed an everlasting hatred to men! "

Chamoureau made a faint grimace at the shepherdess's language; but he assumed that she was the pink domino's maid, and he said to her:

" No, I have never cared for shepherdesses; they're too pastoral for me! My homage is addressed solely to your companion—this fascinating domino."

" But suppose I am ugly, my dear man? for you don't know me! "

" Ugly! you can't be that, with such a shapely head, such brilliant eyes! I am sure that you are adorable."

" You might well be cheated, my boy! there's nothing so deceptive as a mask! "

"For my part," interposed the shepherdess, "I don't try to cheat anyone. You can see at once what I look like; then, if I make a conquest, people know what to expect anyway!"

"*Fichtre!* yes," said Chamoureau to himself, "one can be certain that he hasn't to do with a bluestocking! This shepherdess would do well to leave the pretty domino for a while; but perhaps, when they know me better, they'll consent to separate."

"Tell me, my handsome Spaniard, why do you wear a false nose and moustaches? Are you flat-nosed, that you disguise yourself so?"

"No, I can assure you that I am not flat-nosed."

"Then does your real nose make you so very ugly?"

"I have never been told that I was ill-looking."

"People may have thought so!"

"It is not probable!"

"What a conceited creature!—Well, take off your nose, if you want us to believe you."

"Ah! my pretty domino, you ask me to do something of great importance to me. I have many reasons for not wanting to be recognized!"

"Bosh! you say that to put on airs. Maybe you're some great personage? Are you a State official?"

"No, not exactly; but I have a very good position in society, and I have to be careful." *

---

* Chamoureau says : *j'ai des ménagements à garder.* The shepherdess understands him to say *déménagements; déménager* means to move, to change one's residence.

"Do you move people?" said the shepherdess; "so does my uncle!"

"No, no, I didn't say that. You misunderstood me, little shepherdess."

"Take off your nose, or I shall think you haven't got one underneath."

"Oh! what a shocking supposition! It may be that later, pretty domino, when we are tête-à-tête——"

"Nay, nay, Lisette! My dear man, when you make love to a woman, you must begin by showing her your nose. Isn't that so, Laïde?"

The shepherdess, who answered to the name of Laïde, replied simply:

"How hot it is here! God! how hot it is! And I'm eating dust! My chemise is just sticking to me. I'd like to take something, just the least bit *refreshening.* Ain't you thirsty?"

"Why, yes, I wouldn't mind a sip! My throat's all parched."

Chamoureau realized that that was the moment to show his gallantry; he offered the domino his arm, saying:

"Accept my arm and some refreshments, lovely masker; I will escort you to the buffet."

"I will accept everything! for this invitation proves to me that you are a noble Spaniard.—Come along with us, Laïde!"

They made their way to one of the buffets which were at each end of the foyer.

"What will the ladies take?" inquired Chamoureau.
"Gooseberry wine—lemonade—that's the best thing there
is to cool you off."

"I prefer punch," said the pink domino.

"So do I," said the shepherdess; "it's much healthier
than all those other things, and I can drink two bowls
of it without getting tight."

This naïve admission of the shepherdess made Chamoureau shudder. Luckily for him, punch is ordinarily
served in glasses in the foyer. Three glasses were placed
before the Spaniard and his guests. The domino and the
shepherdess tossed off the punch as if it were champagne, although it was scalding hot. The widower had
hardly wet his lips when the ladies had emptied their
glasses.

"It's hot! terribly hot! I can't swallow it as you do,"
said Chamoureau; "it would burn my throat!"

"Ah! the poor boy is afraid of burning himself. I
say, ain't you a man? But we ain't going to stay on
one leg, I suppose, are we?" said the shepherdess.

"What do you mean by that, girl of the fields?"

"Ah! he don't understand! Where are you from,
old no nose? Did they bring you up in a closet?"

"It means, my dear, that we will take another glass
of punch; that will make the second leg," said the pink
domino, squeezing the Spaniard's arm with great force;
and he, delighted to be squeezed, called at once:

"Waiter, more punch for these ladies!"

"And yourself?"

"Oh! if I should take any more, it would make me dizzy!"

"What an oyster!" whispered the pink domino in the shepherdess's ear.

"We need that kind," was the reply; "they're the attraction of the ball; I have always liked oysters myself."

More glasses of punch were brought, which the two women put out of sight as quickly as the first. Then Chamoureau lost no time in paying the bill and leading his companions away from the buffet, for fear they would express a wish to go on three legs.

Meanwhile, our Spaniard, thinking that the punch with which he had regaled the ladies entitled him to become enterprising, ventured, in the crowd, to place one hand on a spot where the pink domino might have worn hoops. She turned upon him instantly, saying:

"Have done with such pranks, false nose! What sort of behavior is that? what do you take me for?"

"Lovely masker, my hand went astray involuntarily."

"Look out that it don't go astray again in that direction."

"I only did it to find out——"

"Whether I wore steel skirts, eh?"

"Exactly."

"Well, I don't need such things; I'm plump enough not to wear substitutes.—What in the world's the matter with your boots?"

"Nothing. They're too big; they keep falling."

" Why didn't you wear hoop-skirts on your legs? they wouldn't be out of the way."

" Are you free, pretty domino, or under the control of a husband?"

" What makes you ask me that? Do you want to marry me?"

" Why, when one desires to form a loving intimacy, isn't it natural to find out, first of all, the situation of the person one desires?"

" Aha! so you desire me, my tall hidalgo! in that case, you are going to treat me and my friend to a stick of candy; if you don't, I won't allow you to desire me."

" Oh, yes! candy!" cried the shepherdess. " Besides, I promised to take some home to my little brother. And then, all the women have a stick in their hands. It takes the place of a fan; it looks very nice."

Chamoureau considered that the ladies who go to the Opéra ball are decidedly gluttonous, but it was impossible to draw back.

They were near the other buffet at that moment; the pink domino and the shepherdess selected a stick of candy each, and they did not take the smallest.

" How much?" asked the Spaniard.

" Ten francs."

" What! ten francs for candy?"

" A hundred sous each for the sticks the ladies took; two make ten francs."

" Come, my noble friend, pay up!" laughed the pink domino. " You certainly don't mean to haggle, do you?

You'll make one believe you're not a noble Castilian at all, and that you learned all you know of Spain in Vaugirard!"

" No, no, I am not haggling!" said Chamoureau, making a horrible grimace under his false nose. " But I'm afraid I haven't the change."

" We'll change a note for you, monsieur."

While our widower took his purse from under his belt and inspected the contents, the shepherdess said to the pink domino in an undertone:

" My dear, there's our men over yonder, by the door, where we agreed. They're looking for us, no doubt."

" In that case, let's be off, while that tall donkey has his false nose in his purse."

Chamoureau changed a forty-franc piece to pay for his candy, and, when he had received his change, turned to where the two women had stood, flattering himself that his gallantry entitled him to the most delicious reward. But instead of the pink domino, his false nose almost came in contact with the eye of a mustachioed individual, who said to him very sharply:

" For heaven's sake, be careful! Sapristi! do you take my face for a full moon, that you try to bury your nose in it? "

Chamoureau made no reply; he was busily engaged in looking for his conquest; but in vain did he gaze in every direction: his two ladies had vanished.

In his amazement, our Spaniard applied to the woman at the desk.

"Do you know which way they went?"

"Who, monsieur?"

"The two ladies who were with me just now and whom I treated to candy at a hundred sous a stick."

"No, monsieur."

"But they were right here, by my side, only a moment ago. I don't understand it at all!"

A crowd of young men and dominos rushed up to the buffet, pushing Chamoureau aside and shouting:

"Come, off you go, Spaniard! You've had enough to drink; make room for others!"

"I beg your pardon, messieurs, I am looking for a lady."

"Go to the deuce! You won't find your lady! Ohé! what a phiz! Ah! now he's losing his boots! Look out, or you'll lose your nose next! Ha! ha! what a ridiculous figure! Oh! that nose!"

At a masked ball, as soon as a few people begin to jeer at a person in disguise, the crowd collects and swells the chorus; and as the widower was a decidedly laughable figure in his ornate costume, and with his false nose and moustaches, bursts of laughter arose on all sides as he passed, and he was followed by people who shouted in his ears:

"Oh! that nose! Look at that Spaniard's nose!"

"That man has been deceived by women."

"He must have made a fool of himself for them."

"Don't you see that monsieur is a foreigner who has come to France to study refined manners?"

" No, no; he's a joker, who made a bet that he would
look more like an ass than anybody else at the ball."

" Well, he has won! he has won! "

All these remarks were accompanied by loud laughter
which made Chamoureau frantic.

To escape the ovation with which he was honored in
the foyer, he rushed through one of the doors, sought
the place where the crowd was most dense, and succeeded in reaching the corridor. He went up one flight,
and as he neared the top, tore off his false nose.

" I'll take it off," he thought; " if I don't they'll recognize me by it and never stop following me. There—now
that I no longer have that nose, I like to think that I
shall not be noticed. But it's a very singular thing: I
come here masked, or practically so, so that no one may
know who I am, and I have to take off my mask to avoid
being recognized!—After all, I was suffocating with that
nose and those moustaches. I am much more comfortable this way.—But I can't understand the conduct
of my two ladies. I treat them to punch and enormous
sticks of candy, and they leave me! they disappear without saying a word to me! Perhaps they saw their hus-
bands, or lovers whose jealousy they fear. They dreaded
a scene if they were discovered with me. That must have
been the reason for their disappearance. I fancy they
didn't belong to the first society. Their language was a
little free, and the shepherdess's especially wasn't the
purest French; but the pink domino had a very neat
figure—and no hoop-skirts! I shall find her again, I

hope.—With all this I have lost Freluchon and Monsieur Edmond.—But they adore the monster galop, and I am sure of finding them when the time comes for that. —But five glasses of punch at a franc a glass, five francs, and ten for candy,—fifteen francs in all! that's rather high for an intrigue that is hardly begun! If she had éven given me an assignation for to-morrow! I should have exacted that before handing over the candy."

As he pursued these reflections, Chamoureau walked along the corridor on the second floor, looking into every box in search of his pink domino.

He had his face against one of the little panes of glass, when he felt a hand on his arm; he turned; a Norman peasant, masked, was hanging on his arm, and she said to him in a wheedling voice:

"Here you are, Chamoureau, my sweet Chamoureau! Ah! what a good idea to take off your false nose, and how much better-looking you are now! When one has a face like yours, one shouldn't conceal it; do you hear, my friend?"

Our widower felt a thrill of pleasure at hearing such compliments addressed to himself. He would gladly have kissed the mask worn by the Norman, to show his satisfaction, but he contented himself with pressing her hand and arm most tenderly, saying:

"What, my charming peasant—do you know me?"

"Do I know you! Why bless my soul! who doesn't know you, O Chamoureau of my heart? It was wholly on your account, to meet you, that I came here."

"Really? But I had no idea myself that I should come. Our party wasn't made up till very late in the evening."

"But I was certain that you would come; my little finger told me." *

"Is your little finger such a magician as that?"

"Yes, for it told me that you would be disguised as a Spaniard; that you would have top boots which would cause you much annoyance——"

"By Jove! this is marvelous!"

"That you would make love to a pink domino and a shepherdess; I saw you with them just now."

"It's the truth; I don't deny it."

"You even offered them candy."

"Offered! you mean that they asked me for it."

"It's the same thing. You gave them each a stick; so I hope you'll give me one too, as I came to the ball solely to see you."

"If you came to the ball solely to see me, you ought not to care for candy."

"I care to have you as generous to me as to others— as gallant—as attentive—as amorous; will you be? Tell me, O my Chamoureau! for I love you, I am on fire for you, as you see!"

"Really, lovely Norman, you manifest sentiments which flatter me; but how do you know me?"

"If I should tell you, you would be greatly surprised;

---

* *Mon petit doigt me l'avait dit*—a phrase equivalent to the English "a little bird told me."

but I won't tell you—not here, at all events; later, when you come to my house, we shall see."

" You have a house? "

" Yes, my boy, one of the very swellest in the Chaussée d'Antin."

" Then you are rich? "

" Who isn't rich to-day? unless he's as stupid as a pot! "

" True; your reflection is very clever. And you are free? "

" As free as air! "

" And you will receive me? "

" You shall have the entrée every day. Come this way; there's another buffet, where they sell candy."

Chamoureau submitted to be led to the buffet in the corridor on the second floor; he could refuse nothing to a woman who declared that she had come to the Opéra on his account.

The Norman selected a stick of the same size as those selected by the pink domino and the shepherdess; she drank a glass of gooseberry wine, then took the Spaniard's arm again, saying:

" Mon Dieu! how wise you were to take off your nose! you are a hundred per cent. better looking! "

" But you, charming peasant, won't you take off your mask? You must divine my longing to gaze upon your features."

" It's not necessary, you know me already."

" Really! I know you? "

" Yes, and you like me very much."

"As for that, I can readily believe it; however, I would be glad to see you, so that I may recall where I have seen you before."

"You shall see me at my house on Rue de la Pépinière, opposite the barracks."

"What number, and whom shall I ask for?"

"The number's of no consequence, you'll see me at my window."

"But where shall I look for your window? This is rather vague."

"I'll toss you a bouquet."

"Very good; but still I——"

At that moment, a young man who wore no mask walked along the corridor, arm-in-arm with a little woman dressed as a dairymaid, to whom he was talking very earnestly. Instantly Chamoureau's companion stopped, crying:

"It's he! it's Adolphe! Ah! the traitor! the monster! I am sure he's with Malvina!"

And dropping the arm that she held, the Norman peasant ran after the couple and halted in front of the young man.

"Ah!" she exclaimed, "so I've caught you, you villain! you infamous traitor! You couldn't come to the ball with me! Monsieur was sick; he had the colic! And you refused to bring me, to come here with this little minx! But I'm not such a fool, my boy; you don't make me swallow such rubbish; I had an idea that I should catch you here."

"Come, come, Clorinde, don't make a scene; you know how I dislike them! Don't shout so loud!"

"I'll shout as loud as I please, and you can't make me keep quiet, you wicked rascal, for whom I sold my gold chain not a fortnight ago, and who throws my money away on other women!"

"You talk like a fool, Clorinde; if I have spent the money for your chain, I've spent plenty more with you!"

"You greenhorn! you, who had boots with holes in 'em and paper collars! Ah! this is too much, on my word! And you think that I'll let you strut about with your Malvina—for that's Malvina on your arm."

"Not at all, you are mistaken; it's a masker whom I met by chance, and whom I tell you to treat with respect."

"*Ouiche!* I'll treat her with respect; your charmer doesn't seem to have any tongue; she doesn't open her mouth! If it isn't Malvina, why doesn't she speak? But we'll soon see."

During this dialogue, the little dairymaid, who seemed to be all of a tremble, clung to her escort's arm; but the Norman suddenly snatched away her mask and cried:

"Ah! it wasn't Malvina! Ah! I was mistaken, was I? You are caught, traitor! As for you, little one, you know what I promised you if you ever went with Adolphe. I don't go back on my word—take that!"

As she spoke, the peasant dealt the dairymaid a powerful blow on the cheek; the latter attempted to take her revenge and to return the blow she had received from her jealous rival; but as Monsieur Adolphe had taken

advantage of the battle to make his escape, the Norman
ran after him, crying:

"It's no use for you to run away—I'll find you. Come,
Adolphe, don't run; I am not angry any more. Malvina
has what she deserves, that's all I wanted."

And the peasant disappeared in the crowd, while the
little dairymaid replaced her mask and tried to readjust
her disordered costume.

"Oh! the fishwoman!" she exclaimed; "is it possible that there can be such ill-bred women! But she
shall pay me. I'll go to see her man—the fat hosier
who is ruining himself for her; I'll tell him about all
the games she plays on him. Bless my soul! there's
enough of 'em to cover the city wall."

One gentleman had been a silent spectator of this scene,
which, however, seemed exceedingly distasteful to him.
The reader will guess that it was Chamoureau, who saw
his second conquest escape him with the stick of candy
which he had presented to her.

"How is this?" he said to himself at last; "she assured me that she came to the Opéra this evening solely
to see me, and she was on the watch for one Adolphe!
She told me that she loved me, that she was on fire for
me, and she leaves me to go and kick up a jealous row
with that young man—and she beats the girl he has on
his arm!—The deuce! what a wench! it's a bad move
to deceive her. She told me that she was very rich, that
she had a fine house on Rue de la Pépinière. The little
dairymaid declares that she is kept by a hosier. What

am I to believe out of all that? The one thing that is certain is that she has run after her Adolphe. I am very sorry that I bought the candy for her! but she said such pleasant things to me and pressed my arm so affectionately! O these women! I'll not trust them again; and yet it would be very cruel to have come to the Opéra ball without making a single acquaintance! What would those fellows think of me?"

In his disappointment, Chamoureau decided to go up another flight. There were fewer people in the corridor on the third floor, but the couples were more amorous in proportion to their scarcity; they talked into each other's faces, gazed into each other's eyes, held each other's arms or waists; and sometimes in the ardor of conversation, the hand strayed over a shapely figure.

Our widower observed all this, and his regret that he was alone became all the keener.

"All these people are very fortunate!" he said to himself; "they have love-affairs, intrigues under way. I am well aware that I too have been *intrigué*—mystified, —but nothing has come of it; for frankly I believe that I should have been very foolish to walk on Rue de la Pépinière, in the hope that a bouquet would be thrown to me from a window! That Norman must have been lying to me. My wisest course now is to join Freluchon and Edmond, so that I may go to supper with them. Still, it is annoying not to take someone with me to the supper; for I'll wager that each of them will have a little woman! Their luck is beyond my comprehension!

I suppose that it's the same as in gambling: some people always win and others never do!"

As he communed thus with himself, Chamoureau noticed a black domino, also walking alone, who had passed very close to him again and again within a few minutes, glancing constantly in his direction. It was a woman above middle height, very slender—too slender, in fact, because she was so everywhere; a few wisps of fair hair escaped from beneath her hood which came well over her forehead. The black mask was provided with a very ample barb; it was impossible to obtain a glimpse of any feature. The domino was simple and shabby, and the shoes were not elegant. But she was a lone woman, who had every appearance of being in quest of an adventure, and Chamoureau also pined for one.

"I will venture once more," he said to himself; "perhaps I shall have better luck this time!" and he approached the thin domino.

"It's very hot, is it not, lovely masker?"

"Yes, it's extremely warm here."

"Still, there are fewer people here than downstairs."

"True; it's much less crowded; it's more comfortable here."

"But I believe the heat ascends."

"Do you think so? it's quite possible; no doubt it does ascend."

"Otherwise it would be cooler here than downstairs."

"Oh! yes, of course; if it were cooler here——"

"They would feel the heat more downstairs."

" She converses very agreeably," said our widower to himself. " She doesn't try to be bright, to make fun of me, as the others did. I like this way better; I feel more at ease with this stranger, and something tells me that I have at last found what I sought. She doesn't try to mystify me; but after all, I prefer that she shouldn't know me; then, if I choose, I can retain my incognito with her."

The black domino stood beside the Spaniard, apparently waiting for him to renew the conversation. He, after pulling up his boots, decided to offer her his arm, murmuring in honeyed tones:

" Will you take a turn or two in the corridor with me ? "

" With pleasure."

" You are not expecting anybody? "

" No, I am not expecting anybody."

" You are quite sure? Pardon me for asking the question, but, you see, I have been walking with several ladies, and they all left me abruptly, to run after other men! Frankly, I don't care to take the risk of having that happen again."

" Oh! don't be afraid, monsieur; I am not capable of such conduct. I see clearly that I have to do with a *comme il faut* gentleman, and if you knew me better you would understand that you can place entire confidence in me. I have never known what it was to make sport of a man—I can safely take my oath to that; and I flatter myself that I enjoy an excellent reputation in the house where I lodge."

All this was said in the tone of a servant applying for a position and announcing her readiness to refer to her former employers.

But Chamoureau was delighted; he was sure that he had found what he wanted, and he pressed the arm that lay in his as he rejoined:

"What you tell me gives me great pleasure. I believe you; there is an accent of truth in your words."

"Besides, you can ask my employers if they are not satisfied with me."

"Your employers?"

"To be sure—the people I work for."

"Ah! you work—in a shop?"

"Yes, monsieur; oh! I don't set up for a princess myself! I told you that I had no desire to deceive anyone."

"That is very nice of you, and I can only praise your frankness. Might I inquire what branch of trade you are in?"

"I work for a shoemaker, monsieur; I sew ladies' shoes."

Chamoureau was not so well pleased with this admission; he would have preferred a milliner or a flower-maker; however, he said to himself:

"After all, there are some very pretty shoe-stitchers; if she is virtuous enough to have only one lover, I shall have made a lucky find all the same; she's a little thin, but she must be pretty. I'll tell Freluchon that she's in the ballet at the Cirque. She's a blonde, and I don't

dislike blondes.—Tell me, lovely domino," he said aloud,
" did you come to the ball alone?"

" No, monsieur, I came with a friend of mine; but
she was looking for someone, and when she met him, I
left them; I was afraid of being in their way."

" That was most thoughtful! So then you are free?"

" Yes, monsieur, entirely free!"

" And no previous entanglement—no liaison?"

" Oh! none at all! absolutely none! I can safely
swear that it's two years since I have walked alone
with a gentleman."

Chamoureau was in raptures at the thought that he
was walking with a woman to whom such a thing had
not happened for two years. In his enthusiasm he said
to himself:

" With this one I can safely try a stick of candy; she
deserves it more than the others did; her frankness and
innocence are worthy of the prize of virtue!"

And he escorted his domino to the buffet, saying:

" Pray, take something."

" Oh! you are very kind, monsieur, but I am not
thirsty."

" She isn't thirsty!" said Chamoureau to himself; " I
doubt if I could find another like her in the whole ball!"

And he became the more urgent:

" But do at least take a bonbon."

" You are very polite, monsieur; I don't like to keep
refusing."

" I trust you will not."

" I will take a stick of candy."

And the black domino selected one of the smallest, which cost only three francs, thereby putting the finishing touch to Chamoureau's delight. He offered his arm to his conquest once more, saying:

" In that case, if you are free, charming stitcher, will you do me the honor to sup with me and a few of my friends, who will also have ladies with them—that is to say, I assume that they will."

" Yes, monsieur, certainly, and with pleasure."

" You are fascinating! I feel that I love you dearly already."

" And I, too; I shall be very glad to make your acquaintance."

" Do you mean it? Then my appearance is not disagreeable to you? "

" Ah! I should be very hard to suit, if I did not think you a very handsome man! Monsieur must be accustomed to attracting women! "

Chamoureau turned redder than his rouge; the corridor had become too narrow for him; he placed his cap more on one side, pulled up his boot-flaps, and seemed to be walking on a spring-board, ready to jump.

" I don't know whom those fellows will bring to the supper," he said to himself, " but I'll wager that their conquests won't hold a candle to mine! I have an idea that this slender creature resembles the Madonnas we see in the pictures of our greatest masters. However, I'll find out about that; she's a good-natured body, and I am sure that she'll unmask as soon as I ask her to.—Let's go down to the ball-room," said our widower, taking his domino's hand; "we shall find my friends there; they are great jokers; they like the galop and are quite capable of dancing it.—Are you fond of dancing, my dear?"

"I am willing to do whatever anyone wishes, monsieur."

"That's very pleasant in company. In that case, if I ask you to remove this mask—that conceals your features, you will not refuse, will you?"

"Take off my mask! oh, no! I won't take off my mask here; I will at home."

"I presume that you don't keep it on at home; but what is there to prevent your taking it off a moment here, while we are walking in this corridor? You may put it right on again, if you please."

"But why do you want me to take it off?"

"I have just told you: because I long to look upon your features. That is a very natural desire—and since you have admitted that my face was not displeasing to you——"

"Oh! no, monsieur! far from it!"

"I am persuaded yours will be most pleasing to me."

"Oh! I am not very beautiful!"

"I will wager that you say that from modesty; at all events, it is not necessary to be very beautiful in order to please; there are some bright, saucy little faces that are far preferable to regular beauties."

"I have an odd face."

"Well! odd faces are included in what I have just said. Do take off that horrible mask!"

"Oh, no! I don't want to; I won't take it off till after supper, because I am a little less bashful when I have drunk a little pure wine."

"What! do you intend to eat supper with your mask on?"

"Why not?"

"It would bother you a good deal while eating."

"Oh, no! I can turn up the barb."

"Take off your mask, pretty stitcher! I am sure that you're lovely enough to paint, and you postpone it only to make your triumph all the greater."

"I won't take off my mask now; no, monsieur, I'm determined on that!"

"She's very obstinate about it!" said Chamoureau to himself, as he escorted his conquest to the ball-room; "it's simply to increase my desire, to inflame my imagination! Female cunning! I know what that is!"

At the moment that the Spaniard and the domino stepped into the space between the ball-room and the stage, a general galop began—one of those monster galops in which the torrent of dancers rushes and leaps and roars to the strains of music which would make mummies dance. Freluchon and Edmond soon whirled by Chamoureau, the first with his arm about a Marquise Pompadour, the second with his little *débardeur*. The sight electrified our widower, who said to his domino:

"Suppose we venture? what do you say?"

"I ask nothing better."

With that, the lady threw her arm about her escort and they plunged into the infernal galop. Then they had no choice but to go with the crowd, the torrent; for woe betide the man who stops! He is instantly thrown down by those who come behind.

But the Spaniard's bosom swelled with a noble ardor; he was pushed and jostled, but he went on and on. The heat was extreme, however; and from time to time his domino murmured:

"I am stifling! suppose we stop a minute?"

"No, no; we must keep on!" Chamoureau replied; "don't be afraid; I'm holding you tight; you shan't fall."

But after they had danced for some time, the lady's hood fell back, disclosing a tight fitting black cap on top of which the tower of fair hair was mingled with locks of gray hair combed up from behind. A moment later the tower fell to pieces; then it was the mask's turn to fall—and our widower discovered that he held in his arms a woman of fifty, ugly as the mortal sin, with a thin, sallow, vulgar face that would have been disgusting even in a concierge.

Dumfounded, furious at what he saw, Chamoureau did not hesitate an instant; he dropped his partner, who rolled on the floor among the feet of the dancers; and he lost himself among the spectators.

"I am not surprised now that she proposed to sup in her mask!" he said to himself.

VI

A GENUINE INTRIGUE

The pearl-gray domino had entered the enclosure reserved for the dancers, walking boldly through the crowd, well able to repay in kind those who pushed and jostled her, and paying no attention to the men who spoke to her and tried to detain her by the usual phrases, which such gentlemen do not vary enough.

"Where are you going, lovely domino?"

"Listen to me, my deserted beauty!"

"You are running after him—better come with me."

"If your face resembles your figure, you are the phœnix of dominos."

To all these pretty speeches, tall Thélénie replied only by a very expressive shake of the head. When a man attempted to detain her by taking her arm, she had no difficulty in releasing herself by a sudden movement, saying in a far from encouraging tone:

"I advise you to let me alone, for I assure you that you are wasting your time with me; and that would be a great pity, if you came to the ball with the purpose of making good use of it."

Thélénie's black eyes, full of fire, looked about on all sides for the little *débardeur* with whom she had seen

Edmond Didier talking. She was certain of recognizing her, although there were many similar costumes at the ball; a woman guided by jealousy takes in at a glance the figure, the carriage, the foot, the hand and the slightest movements of the person she believes to be her rival.

In a corner of the ball-room, near the orchestra, the pearl-gray domino, convinced that she was not mistaken, halted in front of a little masked *débardeur* and said:

"I was looking for you."

"You were looking for me!"

"Yes, you."

"What for?"

"To speak to you, naturally."

"What can you have to say to me? I don't know you —at least, I don't think I know you. But perhaps you're that big Julie who goes to the Café du Cirque so often, near the Folies-Dramatiques, and who always wins at dominoes."

"I am not big Julie; I never go to the Café du Cirque, and I don't play dominoes. But you evidently go there, and I am not sorry to know it."

"I go where I please—what business is it of yours? What are you talking about? If you were looking for me just to say that, it wasn't worth putting yourself out, charming domino."

"I have something much more interesting to say to you; but first tell me this: what do you do? who are you? Not of much importance! I can see that by your manners and your language. No matter—I want to

know; are you a milliner, flower-maker, seamstress—
or something much lower down? Come—answer me."

"Ha! ha! ha! this is too good, on my word! Madame questions me, and with a tone of authority!—one
would think she was talking to a slave! By what right
do you ask me all this?"

"By what right? Oh! I'll show you that I have a
right. Listen: you are Monsieur Edmond Didier's mistress."

"Oho! so you know that, my tall beauty! Very
good! I understand it all now; you're one of Edmond's
old ones; a poor creature whom he abandoned for me!
Ha! ha! and you've come here to make a jealous row!"

"Well, yes, I was Edmond's mistress, I still am; for,
if he has had a caprice for you, it's not what can be called
love!"

"Really! you believe that? you think that a man may
not love me? Well! you are mistaken, my dear; on
the contrary, he loves me dearly, he adores me; he told
me so just now."

"Listen, girl, remember what I am going to say."

"If it's a song you are going to teach me, I'll remember it if I know the tune."

"Don't jest, for my words are most serious."

"I don't care if they are; I am never serious myself."

"I forbid you—do you understand?—I forbid you to
go to Edmond's rooms again; and if you disobey me,
beware! you have no idea to what length jealousy may
drive me."

"If it could drive you home to bed now, what an excellent thing it would be!"

"You have heard me—and you will obey."

"Not much! This was a foolish step of yours, my dear; for I have quarrelled with Edmond and I didn't intend to see him again; just a minute ago he begged me to go to supper with him, and I refused; but now that you forbid me to—oh! that puts a different face on the matter; I will accept. I'll make it up with him, and we'll be like turtle-doves again."

"Beware! don't drive me to extremities, you little strumpet!"

"Oh! if I'm a little strumpet, you're a big one! Let me tell you that I snap my finger at you and your threats; and to prove it, there's Edmond now, looking everywhere for me, and I'm going with him."

Edmond Didier was, in fact, coming toward them; he was still looking for his little *débardeur*. Mademoiselle Amélia ran to him and seized his arm, saying:

"I'm not angry any more, dear boy; I love you more than ever, and I'll go to supper with you. You're glad of that, aren't you?"

The young man, thunderstruck by the sudden change that had taken place in the grisette's humor, stared at her and tried to read in her eyes whether she really meant what she said.

But she continued:

"You're surprised that I am not sulky any longer? Well! who do you suppose you owe it to? I'll tell

you; it's that tall mouse-gray domino who's looking at us
over there, and glaring at me as if she'd shoot me! She
forbade me to go with you! That instantly made me
want to do it."

Edmond looked at the masker the girl pointed out; it
was a fact that in the eyes which were fixed upon his
companion and himself there was a gleam which had
in it something fascinating. Those eyes were easily
recognizable, for, as Monsieur Beauregard had said,
there were no others at the ball which could be compared
with them.

Edmond divined therefore who the person was who
glared at him so, and, in spite of himself, he was disturbed and embarrassed for a moment beneath Thélénie's
burning glance.

"Oh!" he stammered, "that domino told you—forbade you to speak to me, did she?"

"Yes, she's one of your old ones, you must recognize
her. Madame is jealous, but I don't care a fig! You're
through with her, I hope. At all events, I'm not jealous
—I'm no such fool! I prefer to dance. You are going
to galop with me."

The pearl-gray domino, whose eyes were still fixed on
the young couple, suddenly walked toward them, stopped
beside Edmond and said in an undertone:

"So this is the creature for whom you abandon me!
She doesn't do you credit!"

"Eh? what's she saying to you?" demanded Mademoiselle Amélia; "some nasty thing about me, I'll bet."

" No, no! nothing at all! " Edmond replied, as he
watched Thélénie disappear in the crowd.

" I say yes; that tall giraffe spoke to you! "

" She called me a—monster! "

" Ah! how new that is! "

" Let us galop."

It was toward the end of this galop that Chamoureau
had dropped his partner, who lost her mask, her hair
and her cap, and had fled as far as possible, leaving the
ball-room and rushing aimlessly into the foyer, so great
was his fear of being pursued and overtaken by his new
conquest.

When he reached the foyer, the unlucky Spaniard
dropped upon a bench, saying to himself:

" I have too hard luck! I am pursued by cruel fate!
What a face! great God! what a horrible face! I
wouldn't have her for charwoman! Why, if I, a business agent, had such a woman in my house, she'd frighten
all my clients! And such an old thing! all skin and
bone! and a profile like an embroidery frame! When a
woman has no more flesh than that, she must be very
bold, to go to the Opéra ball, and try to make an acquaintance! I am not surprised that it hasn't happened
to her for two years—she must have meant ten!—And
I treated her to candy! It's very lucky that her mask fell
off when it did! if it hadn't been for that, she'd have
come to supper, she'd have unmasked afterward, the
wretch! and God knows all the jokes the others would
have made at my expense, especially Freluchon, who's

a connoisseur in pretty women; for he often used to say to me: ' Chamoureau, your wife's too handsome for one man, it's downright murder!'—He was dancing the galop just now with a handsome wench dressed *à la Pompadour,* and Edmond with a *débardeur;* they both have what they want, I'm the only one who has nothing, after paying for so many sticks of candy. But I am done; I have had my fill of intrigues, and if I weren't waiting for those fellows I'd go home. But I can't go without Freluchon, as my clothes are at his room. We are to meet here in the foyer, under the clock. It must be very late. I have had very little sport here, and I've lost my false nose."

And Chamoureau watched the promenaders with a woe-begone expression. He did not notice that a blue domino pointed him out to one of pearl-gray, whispering:

" That's the man; he came with them."

The pearl-gray domino, with whom we are well acquainted, but whom our widower did not know as yet, immediately seated herself beside him and motioned to the blue domino to go.

At first Chamoureau simply moved away a little, to make room for the person who had taken a seat by his side; then, allured by the perfume that emanated from his neighbor, he glanced furtively at her, saying to himself:

" Sapristi! this domino smells good; it's as if a bouquet had sat down here. I ought to have guessed that that other woman didn't amount to anything; she smelt of garlic, and when she got warm dancing—then it was much worse!"

Chamoureau's examination of the pearl-gray domino was wholly to her advantage; in addition to the perfume she exhaled, everything about her was refined, stylish and in good taste. But when Thélénie fastened her great black eyes on him, our widower was speechless with admiration, and in his confusion he could think of nothing better to do than to pull up his boots.

Thus far, Chamoureau had not addressed a word to his neighbor, although he was dying to do so; she, however, saved him the trouble by opening the conversation herself.

"Well, Monsieur Chamoureau, are you enjoying the ball?"

"What! how! madame knows me? I have the honor of being known to madame?" murmured our widower, utterly bewildered to hear the stylish domino call him by name.

"Yes, monsieur, I know you—not very well, I must admit; but well enough to tempt me to seat myself here so that I might talk with you."

"Oh! how flattered I am, madame! What! it was to talk with me that you came here to sit? that is extremely amiable on your part!"

"Oh, no! it is quite natural! Sometimes one passes the whole night here without meeting a person with whom one can talk freely; for, to speak frankly, the company is very much mixed at a masquerade."

"You don't know how fully I realize it, madame! for I myself, a moment ago, was misled by a—a—less than nobody! But you understand—when people are masked!"

"In spite of the mask, monsieur, there are always a thousand things which enable one to recognize the well-bred woman, and which betray all these grisettes, all these prostitutes who come here masked, to try to make dupes."

"That is perfectly true, madame; there are a thousand things that betray one's identity; and, as I sit beside you, madame, those things lead me to believe that I am talking with an extremely *comme il faut* person."

"Take care, Monsieur Chamoureau, you may be deceived again."

"Oh, no! this time I am sure of my ground!"

"You did not come to the ball alone, did you, monsieur?"

"No, madame, I came with two young men, friends of mine."

"Yes, Messieurs Freluchon and Edmond Didier."

"Ah! madame knows them also?"

"Very little; but I have a friend, a lady, who is very intimately acquainted with one of them."

"Yes, I understand; and it's with Freluchon, I suppose?"

"No, with Monsieur Edmond; and between ourselves, I think that my poor friend has bestowed her affections very ill."

"Yes, indeed, I should say so! If she relies on that young man's fidelity, she is completely taken in."

"He has to my mind every appearance of a ne'er-do-well, hasn't he, monsieur?"

"He's the worst ne'er-do-well in the world! one of those blades who make love to the first woman they see; who have three, four, five mistresses at the same time— I don't know how they manage it! I love the fair sex, there's no doubt of that, and I cultivate it assiduously, but I don't scatter myself about like that. *Ne quid nimis!* That Latin axiom is my motto. Forgive me for using a dead language, madame; it slipped from my tongue."

"I congratulate you, monsieur, for not behaving as Edmond does."

"Freluchon's no better! Indeed, I think perhaps he's worse! He's a thorough scapegrace, and, as he's rich, he can do more than others; but he's an intimate friend of mine, and I don't propose to speak ill of him, especially as my late wife had much esteem for him."

"Are you a widower, monsieur?"

"Alas! yes, madame; I have lost my Eléonore, my sweet better half! my faithful companion!"

Chamoureau was on the point of blowing his nose, but he checked himself, reflecting that it would be unwise to appear grief-stricken in that lady's company; and, laying aside his melancholy, he assumed a sprightly air.

"Does not madame dance?"

"Oh, no! monsieur, never at a masquerade. But what have you done with your two friends?"

"They are dancing, madame; they must be on the floor."

"Between ourselves, Monsieur Chamoureau, it isn't good form to dance here, unless one is disguised as you are; then anything is allowable; but those gentlemen are not."

"True; but they are not exactly dancing; the galop is the only thing they dance—the infernal galop."

"Oh, yes! I remember: I saw Monsieur Edmond pass just now with a woman dressed as a *débardeur*—his mistress, I suppose?"

"Yes, that's one of his mistresses; it must be little Amélia; he was looking for her."

"Who is this Amélia?"

"A young flower-maker: nineteen years old, with a piquant, roguish face, eyes full of fire and a lovely figure!"

"You seem to know her very well!"

"I! oh! I don't know her at all; I am simply repeating what Edmond told me about her a little while ago."

"Then you haven't seen this woman?"

"Not yet; but I shall see her before long, as we are all to sup together; Freluchon arranged it all at the costumer's."

"Ah! you are to sup together!"

Thélénie was silent for some moments, apparently lost in reflection. Meanwhile Chamoureau cudgelled his brain to think of something clever to say to her; having had no success, he confined himself to adjusting his cap and pulling up his boot-tops.

"Monsieur Chamoureau," said Thélénie at last, in her sweetest voice, "will you give me your arm for a little promenade—not here in the foyer, for there are too many people here."

"Will I, madame! why, I am only too happy that you should deign to take me for your escort."

And the Spaniard, springing to his feet, offered his arm to the pearl-gray domino, who took it with that lack of formality which a mask sanctions.

Before leaving the foyer, Chamoureau, as proud as Lucifer to have on his arm a stylish woman who left an odor of violets and patchouli as she passed, said to himself:

"Faith, I don't care what happens! I propose to risk another stick of candy!"

Whereupon he led the lady toward a buffet and urged her to take something; but Thélénie dragged him away, saying:

"I am obliged to you, monsieur, but I never take anything here; besides, I think that carrying about sticks of candy is very bad form.—Come, I long to be out of this foyer."

Thélénie had just noticed the tall Beauregard, who was gazing at her with an air of surprise, and with a mocking smile which seemed to say:

"What! you, elegance personified, on the arm of this Spaniard who looks like a genuine buffoon!"

Chamoureau, who had a most exalted opinion of his new acquaintance since she had told him that she never took anything at a ball, walked with her into the corridor, where the domino guided him toward the staircase, saying:

"Let us go up, there are too many people here."

"With pleasure; let us go up."

When they reached the second floor the domino continued to ascend, saying:

"Let us go up farther."

Nor did she stop at the third, but said to her escort:

"Let us keep on."

And Chamoureau made no objection.

"Does she mean to take me up to the small boxes in the dome?" he said to himself. "Have I inspired her with a frenzied passion? But I believe the small boxes aren't open on ball nights. No matter, let her take me where she will; she's a beautiful woman, her figure is enchanting, her hand small, her language distinguished. God grant that I may not find behind her mask any resemblance to that horrible shoe-stitcher! Gad! I am distrustful now!"

The gray domino stopped in the passage leading to the amphitheatre and said to her escort:

"Excuse me, monsieur, for making you come up so high, but I was anxious that we should be alone for what I have to say to you."

"I would have followed you up in a balloon, madame, if you had asked me."

"Oh! you go much too fast perhaps, monsieur, for, after all, you do not know me."

"But I desire most ardently to make your acquaintance."

"Well, monsieur, I shall surprise you, no doubt, but I will not deny that I too should be very glad to know you better, and that it was with that end in view that I took my place by your side just now in the foyer."

"Is it possible that I am so fortunate as to be distinguished by you—so fortunate that a fond hope may be permitted to take root in my heart?"

"Oh! don't go so fast, monsieur; do you think that none but sensual liaisons may exist between two persons of different sexes?"

"I don't say just that; but I have reached the age when love is as necessary to men as the bottle to a child; I say the bottle as I might say the nurse! Madame, should I be too presumptuous if I asked to see your face?"

"It was for the express purpose of showing you my features that I brought you here, monsieur. I am very glad to have you know what sort of person you have to do with."

As she spoke, Thélénie removed her mask and Chamoureau uttered an exclamation, this time of admiration.

Indeed, the first sight of her face might well arouse that sentiment. All her features were beautiful and clean cut; her teeth were beyond reproach, her hair as black as the crow's wing, and her eyes, whose brilliancy

we have already noted, were unusually large, fringed
by long black lashes, and surmounted by perfectly arched
eyebrows. Perhaps that face would have lost a little of
its brilliancy in the daylight; there were circles round
the eyes and the complexion was a little sallow; but in
the gaslight these slight blemishes vanished and left only
lovely features and a countenance instinct with animation.

Chamoureau was fairly dazzled.

"Oh! madame!" he stammered; "on my word—I
did not expect—I mean—yes, I did expect to see a pretty
face—but yours passes all understanding—you are a
goddess! I am compelled to admit that Eléonore was
only small beer beside you."

This unique compliment brought a faint smile to the
lovely brunette's lips.

"Now that you have seen me, monsieur," she rejoined, "do you still desire to make my acquaintance?"

"Do I desire it, entrancing creature! Ah! it is more ·
than a desire now, it is a craving! it is more than a
craving, it is——"

"Well, monsieur, I give you permission to call on me,
I will receive your visits—but only on one condition."

"I agree beforehand to all conceivable conditions."

"There is only one, monsieur; but you must swear
to abide by it; if you should fail, my door would be
closed to you instantly."

"That fact should assure you of my obedience, madame; pray tell me what the condition is."

"First of all, monsieur, I must tell you my name: I am Madame de Sainte-Suzanne."

"De Sainte-Suzanne—what a charming name! You must be descended from that Suzanne whom two rakes tried to catch a glimpse of as she left her bath."

"My condition is, monsieur, that you will tell nobody —*nobody,* you understand—that you know me and that you call on me."

"Agreed, *belle dame;* although certainly one may well be proud to know you, although one is entitled to be vain of your acquaintance, from the instant that you forbid me to speak, I will not lisp a word."

"Do not forget that promise, monsieur, especially when you are with your friends Messieurs Edmond Didier and Freluchon."

"Oh! I'll be very careful, I know that they are terribly garrulous, especially Freluchon."

"And if my name should happen to be mentioned in your presence, if I should be the subject of conversation, you will listen and keep silent."

"If you wish, I will not even listen."

"I beg your pardon, monsieur, you will listen and remember everything that is said; for I am inquisitive and am anxious to know what people think of me."

"In that case, never fear; I'll open both my ears so wide that I won't lose a word."

"Now, monsieur, I must leave you. See, this is my address;—you may return to your friends and sup with them."

As she spoke, Thélénie handed Chamoureau a card,
then hurriedly replaced her mask.

"What is this, fascinating woman! are you going to
leave me?" said the Spaniard, tucking the card under
his doublet. "I hoped—I dared to think that you would
allow me to escort you to your home."

"No, monsieur, it's impossible; I have friends here,
and I must join them again. The day after to-morrow,
between two o'clock and five, I give you permission to
call. Now, adieu; I forbid you to follow me."

And Thélénie ran rapidly downstairs.

"All the same," said Chamoureau, pulling up his boot-
tops, "I have made a fine conquest!"

VII

THE DANGER OF FALLING ASLEEP IN COMPANY

Thélénie found Mademoiselle Héloïse in the balcony
box; she motioned to her to come with her.

"Do you mean to say we are going already?" asked
the little black domino.

"Already! why, it's very late. See, the dancers have
plenty of room now, which means that the ball is nearing
its end."

"Have you spoken to Monsieur Edmond?"

"No, no, it's of no use; I leave him with his mistress —a flower-maker, my dear; really, it makes me blush to think that I was jealous of such a creature."

"But there are some very pretty flower-makers!"

"What of that? she's a grisette, all the same, and that sort of an affair won't keep Edmond in chains for long. I say again that I regret having lowered myself by speaking to that girl. However, I have just made the acquaintance of a person who will keep me advised concerning my faithless lover's intrigues."

"It's that tall man dressed as a Spaniard, I suppose, that that woman came to tell you about?"

"Exactly; an idiot who thinks he's made a conquest of me.—Come this way, we'll get down more quickly."

As the two women started downstairs, the tall man who had talked with Thélénie in her box, happened to be directly in front of her. He stopped her, saying:

"How is this? you have left your hidalgo? Oh! my dear, you were very foolish to leave him, for you won't find his like at this ball."

"And I am not looking for him, you see, as I am going away."

"Without Edmond Didier?"

"Without Edmond Didier!"

"Whom you leave behind in the company of an extremely pretty little *débardeur*."

"I am absolutely indifferent to that, as you see!"

"Oh! you conceal your thoughts; it certainly was for some purpose that you consented to pass your arm through that fellow's,—that man had the appearance of a mustard sign."

"That doesn't concern you; adieu!"

"You are in a great hurry."

"I don't see that we have anything more to say to each other."

"Nothing more to say to each other! You always forget that we have, on the contrary, a very serious subject to discuss. But I will come to see you."

"Very well, I am horribly tired. Adieu!"

"You run away as if you had seen Paul Duronceray here."

The name of Duronceray caused the fair Thélénie a painful shock; despite the mask that covered her face it was easy to detect the perturbation which that name aroused in her mind.

She soon succeeded in recovering herself, however, and rejoined in a harsh voice:

"You are mistaken, Beauregard, I run away from nobody; and if Monsieur Duronceray were here, I should not be the one to run away—but you!"

"I! oh, no! for now he ought to thank me, instead of bearing me a grudge."

"Very well! hunt him up then!"

And the pearl-gray domino disappeared with her companion.

Monsieur Beauregard stood for some moments lost in thought; then he shrugged his shoulders and returned to the foyer, saying to himself:

"The fact remains that I have no one to sup with; it is time to be thinking about that."

Chamoureau, having discreetly allowed a few minutes to elapse, that he might not appear to be following the pearl-gray domino, who had forbidden him to do so, decided at last to descend from the amphitheatre passage. Now that he had an intrigue fairly started with a lady as elegant as she was lovely, the widower had none but contemptuous glances for all the women who passed him. He puffed himself out in his ruff, held his head erect with much dignity, squared his shoulders under his cloak, and no longer took the trouble to pull up his boot-tops. He was a man who had *arrived;* in other words, a man who had what he wanted and who no longer needed to put himself out in order to gain his ends.

Meanwhile he desired to find his intimate friend Freluchon and young Edmond, because he began to feel an inclination to sup.

In the corridor on the first floor a domino stopped him, and Chamoureau shuddered as he recognized the shoe-stitcher's false light hair.

"Ah! I have found you again at last, my dear monsieur!" cried the scrawny creature. "I am so glad! I have been looking for you ever since that unlucky galop, when I fell; you let go with your left arm, I was a little dizzy, and—*patatras!* And I lost my cap, too, and had hard work finding it; I bruised myself somewhere when I fell, but it won't amount to anything."

" But why were you looking for me, madame? " rejoined the Spaniard, wrapping himself in his cloak, with
a savage glare. " I was not looking for you."

" Why, as it's pretty late, I was thinking about supper,
as you asked me to take supper with your friends."

" I think I see myself taking you to supper! You had
a stick of candy from me, and that's all you will get;
for it's not decent to deceive everybody as you do. At
your age, and with a face like yours—to try to make
a conquest! Go and hide yourself! "

" Let me tell you that you're an impudent wretch, monsieur, and that a man don't talk like that to a woman.
When a man has such spindleshanks as yours, he
shouldn't put on so many airs. Did anyone ever hear of
such a thing! This blockhead flinging a miserable stick
of candy in my face! You might stuff it into your nose,
your sweetmeat; it would go in. I'll show you what I
think of it! "

And the domino hurled her stick of candy at Chamoureau's legs and angrily turned her back on him.

While the widower gazed in stupefaction at the shat-
tered fragments of the bonbon, Freluchon took his arm.

" What the deuce are you doing here," he said, " in
rapt contemplation before these broken bits of candy? "

" Faith! I was thinking, as I looked at them, what a
pity it is to waste good stuff like that."

" Pshaw! let's go to supper; that will be better fun
than staying here. We are just going; we are all downstairs, and I left my Marquise Pompadour to come in

search of you; I should say that that was rather kind
on my part, eh?"

"Parbleu! you couldn't leave me here and go off without me, when my clothes are at your rooms."

"Come, come; we are going to have supper at Vachette's."

"Why not at the Maison d'Or? it's nearer. You see
I never thought to bring a cloak or an overcoat to wear
over my disguise. You have a carriage, I trust?"

"A carriage, when there are eight of us! We will
run; the weather's fine and that will warm us up."

Edmond was in the vestibule with his little *débardeur*
on his arm; two young men, friends of Freluchon and
himself, each accompanied by an unmasked domino, and
the little woman dressed as a Louis XV marchioness completed the party. The merry band walked away, shouting *oh!* and *éh!* as the custom is during the Carnival,
each with his chosen companion on his arm; our widower
alone had no one, which fact did not prevent his shouting louder than the others, for he said to himself:

"If I haven't a woman on my arm at this moment, I
flatter myself that the one I have captivated is worth
more alone than all four of their supper companions."

They arrived at Vachette's, where Freluchon, being a
man of forethought, had engaged a private room beforehand. The table was laid; the ladies removed their
hoods, caps, gloves, everything that would interfere
with their eating; and they all whispered and laughed
as they glanced at the Spaniard.

"Who on earth is this tall scarecrow without a lady?"
they asked Freluchon; "is he a provincial on his first
visit to Paris?"

"No, mesdames," Freluchon replied, "he's a widower
who has sworn to remain faithful to his defunct spouse;
he's a male Artemis; he is Orpheus, who has lost his
Eurydice and is constantly looking for her. If you wish,
I will make him weep in a moment."

"No, no, thanks! we prefer to laugh. But why does
he wear a disguise if he's so grief-stricken?"

"To disguise his grief; he is persuaded that he has no
right to divert himself except in that costume."

"Mesdames, don't you think Freluchon is stuffing
us?"

"To table! to table!"

"See, there are ten places, and only nine of us," observed one of the young men.

"True," replied Freluchon, "I ordered supper for ten
because I thought that Chamoureau would bring a lady."

"That's so!" cried Edmond; "I hadn't noticed.
How's this, my dear Chamoureau, didn't you make a
little acquaintance at the ball? What does this mean?
how, then, did you pass the time?"

Chamoureau drank a glass of chablis and replied with
a triumphant smile:

"I beg pardon, messieurs, I beg pardon! if I haven't
brought a lady to supper, that doesn't prove by any means
that I am not so highly favored as you are by—by
Cupid!"

"The deuce! do you mean it, Chamoureau?" cried Freluchon; "you've been favored by Cupid! Come, tell us about it! When I found you in the foyer, looking, as if stupefied, at the remains of a stick of candy, I supposed that your presents had been repulsed with loss."

"Oh! not by any means! on the contrary my candy was not once repulsed; in fact, I have given away a great deal of it during the night!"

"Really! then you have had a number of intrigues."

"I have had nothing else all night long; I left one woman to take another, and vice versa!"

"What a Lovelace!"

"How is it, monsieur," said the little Pompadour, "that after making so many conquests at the ball, you haven't brought a single one to supper? That is not very gallant for a hidalgo!"

"Pardon me, pretty marchioness," rejoined Chamoureau, after tossing off another glass of chablis, with which he constantly watered his oysters, "my first conquests were worth little more than a stick of candy. Frankly, I found that they were not what I was looking for, so I dropped them, as Henri Monnier says in his *Famille Improvisée.* But the last—oh! the last——"

"She dropped you, I suppose," said Freluchon.

"No indeed! *Diantre!* let us not joke about her! it's a very serious affair with her. Ah! Dieu!"

"Ha! ha! what a touching sigh!"

"Well, monsieur, why didn't you bring that one to supper—the one who is responsible for that groan?"

"I promise you that I would have asked nothing better; indeed, I invited her, but she refused—she couldn't come."

"Perhaps she was afraid of compromising herself?"

"I don't say that; and yet I can understand that in her position——"

"Ah! she's a woman with a position! Is she on the stage?"

"Well, hardly! no, no! she's a very great lady."

"About five feet six?"

"I am not joking; she's a lady of the very best society."

"Ha! ha! you rascal of a Chamoureau! I believe you are laughing at us."

"Or that she laughed at him!"

"I assure you that she did not laugh at me! In the first place, she unmasked, and I saw the most captivating face. These ladies are very pretty most assuredly, but my superb brunette would throw them all into the shade!"

"I say, Spaniard, do you know that you make us tired with your brunette!"

"If she wouldn't come to supper with you," said little Amélia, "that proves right away that she was intending to take supper with someone else, doesn't it, mesdames?"

"Yes, yes; Amélia is right."

"Oh! you are mistaken, mesdames; it isn't at all as you imagine."

"Well, Chamoureau, where do you expect to see your wonderful conquest again? has she given you an assignation?"

"She has done more, my dear fellow: she has given me her address, with permission to call on her—at her hôtel!"

"So she has a hôtel—furnished probably."

"And when he goes to ask for his charmer, the concierge will say: 'It's on such a floor, monsieur, such a number; the numbers are on the doors'—Ha! ha!"

"Laugh away! laugh all you please! 'He laughs best who laughs last!'"

"The moment you begin on proverbs, I haul down my flag. But where does your conquest live? Perhaps I know her house."

"Freluchon, ask me for my fortune, ask me for my life——"

"You wouldn't give 'em to me, I know; go on."

"I would give them to you rather than tell you the name and abode of my fascinating brunette!"

"Oho! is it as bad as that?"

"I have sworn to be discreet, and I shall keep my oath! If I hadn't promised, it would be a different matter."

"Inasmuch as you have sworn—you will tell us the whole thing at dessert!"

"Never!—better a thousand times to be a widower!"

"Bravo! that's not bad! I'll remember it!"

"You are making me talk nonsense, Freluchon; but in Carnival time——"

"Join me, mesdames and messieurs; I drink to Chamoureau's mysterious conquest!"

"Good! here's her health!"

"For my part, I won't drink it," said the marchioness; "don't you do it, mesdames; he had the face to say that she was prettier than we are!"

"Forgive him, mesdames; passion makes him blind."

"I am rather inclined to think that he's drunk."

Chamoureau did not stint himself while the young men were talking and laughing with their companions, but addressed himself constantly to the decanters within his reach, saying to himself:

"Ah! these strumpets won't drink to my conquest! All right! I'll drink to her myself, in madeira and champagne! To your health, seductive, enrapturing Sainte-Suzanne! You are as far above these lights-o'-love as the oak is above the weed! You could crush them by a single glance; your eyes shine like real diamonds, whereas all these creatures are simply white topazes—To your health again, divine woman! I drain my glass to you."

By dint of drinking of healths and draining his glass, Chamoureau fuddled himself completely; then his head grew heavy, his eyes closed, and he fell asleep.

Our sleeper was awakened by a succession of light taps on his shoulder. He opened his eyes and looked about him. He was still in the small room where he had supped, surrounded by the remains of the feast; but all his table companions had disappeared, and he saw nobody but the waiter who had roused him.

"Hallo! what's the meaning of this?" murmured Chamoureau, rubbing his eyes. "Where are my friends —those gentlemen—and their ladies?"

"They all went away just a minute ago, monsieur."

"What! they went away without me, without waking me!"

"Yes, monsieur, they did it on purpose. I was going to wake you, but Monsieur Freluchon said: ' No, don't wake him till we're gone; that will teach him to go to sleep in our company!'"

"Oh! how stupid! some silly nonsense, some wretched joke all the time! Why, bless my soul! it's broad daylight!"

"Parbleu! long ago, monsieur! it's nearly eight o'clock."

"Sapristi! and I have to go to Freluchon's to change my clothes! However, there are plenty of cabs, luckily. Is there anything for me to pay, waiter?"

"No, monsieur, it's all paid."

"Good!—To think that I haven't an overcoat to hide this costume! Freluchon is to blame for that; ' you won't be cold,' he said.—It isn't the cold I'm afraid of, but the street urchins.—Call a cab, waiter; have it come as near the door as possible."

"Bless me! monsieur, they ain't allowed to come on the sidewalk."

"Well, then, right in front of the door."

Chamoureau covered himself with his cloak as well as he could; he pulled his cap over his eyes, drew his

chin inside his ruff, pulled up his boot-tops, and when
the waiter announced that the cab was waiting below,
rushed down the stairway and across the sidewalk so
recklessly that he nearly overturned a woman carrying a
tray of bread.

The woman shouted after Chamoureau, who had
knocked off three loaves, calling him: "Beast, brute,
dirty scum!" But he let her shout, for he was already
out of sight inside the cab; he gave Freluchon's address and the cab drove away followed by the hoots of
the urchins who had gathered to see a masker, and by
the shrieks of the woman with the tray on her head, who
was obliged to pick up her loaves.

They soon reached the house on Rue Saint-Georges
in which Freluchon lived. Chamoureau leaped out of
his cab under the porte cochère, and hastily paid the
cabman and dismissed him; because, in his everyday
clothes, he could easily walk home.

That transaction completed, the widower said to the
concierge:

"I am going up to Freluchon's room."

"What for?" demanded the concierge, eyeing the
Spaniard from head to foot.

"What for? why, don't you know me? I am Chamoureau, Freluchon's best friend."

"Yes, I recognize monsieur now, in spite of his masquerade."

"I am going up to my friend's room to get my clothes
—unless Freluchon left them with you."

" Monsieur Freluchon left nothing with me, and it ain't worth while for you to go up, as there's no one there. Monsieur Freluchon didn't come home to sleep."

" What's that you say, concierge? it's impossible."

" It's the truth, monsieur."

" Then you have my clothes here? "

" No, monsieur. Last night, if you remember, Monsieur Freluchon came in with a boy who had a bundle—your clothes, no doubt."

" Well, yes; what then? "

" The boy was going to leave the bundle here, but Monsieur Freluchon had to go upstairs to get some money, so he took the bundle up, saying: ' Chamoureau would rather dress in my room than in yours. ' "

" Very good; then my clothes are upstairs. Let's go and look for them; if Freluchon isn't there, you must have his key."

" That's just what I haven't got; sometimes he leaves it with me, but he generally takes it with him; and he didn't leave it last night."

" By Jove! this is too much! my clothes are in his room, he knows it, he has his key in his pocket, and he doesn't come home to sleep! What is going to become of me in my Spanish costume? It's an outrage to have to go home dressed like this! "

" Monsieur can take a cab."

" I know that well enough; it wasn't worth while to send the other one away. But I've got to get out of the cab; and I live on Carré Saint-Martin, where there are always lots of people passing. If my house had a porte cochère, I would have the cab drive under it; but no— it's a house-door; and my concierge and all the neighbors will see me come home in this state! Sapristi! this is an infernal trick for Freluchon to play on me.—But I have an idea. Concierge, suppose you lend me some of your clothes?"

"Oh! they wouldn't fit, monsieur; I am short and thin, and monsieur is tall and stout."

"That's so; I'm a fine man, and you are not. Well, I must swallow the absinthe. Concierge, be kind enough to step out and find me a cab."

"But I am all alone, you see, monsieur; my wife has gone out to work and I can't leave my post."

"I will look out for your post—never fear."

"But that isn't the same thing; you don't know the tenants."

"That's of no consequence. Go; my reputation is at stake. Here's forty sous for your trouble; I pay well, you see."

"All right, I'll go; I hope I'll find one on the stand."

"A cab I must have, dead or alive! do you hear?"

The concierge decided, albeit regretfully, to desert his post, and Chamoureau stepped inside.

"Luckily the porte cochère is open," he said, "I shall not have to pull the string!"

VIII

A FALSE CONCIERGE

Chamoureau concealed himself in the farthest corner of the concierge's room, in an old armchair that
might have served the purpose of a couch. He placed
himself with his back to the window through which
visitors addressed the functionary whom he represented,
and, in order that he might be observed less easily, he
removed his plumed cap and replaced it with an old cap
that he found on a table.

So long as people simply passed and repassed the lodge,
the false concierge did not put himself out; he did not
turn his head, but contented himself with cursing Freluchon, who had put him in that embarrassing position.

But soon someone opened the window, a man's head
appeared, and a loud voice inquired:

"Is Monsieur Delaroche in?"

Chamoureau did not stir and did not say a word. The
voice repeated, louder than before:

"Is Monsieur Delaroche in?"

The same immobility and the same silence on Chamoureau's part. Whereupon the voice assumed a formidable intonation, capable of breaking all the panes of the
window.

"Sacrebleu! are you deaf? are you still asleep? This is the third time I've asked if Monsieur Delaroche was in, and you don't answer! What kind of a damned concierge is this!—Wait a bit, till I come into your lodge; I'll shake you and teach you to sleep at this time of day!"

Chamoureau, who was not at all anxious that that gentleman should enter the lodge and shake him, decided to answer without turning:

"He's in! yes, yes, he's in!"

"Why didn't you say so then, you old fool?"

"He's in! he's in!"

The loud-voiced individual went upstairs, and our widower hurled himself in his chair once more, muttering:

"After all, I was a great fool not to answer. Probably no one has gone out so early as this, and I don't risk anything by saying they're in; and then, even if they should be out, what do I care?"

Soon various other persons appeared at the window.

"Is Madame Duponceau visible?"

"Yes, yes, she's there."

"Is Monsieur Bretonneau in?"

"He's there, he's there."

"Is there anybody at Mademoiselle Crémailly's?"

"She's there, she's there."

"Then she's back from the country?"

"She's there!"

"In the country, or here?"

"She's there, she's there!"

" Sapristi! tell me what you mean, concierge: is Mademoiselle Crémailly still in the country, or has she come back to Paris?"

" She's there, she's there!"

" Very well, then I'll go up. Still on the fourth?"

" She's there!"

" Heavens! what a donkey that concierge is! one would say he was a parrot—repeating the same thing over and over again."

" I'm beginning to get infernally tired of this!" said Chamoureau to himself; " altogether too many people come to this house. The deuce! now it's raining great guns! and my cab doesn't come! Can it be that there wasn't one on the square? that's usually the way when it rains hard. O Freluchon! you shall pay me for this! The rascal probably went home with his Pompadour!"

Soon a lady's maid appeared at the window.

" Madame's paper, please, Monsieur Mignon," she said. " I am a little late not that madame's hair is dressed yet, but I must have time to read the paper before she does, as usual; especially as there's a most intensely exciting *feuilleton* just now. It's too splendid for anything, I tell you: four killed already, and one that they're getting ready to poison! and a woman who always has a dagger hidden in her belt! and a château where there are subterranean vaults with instruments of torture, and the author describes the way of using them! There's an interesting executioner and there's corpses and tortured people on every page! Oh! such a lovely

novel! Now that's what I call literature, and I know
what I'm talking about; I don't read all this mawkish
stuff, not me! I want a crime, a murder, in every
chapter; then I say: 'there's an author who has a
wonderful talent and who has studied murders to some
purpose.'—But look here! I believe you're not listening
to me! And where's my paper? God bless my soul! he's
still asleep! Well, I'll come in and get it myself."

The young servant entered the room, looked over several papers that lay on the table, and took her own,
saying:

"You must have been kept up late last night, old
Mignon? I'll bet it was because Madame Duponceau
went to the ball. There's a woman who's up to snuff;
she tells her old beau that she has a sick headache or one
of her nervous attacks, and means to go to bed at nine
o'clock; so she dismisses him with an: 'I'm going to
dream of you, my loulou!' and he's no sooner out of sight
than she skips off to the ball with another man. But
still it's the custom, it's done everywhere, as the song
says:

> "Trompe-moi, trompons-nous,
> C'est un plaisir assez doux!"

Bless my soul! he's really asleep.—Au revoir, Père Mignon. Take this, to wake you up, as you haven't anything to say to me."

And the girl brought her fist down hard on the old
cap that Chamoureau had put on his head; then she ran
laughing from the room, while the unlucky widower, who

dared not stir and had taken the blow without a word, with difficulty extricated himself from the cap which was jammed down on his nose.

"That servant is very familiar with the concierge," he muttered; "if I were Madame Mignon, I would keep an eye on her.—And that cab doesn't come! It seems as if everything was against me!—But what's all this noise in the house? One would think there was a row on every floor. Gad! I wish I were a long way from here!"

There was, in fact, a great shouting on the second floor, a quarrel on the third, and a lively exchange of insulting epithets on the fourth. One would have thought that the house was given over to pillage; all the tenants were in the halls, the uproar increased momentarily and seemed to approach the concierge's lodge. Soon the voices became distinct; everybody seemed to be coming downstairs. Some persons went out; but the tenants collected in front of the concierge's window and began to abuse him.

"So this is the way you carry out my orders, is it, you blockhead of a concierge?" cried a young man wrapped in a handsome dressing-gown. "It seems to me that I pay you well enough for you to give some attention to what I say to you. I told you last night that if anyone should ask for me this morning, I was not at home, not at home to anybody! it was impossible to misunderstand me. I added simply: 'You will not let anything come up but my breakfast, my chocolate, which they make for

me in the restaurant close by.'—A child always brings it,
so that you couldn't make any mistake about that. But
lo and behold! someone rings; I say to myself: ' there's
my chocolate.' I open the door, and what do I see? my
tailor! A creature whom I left because he dressed me
wretchedly, and now he insists on my paying him a regular apothecary's bill—a bill in which he charges sixty
francs for a waistcoat! And that fellow shrieks and
threatens me! I was tempted to pitch him over the stair-
rail.—And it's you, you idiot, who are responsible for
this scene! Pay a tailor! In God's name, what do you
take me for? "

Next came a lady's maid in a frenzy.

" Why did you let anybody go up to Madame Duponceau's? You know very well that madame is never visible before one o'clock at the earliest. You have been
told enough times! I had gone out to buy some rolls;
the bell rang; madame thought I had forgotten my key
and opened the door, and there was a strange gentleman
who's paying court to madame and has never seen her
except by candle-light. You can judge of my mistress's
despair, for her face wasn't made up; every morning she
puts on white and pink and red and black—paints herself all colors—to say nothing of the false hair and arti-
ficial teeth and substitutes of all sorts.—And to show herself to monsieur in that state! she was furious; she
slammed the door in his face, saying: ' I'm not in!'
But the trick was turned all the same; the stranger stood
like a statue on the landing, and when I came back my

mistress paid me and discharged me; I've lost my place
—and all because this old goose of a concierge said
that Madame Duponceau was visible at this time of the
morning! But this ain't the last of it; I must have another place or else I'll complain to the landlord and have
you sent about your business."

" I," said a man, " asked him ten times if Mademoiselle
Crémailly had come back from the country; he finally
said yes, so I went up to the fourth floor—and when
one's lame, it isn't pleasant to go up four flights of stairs
—and I found nobody but the cook, breakfasting with a
soldier. Very pretty, on my word! I'll let Mademoiselle
Crémailly know about it."

" I was breakfasting with my cousin, monsieur; that
ain't a crime. He was on duty last night at the Opéra,
and he looked in this morning to say good-day; where's
the harm? I asked him to breakfast with me—just a
boiled egg—there's no need of making a long story out of
that. You can tell Mademoiselle Crémailly if you want
to. I'm not afraid of her discharging me for such a
little thing as that. This concierge hasn't got two sous'
worth of common sense, to tell you mademoiselle had
come back from the country, when she's going to be there
at least two weeks longer! He must have had too much
white wine this morning."

A lady enveloped in a simple *peignoir* cried even louder
than the others:

" You are a miserable villain, concierge! You will be
the cause of a duel. Moncornu found Hippolyte in my

room. To be sure, Hippolyte was doing nothing wrong
there; he had taken off his overcoat, it is true, but only
so that he could light my fire better. Every day a man
takes off his overcoat to kindle a lady's fire. That's the
way the most harmless actions are twisted into crimes in
a jealous rival's eyes. Moncornu rushed upon Hippolyte,
using language which I will not repeat. Hippolyte is
not the man to allow himself to be insulted without reply-
ing. I tried in vain to pacify them. From words they
came to threats, and finally they went out to fight. O
God! if Hippolyte is killed, I shall not survive him!
If Moncornu is the one, I shall never be consoled; still
I would rather it should be Moncornu than Hippolyte.
—You horrid brute of a concierge, you are the cause of
all this! Your orders were to say: ' Madame is at the
bath,' as usual, and you said: ' She's there, she's there! '
You're a blockhead, a donkey! you never were fit to keep
a door! ' "

All these clamors and upbraidings assailed Chamoureau's ears without inducing him to turn his head; on
the contrary, he slunk down still deeper into his chair
and tried to show nothing but his cap. But the obstinate
silence of the person whom they all supposed to be the
concierge simply intensified the general indignation.
They shouted at him:

" What have you to say to all this? "

" Come, speak! "

" Tell us why you did it."

" You see, he won't say a word! "

" Monsieur doesn't even condescend to answer us."

" Don't you hear us, concierge? have you suddenly gone deaf ? "

" Can it be that he's still asleep ? "

" That isn't possible; we've made noise enough to wake the dead."

" This silence isn't natural ! "

" He doesn't move; can he have had a stroke of apoplexy ? "

" We must find out what the matter is. The poor fellow ! here we are abusing him, and perhaps he is dead ! "

Meanwhile someone had opened the door, and several persons rushed in at the same moment. They ran to the easy-chair and began by turning it round so that they could see the person seated in it; whereupon there were exclamations of surprise on every side.

" It isn't Père Mignon ! "

" It isn't the concierge ! "

" It's a false concierge ! "

" Just look at the costume; it's a Spaniard of the time of Louis XIII."

" It's a masker."

" He isn't masked."

" It's a masker, all the same; that's what they call people disguised."

" It's a thief who broke into the lodge while the concierge was away."

" He's taken his cap already."

" Answer; what are you doing here, merry-andrew ? "

Chamoureau decided to rise; he tossed the concierge's cap aside, resumed his own cap with the plumes, and replied, affecting a dignified air:

"In the first place, messieurs and mesdames, I am not a thief and you will soon have proof that I am not. I am waiting for the concierge to return; he has gone to get me a cab, for you will understand that I could not go home on foot in this disguise."

"But you don't belong in the house. Why did you come here?"

"I came here, intending to go to the apartment of my intimate friend Freluchon, on the fourth floor, opposite Mademoiselle Crémailly, because my clothes are there and I expected to put them on. But Freluchon did not come home, which was very wrong on his part, as he has my clothes."

"Oh! it very often happens that he doesn't come home at night," murmured the young servant who came for the newspaper, smiling as she said it.

"You understand now, messieurs and mesdames, why I let everybody go up; Père Mignon did not tell me his orders, he didn't have time; besides, even if he had, I should probably have made mistakes, for I am beginning to realize that the trade of concierge demands strict attention as well as memory."

Chamoureau's explanation seemed plausible, but no one was willing to go away until the concierge came. His wife arrived first, however, and when she saw the gentleman in fancy costume in her room, she exclaimed:

" Mon Dieu! my husband has been changed! Who in the world is this Spaniard? What's happened to Mignon? I want my husband! He's never been to Spain!"

They strove to pacify the concierge's wife by repeating what Chamoureau had just told them, but she refused to credit the Spaniard's story and continued to cry:

" That ain't true, I say. Mignon wouldn't have left his post for this disguised man that nobody knows. He took Mignon's place; what's he done with him? If my husband don't return soon, I'll have this carnivalizer arrested!"

But the concierge's return put an end to his wife's shrieks and to the tenants' suspicions.

" Faith, monsieur," he said, going up to Chamoureau, " I had lots of trouble finding a cab for you; I went to at least four stands, and not a cab to be seen! I met an empty one at last, on Rue de Provence a minute ago, and brought it here. But if I'd known I should be away so long, I certainly wouldn't have done your errand for you!"

" Especially as your substitute does such nice things!" cried Madame Duponceau's maid.

" Let me hear no more of all that nonsense!" said Chamoureau, leaving the room.—" Your husband isn't lost, you see, Madame Mignon.—Messieurs and mesdames, you must be convinced now that I am not a thief. I have the honor to salute you."

With that, Chamoureau hurried to the sidewalk and was stupefied to find there an open *milord*.

" Why, concierge," he cried, in dire distress, " I asked you to get a closed cab, so that I couldn't be seen."

" Go and get one for yourself and leave us in peace! " exclaimed Madame Mignon, who was still in a bad humor.

Chamoureau made the best of it, jumped into the *milord,* gave the driver his address, and throughout the journey held his cap in front of his face, like a fan.

IX

A BUSINESS AGENT'S OFFICE

Chamoureau occupied a very comfortable apartment on what is called the Carré Saint-Martin, that is to say, the junction of Rue Saint-Martin and the boulevard. There he carried on the profession of business agent; he undertook the purchase or sale of houses, the investment of funds, the recovery of old debts, in short, everything which business agents—*hommes d'affaires*—generally undertake; most of them having passed the examination for admission to the roll of advocates, and some having even assumed that title, they are generally familiar with the laws and with all the tricks of the profession.

Chamoureau did not lack clients, for he had the reputation of being an honorable man, and was one in fact; in his case that quality was an advantageous substitute for cleverness, which unfortunately is not always a guaranty of uprightness. By which we do not mean that a man may not be both a fool and a knave. Nature is sometimes as lavish of evil as of good qualities.

Several persons had already called to confer with the business agent on the morning following the Opéra ball. They had found no one but the woman employed to do his housework, who always found the key at the concierge's lodge. Not finding Chamoureau, she assumed that he had gone out very early on business.

At eight o'clock, a man from the country made his appearance. He seemed to be half-bourgeois, half-peasant; he was about fifty years of age, short and thickset; his head was set low between his shoulders; his features were ugly and without distinction, their only expression being that distrust so customary among country people, who are always suspicious of those who live in cities and believe that they are always trying to cheat them; probably because when they themselves are at home they have no scruples about cheating city folk.

This man asked the concierge if Monsieur Chamoureau, business agent, was at home, and the concierge replied:

" He must be; I haven't seen him go out;" the fact being that he had not seen him come in; but concierges do not always notice the goings and comings of their tenants.

The little stout man started upstairs, but thought better of it and returned to the concierge.

" I say—between you and me—this Monsieur Chamoureau who keeps a real estate office—can I trust him?
is he a good business man? You see how it is—I'm
from the country, but I don't want to get cheated here in
Paris! And, you see, I've heard as how your business
agents was as likely as not to be thieves who did their
business at the expense of the poor devils who put theirs
in their hands."

" Oh! monsieur, you needn't have any fear about Monsieur Chamoureau; he's a very square man! nobody's
ever said a word against his honesty. He pays everybody cash—even his baker; he don't owe the least bit
of a debt in the quarter!"

" Well, well! that's good enough! and he ain't a
woman's man—a rake—a spendthrift?"

" Not at all; he leads a very quiet life and don't put
on any airs; he don't stay out too late—always comes
home when the theatre's out, when he goes there. To
be sure, the theatres keep it up nowadays till an hour
that makes it unpleasant for concierges—but still, that
ain't Monsieur Chamoureau's fault."

" That's good too! and is he married? has he got a
wife and children?"

" No; he was married, but he's been a widower a
short time; and he keeps up his regret for his wife, which
is very noble on his part; he can't talk about her without
crying."

" Oh, well! if he cries for his wife, I see that I can
trust him. So I'll just go up and hand over my papers

to him. You see, it's about collecting some money for me at some of the departments and from notaries. They told me like this: ' You just give some business agent a power of attorney and he'll attend to it all for you.' —So I had the power of attorney made out with the name left blank; and you think I can safely turn it over to your Monsieur Cha—Chamouilleau? "

" You can, monsieur; you needn't have any fear."

" In that case, I'll go up. Good-day, monsieur le concierge."

The little man arrived at Chamoureau's door on the second floor.

" Monsieur went out early," said the charwoman, " but he'll certainly be back soon; if you'd like to wait, please take a seat."

" I'll wait as long as I've come; I'd rather wait than go back."

The countryman sat down in a sort of reception room lined with shelves which were filled with boxes, all of which gave the room a sort of resemblance to a solicitor's office; only the clerks were lacking. But the sight of boxes and of docketed files of papers always produces a great effect on clients of the type of the little thickset man. He looked around, evidently impressed, and said to himself:

" Yes, yes! this must be a famous business agent; there's lots of papers in them boxes! "

The countryman had been awaiting Chamoureau's return about fifteen minutes, when another person arrived.

This was a man of middle age, with a bald head, long face and bumptious manner, who at once reminded one of the Joseph Prudhomme so well delineated by Henri Monnier.

This gentleman, who was dressed all in black, with a white cravat, which did not prevent his having a decidedly dirty look, entered the room with his head in the air, saying:

"I wish to speak at once with Monsieur Chamoureau, business agent; announce me, servant; I am Aimé-Désiré-Jules Beaubichon, professor of bookkeeping; however, your master knows me; I have seen him twice —in this domicile,—concerning the delicate affair, the purport of which I have succinctly laid before him. It relates to the subject of marriage; he has told me of a young woman whose virtue and morals he will answer for; and I am most particular touching those qualifications, provided that a suitable dowry be added to them, the face and form being in my eyes mere superfluities of little importance to a housewife in watching her soup-kettle!—I am disposed to take upon myself the bonds of matrimony once more if all the conditions are in accord with my social position, which, I venture to say, is as honorable as it is lucrative; fifteen hundred francs a year, without counting gifts from pupils—when they make any!"

The servant continued to dust the furniture as she listened to this harangue; when it was at an end, she replied:

" Monsieur Chamoureau went out early; he's sure to be back soon; if you'd like to wait—monsieur here has been waiting a quarter of an hour."

Monsieur Beaubichon cast a sidelong glance at the man from the country, who put his hand to his hat; whereupon the professor concluded to touch his own slightly and to address his companion.

" Is monsieur also awaiting Monsieur Chamoureau? "

" Yes, monsieur, with your permission."

" I have no intention of objecting. Would monsieur care to learn bookkeeping, double or single entry? "

" Me! learn bookkeeping! God bless me! what for? "

" What for? why, in order to know it."

" And what use would it be to me? "

" Why, to keep your books; to have everything down in black and white! "

" In the first place, I haven't got any books—oh, yes! except the *Country Cook* for the women, and fairy stories for the young ones, and their catechism for 'em to learn their lesson out of ; but all of them keep themselves in a closet; there ain't no need for us to learn to keep 'em."

" Dense ignorance! " muttered Monsieur Beaubichon, shrugging his shoulders.—" Then you are not in business, monsieur? " he continued, aloud.

" Oh, yes! I sell wine from my own vines, and fruit from the orchard when there's a good crop! "

" Well, then you must have books to write in—' sold Monsieur So-and-So so much; received from Monsieur Thingumbob so much.' "

"It ain't worth while, for I almost always sell for cash, and then, if anyone does owe me money, why, there ain't no danger of my forgetting it before he pays me."

The professor gave another shrug and began to pace the floor.

"And people say that we are going forward, they declare that our progress is constant! But where is this boasted progress, I pray to know, when this countryman has no ledger wherein to keep a running account with his apricots and his pears!—Servant, your master does not return; a pupil awaits me; I go to place my learning at his service, to instil my knowledge into him. I will return. Beg Monsieur Chamoureau to wait for me, and may he be pregnant with information concerning the marriageable young lady!"

The gentleman in black having retired, the country-man said to the charwoman:

"Who in the devil is that fellow who puffs himself out when he talks, just exactly like a bladder when you blow it up? He looks like a schoolmaster—with his books he wants to learn me to keep. And then I saw how he hoisted up his shoulders and called me ' dirty ' * under his breath! But just let him come down our way, and I'll bet he don't so much as know how to plant beans or hoe potatoes! All these fellows that put on so many airs in the city ain't good for nothing in the country; they don't know how to use a spade nor yet a pickaxe!

* The professor said, a few paragraphs earlier, *ignorance crasse*—dense ignorance !—the countryman understood him to say *crasseux*—dirty !

But it's my opinion that the man what makes the veg-
etables grow that you eat deserves to be thought just as
much of as that critter what makes scrawls on books."

The servant continued to dust the furniture, nodding
her head approvingly.

" I'd like to know if your master, Monsieur Cha—
Chabouleau puts on airs and eyes country folks like that
crow that just went out; because if he does, why, I
wouldn't give him any business of mine, d'ye see."

" No, monsieur, no; never fear. Monsieur Chamoureau is too well-bred not to be polite to everybody, especially his clients. He'd take off his hat to a child two
years old, if the child should give him his business."

" All right! but seemin' to me your bourgeois is staying
out a long while."

" In Paris, monsieur, one can never be sure how long it
will take to do an errand."

" That's so; because there's so many carriages passing—that delays you. Well, here it is raining now!"

" And monsieur didn't bring his umbrella."

" They told me nobody used umbrellas in Paris now,
as there's so many busses that folks never walk."

" That's an exaggeration, monsieur; people still go
on foot when they prefer to walk."

" They told me that there's going to be a railroad underneath Paris, so's you can take the underground and
go quicker when there's too many people on top. That
ain't a bad idea.—But, sapristi! the bourgeois don't seem
to come back."

Twenty minutes more had passed, when there was a great uproar in the street; hoots and shouts of laughter, and yells from the street urchins. The servant opened a window on that side to ascertain the cause of the tumult.

The *milord* containing our widower had stopped in front of the house, and before he had had time to alight, a crowd had collected round the cab, because its occupant was in plain sight.

Shouts of *" à la chienlit!"* went up on all sides. The concierge stood in his doorway, looking on with the rest. Chamoureau, having paid his driver, could hardly force his way through the crowd, which yelled at him:

" Oh! you Spaniard!"

" Just look at him! ain't he dazzling with his spangles!"

" He's a Spaniard—he's a regular sun!"

" But he'll lose his boots; he's treading on 'em!"

At last, by dint of pushing this way and that, Chamoureau reached the door; he tried to enter in a hurry, but the concierge barred the way, saying with an air of importance:

" What do you want? where are you going?"

" What's that? where am I going? Why, to my rooms, parbleu!"

" You have evidently made a mistake; we don't let rooms to buffoons!"

" On my word! this is too much!—How is this, concierge? don't you recognize me—Chamoureau?"

The concierge was stupefied; he could not believe his eyes and his ears; he could not conceive that that sedate and orderly tenant, who always wept when his wife was mentioned, could come home at ten o'clock in the morning, dressed as a Spaniard.

But Chamoureau left him to digest his amazement and hurried upstairs. The servant, who had not recognized her master, had just left the window, saying:

"It's a masker coming home from the ball! The deuce! he has made a night of it and no mistake! this is none too early to come home!"

"Do you mean to say that balls last till the next forenoon?" asked the countryman.

"No, monsieur, they end at daybreak, but after that the maskers go to supper and raise the deuce at wineshops; three-quarters of 'em get tight and don't go home till they haven't got another sou to spend, like this fellow who's just come into the house, I suppose. I'd like to know who he is. He must be a regular loose fish, to come home from the ball after ten o'clock in the morning. I'll ask the concierge who he is."

The bell rang and the woman ran to open the door.

"This time it's monsieur, sure!" she said.

But seeing before her a man in fancy costume, she was about to prevent his entrance, as the concierge had done. But Chamoureau pushed her aside with some force.

"Are you going to make a fool of yourself like the concierge?" he cried, "Sapristi! here I am at home at last! thank God for that!"

He fell into a chair, snatched off his cap, unbuckled his cloak, and shook his feet to rid himself of his top-boots, and as they were far too large, he sent one in the face of the countryman who had been waiting so long for him, and whom, in his hurried home-coming, he had not noticed.

The little thickset man, who was staring at Chamoureau with wide-open eyes, like a fisherman who thinks that he sees something at the end of his line, seemed far from pleased at receiving the Louis XIII boot in his face, and cried out:

"Well, look here, you—Carnival—do you take my face for a boot-jack? What sort of an animal is this, anyway?"

Thereupon the business agent, perceiving that there was a man seated in one corner of the room, made him a low bow.

"I beg pardon, monsieur, a thousand pardons; I didn't see you.—Madame Monin, my slippers, at once. What does monsieur wish?"

"What I wish is to speak to the master of the house, the business man—because I have business—and it ain't a small matter either—to put in his hands."

"I, monsieur, am the master of the house, Chamoureau,—at your service. We will step into my office, when I have my slippers and dressing gown.—Come, Madame Monin."

"I'm looking for 'em, monsieur, but I don't know where you've hid 'em; I can't put my hand on 'em."

"What's that! is that the truth? you're the business agent?" said the countryman, scrutinizing Chamoureau from head to foot.

"To be sure, monsieur, I am the man."

"Are you always dressed like this—with spangles all over you, and such a funny-looking cravat?"

"No, monsieur, this is a disguise which I assumed, contrary to my custom; it must not be regarded as establishing a precedent."

"Ah! so you spent the night at the masquerade, and then you went round drinking at wine-shops—raising the devil, as your servant said just now!"

"You are mistaken, monsieur; a man may go to the ball by chance—there's no law against it—but that is no reason why he should visit wine-shops and raise the devil afterward."

"Well then, as your fandangoes end at daylight, what have you been doing since then that makes you come home so late, if you haven't been the rounds of the wine-shops?"

"It seems to me that these are rather unusual questions, monsieur."

"Damnation! monsieur, let me tell you that what I've seen sets one to thinking. Do you suppose I'm going to put my business in your hands, and give a power of attorney to collect a plump little sum of money to a man what dresses like this and shows himself in the streets in such a dress at this time of day—goes on sprees in short, at an age when he ought to behave himself! *Nenni,*

nenni! this sort of thing don't give me confidence in you. I'll go and look for a business agent who ain't up to such tricks!"

And the countryman rose and prepared to leave the room.

Chamoureau, who was very uncomfortable because he had taken off his boots and had not received his slippers, none the less ran after the client who was about to escape him, and seized his arm, saying:

"For heaven's sake, monsieur, don't judge by appearances; I am not a frequenter of balls. Besides, here in Paris a man may amuse himself a little and still attend to his business; indeed, it often happens that you meet at a ball or at the theatre the very persons you want to see. —Madame Monin! sapristi! my slippers!"

"Tell me, then, where you hid them, monsieur."

"Look under my bed.—Entrust your business to me, monsieur, and rest assured that I will look after it with all the zeal that I always display in behalf of my clients, who, I venture to say, have never had occasion thus far to do anything but congratulate themselves on having placed their interests in my hands."

"*Ouiche!* that's all very fine talk! but I believe what I see.—They told me that Monsieur Chamoureau was a widower, but that he still cried for his wife."

"That's the truth, monsieur, the exact truth.—O Eléonore! why are you not here to defend your husband!"

"They ain't under the bed, I just looked there."

" Look in my somno.—Yes, monsieur, I mourn for my wife! If she were alive, she'd have found my slippers before this!"

" When a man mourns for his dead wife, he don't go masquerading round the streets in broad daylight! No, no! I don't trust you!"

At that moment they heard loud talking on the stairs. The door, which was not locked, was thrown open with violênce, and the professor of bookkeeping rushed into the room, shouting at the top of his voice:

" What have I learned? Great God! He has worn a disguise, attended public balls, and carried disregard of propriety so far as to appear in broad daylight and in his own neighborhood, dressed in a costume to which it is impossible to give a name.—Yes! it is not a falsehood, a fable, a false rumor; here he is, still in that absurd costume! and he, a man who keeps a business office, abandons himself to such libertinage—and without his shoes! —What a shocking disguise!"

" Ah! good-morning, Monsieur Beaubichon, I am at your service in one moment.—Come, Madame Monin, will you give me my slippers or not?"

" They ain't in your somno either, monsieur."

" You are at my service, monsieur!" rejoined the professor, puffing like an ox; " but I, monsieur, I am not at your service! I no longer propose that you shall dispose of my destiny and my future.—Upon my word!—I have come to tell you, monsieur, that I withdraw my confidence from you and that you shall find no wife for me

—for me, Aimé-Désiré-Jules Beaubichon; the idea of
my taking a wife on the guaranty of a pseudo Spaniard!
of a man who so far forgets his manhood as to deck himself in tinsel that gives him the aspect of a mountebank!"

"I do the same, monsieur," said the countryman; "I
withdraw my confidence from him; to be sure, I hadn't
given it to him, but I withdraw it all the same. I was
going to give him my power of attorney. But nay, nay,
Lisette! he won't have a chance to throw my money away
at balls!"

"He was employed to find me a spouse, monsieur;
but where would he go to find one? to *Valentino,* or the
Salle-Barthélemy? For me, who desire good morals and
virginity before all things! He would arrange a marriage for me with one of those little women whom all
Paris knows, a *girl of marble,* monsieur; when I say
marble, I use a theatrical form of expression—do you
understand?"

"Faith, no!"

"I am not surprised."

While these two gentlemen indulged in their recrimina-
tions and reflections, far from flattering to the business
agent, the latter, finding that his slippers did not come,
and being averse to standing on the floor in his stockings, decided to get down on his hands so that he might
more easily look under the furniture and find that indis-
pensable portion of his costume. His position, as he
crawled around his room on all fours, was ill adapted to
restore the confidence of the persons whom the sight of

his disguise had so exasperated. Monsieur Beaubichon therefore wrathfully jammed his hat over his eyes, crying:

" Observe, monsieur, observe the results of dissipation! A man who should be as serious as the law itself, is obliged to crawl around his room on all fours, in search of objects which should be at his hand!—I go, and never in my life will I set foot inside this office! Keep your marriageable women, monsieur, or marry them to your clients—this professor of bookkeeping will not endorse them. Good-day!"

" I follow your lead, monsieur; I'll keep my power of attorney and try to find a business agent who won't fling yellow boots in my face. Good-day!"

" Go to the devil! and leave me in peace! for I'm sick of you both!" retorted Chamoureau; and, weary of his unsuccessful search, he sat on the floor in the middle of the room. But at that moment the servant returned with a victorious air, holding the slippers in her hand.

" They were in the sideboard, monsieur," she cried; " you must have been very absent-minded to put 'em there."

X

AGATHE AND HONORINE

Chamoureau thrust his feet into his slippers, then ran to his office, which was also his bedroom, and made haste to divest himself of his Spanish costume, saying to himself:

"That infernal disguise has cost me dear! it has already caused me to lose two clients, and I shall have to grease my concierge's paw to keep from telling all over the neighborhood that I came home this morning in Carnival costume after passing the night away from the house!—And then he'll promise not to talk, and he'll tell everybody! Anyway, all the neighbors saw me—the fruitwoman and the grocer.—Ah! this will be a very bad thing for my business.—That was a vile trick for you to play on me, Freluchon! Still, it is possible that he didn't do it purposely. In his Pompadour's company, he probably forgot that he had his key in his pocket. Now I have got to send all this stuff back to the costumer; another messenger to pay! Gad! I spent a lot of money last night!"

Our widower heaved a deep sigh; but in a moment his face lighted up, and the clouds that darkened his brow vanished. The memory of the pearl-gray domino had

changed the color of Chamoureau's thoughts from black
to rose; he rubbed his hands and reflected:

" I am an ungrateful wretch to curse this costume.
Even if it has caused me the loss of Monsieur Beaubichon's confidence—a trivial loss, for the fellow would
give me only twenty-five francs to arrange a good marriage for him!—to make up for that, do I not owe to it
the conquest of that magnificent brunette—a fascinating
woman! fine figure, fine waist—and such features! *She*
wasn't afraid to show me her face! I am very seriously
in love with her.—Madame de Sainte-Suzanne! She
must be a great lady! What a pity that I am not of
noble birth; but love knows no distances, and the proof
of it is that she urged me to come to see her. Let's see
where she lives: Rue de Ponthieu, Champs-Elysées
quarter—the swell quarter! the most *comme il faut*
quarter of Paris!—Freluchon and Edmond laughed at
me; but they would have liked right well to know my
conquest's name. I swore to be close-mouthed; that's
a pity, for when one has a beautiful mistress, she does
me credit; but I promised. To-morrow, about three
o'clock, I will call on Madame de Sainte-Suzanne; I
will be careful about my dress. By the way, I hope Freluchon will send back my clothes, he has my new coat.—
Ah! I wish it were to-morrow now!"

Chamoureau sent his servant to the costumer's with
the Spanish costume, and told her to go thence to Freluchon's, inquire if he had returned, and if so, to bring
back his clothes; then, enveloping himself in his dressing

gown and stretching himself out in his great easy-chair, he abandoned himself ecstatically to his dreams. He fancied himself already at the feet of the glorious brunette, who had crowned his passion; he drove with her in a calèche in the Bois de Boulogne, and his excessive happiness finally put him to sleep.

The ringing of the door-bell roused the business agent. He remembered that he had sent his servant on an errand, and that there was no one to open the door. Making up his mind regretfully to leave his chair, Chamoureau went to the door and instantly became wide awake when he saw two ladies of most respectable appearance, and both very good-looking. The elder lady, who seemed to be twenty-seven or eight years of age, was of medium height, slender, perhaps a little thin, but exceedingly graceful. Although her face was not very pretty, it was charming; her blue eyes were at once soft and intelligent, her nose, slightly retroussé, gave a touch of archness to her expression; her mouth was not small, but it was not stupid either; her chestnut hair, which was combed smooth and with care, formed a suitable frame for the face, which was slightly pale and seemed to indicate delicate health.

Her companion, who was much younger, was evidently unmarried. She was a lovely blonde, as fair and rosy and fresh as a bud just about to open; her refined, regular features recalled the exquisite vignettes with which the English embellish their *keepsakes.* Her great dark blue eyes were almond-shaped, and shaded with long

black lashes; a combination rarely seen in a blonde; her
mouth was garnished with a double row of little pearls,
and when she laughed, which she did very often, two tiny
dimples appeared in her cheeks. Her abundant light
curls played about that charming face. She was shorter
than her companion, and constantly looked up into her
face with a sweet, affectionate expression.

They were not mother and daughter, for there was
only ten years' difference between them; but the elder
was evidently a sincere and beloved friend, and the
younger almost a cherished daughter.

Chamoureau bowed very low, and the elder lady said
to him:

" Is this the office of Monsieur Chamoureau, business
agent?"   •

" Yes, madame, I am Chamoureau. Won't you be kind
enough to step inside?"

The two ladies were ushered into the office, where Chamoureau offered them chairs, and the elder continued:

" A person for whom you have done some business,
monsieur, told me that through your agency I might be
able to find a small country house for sale. I know that
they are to be found in the *Petites-Affiches;* but I
thought that by applying to you, monsieur, I could obtain more precise and definite information, and that you
would undertake all the necessary negotiations, which a
woman does not understand."

" Certainly, madame, and with the greatest zeal, I
beg you to believe. I presume that madame desires to

purchase a large house, a handsome villa, with a view
to passing the summer there?"

"No, monsieur, no, I do not wish to purchase a fine
house; my means will not permit it. I want a modest,
unpretentious place, but as attractive as possible, where
we shall have everything that is necessary when one
lives in the country all the year round; for it is with
that purpose that I am looking for a house for my friend
and myself, at some distance from Paris."

"Ah! you intend to leave Paris altogether! Are you
not afraid of ennui?"

"Oh, no! far from it, monsieur! we don't care at
all for Paris, do we, Agathe?"

"For my part, my dear friend, you know that I look
forward with pleasure to living in the country! to have a
garden, flowers to care for, and birds and hens—oh! it
will be such fun!"

"I have two reasons for wishing to live in the country,
monsieur: first, my health, which is not very good, and
the doctors say that the pure country air will cure me
entirely."

"Yes! yes!" cried the girl, taking her friend's hand,
"I am perfectly sure that you will soon be as stout as I,
who am a regular little ball. You won't have any more
pains in your chest, you'll have a good appetite, and
we'll walk a lot and eat all day long! Oh! you won't
be sick any more, Honorine, I promise you; you'll get
back your strength and color and be in magnificent
health!"

"I trust so, my child; at all events, we must always hope for what will make us happy; the happiness we have in anticipation is sometimes the only happiness we have at all.—But I haven't told you my second reason, monsieur. Unfortunately it is one of those to which everything must give way. It concerns the state of my purse. My means are very modest, monsieur, and in order that they may be sufficient for our needs, that we may have to undergo fewer privations, it is most important that we should leave Paris, where it costs so much to live in these days!"

"Dear Honorine, if you didn't have me with you, if you lived alone, you would be very comfortable, and you could have a lot of things which you deny yourself in order to give them to me!"

"It is unkind of you to say that, Agathe. You forget that you are my ward, my only companion; that you are a sister, a child, and a friend to me, all in one! That, if I am able to be of some little service to you as a guide, to protect you and to take the place of a family, your mother once did as much for me, and that I am simply paying my debt by giving you what I received from her. Lastly, what you forget above all—and I did not expect to have to remind you of it—is that without you, who have been for so long my faithful companion, I should be alone, I should have no one to love, no one to whom I could tell my thoughts, my memories, my dreams; no one to nurse me when I am sick; in short, that I should be very unhappy! Now say that you are a burden to me!"

The young woman's eyes were wet with tears. Agathe threw her arms about her neck and kissed her again and again.

"Ah! I was wrong, I was wrong!" she cried. "Forgive me, Honorine; you know that I don't know what I am saying, that I speak without thinking, I won't do it any more! Why, I know well enough that it would be as impossible for you to part with me as for me to live away from you."

"Well, it's all over now; let us forget it and apologize to monsieur, for we are wasting his time by forcing him to witness a scene which can hardly interest him."

The young woman was very generous to apologize to Chamoureau, for he had been paying no attention to their conversation for some time. He was thinking only of his clothes,—of the new coat left at Freluchon's, which Madame Monin did not bring back.

"I must have my coat to call on Madame de Sainte-Suzanne," he was saying to himself; "for I certainly will not appear there in a sack-coat."

"Well, monsieur, let us come down to business," continued the young woman. "Do you know of any modest house for sale in the outskirts of Paris?"

"There are plenty of them, madame; but first of all, in what part of the suburbs do you wish to live?"

"It makes no difference, monsieur."

"That will simplify matters."

"However, I should not care to live in one of those neighborhoods which have become the rendezvous of equestrians and driving parties; for in those places, if one leaves the house, one must dress as carefully as in Paris. That is not what we want; we want genuine country, where there is no formality, no ostentation, where one meets more peasants than city folk."

" I understand; in that case, madame would not care to purchase at Passy, Auteuil, or Enghien?"

" No, too many people go there."

" And the distance—is that a matter of indifference to you, also?"

" Yes, although I should not want to be too far from Paris; I may have business there occasionally; and then, ladies must keep abreast of the fashions, and if it were a long journey it would be tiresome and expensive."

" Wait, madame; I believe that I have just what you want."

Chamoureau took down a pasteboard box, looked over some papers, and read:

" ' A pretty country house for sale on easy terms, at Créteil, on the bank of the river.' "

" Oh! my dear friend, the bank of the river!—that's lovely!"

" Yes, but it isn't healthy."

" ' Large house, six bedrooms——' "

" Oh! we don't need so many, monsieur!"

" ' Billiard-room, stable, poultry yard, a garden of an acre——' "

" But the price, monsieur, the price?"

" Thirty-five thousand francs."

" That is too dear for me; I can hardly afford more than twenty thousand."

" Let us see if we can find something else then. Ah! it just occurs to me that a client of mine, who has just made a large amount of money on the Bourse, is looking for a small château now, and told me to sell a country estate of his a few leagues from the city, which is too modest for his present circumstances. Let us see if that would suit you; I imagine that we could get it at a bargain. I have a little memorandum here that he gave me—yes, here it is; listen, madame.

" ' A small house at Chelles, six leagues from Paris, near the main street and just on the outskirts of the town. Ground floor, first floor and attics; four rooms on each floor. A nice lawn in front, and yard behind, with hencoop, pump and a large shed; a pretty garden entirely planted, and a wall around the whole place.' "

" A garden all planted! Then we should have fruit. Honorine, I will be the one to take care of the garden. Chelles—in which direction is that? "

" Chelles, mademoiselle, formerly celebrated for its abbey, is just beyond Montfermeil and the village of Couberon. It used to be a heavily-wooded district, but I believe the wood has been pretty well thinned out in the forest; however, there is still the Forest of Raincy, which is not far away. They do some cutting there also, it is true, but there will always be a little left. It's a very uneven, picturesque country. You desire a country house where you will be free from anything like etiquette;

in that neighborhood you will imagine that you are a hundred leagues from Paris."

" That place might suit us, but the price——"

" I beg pardon, madame, I have not read it all.—' The house is all furnished, and the owner desires to sell it in that condition. Whoever wishes to see it may apply to Père Ledrux, gardener and florist, who lives nearby and has the keys; he is instructed to show the place. Père Ledrux is well known in the town and anybody will point out his house. The place will be sold for twenty thousand francs.' "

" Twenty thousand francs and all furnished. Why, that is just what you wanted, Honorine! "

" I must say that it does not seem to me a high price. I know Montfermeil—it's a delightful country."

" As I told you, madames, this is a rare chance. Do you pay cash? "

" Yes, monsieur, the whole amount in cash."

" Oh well! in that case perhaps we may be able to obtain a reduction in the price; my client is very good-natured since he made a fortune, wherein he doesn't resemble the majority of new-rich people."

" The next thing is to find out whether the house will suit me; you will understand, monsieur, that I don't wish to buy it until I have seen it and found out whether it is pleasantly situated, not too lonely, and whether it has a good view."

" Very well, madame, you must go and see it. Chelles isn't far away; there's a railroad station there; I think it's the Strasbourg line that runs through the town, or very near it. You will be there in an hour; inquire for Père Ledrux, gardener and florist, and he will show you Monsieur Courtivaux's house—that is my client's name."

"Yes, yes, that's right; let us go to Chelles, Honorine, and see the house. If you like it, we will buy it immediately."

"The weather isn't very inviting for a trip to the country; no matter—if it's fine to-morrow, we will go there; and if the house suits us, we will return, monsieur, and arrange about the purchase."

"If madame will kindly leave me her address, I shall have the honor to call and thus save her the trouble of returning."

"Here is my address, monsieur; but if we see the house to-morrow, we may not wait for you to call; especially if we like it, for we shall be in a hurry to conclude the bargain, and we shall come to see you at once."

"As you please, madame; I shall always be at your service. Would you like me to write the names for you —Ledrux and Courtivaux?"

"It's not necessary, monsieur; we have good memories."

Chamoureau escorted his new client to the stairs. When he returned to his room he looked at the card she had handed him and read:

"Madame Dalmont, 40 Rue des Martyrs."

"Madame!" murmured the agent, "they are two ladies who live alone—one unmarried; the elder is evidently a widow, unless she is separated from her husband. An interesting and distinguished face, and most refined manners. The young lady is exceedingly pretty! refined, regular features—not red like most blondes; but with all that she doesn't come up to my enchanting brunette, who expects me to-morrow between two o'clock and five—at her hôtel.—Ah! I hear Madame Monin at last."

The servant returned without a sign of a bundle. Her master began at once to question her.

"Well, Madame Monin?"

"I did your errands, monsieur; I carried the Spanish costume back to the costumer, who said that monsieur had lost lots of spangles off the cloak."

"Indeed! he proposes to count the spangles, does he? Skip the details. Freluchon hasn't gone home, I suppose, as you haven't my clothes?"

"I beg your pardon, monsieur, your friend has been home, but he didn't stay long; he just changed his clothes, and then went right away again, saying to the concierge: 'I'm going to Rouen; I'll be back in four days.'"

"What! he's gone to Rouen? that's a good one! But didn't the concierge tell him that I had been there to get my clothes?"

"The concierge didn't think to tell Monsieur Freluchon till just as he came downstairs. But he was in a great hurry then; a lady was waiting for him in his cab and he drove right off. All he said was: 'That's all right!

Chamoureau won't need his coat; he's got plenty of others.' "

" On my soul! this is too much! Freluchon is a villain! If I only had him here! Of course I have other clothes, but as one rarely has occasion to wear a frock coat, I have only one; that's quite enough; and now, thanks to Freluchon, I haven't that! I can't go to Rouen to ask him for his key, especially as I shouldn't know where to look for him in Rouen. Didn't he leave his key with the concierge? "

" No, monsieur, he didn't leave anything."

" A tailor will never have time to make me another coat for to-morrow; he might promise it, but he wouldn't give it to me. What am I to do? To call on that lady in a sack coat or an overcoat would be much too un-ceremonious, especially for a first call! it would give her a very poor opinion of my breeding. Well, there's only one thing for me to do—go to a ready-made clothing house and buy a frock coat there. I trust that I may find one that fits! It's an absolutely unnecessary expense especially as I am still in mourning and shall have to get another black one. Two black frock coats! how stupid! But a glance from my charmer's eyes will recompense me; still, it's an infernally mean trick for Freluchon to play me all the same."

And Chamoureau went out to buy a new coat.

XI

DRAWBACKS OF NEW CLOTHES

In a handsome apartment on Rue de Ponthieu a lady was putting the finishing touches to one of those coquettish morning toilets which are called *négligé,* but which are the object of quite as much art and painstaking as full evening dress. Why should not ladies be as assiduous to please in their own homes as in society? For my part, I believe that that is their aim at all times, even when they expect no visitors; for even then they seek to please themselves by looking into their mirrors.

In their own homes, you will say, they are not subjected to the fire of a hundred glances, they receive only a few privileged friends; but these latter, seeing their hostess at closer quarters, are able to examine her in detail and at their leisure. So I say that much more care, much greater attention to every detail of the toilet is necessary to produce as much effect in the boudoir in the morning, as at a ball or the theatre.

Thélénie, however, for it is the lovely brunette's apartment to which we now introduce the reader, seemed absorbed by thoughts altogether distinct from her toilet; and, after a careless glance at her mirror, she dismissed her maid.

" That is all right, Mélie, I don't need you any more."

" Will not madame put something in her hair—not a single flower? "

" No, it's not necessary; I am well enough as I am, for the person I expect."

" Oh! madame certainly does not need flowers to make her beautiful. When one has such lovely hair as madame's, it is the loveliest of head-dresses; but as madame sometimes wears a pomegranate flower or a poppy——"

" I tell you that I want nothing more; leave me."

The maid left the room, and the fair Thélénie paced the floor a few moments, then paused in front of a mirror, talking to herself all the while.

" It was to please him that I wore a pomegranate flower in my hair; he liked it; he said that the deep color of the flower blended beautifully with my glossy hair. He called me his lovely Andalusian then; and now he no longer loves me. Have I changed? Why, no, no; I am just as I was three months ago, when I captivated him. As if one had changed in three months, when one has not been sick! Oh, no!—But if this goes on, I shall have changed in three months more: anger, jealousy and ennui will have made ravages on my face. I shall have grown old and he will be the cause of it.—False Edmond! Oh! what a fool I am to think of him still! conceited little fop, who never loved me! And I, I who had never before known a deep-rooted sentiment, who laughed in my sleeve at all the men who sighed at my feet—by what fatality did I allow myself to be bewitched by that little

fellow?—After all, that love could never have led to anything; on the contrary, it was a disadvantage to me; it
kept men away from me who might have made my fortune; and I want to be rich!—I have no desire to imitate
those women who, after dazzling Paris by their mag-
nificence and their follies, die at the hospital or become
box-openers at a second-class theatre.—I am in a position now to be at ease in my mind concerning the future;
I have got together about ten thousand francs a year.
That is something, but it isn't enough; I can't have a
carriage and a handsome place in the country on ten thousand francs, and I want those things. Edmond isn't rich;
he never gave me anything; indeed, I believe it was that
that made me love him! Mon Dieu! what a fool I am!
Of course I no longer love him, but that is an additional
reason for wanting to be revenged on him. He left me
first; that is one of those affronts which I never forgive."

The door-bell rang; a moment later the maid appeared.

" A gentleman wishes to see madame."

" Did he give his name? "

" Monsieur Cha—Chamoureau."

" Very well; show him in."

Chamoureau was in full dress; he had bought a new
coat and trousers. The coat was much too small in the
armholes; the trousers were uncomfortably tight around
the waist and had straps under the feet; but our widower
was not sorry to have a genteel figure and to conceal a
part of his embonpoint. Anyhow, he could find nothing

better at the ready-made clothes shop the day before. A
snow-white cravat and waistcoat completed the agent's
resemblance to a bridegroom; he lacked only the white
gloves, which were replaced by a pair of light yellow ones.

In this costume he had driven to Rue de Ponthieu in a
cab, for he did not propose that his clothes should be
marred by the slightest speck of mud.

"Madame de Sainte-Suzanne?" he said to the concierge with a self-assured air; and as he went up to the
second floor by a handsome staircase, he said to himself:

"I must present myself with ease of manner; I must
not be timid; women like men with plenty of self-possession. Now, as this lady herself invited me to call on
her, it must be that she was pleased with me; consequently, that being so, I can afford to be enterprising;
she will certainly forgive me. Damnation! this coat is
infernally tight under the arms; the dealer assured me
that it would be all right, and it fits me perfectly everywhere else. The waistband of the trousers rather takes
my breath away, and when I sit down, they're too tight;
but I am much thinner; the straps suit me better; I
have almost no stomach at all. How stupid it is to have
a stomach at thirty-eight! I shall have to take white
mustard seed; they tell me that that makes you thin or
fat, just as you choose. Ah! this must be the door! My
tie isn't rumpled; good!"

Although he did his utmost to be self-possessed, Chamoureau was intensely agitated when he entered Madame
de Sainte-Suzanne's apartment. Seeing an immense

room, elegantly furnished, contributed not a little to increase his confusion, and as his feet sank into the soft carpet, he said to himself:

" I made no mistake; she's a great lady—a person of the highest station. The devil! I mustn't be enterprising at the start; this is no grisette; I must proceed in due form."

Thélénie wore a sort of blouse of lilac plush, with a girdle about her shapely waist. With that négligé costume, she wore no hoops, and the soft, yielding fabric of the blouse seemed at times to be glued to her beautiful hips, as if to disclose their perfect symmetry. Thus it was easy to see that nature had favored her in every way, and she was a hundred times more seductive than in one of those gowns which, being worn over extravagantly large skirts, make a woman resemble a balloon. The hoopskirt must surely have been invented by women with bad figures, for those who have shapely forms lose far more than they gain by them.

Chamoureau stood speechless with admiration before Thélénie; she seemed to him even lovelier than at the ball, and in his enthusiasm he bowed so low that he caused his coat to split in the back.

He drew himself up in haste, sorely perturbed by the sound, but afraid to put his hand behind him to ascertain what had happened to his coat. Besides, he was obliged to answer the lady, who said to him:

" You are very good, monsieur, to remember my invitation. I was thinking that you had forgotten it."

"Oh! madame! forget to come to you! to seize an opportunity to see you once more! That would be like forgetting to be happy."

And Chamoureau, well pleased with his reply, ventured to explore the back of his coat with his right hand; but he had to cut short his exploration, for Thélénie seated herself on a couch and motioned to him to sit by her side.

"Won't you sit here, monsieur?"

"With the greatest pleasure, madame, if it will not incommode you."

"But I ask you to."

Chamoureau placed his hat on a table, taking care not to turn his back, so that Thélénie might not see the accident which must, he knew, have happened to the back of his coat. Then he took his seat beside her on the couch, thinking what gallant speech he should make to her. Now, when a man tries to think what he shall say, he usually says nothing. But the beautiful brunette came to the assistance of the visitor who was at such a loss for language.

"Well, monsieur, how did you wind up the night before last? did you stay much longer at the ball?"

"At the Opéra? Oh, no! madame, I didn't stay long; what pleasure could I have had there when I could no longer see you? And as you forbade me to follow you, I didn't follow you, despite my longing to do so; for I did long to, terribly!"

"But you joined your friends, I suppose."

" My friends—yes; first I found Freluchon, who was looking for me; I confess that I was not looking for him; I had no thought for anything but the delightful conversation I had just had with you, and the remembrance of your face."

" Well, you went to supper with those gentlemen. Was there a large party? "

" There were five men—Freluchon, Edmond Didier, and two friends of theirs; but there were only four ladies, for I didn't take one; you had refused to sup with me, and what other woman could have taken your place? There were not two like you at the ball—I would lay my life on it! And when one has had the happiness of seeing you——"

" So each of those gentlemen took his mistress? "

" His mistress, if you choose. As for me, I don't call that a mistress; if I had a mistress, I would devote all my thoughts to her, every moment of leisure that I could spare from my toilet-room—I mean my office; I am so confused, so happy with you, that I cannot think of even the most common words."

" Pull yourself together, monsieur; really, I don't see what there is to confuse you."

" You do not see! Ah! madame, if you would but condescend to read in the depths of my heart you would ·see there the flame which——"

" But the supper! was it very lively? And that flower-maker, that young Amélia, Monsieur Edmond's inamorata—is she as pretty as the portrait he drew of her? "

Chamoureau began to be conscious that the lovely brunette cut him short whenever he attempted to speak of his love for her. These interruptions annoyed him, and he put his left hand behind his back, saying to himself:

"Where in the devil did that split?"

"Well, monsieur, you don't answer. I asked you if that little Amélia seemed to you as piquant as Monsieur Edmond described her?"

"Little Amélia? who is she, madame?"

"Why, Monsieur Edmond's mistress; you know perfectly well, you told me it yourself at the ball. You are very absent-minded, aren't you, monsieur?"

"Absent-minded!—why, that is natural enough when you talk of any other person than yourself; for I think of you, of you alone."

Thélénie made an impatient gesture and moved to the extreme end of the couch. But Chamoureau interpreted that pantomime as a proof of intense agitation on the part of the lovely brunette, who evidently feared to yield too quickly to the man who attracted her. Thereupon, determined to take advantage of that agitation, our amorous swain threw himself at the lady's feet, crying:

"Ah! madame, I can no longer restrain——"

But a cracking sound infinitely more prolonged than the former one interrupted the declaration which the agent was on the point of making. This time there was no possible doubt as to the locality of the tear; his trousers had followed the example of his coat, and a cool breeze blowing upon a spot ordinarily covered informed him that there was danger in store.

Our widower was stricken with consternation. Thélénie roared with laughter as she looked at him on his knees; and he, fearing that the noise occasioned by the accident might be interpreted in a way even more humiliating to him than the reality, made haste to say:

" My trousers have split, madame, that's all."

" Mon Dieu! I had no doubt of that, monsieur."

" It's the first time I ever wore them; they have straps under the feet, and they're a little tight; that is why, when I stooped—you understand."

" Perfectly, monsieur; pray rise."

" I believe that the same thing has happened to the back of my coat; it's the first time I have worn that, too. It is all Freluchon's fault; he has a black coat and trousers of mine in his room, and he has gone off to Rouen without sending them back to me."

" These are trivial annoyances not worth a thought, monsieur. Rise, I beg; what on earth induced you to throw yourself at my feet like that? Rise, monsieur, I insist."

Chamoureau decided to rise, putting one hand over the place where his trousers had torn. But he was covered with confusion by what had happened, and he did not know how to resume his declaration.

" Well, monsieur," said Thélénie, who could hardly resist the desire to laugh anew at her visitor's embarrassment, "you seem to be unwilling to tell me whether this little Amélia is pretty."

"The girl in a *débardeur's* costume? she is rather attractive—one of those roguish grisette faces. There are some better-looking ones among young women of her class, but there are many inferior to her."

"Tell me what happened at your supper. Did you laugh much? did you have much sport? Was Monsieur Edmond very devoted to his little flower-maker?"

"The supper, madame; you persist in wanting to talk about the supper—after the ball!"

"Well, yes, monsieur, I do. Sometimes I am very curious; where's the harm?"

"I see none, madame; but I must admit that I am hardly able to satisfy your curiosity."

"Why so, monsieur, as you were with your friends?"

"I was there, madame, it is true, but it was almost as if I were not there. I don't know how it happened, but after the oysters I felt very dizzy; I suppose the wine was not pure! In fact, while my friends were chatting with the ladies, I, who did not take the slightest interest in what they said, as I could think of nothing but you— I fell asleep, yes, sound asleep."

"Indeed! you fell asleep thinking of me; that is very flattering!"

"That proves, *belle dame,* that your image transports me from the earth, that I dream, and——"

"And that you fall asleep. But still, you didn't sleep all the time, of course; and when you woke——?"

"When I woke, they had all gone; which was the more unkind of Freluchon, because he had my clothes at his rooms! You cannot imagine all the annoyance that has caused me—to say nothing of the embarrassing plight in which I find myself at this moment."

For several seconds Thélénie had not been listening to Chamoureau. Her brow had become grave, her features expressed dissatisfaction. She rose and paced the floor, apparently quite oblivious of her guest's presence. For his part, Chamoureau was no better pleased with his tête-à-tête. She seemed unwilling that he should talk to her of love; she questioned him concerning things which did not interest him in the least, and now she left him alone on the couch and strode about the room regardless of him. He said to himself that if he had torn his coat and trousers simply to obtain that result, it was not worth while to go to so much expense. He was strongly tempted to rise in his turn and walk beside his hostess, who seemed to have the fidgets in her legs; but he feared that if he did so he might add to the rents that he had already made in his garments, and that fear cast him into the most painful perplexity.

At last Thélénie seemed suddenly to remember that she was not alone. She halted in front of him, then resumed her seat on the couch, saying:

"Excuse me, monsieur; you must consider me most impolite, but I am sometimes extremely absent-minded; ideas come into my head which absorb me completely. It is a part of my temperament."

"You are forgiven, *belle dame;* indeed, I myself have moments when I am downright stupid! Really, I don't know how to explain it."

"And then I will admit that I am angry with you for falling asleep at that supper after the ball. I had asked you to report to me all that you heard. If that is the way you perform commissions that are entrusted to you——"

"Forgive me, madame; in future I will keep awake, if that will give you pleasure; and it will be all the easier for me, because I feel that you have robbed me of repose forever!"

Thélénie looked at him severely, and said:

"So you absolutely persist in talking to me about love, do you, monsieur?"

"Insist upon it! Why, madame, I came here for no other purpose."

"Ah! that is true frankness! I am going to be as frank with you, monsieur: perhaps you hope to make me your mistress?"

"Oh! madame, I dare not say that I hope it, but I may at least confess that it would be to me the height of felicity! And if the purest love, the most immovable constancy will avail me anything, put me to the test."

"I had an idea that you were in mourning, monsieur. Yes, there is a band on your hat. You are in mourning for your wife, are you not?"

"Yes, madame, for my wife, whom I regret; that is to say, I did regret her profoundly and weep bitterly

G. FRAIPONT

for her; but it was for the very purpose of putting an end to my grief that I welcomed with joy this new love which has taken possession of my heart, my senses, my——"

"What do you take me for, monsieur?"

Chamoureau was embarrassed; that seemed to him an artful question.

"Why, madame," he stammered, looking down at his trousers, "I take you for a lady of the best society—ex—exceedingly well-bred—er—with much wit—in short—er—created to attract the homage of all mankind."

"You don't say all you think; you met me at the Opéra ball, and you said to yourself: 'A woman who comes to the masquerade is sure to be an easy victim. She began to talk to me, consequently she won't make a long resistance.'"

"Oh! madame, I beg your pardon——"

"Monsieur Chamoureau, it is my duty to inform you that you are entirely mistaken in your conjectures. I will not be your mistress, monsieur. In fact, I do not propose to be anyone's mistress. Oh! I won't pretend that I am of the most rigid virtue. I have had a very stormy youth, I don't deny it; but now I am growing old, I must be prudent——"

"You, growing old, madame! what a mockery!"

"I am past thirty, monsieur; at that age one must think of the future; one must think about obtaining a name, a position in society. Do you understand, monsieur?"

"I think that I understand you, charming creature; but if you will deign to accept my name, my hand, my office, I will place them all at your feet by becoming your husband."

"Your offer touches me, monsieur, but between ourselves, marriage is a business matter, and a matter of the greatest importance! What is your fortune, monsieur? How much is this office worth that you lay at my feet?"

Chamoureau drew himself up, did a little mental reckoning, then replied:

"With what I already have and my office, I do not exaggerate when I place my income at four to four thousand five hundred francs."

The fair Sainte-Suzanne threw herself back on the couch with a mocking laugh. Our widower, disquieted by that laugh, waited until it subsided before he said timidly:

"Don't you think that a neat income?"

"Oh, no! frankly, it isn't neat enough for me. I have ten thousand francs a year, and I would not accept any man for a husband who did not bring me at least twice that. I am fully decided as to that. Let us forget this nonsense, my dear Monsieur Chamoureau; let us think no more about your love, which is not old enough to have taken very deep root yet; but come to see me sometimes as a friend. In that capacity, I shall be glad to receive you, but, you understand, only as a friend."

" Forget my love! Ah! fascinating woman! Why, you do not know that you have bewitched me, that you have turned my head, that I fairly dote on you! You do not know——"

" I beg pardon, Monsieur Chamoureau, but I do know that I have visits to pay to-day, and that it is time for me to think about dressing. Permit me therefore to bid you adieu."

Sorely vexed to be thus summarily dismissed, Chamoureau rose, grasped the seat of his trousers with his left hand, took his hat in his right hand, bowed very slightly, so that his coat might not split more, and walked out backwards.

But once outside, he pulled his hat over his ears, muttering:

" Much satisfaction there is in spending money for this! Oh! these women!—And I have got to take a cab again! "

XII

AGATHE'S PARENTS

Honorine Dalmont, with her young friend Agathe, occupied a modest apartment on Rue des Martyrs. Their only servant was a woman who came in to do their housework, and went away again after preparing their dinner.

Madame Dalmont's slender fortune would not allow
her to live more expensively in Paris, where living is
so dear, and it was in the hope of being less straitened
and of being able to obtain more of the comforts of life,
that she had formed the plan of going into the country
—a plan which had keenly delighted her friend Agathe.

For women who go into society, who follow the fashions, who pass their evenings at theatres or concerts or
balls, or at fashionable receptions, it seems a terrible
penance to go to the country to live. To them it is equivalent to ceasing to exist, it means the renunciation of all
the pleasures of life, it means, in short, condemning
themselves to die of ennui.

But it is not so with those who, although they dwell
in Paris, pass their lives in their own homes, seldom go
out, and know nothing of that splendid capital save the
uproar, the crowd, the vehicles which constantly threaten
them with destruction out of doors, and the tumultuous
throng that blocks the popular promenades on Sundays
and holidays. To them there is nothing painful about
leaving the great city. On the contrary, when they turn
their backs on the tumult, the confusion, the incessant
whirl of business and pleasure in which they have no
part, they breathe more freely; they feel more at liberty
to raise their heads, they find in nature something that
they had lost; they have their places there, whereas in
Paris they were nothing at all!

Honorine's past life had been uneventful. The
daughter of respectable people who had not succeeded

in business—there are many respectable people who
do not make a fortune—she had nevertheless received
a careful education. She had learned music and draw-
ing; she was blessed by nature with that fortunate temperament which enables one to learn quickly and without much difficulty that which others often spend long
years in studying.

Honorine, who was a very intelligent girl, would have
liked to marry an artist, but circumstances did not permit her to choose. She was fain to be content with a
simple government clerk, an honest fellow who had nothing poetic in his nature, but who attended punctually
at his desk and performèd his duties promptly.

Honorine longed to become a mother; that would at
least afford some occupation for her heart, which longed
for someone to adore; for, with the best will in the
world, she could only esteem her husband.

After she had been married two years, she had a son;
but she was denied the joy of rearing him; he died at
the age of twenty months, when he was just beginning to
stammer his mother's name and to take his first tottering
steps. Honorine's grief was so intense that it affected
her health. From that moment she began to lose her
color, and her lungs seemed to be impaired. Another
child alone could have consoled her for the loss of the
first; for the heart is of all the organs most amenable to
homœopathic treatment; but she had no other child, and
a few months later her husband died suddenly of inflam-
mation of the lungs.

At twenty-one, Honorine was left alone—a widow and an orphan, for her parents had died long before.

Then it was that she made the acquaintance of Madame Montoni, the mother of Agathe, at that time a child of nine.

Madame Montoni, who lived in the strictest retirement, happened to occupy an apartment in the same house as Madame Dalmont; she had seen her grief when she lost her child, and had been deeply moved by it. When she learned that she had lost her husband suddenly, she hastened to offer her consolation and attentions.

Honorine received her advances gratefully. Being without experience and entirely unacquainted with business, she was in danger of being deprived of the small property which her husband had left her, and which was claimed by collateral relations. But Madame Montoni had strength, courage and resolution; she took all the necessary steps, and the young widow was enabled to enjoy in peace the two thousand francs a year which her husband had left her.

As for Madame Montoni herself, she supported herself and her child with her hands. She made those pretty pieces of fancy work which bring in so little, and require so much time and care. Luckily she was very skilful. But she often passed whole nights over her embroidery frame, in order that she might buy a new dress for her daughter.

Honorine had tried to assist her new friend a little; but Madame Montoni was proud; she would accept nothing from her to whom she had, however, rendered material service.

Incessant toil exhausts vitality. Moreover, Agathe's mother had in the depths of her heart a mortal sorrow which was crushing her; she had confided it to Honorine, who could only weep with her. There are sorrows which admit of no consolation.

Little Agathe used often to ask her mother:

"Why don't we ever see papa? what can have become of him? When I was a little girl, I remember he used to come to see me often; he used to take me out to ride and to dine at restaurants; you used to be very bright then, mamma; you didn't work all day long; and then papa always brought me nice presents, and you too; and he used to kiss me a lot and tell me he loved me with all his heart. And then he stopped coming all of a sudden, and then you cried every day, yes, every day.—Is my papa dead?"

When Madame Montoni heard that question she always wept and strained the child to her heart as she replied:

"Alas! dear child! I don't know what to tell you! I have no idea what has become of your father; I do not know if he still lives, and that is the cause of this grief that is wearing my life away! —Adhémar loved me so dearly! and he adored you! How can I believe that he could have determined to abandon us for no reason whatever?—that he, who promised me such a lovely future,—certain happiness—would have left us suddenly without means, without resource, without support—oh, no! no! he would not have done that! Your father must be dead! My Adhémar certainly has ceased to live, since we are so unhappy!"

"How long ago did you last see him?" inquired Honorine one day, when she had become the confidante of the mother and daughter.

"Alas! my Agathe was just six years old when her father came to see us the last time."

"Why, didn't papa live with you?"

Madame Montoni blushed and turned her face away.

"No, my child, he couldn't; his business prevented him."

"My papa was very nice-looking, wasn't he, mamma?"

"Oh! yes, my child! he was as handsome as he was noble and generous; a little hasty only, and quick to lose his temper; that was the only fault I ever discovered in Adhémar. The last time he came to see us, he said to me: 'In a few days we will start for Italy; it is your native land, Julia, and I want to see it with you; then we will return to France and I will leave you no more.'"

"And you have never seen him since?"

"No; and no news of him, no letter! nothing from him! nothing!"

"But you must have made inquiries, have tried to learn something?"

"When a week had passed without my seeing Adhémar —ordinarily he never let more than two days pass without coming to us—I decided to go to the hotel where he had told me that he lived; it was one of the finest hotels in Paris. I asked for Monsieur Adhémar de—I asked for Monsieur Adhémar, and the concierge assured me that he had left the hotel six days before.

" ' He can't have gone away,' I said; ' if he has, where has he gone?'

" As that man knew nothing, I went to the hotel-keeper himself, who said to me:

" ' Madame, I am quite as surprised as you are at the absence of Monsieur de—of Monsieur Adhémar. I know that he intended to go to Italy, he had spoken of it several times; but when he left the house six days ago, he said simply: "I am going into the country; I shall return to-morrow morning." '

" ' And he has not returned since?'

" ' No, madame.'

" ' Where was he going in the country?'

" ' Mon Dieu! he didn't tell me; he had received a letter that morning—probably an invitation.'

" ' And he went away alone?'

" ' Alone, yes, madame. But he will surely return; he has left his linen here, and property of much greater value than the amount of his bill, for he paid every week. He's a young man of orderly habits, and he will return, madame; he is bound to return. The probability is that he's enjoying himself in the country and so is making a longer stay there than he intended.'

" ' I will return in a few days then,' I said, as I went away. And I did in fact go there again the second day

after. But Adhémar had not been seen! So it went on
for a month; until at last I had to abandon all hope."

" But his family—didn't you know them?"

"I knew from Adhémar that his family lived in the
neighborhood of Toulouse; they were uncles and aunts,
all proud of their rank and titles, and they did not condescend to answer the letters I wrote them. At last,
someone who was going to that part of the country was
obliging enough to make inquiries of several persons,
and they told him that Monsieur Adhémar had not been
seen by his relations, but that they took little interest in
his fate, for they knew that, heedless of his name and
his birth, he had contracted in Paris a liaison unworthy
of him; and if he did not break off that liaison, he would
never be received again by his noble family. That is all
that I learned concerning him whom I loved better than
my life. Ah! if it had not been for my daughter, his
disappearance would have killed me; but what would
have become of my little Agathe, without friends or
kindred on earth? I felt that I must live for her, for
her whom her father loved so dearly! And that is what
I did; I lived, but I have never been comforted!—Alas!
suppose that he died far away from us—unable to embrace us once more, to bid us a last farewell, and above
all, to ensure the future welfare of his daughter! Poor
Adhémar! think what his anguish must have been, his
despair, at the thought that he left us here in misery!
Oh! that idea haunts me incessantly and intensifies the
bitterness of my regrets."

This conversation was often renewed between the new friends, for Madame Montoni was never tired of talking of her Agathe's father. In those soothing outpourings of her soul, she concealed nothing from Honorine, whereas she kept one thing secret from her daughter.

Several years passed; Madame Montoni, exhausted by toil and grief, soon lost her little remaining strength. Feeling that she must soon say farewell to life, she placed in Honorine's hand the hand of her daughter, then twelve years of age, and said to little Agathe:

"Honorine will take my place with you; love her as you loved your mother. Heaven has at least vouchsafed that I should leave with you a sister, a friend! Some day, my daughter, she will tell you what your mother has never dared to tell you; and you will forgive your mother, because she loved you dearly and has suffered much for your sake. Now I am going to join my Adhémar, your father, and from above we will both watch over our child. But if fate has decreed that he is not dead, and that you are to see him again some day, oh! tell him that, until my last hour, his image was always here—in my heart!"

Agathe's tears and Honorine's prayers were powerless to suspend the decree of destiny! Madame Montoni closed her eyes forever.

> " Death's rigors have no like ;
> Vain our entreaties all ;
> His tyrant hand will strike ;
> Our plaints on deaf ears fall.''

After Madame Montoni's death, Honorine took Agathe with her, and from that moment they were never separated.

That which at first was only the affection of a guardian soon became sisterly affection; for, by the time she was fifteen, Agathe had become a sister to her companion, who was then but twenty-seven; time abolished the distance that it had at first set between them. The girl's tastes and pleasures were no longer those of a child, but were identical with those of the young woman, who was overjoyed to find a congenial companion in her to whom at first she had been only a second mother.

But Agathe had not forgotten the last words her own mother had said to her. There was a secret which Madame Montoni had confided to Honorine, but which she had not dared to disclose to her daughter. How could that kind and loving mother have feared to tell her daughter anything? Might she not always have felt quite certain that that daughter would never blame any act of hers?

That was what Agathe said to herself, and yet she dared not ask Honorine to reveal that secret, for she was reluctant to offend even her mother's shade.

" As she did not confide it to me while she was alive," thought the girl, " perhaps it is not right for me to try to learn it now that she is no more."

But one evening, after a long conversation between the two friends, in which they had talked about the strange disappearance of Agathe's father, the girl exclaimed:

"If I only owned something that belonged to my father! I have many things that my mother possessed, which I treasure beyond words; but I have nothing of my father's, absolutely nothing! that is very cruel."

"But suppose I should tell you," rejoined Honorine, "that I have something of your father's to give you—something which your poor mother gave me to keep until I should give it to you?"

"Mon Dieu! is it possible? you have something that belonged to my father, and you have not given it to me in all the time since my mother died? Oh! Honorine, then you did not want to make me very happy!"

"My dear Agathe, when I give you this object which was confided to me, I must also tell you the secret which your mother dreaded to tell you—because she did not wish to blush before you."

"Blush before me!—my dear mother!—why, that is absurd! Come, speak, Honorine, speak; do not conceal anything from me now."

"I will speak; indeed, it seems to me necessary that you should know the truth, that you should learn your father's name at last; otherwise you might stand by his side some day, and not know it."

"My father's name! Why, his name was Montoni, of course, as my mother's was Madame Montoni."

Honorine sadly shook her head.

"No," she murmured. "And that is the whole secret: your mother did not bear his name—for they were not married."

" Not married! Oh! poor mother! poor mother! And that was what she dared not tell me! Am I any less her child on that account? "

" Now, Agathe, listen to the story of your mother's love, as she herself told it to me.

" She was born in Italy, but she left that country when she was very young, with her parents, who settled in Switzerland. They died just as she reached her sixteenth year. She lived then with an old Swiss woman, who treated her very badly and reduced her almost to the condition of a servant. She was keeping a flock of goats, which she drove to pasture on the mountains, when she fell in with a young foreigner who was travelling in Switzerland for pleasure. He was a Frenchman, named Adhémar de Hautmont; he was rich and of noble birth; but he was young, handsome, attractive and susceptible; and it seems that your mother, although a goatherd, was exceedingly pretty. In a word, the two young people were attracted to each other, fell in love and exchanged their vows; and your poor mother had no one to watch over her but the goats that she herself guarded!

" This liaison had lasted two months, and young Adhémar could not make up his mind to part from Julia. It became much harder when she told him that she bore within her a pledge of his love. At that, the young Frenchman said to her:

" ' You cannot stay in this region, exposed to the cruel treatment of a woman who is harsh enough with you

now, and will be much more so when she learns of your
misstep. You must go with me; I will take you to
France, to Paris, and you shall live there; I will take
care that you lack nothing when I am obliged to leave
you and go back to my family. And then I shall not be
away long; as they allow me to travel often, for my
education, instead of visiting Germany, Spain and England, I will pass my time with you until the moment when
I can call you my wife and then I shall never have to
leave you again.'

" You can imagine that your mother joyfully assented
to her young lover's plan. So they left Switzerland together and came to Paris; young Adhémar installed his
Julia in a small apartment, simple and retired, but provided with everything that she required. Then, having
supplied her with all the money she was likely to need
in his absence, he started for Toulouse; for he was not
yet of age, and he had everything to fear from his family
if they should learn that he had abducted from Switzerland a young girl who was with child by him.

" But everything went well; Adhémar calculated carefully the length of his absences, and he loved his Julia
so dearly that he found a way to come to her when he
was supposed to be far away in some foreign country.

" Then you came into the world, and when your father
pressed you to his heart, he swore again that he would
have no other wife than your mother.

" Several years passed. Some of those talkative people who take delight in interfering in everything, and

who had seen Monsieur Adhémar de Hautmont in Paris
when his relations thought that he was in Vienna, did not
fail to inform them that the young man was in Paris
and had a mistress there. The relations ordered Adhémar to return to Toulouse, but he was then of age
and master of his actions, and he paid no attention to
the commands which they attempted to impose on him.
But he had one great-uncle, who was very old and very
rich, and who was very fond of him; this uncle was
expected to leave him his whole fortune. Your father
often said to his sweetheart:

" ' I don't dare to marry you while he is alive, for it
might make him angry with me and deprive us of a
large fortune hereafter. But when he is dead, there will
be nothing to delay our union '; and your mother, who
was very, very happy because your father still loved her
as much as ever, replied: ' Do just as you think best,
my dear; my daughter and I will always be content, so
long as we have your love; to us that is the greatest of
blessings.'

" At last, a few days before his disappearance, your
father learned that his great-uncle had become more indulgent; that he seemed disposed to forgive his nephew
his secret love-affair. Adhémar instantly set about pro-
curing from his native place all the documents that he
required for his marriage, saying to your mother:

" ' As soon as the ceremony is at an end, we will start
for Italy with our little Agathe. We will pass a year there
and then return to France, where my family, knowing

that you are my wife, will understand that there is nothing for them to do but to forgive me, and to love you when they know you.'

" That, my dear Agathe, is the whole story of your mother's love. Many women bear their lover's name without right, and assume in society the title of lawful wife; your mother would never have stooped to do that. The name of Montoni was her father's; it is the only one she has left you. Poor Agathe! why did fate decree that, just when you were on the point of obtaining a noble name, when a brilliant future opened out before you, he to whom you were to owe it all should suddenly disappear? "

" Dear Honorine," said Agathe, " the name and wealth are not what I regret, but my father's love, my father's kisses—But what is it that you have to give me? "

" The letters he wrote to your mother when he was away from her, which she always preserved with care."

" Oh! what joy! my father's letters! Give them to me! give them to me! "

Honorine took from her desk a small package which she had kept in safety there, and handed it to Agathe.

She received with a trembling hand the only heritage her father had left her; she hastily opened one of the letters, put her lips to it and wet it with her tears as she faltered:

" My poor father! "

Then she wiped her eyes, so that she could read, and said to Honorine:

" See—what a pretty hand my father wrote! Ah! I can read this easily; listen:

" ' My beloved Julia, the time seems very long when I am far from you; the days are endless; and what people call amusements—cards, hunting, concerts and balls— all seem very dull to me and are not worth a glance from you or a smile from my little Agathe, who, I love to believe, is still as fresh and rosy as ever, and strong and well. When shall I be able to embrace you both! My child was beginning to stammer a few words. You told me that on my return she would give me that sweet title of father, which I shall be so happy to hear from her lips. In a fortnight I shall start; I shall pass two days in England, then hasten to you. Patience, my Julia, patience; the time will come when I shall leave you no more, when you will be my wife before men as you now are before God. Be careful of your health; do not tire yourself by carrying your child; I told you to hire a servant, and I trust that you have done so. *A bientôt,* and then *à toujours,* your

'Adhémar, Comte de Hautmont.' ''

Agathe read the letter almost at a breath; then she looked up at Honorine and said:

" My dear friend, a man doesn't write thus to a person whom he means to abandon some day. Ah! it must be that my father is dead, as he never returned to us."

The package contained sixteen letters, all of which gave eloquent expression to Adhémar de Hautmont's love for

Julia Montoni and for their child. Agathe read them all
with deep emotion, then exclaimed:

"Ah! thank you, dear mother; this is indeed a treasure that you left for me; and it is much more precious
than money. Henceforth, when I want to reward myself, I will read over these letters and imagine that I am
between my father and my mother."

Now that we are fully acquainted with the antecedents
of Honorine and Agathe, we may go with them to inspect
the little house at Chelles.

XIII

THE LITTLE HOUSE AT CHELLES

It was the middle of March. There were no leaves
on the trees as yet, but there was plenty of sunshine; it
was already soft and penetrating and announced the return of spring, of that lovely season of the year when
everything seems to be born again—even those persons
who are on the downward path.

Ah! why do not men grow green again like trees
and shrubs? To be sure, their springtime lasts more
than three months, but so few of them know how to
make use of it! they do not appreciate it until they have
thrown it away, and then they regret it in vain; decidedly
the trees are wiser than mankind.

Honorine and her young companion dressed in haste in order to arrive early at the railroad station at the farther end of the Boulevard de Strasbourg, whence they were to take a train for Chelles. The two women were ready in a very short time. Agathe, whose quick and cheerful imagination saw something everywhere to give her pleasure, took the keenest delight in going into the country, although the season was not far enough advanced for the fields to have resumed their robes of green. It was a great diversion to her even to take a short journey by rail.

When one rarely indulges in any amusement, one is not surfeited with all the different forms of distraction; and the shortest walk is a pleasure to one who rarely goes out. This is a compensation to those persons who do not often have an opportunity for enjoyment; little is required to satisfy them, whereas ennui sometimes besets those who are always holiday-making. There are compensations everywhere.

In an hour the two friends had reached their destination. When one arrives at the Chelles station from Paris, the village or hamlet is at the left on a low hill; it is distant about ten minutes' walk; but then it rarely happens that the railways take you just where you want to go. When you arrive at a station, you almost always find yourself in the open fields. You look about in search of the place at which you are supposed to have arrived, and you are surprised to see, instead of houses, fields of cabbages, turnips or potatoes.

Agathe, overjoyed to be in the country, leaped and frolicked about like a child.

" Oh! how good the fresh air feels! " she cried. " One can run about here without dread of those horrid omni-buses that are always behind you or in front of you in Paris! And when everything is in leaf and flower, when the trees give shade, when there are poppies among the wheat, lilies of the valley in the woods, and violets in the hedgerows—oh! then it will be perfectly enchanting! Honorine, don't you think that you'll like it—doesn't all this delight you? "

" Yes, yes, I am very fond of the country."

" Well, why do you sigh then? why do you look so sad when you say it? "

" Because I am thinking of my poor little boy. If he had lived, he would be seven years old now. Can't you understand, Agathe, how happy it would make me to have him by my side, to take him by the hand, or to watch him running along the road like you? He was such a pretty boy! I am sure he would have grown to be very fine-looking—my poor little Léon! "

" Mon Dieu! Honorine, if you are going to mourn over that, you will be sad and sigh—and the doctor said that would make you sick."

" It's over, Agathe—you are right; I do not mean to disturb your joy; but, you see, when I think of the new life we are going to lead here, of the sweet peaceful life that is to be ours, when we have left Paris, oh! then I can't help thinking of my son, who always had a place

in my dreams of happiness and of the future. You have
no idea, Agathe, of a mother's love, and you cannot understand the incurable wound that the loss of that child
has made in my heart! But it's all over now, poor love!
Now you are sad, too. Come, let us turn our thoughts
to finding the house that's for sale; we are to apply
to——"

"Monsieur Ledrux, gardener and florist, to see Monsieur Courtivaux's house."

"That's it. We will inquire of the first peasant we
meet; in the country everybody knows everybody else."

When the two young women reached the village they
soon met a laboring man, to whom they said:

"Can you direct us to the house of Monsieur Ledrux,
gardener and florist, please?"

"Ledrux! Well! is it a Ledrux Cailleux or a Ledrux
Leblond, or just plain Ledrux? There's lots of Ledruxes
hereabout, you see, and we give each of 'em a nickname
to tell 'em apart. It's like the Thomases and the Gaillots,
there's a swarm of 'em! there's some families where
they've had heaps of children."

"The Monsieur Ledrux whom we wish to find is a
gardener and florist."

"Oh! but everybody's a gardener round here; you
see, we don't go after our neighbor when we want to trim
our trees or vines."

"But they told us that Ledrux——"

"Then it must be plain Ledrux; yes, he takes care of
orange trees for the folks that go to Paris for the winter.

You want to take this road here in front of you and go straight ahead till you turn to the left; and then, on the corner of a lane, you'll see a little house with only two windows in front—and that's where plain Ledrux lives."

" Much obliged, monsieur."

And the two ladies walked on, Agathe saying:

" How funny it is that people in the country should all have the same name! "

" That speaks well for them; it proves that the members of these families have never left their native place to seek fortune elsewhere. My father often used to say to me: ' My child, you may always have confidence in old families, in old business houses, and in old servants.' "

" Here's the lane, and I see the little house with two windows."

" I trust that it's where our Ledrux lives."

They reached the house and found a small gate which opened by turning a knob; they passed through the gate and found themselves in a large and well-kept garden, cleanly raked, where numerous boxes of pomegranates, laurel-bushes and rhododendrons were taking their first breath of the spring air. But they saw nobody.

" Let us go in," said Honorine.

" Let's call," said Agathe; " he must be either in the house or in the garden.—Monsieur Ledrux! " ˙

" Monsieur Ledrux! "

" Perhaps we ought to say: ' plain Monsieur Ledrux.' "

" What a child you are! It seems to me that if he were in the house he would hear us, for it isn't large,

and the gate rang a bell when we opened it. Let us look
around the garden."

" See, there's a man at the further end of the garden;
he sees us."

The master of the house was a little old man, thin and
wrinkled, tanned by the sun, but whose face was at
once kindly and shrewd. He came toward them humming between his teeth, which promised well for his disposition.

Honorine walked forward quickly to meet the singer.

" I beg pardon, monsieur, but we were told to apply
to you to show us a house that is for sale in this neighborhood."

" What's that! a house for sale? "

" Monsieur Courtivaux's."

" Ah! you want to see Monsieur Courtivaux's house,
do you? "

" We do."

" Do you think of buying it? "

" Why, we may buy it if it suits us."

" Ah, yes! that's so; you must see it first. I'll show it
to you."

" We are sorry to give you so much trouble."

" Oh! it ain't very far. And then, you can't go there
alone, for you don't know where it is. Wait a bit, while
I go and fetch the keys."

And the little old man walked away, humming: " Tutu
—turlututu—lututu! "

" You see, my dear love, we came to the right place."

"Yes; and this old peasant seems a merry old fellow; I like him already."

"We will take him for our gardener."

Père Ledrux returned, still humming.

"Are you looking at my garden?"

"Yes; it's extremely well kept."

"Oh! it'll be much prettier when the orange trees are put out; but it's too early yet."

"Aren't you afraid for the pomegranates and laurels?"

"Oh, no! we shan't have any more hard frosts, and they ain't so delicate."

"You have some very fine espaliers."

"Well! that's because they're well looked out for; but they have to be. Trees, you see, are just exactly like people; if we didn't give 'em a bit of a touch-up now and then, what would we look like?"

They left the garden, crossed one broad street, then another bordered by garden walls.

"Chelles is a large place!" said Honorine.

"Oh, yes; it ain't so small! Bless me! this used to be a famous country; it used to have a name of its own. Oh! you ought to hear Monsieur Antoine Beaubichon, the doctor here, talk about it; he's a scholar and knows a lot—to say nothing of a brother of his in Paris, who's very famous too for his knowledge of business and teaches you how to manage books."

"I know the history of this village," said Honorine with a smile; "I know that the Abbey of Chelles was very famous; that under the first race of French kings religious establishments were founded here. King Chilperic often resided here, and was assassinated here."

"I say! I say! madame knows as much as our doctor!" exclaimed Père Ledrux, opening his eyes.

"One need only read history to learn that."

"But I am very ignorant, my dear friend; do tell me how King Chilperic was assassinated here."

"It's a very old story, my dear Agathe; it happened in the year 584, and between ourselves, all the narratives that we have of those days are somewhat apocryphal. But this is the way the story runs:

"A mayor of the palace—there were prime ministers then, called mayors of the palace; this one, whose name was Landry, was, if history is to be believed, the lover of Queen Frédégonde. Now the king, happening one day to enter his consort's chamber when he was not expected, found her leaning over and washing her head; he amused himself by striking her from behind with his staff. A strange amusement for a king! but in those days there was very little refinement.

"The queen, not seeing who it was who had entered the room, thought that none but her favorite would venture to use such freedom, so she said: 'Why do you strike me, Landry?'

"But, on turning her head, she saw the king, her spouse, instead of her lover; she was stupefied with terror. As for Chilperic, he went off hunting, without a word.

" When the king had gone, Frédégonde sent for the
mayor of the palace and told him everything that had
happened. As they both feared torture and the death
they had merited by their treacherous conduct, they resolved to kill King Chilperic. He did not return from
the hunt until nightfall, and when he arrived at Chelles
and was dismounting from his horse, cutthroats in
Frédégonde's pay stabbed him again and again with
knives; he died on the spot.

" The queen, after causing the report to be spread
abroad that the crime was instigated by King Childebert,
had the courage to attend the obsequies of her deceased
husband, which she caused to be celebrated with great
pomp at Paris.

" That, my dear Agathe, is what history tells us; it
is not a moral tale, far from it! and unhappily that sort
of thing was too common in those days, which cannot
have been the 'good old days' that so many poets have
extolled. I will not tell you anything more about Chelles,
for in truth it would be even less edifying than what I
have just told you."

" My faith! " exclaimed Père Ledrux, who had re-
frained from humming while the young woman was
speaking; " you do know a lot, all the same; and you
tell it plainer than the doctor, because he uses such long
words—words I don't know; so that he always has to
tell us a story seven or eight times to make me understand
it."

" But the house—we don't seem to get to it? "

"Here we are, madame. Look, when we pass this
wall which makes an elbow. There! do you see that
building with green blinds? that's Monsieur Courtivaux's house."

"Oh! my dear friend, just look! how lovely it is!
There's a railing in front, and vases of flowers on the
pilasters; it's all very fine!"

Madame Dalmont smiled at her young companion's
enthusiasm, but the aspect of the house pleased her
greatly as well, and the nearer they approached, the better pleased they were.

There was an iron fence in front, through which they
could see a pretty lawn, which stretched in front of the
house and formed a charming carpet of verdure.

"Oh! Honorine, see what lovely turf! Why, monsieur, how is it possible to have such green turf so early?"

"Pardi, mamzelle—for I see that you're the unmarried one—there's green turf here all winter, even under
the snow. The folks in Paris don't believe it, but grass
grows all the time, you see."

The peasant opened the gate; two paths skirted the
lawn and led to the house; and on both sides were tall
trees, whose branches extended over the grass, so that,
in summer, their foliage protected it from the sun's heat.

Agathe walked beside Honorine, saying every instant
in an undertone:

"Oh! how lovely it is! see those fine trees, and those
lilac bushes, with great buds already, and those syringas!
Oh! how lovely it must be in summer!"

" There's a dozen boxes that we put round the lawn,"
said the gardener, " six oranges and six pomegranates;
but I carried 'em home because I take care of 'em; in
another month I'll put 'em in place. Oh, my! then it
looks nice; it's a pretty sight, I tell you."

The house consisted of two stories and attics. The
ground floor was about three feet from the ground, so
that one had to ascend a flight of steps to the front
door. The peasant opened the door and they found themselves in a handsome hall in which there were four doors.
One opened into a dainty salon, very comfortably furnished; couches filled a large portion of the space; they
and the chairs were covered with light blue material,
and the wall paper was of the same shade.

Agathe uttered a cry of delight.

" A blue salon! my favorite color and yours too, Honorine; if they had asked us what we liked they could not
have suited us better!"

" There's just a crumb of dust on the furniture," said
the gardener, " but you understand—when a house ain't
occupied, the dust collects in a jiffy! I come here every
day myself to feed the hens and rabbits, but you can
understand that I don't have time to clean the rooms."

" What! are there hens and rabbits here, too?"

" To be sure! Monsieur Courtivaux was very fond of
rabbits; he used to have one killed every week to eat."

" That's a curious way of loving animals!" said Madame Dalmont; " for my part, I could never make up my
mind to kill a poor creature that I had fondled."

"Oh! nor I to eat one!" said Agathe.

"And then I am not wild for rabbit as food; and so, Monsieur Ledrux, if I buy the house, I will begin by making you a present of all there are here."

The peasant seemed greatly pleased by that promise; he put his hand to a little round hat which had lost both its color and its brim, and which did duty as a cap, and murmured:

"Madame is very good; I won't refuse 'em. Bless me! there's two females that breed; but still, if you don't like rabbit, I can understand your getting rid of 'em. They smell bad in the first place, and they ruin everything if you're unlucky enough to let 'em get into the garden. My word! what a wreck!—And what about the hens? if madame don't like them any better, I could take care of them too; they ain't very clean, the little devils; they go pecking round everywhere."

"Oh! hens are very different," said Honorine; "they give one fresh eggs, which are always very pleasant."

"Besides, it must be such fun to hunt for the eggs— to see if there are many of them. I'll take care of the hens, my dear friend. And then, they don't kill those poor creatures."

"Oh! yes they do; there's folks who fix 'em up with rice or little onions; and they're good too. And then you sometimes have some that won't lay or that fight with the others; them you don't keep—you eat 'em!"

"Ah! Monsieur Ledrux, you are very pitiless to everything that can be eaten! However, we will see, and when one of our hens maltreats her companions, why, you shall carry her off, that's all; but I don't propose to have any inhabitant of my poultry yard killed on my premises."

"All right; if that's your idea, never fear, I'll carry off the poor layers; madame can do as she pleases. Well, well! here I am saying 'madame' and 'mademoiselle'; but it seems to me that you can't be mother and daughter; one of you's too young, and the other too old."

"That's so, it would be hard; but Agathe is only my friend. I am a widow; I have no—I have no child of my own; we two are all alone."

"Do you think of living here all the year round if you should buy the house?"

"Yes, to be sure, all the year; we shall settle down here."

"Well, I tell you, that'll suit me. Two nice little women in the place—they brighten things up, and they're pleasant to look at."

"Let us finish inspecting the house."

On the ground floor there were, besides the salon, a beautiful dining-room, pantry, bath-room and kitchen.

On the first floor there were four pleasant bedrooms and two dressing-rooms; above that, two servants'-rooms and a loft.

The whole house was furnished very comfortably.

Agathe jumped for joy as they entered each room.

"Look," she cried, "this will be your room, Honorine; see how comfortable you will be here. There's a nice little dressing-room connected with it, and such a view! Oh! do come and look out of the window, my dear friend; it's magnificent! What a glorious panorama! how far you can see! and when everything is green, when these fields are studded with flowers, oh! how lovely it must be! Below us, on this side, there's a little yard, and beyond is the garden, isn't it, monsieur?"

"Yes, mamzelle, that's the garden, and a well-kept garden too, I flatter myself; and there'll be plenty of fruit this year! if we don't have a miserable frost during the April moon."

"Well, let us go to see the garden," said Honorine, "so far, I like the house very much."

They left the house at the rear by a door opening into a small yard. There were the outhouses, the hencoop and the rabbit-hutches. A lattice separated the yard from the garden, which was about a third of an acre in extent and prettily laid out.

Agathe's joyous exclamations redoubled at each arbor, each clump of shrubbery, but her enthusiasm reached its height when, at the end of a path, she spied a mound on which was a pretty little summer-house, standing at a corner of the garden wall. The slope leading to the summer-house was bordered by eglantine and honeysuckle. The building had three windows from which there was an extensive view of the surrounding country; for, as we have said, Chelles stood on a hill and overlooked its whole neighborhood.

"Oh! we'll come here very often!" cried Agathe; "we'll sit at the window and work, won't we, Honorine?"

"Yes, I like this place extremely, I confess. What perfect tranquillity one must enjoy here!"

"And in addition it's sure to be very cool in summer, because of these tall lindens all about. It's a lovely place to come to indulge in a chat and to drink a glass with a friend."

Honorine smiled as she replied:

"We shall hardly come here to drink a glass perhaps; but we may breakfast here sometimes and bring our work here very often. Yes, in two months I should think that this view would be very lovely."

"Oh! in another month the lilacs and syringas will begin to put out leaves," said Ledrux. "And then by that time you'll be having lilies of the valley and violets and tulips and narcissus and hyacinths; there's plenty of them in the garden. You can smell 'em when you walk here.—On the whole, the house pleases you, don't it?"

"Yes, very much; and you too, eh, Agathe?"

"Oh! my dear friend, I am enchanted with it; I would like to stay here now, and not go back to Paris at all! This place seems like a little paradise."

"I suppose they've told you the price Monsieur Courtivaux asks—twenty thousand francs?—But, bless me! very likely he'll take off a little something."

"Yes, we saw his agent. We shall see him again to-morrow to close the bargain."

"Oh! yes, my dear; we mustn't wait till the house is sold to someone else."

"Look you," said the gardener; "as long as this place suits you and you're going to give me the rabbits, if anybody else should come to look at the house these next few days, I'll just tell 'em right out that it's sold; then they won't try to buy it. Ha! ha! Bless my soul! we must be a little sly and help each other a bit."

"Thanks, Père Ledrux, and when we are living here, you must come now and then to look after our garden, trim our trees, and——"

"Pardi! just as often as you say; I shall be at your service, if you pay me! that's my business! Oh! we can settle about that. I ain't stiff myself; when people treat me well, I do the same by them!"

Honorine, who had been looking out over the country, turned to her young friend and said:

"Yes, this house pleases me as much as it does you, Agathe; there is only one reason that might prevent our taking it."

"What is that, my dear?"

"That it is rather isolated, rather far away from other houses; and we are two lone women—Suppose we should be attacked here, who would there be to defend us?"

"Oh! upon my word! Are you so timid as that, Honorine?"

"Without being very timid, I am not very brave."

"Somebody attack you—here at Chelles!" cried Père Ledrux with a laugh. "Well, that is a good one, on my word! As if there was any brigands in this region!

In the first place, they won't steal your rabbits, for you give 'em to me. That's the only thing that does get stolen now and then; oh! yes, there's the hens. But you mustn't let 'em go out. It's a nuisance. But when you come to everything else, there ain't the least danger. This house is on the edge of the open country, to be sure, but there's some very nice places out in the country itself. Look; do you see over here to your right, beyond the mill; it's quite a longish way, on the other side of the Marne; but when the sun's shining on it, you can see it quite plain. First, there's the little village of Gournay, where you go to get *matelotes.* The fish is fresh, they catch it before your eyes. Then, farther on, where the land rises, is Noisy-le-Grand. Do you see, over in that direction, a big square house, with terraced grounds? there's a little tower that stands by itself in one corner, with a lightning rod. You can't see the lightning rod from here, but if you've got good eyes, you ought to see the tower."

" Yes, I can see it," said Agathe; " the house is like a little château. To whom does it belong?"

" Who does it belong to? Well, we know and we don't know. That is to say, no one knows much about who the man is that owns it; to tell the truth, there's two masters to that place—a man and a dog!"

" What do you say? a dog owns that great house? Why, then it must be a dog after the pattern of Puss in Boots."

" Puss in Boots? I say, who's he? I never saw him."

" .Come, Monsieur Ledrux, tell us what you mean. Who lives in that house with a tower ? "

" A very strange kind of man, and his dog. And the master's so fond of his dog, and the beast is so fond of his master, that they're just like two friends, who both do exactly what the other wants him to. When the dog happens to want to go in one direction, why then the master goes in that direction; he lets the animal lead him. And it seems that it's a good thing for him that he does, because the beast is so uncommon intelligent that no one ever saw his like; so that—But who's that going along the road yonder? I believe it's Doctor Antoine Beaubichon.—I beg pardon, excuse me, mesdames, but someone gave me a message for him, and I must find out if he's got it. I'll go out by the little gate yonder, that opens into the road, and I'll come right back. But I must find out whether the doctor's been told to go to Gournay to see the wine-dealer's sick child."

As he spoke, the peasant left the window of the summer-house, from which he had seen someone on the road, and, opening a small gate at the end of the garden, he was soon in the fields.

XIV

PAUL AND HIS DOG

Père Ledrux was no sooner out of the garden than he began to shout at the top of his lungs:

"Holà! Monsieur Antoine! Monsieur le Docteur Antoine!"

A short, stout individual, wrapped in a brown overcoat as long as a surplice, and with a low-crowned, very broad-brimmed hat on his head, which made him appear still shorter, halted in the middle of a cross-road and looked up in the air, saying:

"Who's calling me?" as if he thought that the voice he had heard came from a balloon.

"Pardi! it's me calling you; it ain't a bird, it's me, Ledrux—this way."

"Ah! it's you, is it, Père Ledrux? What are you doing here?"

"As you see, I'm calling you and waiting to ask you if your servant Claudine gave you my message. You wasn't at home this morning when I went to your house to tell you to go to Gournay to see the wine-dealer's child; she's got the scarlet fever, they say."

"Scarlatina—yes, yes. Claudine told me and I am coming from Gournay, as you see."

"Good! then you've cured the child?"

"Not yet; but it isn't anything serious."

"Have you been to Gournay on foot?"

"Yes, the weather was fine, and it does one good to walk; I'm getting too fat."

"But your nag'll get too fat too, if you don't use him! Ha! ha! You'd better lend him to me, I'll give him plenty of work!"

"What are you doing here?"

"I'm showing Monsieur Courtivaux's house to some ladies from Paris; they're very nice, and they act as if they meant to buy it. Look, there they are, both of 'em, at the window in the little summer-house. That's where I saw you from."

Honorine and Agathe were, in fact, still standing at the window. They were looking across the fields, but their eyes turned most frequently toward the house with the turret. The few words that the gardener had said concerning its proprietors had aroused their curiosity to the highest pitch; indeed, as they proposed to take up their abode at Chelles, in the somewhat isolated house in which they then were, it was quite natural that they should desire to know their neighbors.

Doctor Antoine raised his head to look at the ladies; he removed his broad-brimmed hat, disclosing his almost bald head and his cheerful, ruddy face, and made them a low bow, which they instantly acknowledged.

" Look you," said the doctor to the gardener, " as the
garden gate is open, I can shorten my walk home ma-
terially by going through the garden."

" I should say so; it will shorten it by half."

" That being so, I will go that way; and suppose I
should pay my respects to these ladies at the same time?
What do you say, Ledrux?"

" It seems to me that it can't do 'em any harm, even
if it don't do 'em any good!"

" That's so; and then—we shall know each other;
and when they come here to live, if they happen to be
sick, why, they'll send for me."

" Sure enough! especially as you're the only doctor
in the neighborhood."

" Yes; but you see that they sent for me from Gournay; that proves that everybody doesn't take the one
who is nearest."

" Ah! you're a shrewd one, you are! you always have
an eye to the main chance!"

" There's no law against looking after one's business."

" *Nenni!* all the more as it ain't safe to depend on
other folks for that. Ha! ha! ha! tutu—turlututu."

During their conversation the two men had entered the
garden. Père Ledrux closed the little gate, and the two
friends, who had left the summer-house, soon found
themselves face to face with Doctor Antoine, who bowed
again, saying:

" Mesdames, as an inhabitant—and physician—of this
district, I shall consider myself very happy if we are to

have the good fortune to claim you as neighbors, as
Ledrux has led me to hope; for he tells me that you
propose to buy this estate."

" Yes, monsieur, we both like the house very much. It
is well arranged and pleasantly located; the garden is
large enough for us. But just as the gardener caught
sight of you, I was talking with him of the isolation of
this house. We have no man in our family. I expect to
employ a servant, but it will be some young peasant girl!
So you will understand, monsieur, that we must not
incur any risks."

" I have lived at Chelles many years, mesdames, and
I feel justified in assuring you that it is not a region of
thieves."

" I believe it, monsieur, but is the neighborhood as
safe as the place itself? Naturally, when one lives in
the country, one goes out to walk——"

" And very wisely; it is good for the health."

" But it would be very unpleasant if one had to dread
disagreeable accidents on such walks."

" The whole neighborhood is quite thickly settled; and
on my word, except——"

" Except? go on, monsieur."

" Still, I can't say anything definite. When one doesn't
really know—But one thing is certain,—that the fellow is
neither good-humored nor sociable. So far as that goes,
he's a wretched neighbor. I say ' neighbor,' but he's
quite a distance from here. Besides, he won't annoy
you; you'll very seldom meet him, for as soon as he

sees anybody coming he goes another way; he's a wolf,
a bear, a veritable bear-cub, and an ill-licked one!' "

While the doctor was speaking, the gardener pulled
him gently by the coat-tail, whispering:

"What in the devil's the need of saying all that?
you'll scare the ladies, and take away their desire to live
in this house! What you're doing ain't very clever for
a doctor!"

"Well, monsieur, where does this wolf, this bear live?
you must tell us so that we may at least avoid walking
in the direction of his den."

"The person to whom I refer by that designation,
mesdames, lives on the estate yonder at the right,
toward Noisy-le-Grand; quite a handsome house, with
a tower."

"Then it's the man with the dog," said Agathe.

"Exactly, mademoiselle, it's the man with the dog.
Do you know him already?"

"The gardener was just telling us about him when he
left us to call you, monsieur, and the little that he had
told us had aroused our curiosity keenly. It would be
very kind of you, therefore, monsieur le docteur, to tell
us everything that is known about this man; for, frankly,
if he is really an ogre, we shall not be at all pleased
to have him for a neighbor."

"Oho! an ogre!" cried Père Ledrux with a laugh;
"that's a good one, and no mistake. An ogre! they eat
children, ogres do! I never heard tell that Monsieur
Paul or his dog had eaten a child, no matter how small."

"I never intended to imply that he was an ogre," rejoined the doctor. "God forbid that I should attribute such depraved tastes to the man! I simply form conjectures based on what I have heard. And what I have seen is not calculated to give me a very pleasant opinion of him."

Talking thus, the party had returned to the house.

"I'll just take a look at the rabbits," said the gardener, "if you'll rest a bit in the salon."

"Very gladly," said Honorine; "and if monsieur le docteur has the time, perhaps he will tell us what he knows about the proprietor of the house with the turret, whom you call Paul, I believe?"

"Yes, mesdames, Paul; no one knows him by any other name; and as he is always accompanied by his dog, a Newfoundland almost as big as a donkey, they are commonly referred to in the neighborhood as 'Paul and his dog.'"

The two young women entered the blue salon, accompanied by Doctor Antoine Beaubichon, who seated himself respectfully at some little distance from them, and began his story:

"Almost nine years ago the estate called the Tower was offered for sale; but no purchaser appeared. Why was it that no purchaser appeared? People attributed it to a certain circumstance, and that circumstance, mesdames, is too interesting to be passed over in silence. It was like this. Not far from the small park of the Tower, at the beginning of a ravine close to the road

leading to Noisy-le-Grand, in a very lonely spot, a cross
has been erected in memory of a person who, not very
long ago—I forget just when it was, but no matter—in
memory of a person who was assassinated at that spot.
Indeed, it is said that the victim is buried at the foot of
the cross; and as country folk are always superstitious
and love to frighten one another, the people of Noisy-le-
Grand, Gournay, and even those of Chelles to some extent, declare that it isn't safe to pass the cross in the
ravine at night, because strange noises, groans, are heard
there, and you are likely to meet the ghost of the person
who was killed there after the Tower was offered for
sale."

"Oh! mon Dieu! why, this is horrible, monsieur le
docteur," said Honorine; "it's a regular ghost story."

"Pray go on, monsieur," said Agathe; "it interests
me deeply; but you haven't told us who it was that was
murdered. Was it a man or a woman?"

"It was a man, mademoiselle, a young man, who was
found dead in that ravine. How it happened has never
been known, nor were the assassins ever discovered."

"Was it somebody who lived hereabout?"

"No, for no one recognized him; and the strangest
thing was that he had not been robbed; they found a
gold watch on him and a large amount of money."

"But perhaps the miscreants who committed the crime
heard someone coming, and, being afraid of being cap-
tured, ran away before they had had time to rob their
victim."

" The result is that they have set up a cross on that spot, and that the villagers make a long détour rather than go through the ravine at night, for they are sure that they would meet the ghost."

" Bah! turlututu! that's a pretty story!" said Père Ledrux, showing his face at the door of the salon. " What's this, doctor! are you telling these ladies all these old stories so that they'll be afraid to come here to live? Why, it's all fiddle-faddle. I've been through the ravine lots of times at night, right by the cross, and I never met anybody, not the first hobgoblin! The old women say to each other over the fire: ' What can we think up to give us a good fright?' And they invent those old nurse's tales!"

" I am simply telling what everyone says, Ledrux; I am informing these ladies concerning the *chronique* of the place, nothing more."

" The colic of the place don't know what it's saying; anybody can walk anywhere in our neighborhood at all hours; there ain't any danger.—I'll go and take a look at the hens; I think there's one of 'em bothering the others."

" Mesdames," continued the doctor when the peasant had gone, " I hope that you do not think me capable of trying to frighten you; for I should be delighted to have you come here to live."

" We think it so little, monsieur, that we beg you to continue your story; it gives us the greatest pleasure to listen to you."

The doctor rose to bow again to the ladies; then resumed his seat, blew his nose and continued:

"You see, while I don't pretend to be very strong-minded, I don't believe in ghosts, for the reason that I never saw one; if I had seen one, I should believe in them; and in that regard my opinion coincides with that of my brother Désiré Beaubichon, professor of book-keeping in Paris,—a very learned man, of whom you ladies may have heard?"

"No, monsieur, never."

"Nature swarms with curious facts, which the most learned are not always able to explain; and from Apollonius of Tyana, the greatest magician of ancient times, down to Cagliostro, who also was able to evoke the devil, many people, who were not fools by any means, have believed in ghosts. For my part, I declare that I should much rather believe everything than nothing!—I return to the Tower.

"The property is quite extensive, in addition to the buildings, wherein a large number of people can be accommodated, for it is like a small château—there are more than twelve sleeping-rooms. Then there are the garden and a small park—about twelve acres in all. I believe that the price asked was fifty thousand francs, but as I have had the honor to tell you, they could find no purchaser; the nearness of the cross in the ravine, and all the stories that were in circulation frightened the ladies who came to see the property. So that there was great surprise throughout the region when the notary at

Noisy-le-Grand said to his neighbors one morning : ' the Tower is sold ! '

" The news flew from mouth to mouth : ' the Tower is sold ! '

" ' Bah ! it isn't possible ! '

" ' Yes, it's a fact ; monsieur le notaire himself told it.'

" ' Well, to whom is it sold ? '

" ' To Monsieur Paul.'

" ' Paul who ? Paul what ? '

" To all such questions the notary, upon whom secrecy had been enjoined, answered :

" ' To Monsieur Paul ; the purchaser has given no other name, but he pays cash for the property, and is at liberty to take possession whenever he chooses.'

" ' Paul is it ! ' said the country folk ; ' after all, a man may have no other name than Paul and be a perfectly honorable man ; we have had merchants and manufacturers who were called simply Jean or Pierre. If this Paul is an agreeable man, a jovial companion, he'll be a welcome addition to the neighborhood. And then, it's probable that he has a wife and children ; as he has bought that big house, he must have people to put in it. Perhaps he will give a party, a ball to his new neighbors, to become acquainted with them ; then we shall find out what sort of man he is.'

" That, madame, was what the people said here in Chelles and in the neighborhood. But time passed and no one arrived ; the estate of the Tower showed no sign of life, assumed no festal air.

" ' For heaven's sake, isn't the new owner going to occupy his house?' people began to say. ' In that case, why did he buy it?'

"But one morning Jeannette the poulterer informed her neighbors:

" ' Well, the gentleman who's bought the Tower has arrived; he's been in the house a fortnight. What do you suppose his household consists of?—a dog! nothing but a great dog that's always at his master's heels. But I suppose he found out that his dog couldn't get his dinner and do his housework, so he's hired old Mère Lucas, from the village of Couberon, who's almost blind and a little deaf, and she takes care of his house.'

"You can understand, mesdames, that everybody was amazed to learn that the only occupants of that enormous house were a man, a dog and a half-blind and deaf old woman.

" ' The gentleman has come on ahead,' people thought; ' his family is probably going to join him here.' But no one came. And then, the new owner, instead of showing himself to his neighbors and trying to become acquainted with them, never went out to walk, or at all events not in any frequented part of the country; and people said: ' Have you seen the owner of the Tower?' —' No.'—' Nor I; where in the devil does the man keep himself?'—' Doesn't he ever leave his house or his grounds? he must live like a hermit, then?'

"One day, however, one of the townspeople met him and lost no time in letting everybody know that this

Monsieur Paul was a tall, well-built man, neither young
nor old, that is to say, with a full beard which covered a
large part of his face and made it impossible to guess
his age; but that he had a savage, repellent, disagreeable manner; that he was dressed very simply, in hunting costume: jacket, long leather gaiters and a cap with
a broad vizor which concealed all the upper part of his
face. He had a gun in his hand and a large dog at his
heels.

" People said: ' He is probably very fond of hunting
and passes all his time at it; hunters aren't very good-
natured, so we must overlook his peculiarities. But the
hunting season doesn't last forever, and no doubt the
man with the big dog will become more sociable; let us
wait.'

" They waited in vain. However, they saw Monsieur
Paul occasionally, walking in the fields with his faithful
companion. But when anyone approached, he quickly
turned in the other direction to avoid meeting them.

" One day, however, Madame Droguet, one of the
largest land-owners in the neighborhood—Madame
Droguet, having watched to see which roads the master
of the Tower usually chose for his walks, said to her
friends:

" ' I am determined to see our new neighbor and to
speak to him; in short, I propose to find out what that
man has to say for himself; if he's a foreigner, I can
tell by his accent what country he comes from. The
fact is, I propose to find out what we are to think about

him, and it won't take me long to see whether he's a
comme il faut person or an ill-bred one.'

" ' How will you go to work to find out? ' someone
asked Madame Droguet—' As the owner of the Tower
avoids everybody, as he only goes where nobody else
goes, how do you expect to talk with him? '

" ' That's my affair, I shall find a way! you know that
what a woman wants always comes to pass in time.'

" Madame Droguet is a woman who has no doubt of
her ability to do anything, and who fears nothing. There
are some people hereabout who declare that she was a
vivandière in her youth, and that she served in Africa ;
that is a statement hardly worth repeating.

" And so this lady, who, as I have had the honor to
tell you, had carefully observed what roads the master of
the Tower frequented, concealed herself in a dense
thicket at the corner of one of those roads. For four
days in succession she had the resolution to station herself there and to wait several hours for the gentleman to
pass. I presume that she carried her knitting ; one can
knit anywhere, even in a thicket. But the man with the
dog did not pass. On the fifth day, however, her patience
was rewarded ; she saw the hunter coming along a path,
and when he was within ten yards of her, she quickly
stepped from her thicket, so that she was directly in
front of him, in a path so narrow that it was impossible
to avoid the meeting. The gentleman, amazed to see a
lady suddenly appear in front of him, stopped and seemed
disposed to turn back ; but he concluded to step aside so

as to allow Madame Droguet to pass, while his dog
glared at her as if he longed to ask her what she was
doing there.

" But, instead of passing the hunter, Madame Droguet
halted directly in front of him, made a low curtsy, and
said :

" ' I believe that I have the pleasure of addressing the
new owner of the Tower? I am charmed that chance
affords me the pleasure of making his acquaintance. I
am a land-owner at Chelles; I receive all the best people
in the province, and if monsieur will deign to do me the
honor to come to see me——'

" But at that point the hunter abruptly interrupted
the lady and said to her in a sharp and none too courteous
tone :

" ' I go nowhere, madame, and I do not desire to make
any new acquaintances ! '

" With that, he just touched his hand to his cap, which
he did not even raise from his head, and strode away,
followed by his huge dog.

" Ah! if you could have seen Madame Droguet when
she got home! She was perfectly furious! She ran
about to all her acquaintances, saying: ' I know the
owner of the Tower now! he's a boor, a clown, a man
of no breeding whatever! He didn't even raise his cap
tq me! He must be a mere nobody who has made money,
no one knows how. I'll wager that he doesn't know
how to read or write, and if he avoids society, it's because he realizes that he would be out of place therein,

and wouldn't know how to behave himself! Thanks! I shan't undertake his education; it would be too hard work to grub up that fellow.'

" For some time people talked of nothing but Madame Droguet's interview with the newcomer, and the whole district knew that that gentleman needed a thorough grubbing up; Madame Droguet's expression was a great success; she often makes some very remarkable ones. After all, when a person talks a great deal and says whatever comes into his head, it isn't surprising that in the vast output of words there should be a few clever ones—they may occasionally fall from the dullest person's lips.

" Several months passed and the proprietor of the Tower continued to follow the same line of conduct.

" One morning, Monsieur Luminot, formerly a wholesale dealer in wines, who is very well-to-do, and has a fine house and a good deal of land in this region—Monsieur Luminot, I say, took it into his head to make this Monsieur Paul's acquaintance.

" I must tell you, mesdames, that Monsieur Luminot is a lively old fellow, a *bon vivant* and wag, who often gives dinners and entertains handsomely. He is highly esteemed all about here.

" He said to himself: ' The master of the Tower probably divined that Madame Droguet had hidden in a clump of bushes in order to pop out in front of him, and he didn't like it. I can understand that; men don't like to have traps laid for them, or to be watched for and

spied upon. I'll go about it in an entirely different way;
I'll go straight to this gentleman and tell him that I have
come as a neighbor, to call on him, and I will invite him
to dinner. He will say at all events: " Here's a man who
acts honestly, and doesn't lie in wait for me in the
bushes."—I feel sure that he will welcome me more
courteously than he did Madame Droguet.'

" And one fine day, after his breakfast, Monsieur
Luminot bent his steps toward the Tower. He rang
the bell at the main gate which was always kept locked,
saying to himself that if Mère Lucas should answer the
bell, he would ask her to take him to her master. But
it was not the old peasant who opened the gate, it was
the master of the house himself; he stared at Monsieur
Luminot with an air of amazement, and said in his hoarse
voice, not even allowing him to enter his premises:

" ' What do you want, monsieur ? '

" Our quondam wine merchant, who is not easily
abashed, began to laugh as he replied:

" ' Pardieu ! it is you I want, neighbor, for I am sure
that you are the master of the house. I am Luminot, a
landowner at Chelles, a *bon vivant,* always staunch at the
table, always ready to let my friends taste my wine, which
is not bad, I flatter myself. You don't go to see anybody,
you keep yourself shut up here like a bear in his den;
that's not the way to enjoy yourself! and I have come
to ask you to dine with me to-morrow.'

" ' I thank you, monsieur,' replied the man with the
dog, ' but, as I entertain no one here, I do not go to

other people's houses.'—And with that he shut the gate in his face.

"Then it became Monsieur Luminot's turn to feel angry; he came home shouting as loudly as Madame Droguet had:

"'Who in the devil is this fellow that's bought the Tower? The man's worse than a savage! I undertake to be polite to him, to invite him to dinner, and he shuts the door in my face without letting me cross the threshold, without even asking me to sit down and take something! I could have forgiven him for declining my invitation, but he might at least have given me a taste of his wine! Decidedly he's a devilish mean kind of a neighbor.'

"This, mesdames, is the way that people learned to know this eccentric personage; it only remains for me to tell you of my personal experience.

"A year had passed since these incidents, and people were beginning to talk a little less about the proprietor of the Tower—for we become accustomed to everything, and by dint of discussing any one person there comes a time when we have nothing more to say—when, as I was returning one day from Gournay, where I had been to see a patient, I met Mère Lucas, the old woman who composed the whole of Monsieur Paul's establishment. I was passing her without stopping, but she accosted me, saying:

"'Oh! I am glad I met you, Monsieur le Docteur Antoine Beaubichon; it's as if Providence sent you on purpose, for I was just thinking that I'd have to go to your house.'

" ' Do you want to consult me, Mère Lucas?' said I; ' are you sick? what's the matter with you?'

" ' No, monsieur le docteur, I'm not sick; to be sure I'm not very strong, but the cracked pots last longer than the new ones sometimes, you know. It isn't for myself that I was going to see you, but for my master, Monsieur Paul; he's sick, hasn't left his bed for two whole weeks, and he must be feeling very bad, for he's a man that don't take any care of himself, and I had hard work to get him to drink some herb tea.'

" ' Ah! the owner of the Tower is sick, is he? Did he tell you to summon a doctor?'

" ' No, indeed he didn't! on the contrary, every time I say to him: " You ought to have a doctor, monsieur, and if you say so I'll go and call the doctor at Chelles, Monsieur Beaubichon, who's very learned and very skilful," he says: " Let me alone, Mère Lucas! I don't need a doctor, I won't have one; if I have got to die, I can die without doctors, and if it is the will of heaven that I live, they won't be the ones to cure me; nature will come to my assistance." '

" ' Well,' I said to the old peasant, ' as this gentleman doesn't want a doctor, why were you coming to fetch me?'

" ' Why, monsieur, as if we ought to listen to sick folks, especially when they're so peculiar as my master! He don't get any better since he said that; on the contrary, he is much weaker since yesterday, and he seems to be suffering more. So it's my duty to take care of him in spite of him; and as it's your business to cure people, monsieur le docteur, you can't refuse to prescribe for my master.'

" I reflected for some time; I am certainly not so inquisitive as Madame Droguet, and I am not the man to crouch in the bushes for five days in succession watching for a man I don't know. And yet I was not sorry to obtain a nearer view of that strange man who avoided everybody, and to be able to judge for myself whether Madame Droguet and neighbor Luminot had not been a little severe on him. To make a long story short, as the old servant still begged me to go with her to the Tower, I said to myself: ' I may as well go; the man is sick; I am asked to go to see a sick man, and it's my duty to go; that's my profession.'

" So I started off with Mère Lucas. On the way, I ventured to ask a few questions about the proprietor.

" The old peasant's constant refrain was:

" ' Oh! he's a very nice man! an excellent man! '

" As the woman is deaf, I concluded that she didn't hear my questions and that she naturally answered at random.

" We reached the Tower in due time, and I entered the house, which, although well furnished—richly furnished indeed—seemed to me wretchedly kept. I passed through several rooms and at last reached a door which the peasant motioned to me to open, saying:

" ' This is the master's room; you don't need me to talk to him.'

" And she vanished. I glanced at my clothes to see if I was presentable, and was brushing a speck of dust off my trousers, when I heard a dull but prolonged groan.

" ' The devil! ' thought I; ' can it be my patient groaning like that? The man is sicker than he thinks.'

" But the groaning seemed to come nearer; suddenly it changed into a loud barking, and an enormous dog rushed from the room I was about to enter, planted his front paws on my chest, and glared at me with eyes that were far from gentle! I confess, mesdames, that at the first shock I could not control my alarm! As he stood, the dog was taller than I! "

Honorine and Agathe could not restrain a smile at this portion of the doctor's narrative.

" Almost immediately," he continued, " a voice called: ' who is there? there's someone there; who is it, Ami? '

" ' Yes, monsieur,' said I in a trembling voice, ' it is a friend—*ami*—who has come to see you.'—I unconsciously made a pun, for I soon discovered that the Newfoundland's name was Ami, and that it was he to whom the gentleman was speaking. I must say, for the dog's justification, that he did not keep his paws on me long, and that, after contemplating me for a few moments, he walked away from me as from a person who was not at all dangerous.

" As there was no further obstacle to my passage, I entered the sick man's room at last. I saw a man, still

young, lying in bed; he was very pale, with a very forbidding expression; and as he wore a full beard and
enormous moustaches, together with a great quantity of
brown hair which lay in disorder about his forehead,
he really was not unlike a man of the woods or an
orang-outang of the larger species."

" So this man is very ugly, very repulsive to look at? "
inquired Honorine.

" It is not so much that he is positively ugly, madame,
but that savage look—you know. However, he did not
give me much time to examine him, for I had hardly
reached the middle of the room when he cried:

" ' Who are you, monsieur, and what do you want? '

" ' Monsieur,' said I, bowing politely, ' I am Doctor
Antoine Beaubichon, long a resident of Chelles, and
favorably known hereabout, I venture to say. I attend
the whole neighborhood, even a long way beyond the
Marne.'

" ' Well, what difference does it make to me whether
you attend the whole neighborhood? ' retorted the sick
man in an impatient tone. ' Why have you come to my
house? I didn't send for you, I don't need a doctor.'

" ' Monsieur,' I said, ' I took the liberty of coming
here only because I was requested to do so, requested
most urgently.'

" ' By whom? '

" ' Mère Lucas, your servant, who is much concerned
about your health, and who realizes that you are sicker
than you think.'

" ' Mère Lucas is meddling in something that doesn't concern her. I know my own business best. I tell you again, monsieur, that I do not need a doctor, and that you may go.'

" As you can imagine, mesdames, not being accustomed to that sort of reception, I was already near the door, ready to take my leave and sorely vexed that I had put myself out for such a boor, when I heard him calling to me:

" ' Monsieur! monsieur! one moment! '

" ' Aha! ' thought I, ' he thinks better of it; he is in pain, no doubt, and realizes that there is nobody but myself who can relieve him. I will go back, for we must be indulgent to invalids.'

" I turned back toward the bed; the bearded man was sitting up, and his great dog was beside him, also sitting on his haunches. I was preparing to feel the invalid's pulse, when he abruptly drew his arm away, and said:

" ' It isn't for myself, monsieur. My dog here hurt his shoulder some time ago passing through a holly bush, and he still suffers from it. What ought we to put on the wound? '

" When I found that it was for his Newfoundland that he had called me back, I drew myself up to my full height and said to the unmannerly fellow:

" ' Let me tell you, monsieur, that I am no dog doctor! If you called me back on this animal's account, you might have saved yourself the trouble.'

"'Why are you unwilling to prescribe for my dog, pray?' he rejoined in a savage tone; 'your visits will be paid for as generously as if you came for me.'

"'I repeat, monsieur, that I attend men, not beasts!'

"Would you believe that he had the impertinence to reply:

"'In most cases, monsieur, men are the beasts, and dogs are much better than they are!'

"Faith! mesdames, I had no desire to hear any more, so I put on my hat and left the Tower, vowing never to put my foot inside its doors again so long as this Monsieur Paul should be the owner."

"For all that," said Père Ledrux, who had returned to the door of the salon, "if he had asked me for a receipt to cure his dog, I'd have given him one, and a good one, too. Still, his Newfoundland got well by himself, and so did his master, too! Ha! ha! You can't deny that they didn't need you for that, monsieur le docteur!"

"What does that prove, Père Ledrux? simply that nature is sometimes as powerful as science."

"Oh, yes! and if science had taken a hand in it, perhaps the two invalids wouldn't be so smart to-day."

"So you don't believe in medicine, Père Ledrux?"

"I don't say that. I believe in anything you want; but I say just this, that medicine sometimes makes mistakes, but nature—oh! she never makes a mistake!"

"Now, mesdames, from these facts you may form your own opinion of the proprietor of the Tower, and

judge whether he is unjustly called a bear and a disagreeable neighbor."

"It is evident, monsieur, that he avoids society," said
Honorine; "probably he has reasons for that. Doubtless he has had much to complain of at its hands. But,
nevertheless, his old servant said that he was an excellent man."

"Mère Lucas is very hard of hearing; she often hears
wrong.—However, in addition to what happened to me
and to Madame Droguet and Monsieur Luminot, we
have had many other opportunities for judging this
gentleman. On several occasions he has shown that he
is really malicious. Once, Jaquette, Catherine the laun-
dress's daughter, a child of nine, went home crying with
her little sister; one cheek was bright red. They asked
her what the matter was, and she replied:

"'I met the man with the dog and he slapped my face
hard because he said I made faces at him.'

"Another time it was Thomas Riteux's son—a little
boy of eleven, and a very sly rascal—whom my gentleman kicked more than once in—somewhere—because he
happened to be in his way."

"Oh! that is very bad!" cried Agathe. "It seems
that he detests children then."

"Did the parents complain?"

"Nonsense!" said the gardener; "what's the sense
of believing everything this one or the other one says!
There's people who heard Jaquette's little sister say
that Jaquette was beating her and eating her cherries,

and that was why he came up and slapped her. And as
for Thomas Riteux's son, he's a little devil. So far as
he could see Monsieur Paul's dog, he began to throw
stones at him. Monsieur Paul saw it and told him not
to throw any more stones at his dog, because the beast
didn't like it. The little scamp is obstinate, and he began
again when he thought he wouldn't be seen. But the
dog ran at him, and faith! he had him by the breeches
and things looked bad for the boy when Monsieur Paul
ran up and made him let go. That was when he kicked
the boy and said: ' You oughtn't to get off so cheap!' "

" But this puts an entirely different face on the matter," said Honorine. " Don't you agree with me, monsieur le docteur ? "

" It is possible, mesdames ; I know that children sometimes tell false stories ; but I persist none the less in my
opinion concerning the owner of the Tower. He's a
low fellow, whom I believe to be entirely uninformed
and uneducated. And as Madame Droguet—a very
bright woman, by the way—well said:

" ' That man shuns society because he realizes that he
would be out of place in society.'

" I trust, mesdames, that this will not have any influence upon your decision with regard to this house.
Thank heaven, this Monsieur Paul will hardly be what
is called a neighbor to you, for it is fully half a league
from here to his place ; and I venture to believe that you
will find in Chelles ample compensation. Society here
is numerous but select. You will find material for a

game of whist or of Pope Joan. Of late, too, we have
taken up bézique. Madame Droguet gives receptions
which all the notabilities attend; sometimes there is
dancing; she has a piano, and when Monsieur Luminot
brings his flageolet, there is a complete orchestra. Re-
cently they have tried the Lancers quadrille; they haven't
succeeded in dancing it through, but they will in time,
especially as Monsieur Droguet is passionately fond of
dancing."

Honorine rose, as did her companion. The young
woman thanked the doctor for all the information he
had been obliging enough to give them, assuring him
that it had only confirmed her in the plan she had formed
of purchasing Monsieur Courtivaux's estate.

Then the ladies left the house, to return to the rail-
way station, saying to the gardener:

"To-morrow morning we shall see the agent, and
doubtless the bargain will soon be concluded."

"Very good!" said Père Ledrux, "and meanwhile,
as I told you, you know, I won't show the house to anyone, because sometimes it happens—Well! someone who
happened to want it would only have to offer a little more
than you. Men never think of anything but their own
interests, you know; and it would slip out of your hands.
But the way I'm going to do, there's no danger; it's just
between you and me. And then I'm going to keep on
with the garden, and I'll keep an eye on the hens; there's
one black one that fights the others; hum! I'll watch
her! You see, she might keep 'em from laying!"

XV

THE GENTLEMAN WITH THE SARCASTIC LOOK

Chamoureau was in an execrable humor when he left Madame Sainte-Suzanne's. As he could not walk home with his coat all open behind, he had to take a cab, and when he stepped in, the accident that had befallen his trousers was so aggravated that when it was time to alight he was reduced to the necessity of taking off his hat and holding it glued to the unfortunate garment in front.

His concierge, who passed a large part of his time in his doorway, stared with all his eyes again when the tenant of the second floor appeared, this time holding his hat in front of his trousers instead of wearing it on his head.

In fact, even Madame Monin, his servant, seeing her master return with his clothes torn from his head to his heels, said to herself:

" In God's name, what kind of a life is Monsieur Chamoureau leading now, to come home in this state? The man is getting to be very dissipated! "

" She refuses to be my mistress! " reflected our widower, as he changed his clothes. " And she won't be my wife either! In that case, what does she propose to

be to me? And why did she speak to me at the Opéra
ball? Why did she herself urge me to call? She gives
me permission to be her friend—much obliged! At
thirty-five years of age, and with a volcanic temperament
like mine, a man isn't content to be the friend of a fascinating woman! Besides, I love the woman. I adore
her, since I saw her in her lovely velvet robe de chambre
—or was it plush? I am not quite sure, but it doesn't
matter. I feel that my passion has taken a new flight.
It is all over with me; the image of that lovely brunette
is here—engraved on my heart; it has replaced Eléonore's.—Poor Eléonore! If I should want to weep for
her now, I could not. That is some compensation. But
what am I to do? I am going to be very wretched now.
She has ten thousand francs a year, so of course I am
not a very good match for her. But if she adored me!
Sapristi! if Freluchon were in Paris, I would go to him
and ask his advice; nobody but he can tell me how I
ought to act now toward Madame de Sainte-Suzanne."

That evening, Chamoureau did not fail to call at Freluchon's house, to inquire if he had returned. But his
dear friend was still at Rouen.

The next day Honorine and Agathe called early at the
agent's office.

" We have been to Chelles," said the young woman,
" we have seen Monsieur Courtivaux's house and we like
it very much. Be good enough to arrange the matter as
quickly as possible, monsieur; we would like to be living
there already."

" Very well, madame. You know that he asks twenty thousand francs? "

" I am ready to give that, monsieur."

" Yes, but perhaps he would take something off; you pay cash, which is a consideration. Then there are the expenses, the deeds and so forth; they will amount to at least a thousand francs, and are ordinarily paid by the purchaser. If we could induce the vendor to pay them at least——"

" Well, monsieur, do the best you can; I leave it to you."

" Never fear, madame. I will go to see Monsieur Courtivaux to-day; then I will call on you with his answer. I have your address—Madame Dalmont, Rue des Martyrs."

" But do not forget us, monsieur."

" I will devote my whole time to you, mesdames."

But when the two friends had gone, Chamoureau, after sitting for some time lost in thought, suddenly struck his forehead and exclaimed:

" I will see Monsieur Edmond Didier; he's a very enterprising young man with the fair sex! In the absence of that villain Freluchon, who confiscates my clothes, he will give me some advice—most excellent advice."

The agent was really enamored of Thélénie; the lovely brunette's great black eyes had turned his head; he did not cease for an instant to think of her whom he had hoped for a brief moment that he had captivated, and that passion caused him to forget absolutely the business which his clients placed in his hands.

But Edmond Didier was rarely at home. Chamoureau was no more fortunate in that direction than in respect to Freluchon. Thrice during the day he went to Edmond's rooms and failed to find him.

" What is the use of friends?" thought our widower in despair; " they're never at home when you want to consult 'em! What on earth do these fellows do? What good does it do them to have a home? One's at Rouen, the other goes out before ten in the morning and hasn't returned at eleven in the evening! No matter! To-morrow will be the third day since I called at Madame de Sainte-Suzanne's. I'll go again to-morrow—in a *redingote!* One is not obliged to wear full dress all the time. She doesn't want me to talk to her about love; I'll talk about the Boulevard de Sébastopol which is being built—that can't offend her. But for lack of words I'll try to make my eyes terribly eloquent; she can't prevent my having love in my eyes."

And the next day, instead of going to see Monsieur Courtivaux and attending to the business with which Madame Dalmont had entrusted him, Chamoureau passed an hour at his toilet. He tried to scatter over his forehead the tuft of hair that still embellished the back of his head, and having assured himself that he had hair enough for a single man, he perfumed his handkerchief with essence of Portugal and went to Rue de Ponthieu.

When he reached Madame Sainte-Suzanne's residence, our widower, who had been thinking all the way
what he could say to the lady to account for calling again
so soon, and had found nothing satisfactory, walked
quickly through the hall, saying to himself:

"Never mind! I'll offer to take her to the theatre—
whichever she pleases—that can't offend her."

And he ran up the two flights without even speaking
to the concierge. He rang at Thélénie's door. The
maid answered the bell, and could not help smiling
when she recognized the gentleman who had left her
mistress in such piteous guise, and torn in several places.

But our widower, who felt quite safe in his redingote
and had no straps to his trousers, walked with an exceedingly unconcerned air and held his head erect with
much dignity as he asked if Madame de Sainte-Suzanne
were visible.

"My mistress has gone out," replied Mademoiselle
Mélie, with the pert air which servants love to assume
before courteous strangers.

"What! Madame de Sainte-Suzanne is not in?" exclaimed Chamourcau, in a despairing tone.

"No, monsieur; madame has gone out; what is there
strange in that?"

"I don't say that I think it strange; but it annoys me
exceedingly."

"Had madame made an appointment with monsieur?"

"No; certainly she hadn't made an appointment with
me; I did not presume to say anything of the sort."

"Well then, monsieur could not be sure of finding madame, especially as madame often goes out."

"Ah! she often goes out! then it isn't strange that I don't find her in. But will she return soon? If so, I might wait for her."

"When madame goes out, she never says whether she will stay out long. And then I must tell monsieur that she doesn't like to have anybody wait for her; she doesn't want anybody to make himself at home in her apartment when she isn't here."

Chamoureau bit his lip and stepped back.

"That makes a difference!" he murmured; "now that I know that it would vex Madame de Sainte-Suzanne, I will not wait for her; but you will be good enough to tell her that Monsieur Chamoureau came to pay his respects to her. Sapristi! I regret that I did not bring a bouquet—I would have left it. Will you remember my name—Chamoureau?"

"Never fear! If I should forget it, I would say: 'The gentleman who tore himself from head to foot the other day called again.'"

"It seems to me quite unnecessary to recall that unpleasant incident. I prefer that you should simply mention my name—Chamoureau."

"Yes, Monsieur—Chameau."

"*Fichtre!* pray be careful! I didn't say Chameau; you must not confound me with that beast of the desert with two humps. For I flatter myself that I have never had one—although I am a widower."

"Monsieur is quite capable of it; but still a man sometimes wears one without knowing it."

"Do you think so, mademoiselle? If that had happened to me, my wife would have told me; she had no secrets from me!"*

"Oh! that makes a difference!"

"Understand, mademoiselle—Chamoureau, not Chameau."

"I will remember, monsieur."

And the maid, laughing in the gentleman's face, because he seemed to her excessively foolish, was in the act of closing the door, when another person appeared and hastily opened it again; then, elbowing aside Chamoureau, who was still standing on the mat, he entered the reception-room with the air of a master, and said abruptly:

"Is Thélénie here? I want to speak to her."

The agent raised his eyes to look at the person who had pushed him aside so unceremoniously. He scrutinized him with the greatest attention when he heard him ask for "Thélénie" simply, and not Madame de Sainte-Suzanne. Such familiarity was most offensive to Chamoureau, and when he saw that the man who indulged in it was fashionably dressed, he was more incensed than ever.

We will not draw the portrait of the newcomer, as we have already seen him at the Opéra, in the box of the

---

* The point of the dialogue is lost in English. Chamoureau in resenting the maid's naming him camel,—Chameau,—lays himself open to her retort that implies he may have been cuckolded, *i.e.*, "have worn the horns"; the allusion to the humps bearing this signification here.

lady whom he now asked to see. It was Monsieur Beauregard who had applied to the lady's maid, and she,
suddenly become respectful, because he spoke to her in
an arrogant tone, hastened to reply:

"Madame is not in, monsieur; she went out about
an hour ago with her friend Mademoiselle Héloïse. I
do not think that she will return to dinner."

Beauregard walked about the reception-room, then
looked the maid in the eyes as he asked:

"Is it true that your mistress has gone out?"

"Yes, monsieur, it's the truth. But if monsieur wishes
to go into the salon and madame's bedroom, he will see
that I have not lied to him."

"No, it's all right; as she has gone out, I'll be off."

"Will monsieur give me any message for madame?"

"No, what I have to say to her cannot be said by
anybody else. I will see her another time."

"If monsieur will tell me what day he will come, so
that madame may wait for him——"

"It's not necessary. I do not know myself when I
shall come again."

And the gentleman with the yellow complexion, turning toward the door, was about to leave the room, when
he saw the business agent, who had remained standing,
like a milestone, on the mat, and was scrutinizing him
with an expression of mingled amazement and curiosity.

"Who's that?" Beauregard asked the maid, pointing
to Chamoureau. And she replied with a smile:

"It's a gentleman who came to see madame."

Thereupon Beauregard examined more carefully the individual on the mat, and soon exclaimed:

"Ah! I recognize him; I know him now! He's the Spaniard of the Opéra ball, who kept pulling up his long boots. Exactly! yes! that's just who it is!"

Chamoureau overheard all this; but uncertain how to behave before that person who had been eying him for several moments in a most impertinent way, he decided to leave the mat and beat a retreat. He had already gone downstairs, and was leaving the house, boiling over with wrath, when the gentleman whom he had left on the second floor, and who had descended the stairs behind him, appeared at his side.

Our widower had a very great desire to know who the man was who entered Madame de Sainte-Suzanne's apartment so unceremoniously, and asked for her by her Christian name simply. When he saw him so near, he ventured to bow. Beauregard returned his salutation with an air of mockery, saying:

"Your servant, monsieur!"

"Monsieur, like myself, has just come from Madame de Sainte-Suzanne's, I believe?"

"Yes, monsieur, I have come from Thélénie's. The lady's name is Thélénie."

"It is her Christian name, then?"

"As you say, it is her Christian name; didn't you know it?"

"No, monsieur; but, having known Madame de Sainte-Suzanne only a very short time, that is not surprising."

" Why do you call her *de* Sainte-Suzanne? She never had a sign of a *de* before her name."

" Oh! I thought that she was of noble birth."

" You are very much mistaken. In fact, I don't think she is much of a *saint* either! So she ought to be called plain Suzanne; but that isn't sonorous enough for her; so give her the *de* if it gives you any pleasure. I have no objection! "

" Has monsieur known the lady a long while? "

" Oh! yes, monsieur, a very long while."

Chamoureau hesitated awhile, but at last decided to falter:

" And monsieur is—er—intimately acquainted with—er—Madame de—Madame Sainte—er—Madame Suzanne? "

Beauregard laughed heartily as he replied in the satirical tone habitual to him:

" Do you know, monsieur, that your question is just the least bit indiscreet? "

" I beg pardon, monsieur; if it offends you, I withdraw it. I asked it as I might have asked: ' Do you smoke? ' "

" Oh! not at all, monsieur; and it's of no use for you to try to conceal your cunning beneath that affable air. You asked me that because you are in love with Thélénie, and because you are afraid of finding a rival in me! Is not that the truth? "

" Faith! monsieur, you are so good at guessing that I see that it would be useless to try to dissemble with you.—I confess that I consider that lady enchanting, adorable!"

"You made her acquaintance at the Opéra ball, at Mi-Carême, did you not?"

"Yes, that is so; I was disguised as a Spaniard."

"Oh! I know it; I saw you pass with Thélénie on your arm. But how in the devil did you go about it to induce her to accept your arm? that is what I can't comprehend."

"The lady herself offered to walk with me; she spoke to me first in the foyer, calling me by my name, which surprised me greatly as I had never seen her before."

"It is very strange; she certainly did not accost you without some reason."

"Why, the reason was that it gave her pleasure, presumably."

Beauregard laughed ironically as he rejoined:

"Oh, yes! it gave her pleasure; and there was another reason too, I'll wager! Did you go to the ball alone?"

"No, I went with two friends of mine—Freluchon and Edmond Didier."

"Edmond Didier! good! now we are on the track; I understand it all now."

"What! what track are you on?"

"I'll stake my head that Thélénie questioned you closely on the subject of Monsieur Edmond."

"Why, yes; she asked me very often whom he was with, if his mistress was pretty——"

" That s it; and she forbade you to mention her to those gentlemen? "

" Really, it is extraordinary how you guess everything, monsieur; how you read Madame Sainte-Suzanne's thoughts! "

" It's because I've known her a long while, as I told you just now! I have been in a position to study her character, her sentiments and her mind. You asked me if I were intimately acquainted with this lady—Well, my dear monsieur—I beg pardon, but I don't know your name."

" Chamoureau—Sigismond Chamoureau."

" Well, my dear Monsieur Sigismond Chamoureau, I will tell you that I was once, but that I have not been for a long time."

The agent's face brightened, and he cried:

" As you no longer are, it's just as if you had never been."

" It isn't altogether the same thing, but I congratulate you on being so philosophical."

" In that case, monsieur, you don't bear me a grudge for being in love with Madame Sainte-Suzanne, and I need no longer look upon you as a rival? "

" I, bear you a grudge! oh! not the least in the world! I should have had my hands very full if I had been the rival of all those whom that lady's fine eyes have bewitched! "

" She has fine eyes, hasn't she? "

" Magnificent; and they have made many victims! "

" And will make many more ; she is in all the bloom of her beauty ! "

" Ah ! if you had seen her nine years ago ! that was a different matter ! "

" Great God ! what was she then?—For my part, I flattered myself too soon on having made a conquest of the lady; she was very stern with me when I had the good fortune to see her at her home ; she even forbade me to speak of my love. I will confess to you, monsieur, that that drove me to despair."

" Ha ! ha ! poor Monsieur Chamoureau ! "

" Not speak to her of love ! Of what shall I speak to her, pray, that she may listen with pleasure ? "

" Pardieu ! speak of Edmond Didier, who is her lover ! whom she loves to madness—for the moment. That is why she wanted to converse with you at the Opéra ball, —Ha ! ha ! ha ! Do you see now ? "

Chamoureau turned pale; he halted in the middle of the gutter, crying:

" Oh ! monsieur, what are you saying ? What ! Edmond Didier ? "

" I am telling you the truth ; I am opening your eyes ; I am doing you a service."

" It's a service which causes me a great deal of pain, then."

" What difference does it make to you whether she loves that young man or another, so long as she doesn't love you ? "

" But I hoped that she would love me, monsieur."

"If that's your hope, don't despair; who knows? women are so strange, they have such surprising caprices; it is quite possible that she won't always spurn you.—By the way, pardon the question, but are you rich, monsieur?"

· "Not very; I make four or five thousand francs a year."

"In that case, my dear monsieur, you have no great chance of succeeding with Thélénie; and if you are wise enough to follow some good advice, you will forget her and cease to bother your head about her.—But, excuse me—I go in this direction. Good-day, monsieur."

"A thousand pardons, monsieur, but it would be a great pleasure to me to know with whom I have had the honor of conversing."

"Here is my card, monsieur."

"And here is mine, monsieur; I have a real estate office, and if you should ever have any business that hangs fire——"

"Be assured, monsieur, that I shall remember you."

Beauregard walked away, while Chamoureau read the card he held in his hand, saying to himself:

"He was once Madame Sainte-Suzanne's lover! and Edmond is now! and I am nothing at all! I have acted as an information machine, that is all!—Ah! I am not surprised that she expressly forbade me to mention her name. Well! all this doesn't prevent my adoring her. Monsieur Beauregard advises me not to think of her any more; but perhaps he still thinks of her himself;

if he doesn't, why does he go to see her? That is something he would have found it difficult to explain, I fancy.
Perhaps what he told me about Edmond isn't true. That
man has a sardonic expression; I think that I shall do
well to be suspicious of him.—O Eléonore! I am grieved
that I no longer weep for you!"

XVI

AN ELECTRIC SPARK

Chamoureau went home completely overwhelmed by
what he had learned in his interview with Monsieur
Beauregard. He thought of nothing else all the rest of
the day, the result being that it did not occur to him to
go to Monsieur Courtivaux and conclude the negotiation
that Madame Dalmont had entrusted to him. He asked
himself every moment whether he should try once more
to see Edmond, and question him on the subject of his
liaison with Madame Sainte-Suzanne; but he remembered that she had expressly forbidden him to mention
her name to anyone.

" To be sure," he said to himself, " I have already
broken my promise by talking about her with this Monsieur Beauregard; but that wasn't my fault. That man
caught me in Madame Sainte-Suzanne's reception-room,
so I could not deny that I knew her; and the familiar

way in which he asked for her proved conclusively that he knew her very well indeed!"

On the following day our widower was still undecided, hesitating whether he ought or ought not to talk to Edmond about the lady with the beautiful black eyes.

Hesitating people often pass whole days unable to decide what to do, and when, after mature consideration, they say to themselves: "I will decide on this course," you see them suddenly change their minds and pause just as they are about to act. Such characters generally fail in whatever they undertake, because they never do it in time.

In a business agent, this failing is even more dangerous than in anybody else. The agent with whom we have to do had two reasons for not attending to the business placed in his hands: in addition to his habitual indecision, he was in love, passionately in love, with a woman with whom he had no hope of success, which fact necessarily increased his love. It is always the thing that we cannot have for which we crave.

Chamoureau then was at home, saying to himself:

" I think I will go to Edmond Didier and tell him the whole truth; or rather, tell him nothing, but question him shrewdly. I will lead him on to talk of his love-affairs. He will begin about little Amélia, and then I will say: ' No, it's not that one, but another—a very beautiful brunette—that I want to talk to you about.'

" Yes, but then he will reply: ' How do you know that I ever knew a very beautiful brunette? Do you know her yourself?'—Damnation! it's terribly embarrassing!"

At that moment the doorbell rang and shortly after, Edmond Didier entered the office.

" My dear Monsieur Chamoureau," he said, " I understand that you have been to my room several times to see me; I have come to find out what you had to say to me and in what way I can be of service to you?"

Chamoureau was stupefied when he saw Edmond; he recovered himself, however, and composed his features.

" Ah! good morning, Monsieur Edmond; I am very glad to see you; it gives me great pleasure. You are well, I hope?"

" Very well. But I fancy that it wasn't to inquire for my health that you came to see me three times in one day?"

" No, of course not, although I take great interest in it. But Freluchon—have you seen Freluchon lately?"

" He started for Rouen and may have gone as far as Havre, to treat his little Pompadour to fresh oysters; for you know that his taking her to Normandie was the result of a bet that his latest conquest won at that supper of ours, by smoking through her nose."

" I know—or, rather, I don't know—for you must remember that I dozed a little toward the end of the supper."

" Ah, yes! that is true; I had forgotten."

" And that little woman in the Pompadour costume smokes through her nose, does she?"

" That is to say, she holds the cigar in her mouth, like everybody else, but she discharges the smoke through her nostrils; which is rather strong for a woman."

" It is, indeed; I wouldn't do it myself, although I smoke a little. How accomplished women are in this age! If this goes on, I should not be surprised to see them chewing tobacco in time."

" Oh! Monsieur Chamoureau, what are you saying! "

" Bless me! I keep track of the progress of mankind. In the old days, ladies wouldn't allow smoking in their presence; to-day they smoke themselves. From that to chewing tobacco in the shape of pastilles of mint or cachou isn't a very long road to travel."

" Well, let us come to what you had to say to me. I am in more or less of a hurry. It's a fine day, and I promised Amélia to take her to the Bois this morning. We may go as far as Ville d'Avray."

" Amélia! what? the young flower-maker who was at the supper, dressed as a *débardeur?* "

" Herself; I have made up with her; she is amusing and quite bright; on the whole, I like her very well."

" You really like her, eh? And you have no other mistress? "

" Faith, no! not for the moment, at all events."

" Dear Monsieur Edmond! You see, I have been told that you adored a magnificent brunette—a tall, handsome woman, with a fine figure——"

" Ah! you mean Thélénie."

Chamoureau changed color as he stammered:

" Yes, that's the name—Thélénie; that's the name I heard; or Madame—Madame——"

" Sainte-Suzanne? "

" Exactly—Sainte-Suzanne. Then I was not misinformed: you have been—you are that lady's lover? "

" I am not now; I have broken with her; I have entirely ceased to visit her."

The business agent leaped on the young man's neck and embraced him, crying:

" Is it possible? Dear Edmond! You no longer love her; you have broken with her completely! In that case, you are not my rival! "

" Well, well! what then, is the matter with you, Monsieur Chamoureau? what has taken hold of you? whence this outburst of joy? Can it be that you are in love with Thélénie? "

" I—no; I didn't say that; or, at all events, I ought not to say it; it's an impenetrable mystery. But still, if it were true, my dear friend—if I were secretly nourishing that passion in my heart—it would not make you angry with me? "

" I should think not! on the contrary, I would wish you all sorts of good luck in your love-affairs. Ah! I remember now what you said at the supper; that matchless creature, that woman who eclipsed all other women but who did not wish to be known, was she."

" Well, yes, it was she; but she had made me swear not to say that I knew her. I am a wretch, a traitor! I break all my oaths! "

"Bah! in love, you know, that doesn't do any harm."

"Say nothing about it to Freluchon, I entreat you."

"I will be dumb, since that is your wish!"

"Excellent Edmond! Your hand! I congratulate myself on being your friend."

"And I, my dear Monsieur Chamoureau, in the capacity of friend, will venture to give you a little advice, —with which you will do what people generally do with advice—disregard it."

"What is it?"

"Well, it is this: to be a little distrustful of your new conquest. Between us, Madame Sainte-Suzanne is a dangerous woman."

"Really? she is dangerous, you say? In what respect? Does she carry a stiletto about her, like the Italian women?"

"That is not what I mean. But she is very jealous. However, after all, I don't mean to speak ill of a woman who has shown me nothing but kindness; that would be ungrateful.—Au revoir, my dear Chamoureau; I must go to meet Amélia."

"But first, my dear friend, I would like to ask your advice."

"Some other time; I haven't time to-day."

Edmond was about leaving the agent's office, when two ladies entered. They were Madame Dalmont and her young friend, and they had called to ascertain whether Chamoureau had arranged for them the purchase of the little house at Chelles.

The young man courteously stepped aside to allow the ladies to enter, and he had an opportunity to examine them at his ease. He noticed that Honorine was a very attractive person, without being exactly pretty; but when his eyes rested on Agathe, he did not consider her beauty, he did not analyze each of her features; but he was conscious of a sudden thrill of emotion, and discovered instantly in the girl's face an indefinable charm which enraptured him, dazzled him and brought about something very like a revolution in his whole being. He stood as if rooted to the spot, and did not think of going away.

"Monsieur," said Honorine to Chamoureau, who gazed at her with a stupid air, "we have heard nothing from you for three days, and I have come to find out why it is. Does Monsieur Courtivaux no longer wish to sell his house?"

"Oh! pardon, madame, a thousand pardons! Yes, yes! the little house at Chelles; I remember now."

"What! you remember now? Then you had forgotten the matter, had you?"

"I had not exactly forgotten it; but there was another matter which took all my time, and——"

"What, monsieur! you have not been to see the owner of the house? when we said that we were in such haste to conclude the purchase, and that we would like to be settled in the country even now?"

"I was going there this morning, mesdames."

"Oh! it wasn't kind of you, monsieur, to neglect this business," said Agathe, blushing a little, because she saw

that the young man, who was still present, kept his eyes
fixed on her. " My dear friend and I think about that
house every minute in the day; and then they say that
this is just the time to plant seeds and set out flowers.
If it should be sold to anybody else, I shouldn't get
over it."

" How is this, my dear Chamoureau?" interposed Edmond; "you have the good fortune to be the man of
business of these ladies, and you forget the commissions
with which they entrust you. Upon my word, you are
unpardonable."

" It isn't forgetfulness, Monsieur Edmond; it's that
other matter—you know, on Rue de Ponthieu—that is
forever in my head."

" Hush! it is inexcusable. If I had it in my power to
render these ladies the slightest service, I should esteem
myself too fortunate."

" Really, you are very kind, monsieur," said Honorine,
" but you will be of great service to us if you remind
your friend that he ought to conclude this affair."

" Not only will I remind him of it, madame, but I undertake not to lose sight of him until he has taken all
the necessary steps to conclude it.—You desire to purchase a house in the country, madame?"

" Yes, monsieur, and the price is satisfactory to me."

" The owner's name is Courtivaux?"

" Yes, monsieur."

" And this Courtivaux lives in Paris, does he, Chamoureau?"

"To be sure; on Rue Jacob, Faubourg Saint-Germain."

"Very good. We will take my cab and go at once to see this gentleman; from there we will go to the notary to fix a time for passing the papers; and from there to tell madame what day is appointed."

Agathe clapped her hands and cried:

"Ah! that is good! it will soon be done then! Ah! monsieur, how——"

The girl had the word charming on the tip of her tongue, but she checked herself, realizing that it would hardly be proper to use that expression to a person whom she did not know. She lowered her eyes and glanced at her friend, who hastened to say:

"We are very grateful, monsieur, for the interest which you are good enough to take in our affairs, especially as you do not know us."

"Mon Dieu! madame, my interest is quite natural; as soon as one has the pleasure of seeing you, one feels eager—one desires—to be of some service to you."

Edmond also realized that he was getting confused, and that the eyes of young Agathe, which were then fixed upon him, disturbed him to such an extent as to take away his usual self-confidence. To conceal his embarrassment, he turned to Chamoureau.

"Come, my dear fellow, didn't you hear what I promised these ladies? Let us be off at once! We shall find my cab at the door and we will drive straight to the vendor's house."

"What! do you really mean to go to Monsieur Courtivaux's with me?"

"I have told these ladies that I would not leave you
until we have completed their transaction, or at least
appointed a time with the notary for having the documents settled."

"But I thought that you had an appointment this
morning. Just now you were in great haste to leave me
in order to go to the Bois de Boulogne."

"If you have other engagements, monsieur," said Honorine to Edmond, "we should be very sorry to have you
neglect them on our account."

"No, madame, no, I assure you that I have no other
important engagement for to-day. I was going to drive
in the Bois; but one always has time for that."

"Oh, yes!" cried Agathe; "besides, I think it will
be fine all day."

And the girl smiled at Edmond, to thank him for per-
sisting in his plan of accompanying the agent.

"But the person who is waiting for you," muttered
Chamoureau, as he looked for his hat. "You told me
that——"

"It's of no consequence. It's a friend of mine, an
idler like myself, and it makes no difference to him
whether he goes to the Bois to-day or to-morrow.—
Come, are you ready? How slow you are in finding
your hat!"

"You don't give me time to breathe. I can't go to
see Monsieur Courtivaux in a skull-cap."

At last, thanks to Edmond, Chamoureau was ready to start. They all left the office together. The young man would have been glad to offer his hand to Agathe to escort her downstairs; but she was as light and active as a doe, and was at the bottom long before the others.

Edmond had come in a *milord,* which was waiting for him at the door; he bade Chamoureau step in, saying:

" Do you know the address of these ladies? "

" Yes, certainly; I must know it."

But Agathe, fearing that their agent might have forgotten their address as well, hastened to say to Edmond:

" Madame Dalmont, Rue des Martyrs, 40."

" Very good, mademoiselle. I shall not forget, you may be sure. Mesdames, you shall have news of your business before night."

" We do not know how to thank you, monsieur."

" I am too happy to be able to serve you. Driver, Rue Jacob, Faubourg Saint-Germain ! "

" I say ! what about Mademoiselle Amélia, whom you promised to take to drive this morning? " said Chamoureau as they rolled along.

" What do I care for Amélia? Do you suppose that I am going to put myself out for a paltry flower-maker, when I have an opportunity to be of service to such charming women! for they are charming, those two! Tell me, Chamoureau, how long have they been clients of yours? They can't be mother and daughter! Are they sisters, I wonder? Yes, in all probability. And yet they don't at all resemble each other! One of them

is married; what does her husband do? do you know
him too?"

"Sapristi! Monsieur Edmond, you 'bewilder me with
your questions! I don't know which one to answer.—
I have known these ladies a very short time. They came
to my office—ah! I remember only too well it was the
day after Mi-Carême! I had just come home in my
Spanish costume, thanks to that scamp of a Freluchon.
For you know that my brand-new black coat and trousers
are at his rooms! and heaven knows whether he will
ever come back; once at Havre, he's quite capable of
starting for America. If he should do that I'd have his
door opened by the police."

"What in the devil are you talking about?—I didn't
ask you about your clothes; I asked you who those two
pretty women are that I saw at your office just now?
The younger one, especially. She must be unmarried;
I'll wager that she's hardly sixteen. What a fascinating
face! What a sweet expression in her eyes! There is
modesty, playfulness, kindliness in her expression. I
have never met such a charming young woman! What
is her name? The elder lady's name is Dalmont, I
know; but the young lady? tell me—you must know
her name."

"Her namè is Thélénie de Sainte-Suzanne; you know
it well enough, having been so intimate with her; having
had that felicity!"

"Come, come, Chamoureau, pay a little more attention to what I say. I am not talking about Thélénie;

she has nothing in common with the girl I met just now at your office, thank God! "

" Madame Sainte-Suzanne is much more beautiful. She's a grown woman, just in her prime! "

" We won't quarrel about our tastes. Adore Thélénie, my dear Monsieur Chamoureau, it is your right! but tell me the name of the charming girl who was with Madame Dalmont."

" Her name! how should I know it? Oh, yes! I remember now that her friend called her Agathe several times."

" Agathe! her name is Agathe, you say! What a sweet name! "

" Thélénie is a much more distinguished name; and the proof is that it isn't to be found in the Saints' Calendar! "

" Then that lady is her friend, her kinswoman, her cousin perhaps. Is she rich? "

" No, her means are very modest."

" What does the husband do? "

" There isn't one; the lady is a widow."

" No husband; so much the better! "

" Why so much the better? Do you propose to marry the widow? "

" I don't say that. But when there is no man in a house——"

" It is easier to get in, you think, eh? "

" Oh, no! just the opposite; for it is almost always the husband who takes his friends to his house."

" There's no man at Madame Sainte-Suzanne's, but
that doesn't prevent her receiving men. She received
me, indeed she herself invited me to come to see her."

" For God's sake, Monsieur Chamoureau, let us drop
Thélénie! "

" I am in love with her, monsieur, I am passionately
in love with her! "

" So it would seem, as your passion made you forget
the business Madame Dalmont placed in your hands.—
Ah! that was very bad! "

" Here is Monsieur Courtivaux's house; are you going up with me? "

" I should say so! you are quite capable of talking to
him of nothing but Thélénie! "

Edmond accompanied the agent to the apartment of
the owner of the house at Chelles. He was very accommodating; he was anxious to get rid of his little country
estate, and thanks to the eloquence of Edmond, who impressed it upon him that the purchaser was a young widow
of small means, he consented to pay the expenses of the
transaction. He gave them his notary's address, and
suggested that they meet there at three o'clock on the
following day. Edmond declared that Madame Dalmont
would be there punctually, and informed Monsieur Courtivaux that he would go at once to advise the notary.

While the young man hastily made this arrangement,
Chamoureau stood in rapt contemplation before a
woman's portrait, and whispered in Edmond's ear:

" Don't you think it looks like her? "

" Like whom ? "

" Her ! "

" Mademoiselle Agathe ? "

" No, the superb Sainte-Suzanne ! "

" Not in the least. But let us be off. We must go to the notary."

" What ! has Monsieur Courtivaux said that he would be there ? "

" It's all settled, all arranged ; the day and hour were fixed while you were sighing in front of that portrait. Really, it's very lucky for those ladies that I came with you ! Let us go."

Edmond took Chamoureau to see the notary. The young man had now become the agent; he made all the arrangements. Chamoureau's only function seemed to be to sigh.

From the notary's they set off in their cab to go to Madame Dalmont's. As they drew nearer to her abode, Edmond became more thoughtful and silent; he even went so far as to sigh, like his companion.

" I am going to that lady's house," he thought. " She will learn that she is under some obligation to me, since I hastened forward the conclusion of the transaction. She will thank me; but will she ask me to come again? That is doubtful, for she has known me only since this morning. However, I shall no longer be a stranger to them; that is a point gained."

" Is this the place ? " he inquired, pointing to a house.

" I haven't the slightest idea."

" Do you mean that you have never been to see those
ladies ? "

" Never.   But they told us number 40, so this must
be the house.—Are you going up with me ? "

" Am I going up with you!   That's a pretty question!
Why, I settled the business almost unaided; and do you
think I am not going to tell them about it ? "

" Bless my soul!   it makes no difference to me;   I
had no special object in view in asking you that question."

. Agathe opened the door and uttered a cry of joy when
she saw Edmond, for there was something in the young
man's expression that announced the successful result
of the steps he had taken.

In a few words he informed Madame Dalmont that
the business was concluded, that Monsieur Courtivaux
agreed to assume the expenses, and that the next day,
at three o'clock, she was expected at the notary's whose
address he gave her.

Honorine expressed to the young man the gratitude
which the zeal he had shown in her service had merited.
While her friend was speaking, Agathe said nothing;
but it is probable that she too thanked Edmond with her
eyes, for he was radiant with joy.

When the ladies had also said a few words to Chamoureau, who acted as if he had no idea what it was all
about, Edmond said to Honorine:

" As soon as the deeds are signed, madame, you will
be entitled to go with mademoiselle and take possession

of your estate, where, I presume, you propose to pass
the summer."

" Summer and winter too, monsieur. I have bought
the house with the intention of secluding myself there
altogether."

" What, madame! you are leaving Paris for good?
you do not expect to return for the winter? "

" No, monsieur, I shall pass the whole year at Chelles."

" And mademoiselle also? "

" As if I could live apart from my dear friend! " replied Agathe with a smile. " As if I could ever leave
her! Where she is, I shall always be. And then, I do
not care for Paris, and I look forward with delight to
living in the country."

Edmond's face darkened; he already regretted that he
had shown so much zeal in facilitating their speedy departure. There is always more or less selfishness in the
zeal we display in serving other people. In Paris he
thought that it would be easy for him to see Agathe
again, to meet her, even if he were obliged to pass a
large part of the day on the street where she lived. But
he must needs abandon that hope, if she ceased to live
in Paris.

" Are you not afraid, mesdames, of suffering from
ennui in the winter, in a village? " murmured Edmond
at last, looking at Agathe with a melancholy expression.

" One does not suffer from ennui, monsieur," replied
Honorine, " with plenty of occupation for one's time.
Women always have something to overlook, some work

to do in a house. In the country, there are a thousand additional duties to be attended to—a garden, a poultry-yard—And then, for diversion, we have reading and music."

"Ah! are you ladies musical?"

"A little, monsieur. I expect to sell part of my furniture before moving, as the house I am buying is furnished; but I certainly shall not dispose of my piano, our faithful friend; isn't it, Agathe?"

"Oh! if we hadn't the piano, then we should be bored, and no mistake. My dear friend plays very well indeed, monsieur; and she has taught me what I know."

"Do not listen to her, monsieur; I can play accompaniments fairly well, that's all."

"I too am fond of music; I sing a little; and if you ladies had remained in Paris, I should have been very happy if—if—if I——"

Edmond dared not finish the sentence, but it was easy to guess the rest of it.

Honorine could not restrain a smile as she said:

"Since this morning, monsieur, you have placed us under great obligations; you have attended to our business with more zeal than—Dear me! is Monsieur Chamoureau asleep?"

"No, madame, do not mind him; he has something on his mind which engrosses him completely; you must excuse him."

"In fact, monsieur, but for you, nothing would have yet been done toward purchasing Monsieur Courtivaux's house; you will not think it surprising, I trust, that I am anxious to know to whom I am so obliged."

" That is quite natural, madame, and I should have told you before this. My name is Edmond Didier; my father was formerly a clerk in the Treasury and has now retired on his pension, and with my mother is living at his native place, Nancy in Lorraine. They have sufficient means to live modestly, and they are happy. I remained in Paris and had entered a banking house, when an uncle on my mother's side was good enough to leave me sixty thousand francs."

" With your salary, then, you are very comfortably situated."

" I have to confess, madame, that when I found myself in possession of that unexpected wealth, I began by leaving my place; I have invested part of my funds, and I do a little business—not like Chamoureau, I have no office—but I trade a little on the Bourse, and try to speculate on the rise or fall of stocks.—That, madame, is my whole biography, and Monsieur Chamoureau here will bear witness to its accuracy."

" What? what's that? accuracy of what? " exclaimed Chamoureau, who was thinking what he could do to make himself agreeable to Madame Sainte-Suzanne, and who suddenly discovered that he was at Madame Dalmont's.

" Nothing, my dear fellow, except that I was telling these ladies who I am, so that they may not look upon me as a schemer or a nobody."

" We should never have thought that of you, monsieur, but you cannot blame two ladies, who live alone, for desiring to know something concerning the persons whom they receive. Now, monsieur, if the desire for country air should ever lead you in the direction of Chelles, come to our modest abode and rest a moment; we shall be delighted to make you welcome to the house which you have assisted us to purchase."

" Oh, yes! monsieur," cried Agathe, " it will give us great pleasure to——"

Honorine pulled her young friend's dress, whereupon she corrected herself and continued:

" And then you will see the house, which is very pretty, and the garden, of which I mean to take excellent care."

" Your invitation is too kind for me to forget it, madame; and since you give me your permission, I shall have the honor of paying my respects to you at Chelles. —Now, my dear Chamoureau, let us not take any more of the time of these ladies, whom, you remember, you are to meet at three o'clock to-morrow at Monsieur Courtivaux's notary's."

" Three o'clock to-morrow. The devil! I wanted to go to Rue de Ponthieu to-morrow; she won't always be out."

Edmond trod on Chamoureau's foot and whispered to him:

" Hold your tongue! don't mention the name of a Thélénie before these ladies! " Then he added, turning to Honorine: " I will call for Chamoureau myself, madame, and take him to the notary's. In that way I can answer for his punctuality."

" That, monsieur, will put the finishing touch to your kindness, for Monsieur Chamoureau seems to us very absent-minded."

" Pray excuse me, madame; I am in fact very busy concerning—er—it's all Freluchon's fault!"

" Come, Chamoureau, let us be off."

And Edmond took the agent away.

The next day, thanks to the young man's activity, all the parties met at the appointed time at the notary's office, and Madame Dalmont became the owner of the little house at Chelles.

A glance from Agathe amply rewarded Edmond for all the trouble he had taken to bring the affair to a speedy conclusion. And Honorine added to his happiness by saying again:

" You will be welcome, monsieur, at that house of which I am now the owner, thanks to your efforts and your kindness."

XVII

ONE OF THE DREGS

The fair Thélénie returned to her apartment, accompanied by her friend Héloïse, about an hour after Chamoureau had taken his leave under Monsieur Beauregard's escort. As she entered the room she tossed aside shawl, hat, gloves and the rest, with the angry gesture characteristic of her. Then she threw herself on a couch, while her friend Héloïse picked up the hat and gloves from the floor, saying:

"You must admit that you take very little care of your things. Such a pretty hat, almost new! and that's the way you treat it! Why, I would make this hat last till June. Bless me! I haven't the means to buy them as often as you do! How much did this one cost? At least fifty-five francs, I'll bet; milliners are getting to be out of reach. Did I guess right?"

"For heaven's sake! Héloïse, let me alone; you must see that I'm out of humor."

"Oh! you're always out of humor now; you make a great mistake to torment yourself all the time;—it will change your whole appearance, it will make your complexion yellow. If you want to remain pretty, you must never lose your temper. A medical student told me that.

He ought to know a lot, for he attended lectures ten years. He also told me that if I wanted to be well, I must be gay; for there's nothing that's so healthy as gayety."

" Every ten years' student ought to know that gayety can't be administered at pleasure, like a syrup or a drug. To tell a person to be gay is as foolish as to tell him not to have a headache! However, I know perfectly well that I am not sensible; but when I saw Edmond drive by in a cab with his new passion, I could not restrain a spasm of anger."

" Yes, and you nearly caused us to be run over by a coupé."

" But that little flower-maker is a horrid-looking creature; it makes one ashamed to be deserted for such a fright."

" Horrid-looking! oh! that's nonsense. She has a cunning little way with her, and a saucy face such as men like."

" She is as common as one can imagine. If Edmond had left me for a very pretty woman, I would forgive him."

" That is not true; you would be even more put out. Oh! I know all about that; it's always some little compensation to be able to say to yourself: ' I am certainly prettier than she is, and his new love won't last long.' "

Thélénie rang for her maid and Mademoiselle Mélie appeared.

" Has anybody been here while I have been out?"

" Yes, madame, that gentleman who came a few days
ago, and who was so amusing when he went away; who
had torn his coat, and—another part of his clothes."

" Ah! Monsieur Chamoureau? "

" That's the name, madame: Monsieur Chamoureau."

" What did he want? "

" Why, to see madame; he seemed very much disappointed not to find her and asked me if madame would
be out long; he wanted to wait."

" The idiot! does he propose to wear me out with his
calls; however, as soon as he bores me too much, I
shall have no hesitation in forbidding him my door.
Very well; leave me."

" He is the Spaniard of the Opéra ball who kept pulling up his boots, isn't he? " said Mademoiselle Héloïse,
when the maid had left the room.

" Yes, and the great clown, whom I instructed to tell
me everything that happened at a certain supper after
the ball,—I knew that he was to sup with Edmond and
his friends and their ladies. What do you suppose Monsieur Chamoureau did? he went to sleep in the middle
of supper, and when he woke, everybody had gone! "

" He was drunk, probably! "

" And then he comes to see me, and makes me an impassioned declaration of love! "

" Accompanied by diamonds or a cashmere shawl? "

" By nothing whatever! What do you suppose he
proposed to me? Oh! it's enough to make one die
of laughter! "

" To mend his linen? "

" To marry him—to become Madame Chamoureau! "

" Well! you want a position in society."

" A pretty position that would be! My gentleman makes four thousand francs with his office; and as I have ten thousand francs a year, I should be the one to enrich him. Fancy me making Monsieur Chamoureau's fortune! "

" But in that case the fellow isn't as stupid as he looks."

" Oh! he has no selfish designs. He is really very much in love with me—according to what he says, at least. —Madame Chamoureau! what an absurd name! "

" Well, I am not so particular as you are; if he wants to marry me, I'll take him. I am not such a bad writer, I'll be a clerk in his office."

" I had an idea that you weren't very strong in spelling. One day you wrote me, being short of money: ' Are you in funds? can I go to your cash-box? ' And you spelt *cash* with a *q*."

" Well! what difference does it make whether it's a *c* or a *q* so long as the pronunciation's the same? Besides, I've heard it said that nowadays people write as they choose, and that it's much more *comme il faut* not to bother about spelling, because in old times the great nobles didn't know anything about it."

" For my part, I don't consider it good form to make blunders in speaking."

" Why, did you have such a very fine education, Thélénie? I thought you'd never been to school; I had an

idea that your mother sold cooked sausages in a shop
where there was always a long line of people waiting;
there was a stove——"

The lovely brunette flashed a savage glance at Héloïse
and replied, smiling bitterly:

"Ah! so you propose to be nasty too, do you? Be
careful, my poor Héloïse, you won't have much chance
with me."

"I have no intention of saying anything nasty! Between ourselves, you can't make me believe that you're
a duchess's daughter. I have been told that your mother
sold sausages fried on a stove, but I don't see any harm
in it. It's as good a trade as another."

"And you threw that at me because I told you that
you spelt *cash* with a *q*."

"Oh! nonsense! what do you suppose I care for a *q*
more or less! what a fuss about nothing! I assure you,
Thélénie, that I hadn't the slightest intention of making
you angry; that would be very stupid on my part.
You take me to the theatre and to drive with you, and
sometimes you lend me money when I haven't any; so
why should I try to get up a quarrel with you?"

"Then try to curb your tongue, Héloïse, for you may
happen to say before witnesses something that I would
never forgive. Between ourselves, I certainly do not
undertake to make myself any better than I am; my
birth was very humble, I don't deny it; but as I grew
up, and especially when I began to know well-bred men,
with gentlemanly manners, I realized that if I wanted

to *arrive,* I must first of all put myself in a position to hold my own with them. So I hired teachers and studied; I was determined to know my own language. I also learned a little English and Italian, and I assure you that then I felt much more at my ease in the society of men of the world, who are very glad to take a pretty, fashionably-dressed woman to drive in a calèche, but who blush for her when she uses bad grammar before their friends and acquaintances.—What is it, Mélie? what do you want of us now?"

"I beg pardon, madame," replied the maid, who had just entered. "I forgot to tell madame that another gentleman came almost at the same time as Monsieur Chamoureau."

"Who was it?"

"Monsieur Beauregard."

At the name of Beauregard, Thélénie's brow grew dark and she made an impatient gesture, muttering:

"Aha! Monsieur Beauregard! Well, what did he want of me? what did he say to you?"

"The gentleman seemed doubtful at first whether madame had really gone out; he was about to come in without listening to me; but when I told him that he could look into the salon and madame's bedroom, he didn't come in, but went away, leaving word that he would come again."

"That person seems to be very unceremonious!" exclaimed Héloïse; "the idea of his having the face to enter your apartment to see if you were really there!"

" Oh! he's a very old acquaintance—an eccentric fellow; but he would do well to spare me his visits; I confess that I hardly enjoy them. I had not seen him for several years; I don't know what has possessed him lately, and why he has taken to coming again.—Didn't he say anything else, Mélie? "

" No, madame; he went away at the same time that Monsieur Chamoureau did, and I saw them from the window walking away together and talking."

" Beauregard talking with Chamoureau? "

" Yes, madame."

" That is very strange; but after all, it makes no difference to me!—Ah! someone is ringing, I believe."

" Perhaps one of those gentlemen has come back. Shall I say that madame is in and admit him? "

" Yes, if it's Monsieur Beauregard."

" And if it is Monsieur Chamoureau? "

Thélénie had not decided what reply to make when the bell rang again, with great violence.

" The devil! this one's in a big hurry! " said Héloïse.

" I am quite sure that it is not Monsieur Chamoureau who rings like that," said Thélénie. " Go and look, Mélie, and tell me who it is."

The maid opened the door; she was amazed, almost terrified at the aspect of the personage who stood there.

It was a man perhaps forty years old; but his repulsive appearance and dilapidated costume made it difficult to judge of his age. He was of medium height, thin of body and fleshless of face. His small, sunken eyes, rimmed with red, had a very bold and cynical expression, mingled at times with a threatening ferocity. His nose was long and thin and slightly curved like a bird's beak; his mouth, almost without teeth, was pinched and retreating, and the lips were hardly visible; thick eyebrows, red like his hair, bristled over his eyes. His forehead was low and sloping. He had a great abundance of badly combed, or rather uncombed, hair, which fell at random over his shoulders and his forehead; and although he wore a full beard and moustaches, a large scar was visible at the base of his left cheek.

This villainous-looking person was dressed in a long coat which had once been nut-brown, but of which it was now very difficult to distinguish the color. The coat lacked several buttons; it was worn through at the elbows, covered with spots and torn in several places; olive-green trousers, horribly soiled and ragged at the bottom, were in perfect harmony with the coat. A red handkerchief, twisted rope-fashion, served as a cravat; his footgear consisted of immense shoes, covered with mud, one of which was tied with twine and the other not at all. Lastly, on his head he wore one of those shocking low-crowned hats to which one may give any conceivable shape, because they have no shape.

"*Cré nom d'un bouffarde!* my beauty! you take your time about opening the door! Are your stumps asleep?"

As he spoke thus to the lady's maid, the visitor twirled in his hand a stout blackthorn stick, which he handled with the dexterity of a drum-major.

"What do you want, monsieur? You have probably made a mistake; I am very sure that it wasn't our door that the concierge pointed out to you."

While speaking, the maid held the door only half open, as if to prevent the man from entering. But he replied with a smile peculiar to himself, which made his face even more repulsive:

"No, no! I ain't mistaken in the door, *larbine!* otherwise called servant! This is the place where Madame Sainte-Suzanne lives, isn't it?"

"Yes, this is the place."

"Well, then! don't make so much fuss and feathers! Madame Sainte-Suzanne is the one I want to speak to."

"You, monsieur?"

"Yes, me! What in the devil's the matter with the girl that she makes eyes at me like a cat that's been taking physic!"

"What can you have to say to my mistress?"

"What have I to say to her? Look you, my love, that don't concern anybody but her and me, and I won't let my words fly till we are together in the closest possible confinement, as the president of the criminal court says."

"My mistress only receives people she knows, monsieur; and as she certainly doesn't know you, she won't receive you."

"You're crazy, my girl! You stand there chattering like a magpie and you don't know what you're saying. Your mistress knows me and knows me well, too, I flatter myself; consequently she will receive me; and

I don't advise her to refuse to see me, for then there'd be a row at papa's!"

As he spoke, the man pushed the lady's maid before him little by little; and she, being afraid of him, had allowed him to reach the middle of the reception room. There he stopped and glanced about, saying:

"*Bigre!* it's rather neat here! it's bang up! They didn't deceive me when they said there was fat times at Madame Sainte-Suzanne's. So much the better! this suits me! I love luxury and style, I do!"

"One would hardly think so to look at you," said the maid.

"That proves, my beauty, that you mustn't judge by appearances.—Just go and tell your mistress that I want to talk with her a bit; and to make sure that she won't refuse to see me, you may tell her it's Croque who has looked in on her to bid her good-day as he passed."

"What name did you say, monsieur?"

"I said Croque."

"Is that your name?"

"It seems to be!"

"I am very sure that madame won't receive you. Whom do you come from?"

"Whom do I come from? why from myself, and that's enough. Come, come! do what I tell you, girl; and if we are satisfied with you, we'll give you a kiss."

The maid hastily left the room to tell her mistress.

Thélénie was beginning to be impatient because she had not learned who had ventured to ring her bell with such violence as to break the cord; the alarmed expression of her servant redoubled her curiosity.

"Well! who was it? why were you so long about coming to tell me?"

"Oh! madame, it is—if you knew! I am all upset."

"Explain yourself, I say."

"There's a man there, who looks just like a thief; I believe he is one; he has every appearance of it. Oh! what a horrid man! he frightens me to death! He has on a long coat with holes in the elbows, and a face—an expression——"

"Well! what does this man want?"

"He wants to speak to madame—in private; and if you knew how insolently he talks; one would say that he thought he was in his own house."

"Send the man away; it must be some beggar who has come to ask alms; I don't see such people; send him away."

"And quickly, too," suggested Mademoiselle Héloïse, "for he is capable of stealing something in your reception room. I shouldn't suppose your concierge would let poor people come upstairs. Is the man a dumb idiot?"

"I don't know if the man will go away," said Mélie. "'You will tell your mistress,' he says, 'that it's Croque who wants to speak to her.'"

When she heard that name, Thélénie turned ghastly pale; she was evidently deeply agitated; her features contracted; she seemed completely crushed, and muttered between her teeth:

"Oh! mon Dieu! he is still alive! I hoped that he was dead!"

"Croque! what a name!" exclaimed Héloïse; "why not Croque-Mitaine and be done with it? Then we should know at all events that he doesn't mean to scare anyone but children!"

"I will go and tell the horrid man to go away, that madame refuses to receive him," said Mélie.

But Thélénie hurriedly arrested the maid, crying:

"No, no; don't do that, Mélie; on the contrary, go to this—this gentleman, and show him in. I am curious to know what he has to say to me.—Do you, Héloïse, step into the salon a moment."

"What! you propose to receive this man? You are not afraid to be left alone with him?"

"No, I am not afraid; do what I tell you; and you, Mélie, go and bring this stranger to me."

The maid obeyed, not trying to conceal her amazement at her mistress's sudden change of front; and Mademoiselle Héloïse walked toward the salon, remarking as she went:

"Keep your eye on the mantel all the time, and look out that your friend don't pinch something."

When the wretchedly-dressed personage was ushered into Thélénie's bedroom, he bowed to her most respectfully; she motioned to her maid and to Héloïse to leave them, then carefully closed and locked all the doors. Thereupon Monsieur Croque dropped carelessly upon a couch and tossed his hat on the floor, saying:

"Damn my eyes! my dear love, it takes a lot of trouble to reach you! it's worse than it is at a minister's office! What a get-up! what style! what a dust!"

The beautiful brunette gazed loweringly at the person before her, and said at last in a faltering tone:

"What! is it you? I thought——"

"You thought I'd kicked the bucket, didn't you? and I'll bet you didn't weep very much over me. But no, the little man's still alive; and he hasn't the slightest inclination to die. What a pity it would be! at forty years! just the prime of life for a man!"

"But what has become of you these five years past? for it is fully five years since I last saw or heard of you. —Mon Dieu! what do you look like!—how can you possibly show yourself dressed like this?"

"Why, I have to do it when I haven't anything else to put on my back, and not a sign of anything to buy duds with."

"How did you ever allow yourself to fall to such a low condition?"

"How did I allow myself to fall! ah! that's a good one, little sister! the dear sister, who don't throw her arms round her dear brother's neck. Look you, that isn't pretty of you; for, after all, I'm your brother, my dear love, and what's more, your senior, which gives me something very like the rights of a father or an uncle over you!"

"You have rights over me! I don't advise you to repeat that."

"Come, come, let's not get waxy, Titine—for your name used to be Titine, you know; you twisted that into Thélénie, and you did well, for Thélénie's more melodious, it sounds better to the ear. You see that if I had a swell apartment, like you, and a bully lot of togs, instead of calling myself just Croque, I'd take the name of Croquinosky or Croquignolle; but unluckily I haven't got so far as that. You ask me what I've been doing these five years. Bless my soul! my dear love, I couldn't come out, I was in the background."

"Ah! you have been in prison?"

"Something very like it."

"For debt?"

"A little for debt, and for something else too—an unfortunate affair—a theft of shirts in which I was mixed up, although I was most innocent."

"Innocent! you! that is hardly probable."

"Ah! you are as amiable as ever! you doubt your little brother's probity!"

"Because I know what you are capable of!"

"You know—or you don't know; that's a question. I don't say that I won't put you in a way to solve it some day; that will depend on the way you behave toward Bibi!"

"What do you mean? Is that a threat?"

"Oh, no! I never threaten. Come, come! a fellow laughs and jests a bit, and you flare up right away! I should have supposed that wealth would make people more amiable."

"Wealth! why, I have no wealth; I have enough to live on and no more."

"Oh! I expected that; you haven't got any money, and you live in a magnificent apartment, you have splendid furniture and servants at your beck and call, you're dressed like a stage princess."

"What does all that prove? You know well enough that in Paris a person can make a great show without being rich; that sometimes all this display serves simply to cover up debts and straitened circumstances."

"Yes, yes; and another thing I know is that this is no furnished lodging house, and, that being so, you have your own furniture; that everything I see is yours; and look—with nothing but that clock and those candelabra on the mantelpiece, I could get enough to fit myself out new and go on a good long spree."

Thélénie contracted her black eyebrows and made an impatient gesture.

"Come," she cried, "tell me what you want of me? Why have you come here?"

Monsieur Croque lounged easily on the couch and replied, smoothing his beard:

"Oh! you have a shrewd idea, little sister; I won't insult you by thinking that you haven't guessed. After all, isn't it perfectly natural? Your brother is unlucky, he hasn't a sou, he's wretchedly dressed, as you justly observed just now, and it's hard on one's self-esteem to go out in the street like this! But this brother has a sister who is in very happy, fortunate circumstances.

G. FRAIPONT.

G. FRAIPONT.

I don't say she's a millionaire; dear me, no! that would be too grand! but she has enough to dress very stylishly. Well, then; she can't let her brother go in rags. Of course not! that wouldn't be decent! And so this brother goes to see his sister and says to her: 'You've got money, and I haven't; give me some of what you have; I won't give you any of what I have because I have nothing, but I'll bear your image in my heart.'—How's that? do you get my meaning now?"

"Oh, yes! I knew well enough that it was money you wanted."

"If you knew it, what made you ask me what I came here for? You wanted to make me laugh a bit, you rogue!"

"It was money that you came for five years ago, and then you were to obtain employment, to reform and behave yourself."

"Bah! my dear love, are we able to direct events to suit our pleasure? Certain things happened which disarranged the course I had marked out for myself—that's the whole story."

"Nine years and a half, almost ten years ago, I found a suitable place for you; how did you lose it?"

"Oh! you mean the place of secretary to Monsieur Duronceray?"

"It was a pleasant place; you wrote very well, and that was all that was necessary; you had very little to do and a salary of fifteen hundred francs."

"Magnificent!—I aimed higher, I was ambitious."

" And to gratify your passions, you dared to rob——"

" Enough! enough! that affair happened a long while ago, and it's no use to talk about it now; besides, I have something to remind me of it that will never disappear, I'm afraid! "

As he said this, Thélénie's brother put his hand to his left cheek, where the scar was; then he continued:

" However, then as now, nobody knew I was your brother; you had recommended me to that gentleman as a protégé of yours."

" Thank heaven! "

" By the way, what has become of that Monsieur Duronceray? "

" I have no idea."

" Do you never see him now? "

" No, not for a long time."

" Do you know whether he's in Paris at present? "

" I tell you that I know absolutely nothing about him. Why do you ask me all these questions? "

" Oh! because I am not at all anxious to meet that gentleman—although he probably wouldn't recognize me, misfortune has changed my features so! But he had a certain animal that might recognize me.—Ah! that infernal dog! "

And again Monsieur Croque put his hand to his left cheek.

" The villain! if ever I get a chance to settle his hash! But perhaps he's dead! I should like it as well if he was dead. Ever since then I've had a horror of dogs.

—But never mind all that; the present business is to provide for the little brother; that's the most urgent thing; do you understand, little sister?"

The beautiful brunette was silent for some time; at last she muttered:

"To be economical, to take the pains to save enough to live on, by depriving oneself, and then to have that money squandered by lazy vagabonds, by people who do not know what decent behavior is—do you know that that is decidedly unpleasant?"

Monsieur Croque swayed to and fro on his couch, singing between his teeth:

> " When one knows how to love and please,
> What else need one desire?''

"A man says to himself when he has a relation with some little means: 'I don't need to work; I'm a great fool to bother my head about the future; when I am out of funds, I'll go to see my sister, I'll appear before her, covered with dirt and dressed in rags, with a long beard —in fact, in a state to arouse compassion; and then I'll tell her that I've been unfortunate, through no fault of my own, and that she must come to my aid.'—That's about what you said to yourself, isn't it?—But suppose this sister should get tired of always coming to the aid of a man whom she has tried more than once to lead back to a decent mode of life; suppose she should say to him: 'I don't propose to have my savings wasted by you again; I won't give you anything!'"

Croque rose and, walking toward Thélénie with a threatening air, cried as loud as his hoarse, rough voice permitted:

"If you should do that, Titine, why, I would go through your apartment, through the hall, and through the courtyard, shouting at the top of my voice that you are my sister; everybody should know it: the neighbors, your concierge, your servants——"

"Enough, Croque, enough! not so loud!"

"I would add that I haven't anything to eat, and that you refuse me a piece of bread."

"Hush! hush, I say!"

"And I would follow you through the streets, and say to everybody: 'Do you see that beautiful lady covered with silk and velvet; the one who has jewels on her neck, ears, arms, everywhere? Well, that's my sister, and she lets me go barefoot!'"

"Once more, monsieur, hush! and tell me what you need, how much you want."

"Good! well said! Now we are getting to be agreeable again; and that's the way I love you; for I do love you, I feel that nature appeals to me in your behalf, and that the same blood flows in our veins. Would you like to embrace me?"

Thélénie hastily drew back and repeated her question:

"Tell me how much you need?"

"Bless my soul! my dear love, in my present plight, you understand, I need everything; I must get an entire new outfit, and then I must have time to find lucrative employment. I have several things in view, however; but still you wouldn't want me to be obliged to come back in a fortnight and tell you that I have nothing left."

" No, indeed! I want you to promise to leave me in peace hereafter."

" Well then, I won't beat about the bush, but I'll tell you at once that you must part with a thousand-franc note! because with that I shall have plenty of time to turn round and start an industrial enterprise, in shares, —with or without a premium; I haven't decided yet; that will depend."

Thélénie put her hand to her forehead; but at last she made up her mind, opened her desk and then the drawer which she used as a cash-box. She took out a thousand-franc note, saying to her brother:

" This is the only one, monsieur; you may look and satisfy yourself."

But Croque rejoined with a smile:

" When a woman is as pretty as you are, my dear love, you shouldn't worry; when you have no money, there's plenty more to come."

" Here—take this, and forget me from this moment."

" Thanks a thousand times, beloved sister! If you should ever need me for—no matter what—I am game for anything; remember that I am devoted to you, and that I shall be very glad to do you a favor in my turn."

As he spoke, the fellow took the bank-note and bestowed it with care in a pocket of his coat, then picked up his hat, opened the door and went out.

Thélénie followed him, keeping her eye upon him; but, in the maid's presence, he assumed a respectful demeanor, bowed to the floor, and said to his sister:

"Accept once more, madame, the assurance of my profound respect and gratitude."

"At last he has gone!" said Thélénie to herself when the door had closed upon her brother. "The wretch!—But he will come again before long! It will be useless for me to change my residence, he will always succeed in finding me. What can I do to throw him off my track?—Luckily no one knows that he is my brother!"

"No one but me!" muttered Héloïse, who, with her ear glued to the door, had listened to what was said in the bedroom.

XVIII

A SPEAKING HEART

Honorine and Agathe returned from the notary's well content and very happy. The pretty house at Chelles had become their property. They were at liberty to make plans for the future without fear of being unable to realize them.

"Now that the house is ours," said Madame Dalmont to her young friend, "we must go there again to-morrow, to inspect it more carefully, from top to bottom.

I will examine the furniture and see what part of it I can keep and what I must bring from Paris."

" Yes, my dear."

" Then we will come back here; I will sell all I do not need to keep, and we will pack up, leave Paris for good, and settle down in our own home. Oh! how lovely it is to be able to speak of *home!* I can understand already the love of the soil."

" Yes; we can arrange and disarrange our furniture without fear that we shall be found fault with.—By the way, my dear, I fancy that, but for that young man, Monsieur Edmond Didier, the transaction wouldn't have been concluded so quickly."

" I agree with you; especially as that Monsieur Chamoureau, the agent, doesn't seem to listen to anything one says to him. I am very glad to have done with him. However, his charges are not high; he refused to accept any fee, saying: ' We will let it go in with something else.' But as I have no desire to employ him for anything else, I paid him.—Besides, one doesn't buy a house every day."

" He certainly didn't exert himself very much about this affair; Monsieur Edmond was the one who did everything; it was very lucky that he happened to be at Monsieur Chamoureau's the last time we went there; and it was very funny that he should have put himself out as he did, on the instant, to be useful to us; for he didn't know us, he had never seen us.—Had you ever seen him before, dear?"

"No indeed! Where do you suppose I could have seen him? Don't you go everywhere with me?"

"Yes, of course; and I should have seen him too. Everybody isn't as obliging as he is; for he threw over his own engagements; he was to go to the Bois de Boulogne, and he dropped everything to be of service to us."

"That proves that he is very polite."

"It does, indeed; don't you consider it rather extraordinary, Honorine?"

"Why, no; God be praised! there are still some men who take pleasure in rendering a service to ladies! They are becoming rather scarce, especially since men think of nothing but smoking; for courtesy and tobacco do not go well together! but still, you see that one sometimes meets such a man."

"And perhaps Monsieur Edmond doesn't smoke."

"Come, let's make a list of the furniture that I care most for and that I intend to take into the country. I will call it off, while you write, Agathe."

"Yes, my dear."

Mademoiselle Agathe procured writing materials, but she did not choose to drop the previous subject of conversation.

"Honorine, that gentleman is musical.'

"What gentleman?"

"Monsieur Edmond Didier."

"Indeed! do you think so?"

"I am sure of it. Why, don't you remember that he told us that he sang?"

" No, I didn't notice."

" Yes, yes, he sings ; I feel confident that he has a nice voice."

" What makes you think that, pray ? "

" Why, because—because he has a very sweet speaking voice."

" That is no reason ; there are people whose speaking voices are very harsh, but who sing very pleasantly."

" Oh, yes ! but when one's voice is sweet to begin with——"

" Come, write ; are you ready ? "

" To be sure."

" First of all, this little mahogany cradle—the one my poor little boy slept in. Ah ! I shall never part with this cradle !—Next, the little desk, with drawers, downstairs ; I shall keep that, too."

" And the piano, dear ; we mustn't forget the piano."

" That goes without saying ; for we shall not find one there."

" And we will play a great deal, for music must be even more agreeable in the country than in Paris."

" Why so ? "

" Because, in the first place, we can hear each other better."

" This old easy-chair—what they call a *ganache;* it's very convenient when one isn't feeling very well ; you can sleep very comfortably in it."

" We will carry all the music. What do you think about buying some new songs, Honorine ? "

"We have quite enough."

"But we haven't the new ones."

"This somno, which can be used as a table if necessary."

"To be sure, we don't know what the prettiest ones are."

"And my whole library—all my books! One never has too many of them!"

"But then Monsieur Edmond can tell us, as he is coming to see us. Oh! you did well to ask him to Chelles; for it wouldn't have been polite not to invite him after all the trouble he took for us."

"I did what courtesy required. Now, the young man may come or may not; we need not worry about that."

"Oh! he will come, my dear; I am very sure that he will come."

"Why are you so sure of it, pray? what makes you think so?"

"Why—because he looked so happy when you invited him to come; his eyes expressed such pleasure!"

"Very well! if he comes, we will receive him.—Have you put down my library?"

"Yes, it's all down. He has a very courteous manner."

"My *étagère.*"

"And very *comme il faut!*"

"The small dining-table; we may need it."

"He expresses himself very well."

"And this desk, this blotting-pad."

"How old should you say he was?"

" My blotting-pad ? "

" Why, no; Monsieur Edmond Didier."

Madame Dalmont's expression was almost stern as she said:

" My dear girl, don't you propose to think of anything but Monsieur Edmond?"

" I! Why do you ask me that?"

" Because ever since we came back from the notary's, I suppose you are not conscious of it, but you have talked of nothing but him; you are thinking of him all the time."

Agathe blushed to the whites of her eyes and stammered:

" Mon Dieu! if I have talked about that young man, it is only because he was so obliging to—you, that it seemed to me quite natural to be grateful to him. But if it displeases you, that is enough; I won't mention him again."

" Let us not exaggerate things, my dear love; the thing that might displease me would be to see you thinking too much of a person whom we hardly know; who showed himself most willing to be of service to us, it is true; but who is none the less a stranger to us."

" A stranger! why he told us all about his family and his means, and what he did."

" Yes, that is true; and I noticed that the first use he made of the sixty thousand francs left him by an uncle, was to leave his place."

" Because he does business on the Bourse now."

"It would have been much wiser of him to keep the place he had.—But after all, my dear girl, this doesn't concern us. In my judgment, we have had quite enough to say about this gentleman, and I ask you now whether you will or will not help me to prepare an inventory of the furniture I propose to keep?"

"Am I not writing what you tell me to? I am waiting for you to dictate to me. I won't say another word."

Mademoiselle Agathe had assumed a little pout which made Honorine smile.

They went on with the inventory without a word on any other subject; and during the rest of the day Edmond's name was not mentioned; but it was easy to see that Agathe checked herself sometimes as she was on the point of speaking, probably because it was about him.

Early the next morning the two friends went to the station where they took the train for Chelles. It was not a long journey, but they had plenty of time to talk. It was not difficult to discover that the girl was burning to talk about Edmond, but she dared not; and Honorine, who could easily read the thoughts of her whom she had almost reared, made a point of avoiding everything that might lead the conversation to the young man who had been so obliging to them.

But at sixteen years, a girl has much difficulty in concealing what she feels, in holding back what she is burning to say. She has not yet acquired that habit of dissimulation which is the result of experience and of familiarity with the world.

Agathe, consumed with the longing to recur to her favorite subject, said abruptly to her companion:

"Do you know, my dear, I believe that I have guessed why Monsieur Edmond Didier suddenly showed so much zeal in making himself useful to us?"

"Ah! you have guessed why it was? Well, what motives impelled him, do you think?"

"Why, I think that it was probably because he had fallen in love with you."

Madame Dalmont turned toward the girl and looked her straight in the eye.

"Agathe," she said, "you don't mean a word of what you are saying; and it is not kind to lie to your friend in the hope of concealing your real thought from her. Instead of that, why not tell her frankly—what I noticed clearly enough, by the way—that that young man looked at you a great deal, that his expression seemed to imply that he thought you pretty, and that you were flattered by it; indeed that it turned your head a little, so that you have thought of nothing but Monsieur Edmond from that moment? Come, don't tell me any more falsehoods —have I not guessed right?"

Agathe quickly hung her head and took her protectress's hand in hers; and tears began to fall from her eyes. Honorine saw the tears and kissed the girl affectionately, saying:

"Come, this is all mere childishness, let's say no more about it. You will readily understand that a young man may show great alacrity in obliging a person who is most attractive, and the next day forget that person entirely, because he meets others who fascinate him no less; that happens every day; and the young person in question would be very foolish to burden her mind with something which is of no consequence whatever. But my little Agathe must never again conceal her real thoughts from her friend by pretending to have other thoughts.—Now let us think of nothing but the pleasure we are going to have in the country; and here we are at Chelles already!"

As they were now familiar with the road, they went at once to the village and to Père Ledrux's.

" My word! I was looking for you," he cried when he saw them, " and it's well for you that you've come. There's been lots of people to see the house, everybody wants to buy it; but as I promised you, I haven't shown it to anybody. I told 'em all sorts of fibs: that it was almost sold, and this and that; I even refused a good pourboire from a man who wanted to go over the house; but, I says to myself: ' Those ladies will make up to me for it.' "

" Hereafter, Monsieur Ledrux, you will not lie when you say that the house is sold, for the transaction is completed; the house is ours, and here is a letter from Monsieur Courtivaux, informing you of the fact and authorizing you to give us the keys; read it."

" Oho! so it's all fixed, is it? Well, my word! I'm mighty glad to hear it! it makes me feel good. So you've bought it, have you?"

"And paid cash, without even waiting for the mort-gages to be discharged; the notary assured me that I needn't worry about that. But read the letter."

"Oh! it ain't worth while; I'll trust you. Still, I may as well read it; it don't cost any more. Yes, yes—that's what it says: 'You will hand the keys to Madame Dal-mont, the new owner.'—And you're Madame Dalmont, are you?"

"To be sure."

"Then I'll go and get you the keys right away."

"And if you haven't time to come with us this morn-ing, Père Ledrux, we know the way now, and we can go alone."

"Oh! yes, I can go with you all right; I've nothing pressing to do, and then, now that the thing's settled and the house is yours, I might as well take the rabbits right away; then you'll be rid of 'em. Tutu—tuturlu-tutu."

They soon reached the house they had bought, and already they viewed it with more pleasure than before.

While the gardener went to take a look at the rabbits and hens, the two young women entered the house, went through all the rooms, opened the shutters, looked out of the windows, and began to discuss where they would place the furniture they were to bring from Paris.

Then Agathe ran into the garden; she examined it more carefully than before; she called the gardener and made him tell her the name of each tree and each flower; then she went back to Honorine.

"My dear," she said, "we have peaches, apricots, plums, cherries, grapes and gooseberries."

"Yes, yes," said Père Ledrux, "you have 'em when they grow, and they grow when they're well taken care of, well kept, well trimmed. Bless me! a garden requires care. You'll have string beans too if you plant 'em, and now's the time, just the right time to plant, if you want radishes—to tone up the salad—and artichokes."

"Very well; you must plant them, Père Ledrux. You can tell us what we must buy at Paris and we'll bring you the seeds."

"That ain't worth while; I've got all those things at home or right in the neighborhood; I'll supply you with what you want, and they'll be better than you'd get in Paris; because we fellows, you understand, know more about such things than you do; it's our business. Have you come to-day for good?"

"No, not yet; we have many things to do in Paris."

"When are you coming?"

"I hope that in a week, at the latest, we shall arrive, with such furniture as we shall bring from Paris."

"You're going to bring furniture, when it's here already?"

"That makes no difference."

"The devil! the house will be well furnished, in that case."

"But the mere having furniture isn't everything; we need something else that we can't do without; for the house is quite large."

" What is it? "

" A maid, a servant to keep our house clean and to cook for us."

" Ah! you want a maid who can cook? "

" Who can do everything, if possible."

" Do you want a first-class cook, like Madame Droguet's, who's a—a blue ribbon, so they say, and makes *soufflés* and omelettes as big as balloons? "

" No, no, Père Ledrux, we don't ask for such talent as that; just find us a smart young girl, who likes to work and can sew a little. As for the rest, I will teach her what she doesn't know; with the desire to learn, one soon learns whatever one chooses. Let her be honest and virtuous—those are the principal points."

" Well—wait—I believe Poucette would just suit you."

" Who is Poucette? "

" She's Poucet's daughter, who used to work in the quarry and was killed in a cave-in three years ago; her mother died the year before, so the girl lives with her uncle, who's a farmer; but he has children enough of his own, and Poucette would be very glad to get a place."

" Very well; if she's a good girl, I will take her."

" As for being good, I'll answer for that; but when it comes to knowing how to cook, I won't answer for her."

" That makes no difference, I tell you; she will learn. How old is she? "

" Well! she might be about eighteen; but she's strong and solid; she'd make two of you."

"So much the better. With a strong girl in the house,
we shall not be afraid if we are attacked. Tell me, Père
Ledrux, do you think that she will be able to come to us
as soon as we come back? I would like to have her, for
then she could help us to clean house and put everything
to rights. And then, I admit that, for the first few days,
I shall be a little timid if we two are alone."

"Ah! my dear! it seems that I am to be the sensible
one here!"

"Oh! don't you pretend to be brave; you're afraid of
mice!"

"That's very different; mice climb everywhere."

"Tell me, Père Ledrux, can we count upon this girl
for the day of our arrival?"

"Why, you see, I can't answer as if I was her, or as
if I was her uncle; but I'll tell you what you can do:
while you're here, just go and talk to Poucette; then
you'll know what to expect, and whether you can count
on her."

"You are right; that's the better way. But where
shall we find this Poucette?"

"Pardi! at her uncle's, her aunt's husband's. It ain't
very far out in the country; I'll show you the way if you
want me to."

"I should be very glad; I like above all things to
settle matters on the spot.—Come, Agathe, let us go to
see Mademoiselle Poucette; at the same time we shall
see a little of the country where we are soon to live."

XIX

A FARMER'S COTTAGE

Honorine and Agathe followed the gardener, who walked a few paces in front of them, constantly humming his little song:

" Tutu—tuturlututu."

They walked for some distance; the peasant stopped from time to time to point out some pretty house, saying:

" That's where monsieur le maire lives. That's Monsieur le Docteur Antoine Beaubichon's house; it ain't very large, but he has a nice vineyard behind—and such pear trees! Well! they bear the finest pears you ever saw—as big as melons! He gives them to the people he takes care of. In fact, they came near killing Monsieur Jarnouillard! but you may say he made a fool of himself, he ate too many of 'em. And deuce take it! pears are cold for the stomach, especially the grand duchess!—That's Madame Droguet's house—a fine house —two wings! Oh! it's a valuable place, I tell you! and kept up! You ought to see it! There's carpets everywhere, even on the stairs; and everything rubbed till it shines like a mirror; *estatues* in the courtyard, vases of flowers, and a garden, with paths as straight as a string can make 'em; the box is trimmed so that never a branch

sticks out by another. And there's a fine clump of chest-
nuts, where you can stand without fear of the rain; and
a basin with a fountain that plays Sundays! Oh! it's
magnificent! One of the finest places anywhere about.
But then Madame Droguet's one of the swells."

"Isn't she the lady," queried Agathe, "who had the
resolution to hide five days in succession among the
bushes, to get a close view of the owner of the Tower?"

"Bah! it was the doctor who told you that. Well,
yes, they did say at the time that she did that; but I
didn't see her. Suppose she did: she was at liberty to
hide in the bushes if it amused her; she don't have anything else to do."

"True; but one must be very inquisitive to pass five
days in succession in the bushes, watching for someone."

"Bless me! she's rich—she can afford to be inquisitive."

"Has the lady a husband?"

"Oh, yes! a little bit of a man. When he's alongside
of his wife, you can't see him, because Madame Droguet's
a splendid woman; she's a good five feet five, and strong
in proportion; what you might call a fine woman!"

"Isn't she supposed to have been a vivandière formerly?"

"Oh! there's another one of the doctor's tales. You
know, they say a lot of things like that in the country,
—because Madame Droguet's a little quick, and when she
first came here to live she used to give her servants a
slap now and then; and they never failed to say that

she boxed her husband's ears too, and kicked him in the rump, saving your presence, when he undertook to oppose her wishes; but that's all fiddle-faddle!—People saw that she was the mistress in her own house, that nothing was done there except by her orders, so they said: ' She must have been a vivandière, she leads her husband about to the beat of the drum.'—This much is certain, that she's the one that runs the house and says what's to be done and undone, built and pulled down; the husband don't meddle in anything. That's why you hear people say ' Madame Droguet,' and never ' Monsieur Droguet!' But that just suits him; he seems to be satisfied so long as he can dance."

" Ah! so Monsieur Droguet is fond of dancing? How old is he, pray?"

" I guess he's close on to fifty-five; and his wife, too —she must be as old as he is, at least."

" Then she gives balls so that her husband may dance?"

" I don't know whether she gives balls, but she gives dinner-parties and she has lots of company. It seems that they live pretty well there. But she's sure to invite you; she invites all the swell people in the neighborhood."

" I don't know whether she will invite us," said Honorine with a smile; " but it would be a waste of time; for we do not dine out."

" Oh, well! if that's your idea, it's all right. If she invited me, I'd go; but I ain't enough of a bigwig."

" Are we almost there, Père Ledrux?"

" It's just a little farther; Guillot's house—he's Poucette's uncle—is on the other side of the river. But this
walk shows you something of Chelles."

" Do we pass the ruins of the Abbey? "

" No, they ain't on our road; after all, you don't see
anything of the Abbey; it's been made into a farm-house,
and there isn't anything very interesting about it; there's
only a few old walls left. But we're going to pass Monsieur Luminot's house. That's another nice one, I tell
you; not so well kept as Madame Droguet's; but heaps of
land behind: vineyards, arbors, and lots of white grapes."

" Isn't he the gentleman who went to call on the owner
of the Tower, to invite him to dinner? "

" Yes; he's a high-liver, is Monsieur Luminot—used
to be a wine-merchant; he always has good stuff in his
cellar, and he's never stingy about a glass of wine. He's
a friend of Madame Droguet and often dines there."

" Does he dance with Monsieur Droguet? "

" I couldn't tell you. I don't believe he's a dancer, he's
too fat for that; while Monsieur Droguet, who is very
short and thin, keeps his feet going all the time he's
talking to you, just exactly as if he had the St. Vitus's
dance. He must have had it when he was small, and
never got wholly rid of it. He went to Paris not long
ago, on purpose to learn a new dance that's all the fashion, so they say—the lance—lances——"

" Lancers? "

" That's it, mamzelle, the lancers! and when he came
back, he couldn't sleep for a number of nights; he used

to get up and dance the lancers with his chamber-vessel, so that he woke the whole house, and Madame Droguet was obliged to get angry.—Ah! there's Monsieur Jarnouillard's house."

" The gentleman who ate too many pears? "

" Yes, mamzelle. It isn't very large, but there's only the husband and wife; no children and no servants; Madame Jarnouillard does all the work. But people say they've got enough, that they're rich; and what makes 'em think so is that Monsieur Jarnouillard lends money to people who are hard up and are able to pay it back—who have chattels and land, as he says. If you haven't got those things, there's no danger of his accommodating you; and anyway he charges interest that makes you shudder! "

" The man's a usurer then, is he? "

" Faith! I can't say as to that. They say that he used to be a tradesman in Paris, with a shop on Quai des Lunettes. I don't know what kind of *lunettes*—spectacles —he sold, but he must have made a good thing out of it. They ain't liked hereabout, and yet people are very glad to have 'em here; because those who get into difficulty, who need money to pay their rent or to take up a note, go to see Monsieur Jarnouillard, and he lends 'em the money—provided he can make a pretty profit out of it. Still, they're people who don't put on any airs, and the Lord only knows what they live on. The wife buys one mutton cutlet for herself and her husband. Bless me! but they're miserly! they eat crusts of bread, old roosters, and fish the husband catches in the Marne; in fact, he's been arrested twice for fishing without a permit. In summer he tries to catch birds with birdlime; they eat whatever he catches; but when they dine out they near kill themselves with indigestion; and besides that, Madame Droguet's maid tells me that they stuff their pockets with things from the table. Ha! ha! that gives them a royal feast the next day. But you understand that all I'm telling you is just gossip; I don't bear those people any grudge; I don't want anything of 'em.—Tutu—tutu—turlututu."

"Ah! my dear Agathe!" said Honorine in a low tone, "people are no more generous in the country than in the city, and he would be bitterly disappointed who should go into the country to live, in the hope of finding purer morals, more agreeable relations, more sincere friendships, and more obliging neighbors! No, men are the same everywhere; but their failings, their vices show more plainly in small places than in the large cities. The only thing one can be certain of having in the country is pure air."

"There's Guillot's house!" said the gardener, halting in front of a wretched hovel of earth and stones, the roof of which was in such bad condition in several places that when it rained the occupants were but partially sheltered.

There was a small garden, hardly separated from the fields by a scrubby hedge of elder-bushes, at the right of the hovel, and in it a few stunted trees shading cabbages and potatoes. Everything was growing haphazard in the little enclosure, which seemed in as wretched a condition as the house.

The two women entered a large room, which was not floored either with flags or boards. It was used as a kitchen, and also as a bedroom, for there was a dilapidated cot in one corner. On the walls, innocent of paper, hung divers kitchen utensils; there were also shelves, upon which were dishes, mainly earthen bowls.

A large walnut *buffet,* several chairs without seats, some stools and a table composed all the furniture of that room, which, moreover, was not very clean and presented an appearance of wretchedness that made the heart ache.

And yet that hovel sheltered a whole family: Guillot the farmer, his wife and four children, the eldest of whom was only eleven, while the youngest still lay in his mother's arms, and another, two years old, still dragged at her skirts.

Nevertheless it was in that family, whose head earned barely enough to support his own children, that Poucette was made welcome. The worthy man considered that his niece, being an orphan, was also his child; and he took her into his home.

"I will try to work a little harder," he thought, "and God will provide."

If the country people are envious and evil-speaking, we also find among them such touching examples as this of humanity and kindliness: the latter should induce us to forgive the former.

When Agathe and Honorine entered the house, the farmer's wife was nursing her youngest child; another little fellow was rolling on the ground, gnawing a piece of black bread. By the fire, a girl of eight was trying to make the water boil in the kettle by blowing with her breath two or three small sticks that smouldered on the hearth. The two young women stood lost in amazement at the sight of those wretchedly-clad children in that tumble-down hovel. The picture of destitution is always more painful to look upon when it embraces children.

Guillot's wife looked up with a surprised expression at the two ladies who had entered her home; but it did not interfere with her maternal duties.

A moment later, however, Ledrux put his head in at the door and shouted, as if he were speaking to deaf people—as was his habit with everybody:

"I've brought these ladies to see you, Mère Guillot; they're the ones who've bought Monsieur Courtivaux's house, and they're coming to live in it. They're looking for a girl to do their housework and their cooking; in fact, the whole business; and I thought of Poucette, who hasn't got any place. Would it suit you to have her work for these ladies, who are bourgeoises and well off——"

Honorine interrupted the gardener.

"Madame," she said, "we are told that your niece is a good girl, and we will treat her so that she will be happy with us; but if she is useful to you, if you prefer to keep her with you, we will look elsewhere."

" Oh! Poucette ain't so very necessary to us," replied the peasant; " because Claudine, our oldest, is old enough to look after her little brothers while I go to work in the fields."

" Is that Claudine?" asked Honorine, looking at the child who was still blowing the sticks with all her strength.

" No, that's Mariette, our second one; Claudine's eleven; she's big and strong. As for Poucette, she's a good girl, but let me tell you, if you count on her to do your cooking, why you mustn't expect too much! Well! she ain't very subtle about cooking."

Honorine smiled at the word " subtle " which the peasants are very fond of using, often without any clear idea of its meaning.

" I am not disturbed about that," she replied. " All I shall ask of Poucette are zeal and willingness."

" Oh! as far as that goes, she's got plenty. And you will give her her keep?"

" Naturally."

" And her washing?"

" She will have to spend nothing but for clothes; and Agathe and I will often find something to give her among our old dresses."

" I will give her my blue striped dress at once," said Agathe, " for it's too small for me. I am still growing."

" If it's too small for you, it will be even smaller for Poucette, who's taller than you," said Père Ledrux, with a laugh.

"Oh! that don't make any difference," rejoined the
farmer's wife; "dresses can be let down and pieced out;
we ain't ladies, you know. How much will madame pay
my niece to do her work?"

"Tell me yourself what you think it will be worth."

"Bless me! if the girl has her lodging and keep and
washing, it seems to me that if you give her a ten-franc
piece every month she'll be satisfied. Do you think that's
too much?"

"No, it's not too much; and I promise you to increase
her wages if she serves me faithfully."

"Then it's all fixed, unless Poucette don't want to go
into service; but if she don't want to, why, we wouldn't
like to vex the child. She'd think we was doing it to get
rid of her; she'd think we didn't love her any more; and
that would make her unhappy, and us too!"

"Poor people!" said Honorine, looking at Agathe,
"how devoted they are to one another! Their hearts
are rich at all events! And the people who roll in wealth
are sometimes very poor in that respect.—Might we not
see Poucette, madame," she asked the peasant, "so that
we may find out at once whether or not we may count
upon her?"

"Well, yes! but just now she's at our little piece of
land with Claudine, planting potatoes, because Guillot's
got some work at Monsieur Luminot's."

"Is your piece of land far from here?"

"Oh, no! not so very far; if you'd like to go there—
you see I can't show you the way myself, and Mariette

is doing something for me just now.—Père Ledrux, you know where our field is."

"Let me see! Pardi! to be sure I do; it's right alongside of Gros-Pierre's field, where he's set out plum trees that don't grow."

"That's right; then you can take these ladies there."

"Yes, yes! Pardi! while I'm about it, I might as well lose my whole day; it will go in with the rest."

"Very well; continue to be our guide, Père Ledrux, and let us go to find Poucette. After all, it will make us acquainted with the country.—Good-morning, madame; we are going to see your niece, and if my proposition is satisfactory to her, that arrangement will be made."

"You won't be sorry, for she's a good girl. Your servant, mesdames."

The two friends set off once more, still preceded by the gardener, who led them across the country, saying:

"This time it's in just the opposite direction; we have got to go toward Gournay."

"Is it a long distance?"

"Faith! it's quite a little piece."

"How does it happen," said Agathe, "that a man buys land so far from his house?"

"Well! mamzelle, sometimes one inherits it, or else he gets it at a bargain. I believe that Guillot got this piece of land of his from his father-in-law, but I'm afraid he won't keep it long."

"Why so?"

"Oh! I have an idea that it's pretty well mortgaged! I've often seen Guillot going to Monsieur Jarnouillard's, and bless me! round here, when you say: 'He goes to Jarnouillard's,' that means that his affairs are in bad shape, that he needs money!"

"Poor people! But Poucette's uncle is a hard-working man, you said?"

"To be sure; but you understand, when you have to feed so many mouths—and then the potatoes being bad last year, and that was Guillot's only crop! When you count on a thing and it goes back on you, why, it's rather upsetting!—Tutu—turlututu!"

XX

THE ENVIRONS OF CHELLES.—POUCETTE.—AMI

"We're heading now as if we was going to Gournay," said the gardener, trotting in front of the two ladies; "this will help you to know the way when you want to go to walk in the neighborhood; and especially if you happen to feel like eating a *matelote;* for Gournay's famous for them, you know."

The peasant led them past the railroad station, which is on the road from Chelles to Gournay. Beyond the station they found themselves on a fine road bordered by tall poplars and enclosed by ditches filled with water,

which prevented passers-by from walking in the fields
on the other side of the ditches.

Both to the right and left the country was flat for
some distance; it was a beautiful valley interspersed
with coverts arranged for the express purpose of afford-
ing the game a place of rest and shelter.

" This is a very fine road," said Agathe, after they
had been walking on it for ten minutes, " but it is too
straight, too monotonous; I don't like roads where you
never can tell whether you are going forward; is it like
this very much longer? "

" No, mamzelle. Look; where you see that stone on
the left, we make a turn, and then we shall have Gournay
before us, and the view is more varied."

In fact, after turning to the left, they could see the
Marne, whose placid green waters conceal many rocks
dangerous to vessels and to bathers. The outlook was
charming: on the left they saw a mill which reached
boldly to the very centre of the river, supported by numerous piles. There were obstructions, too, to warn
boatmen that they must not venture near, and that the
passage was dangerous when it was not impossible. And
the water, passing over these obstructions, formed cas-
cades and waterfalls which gave life to the picture; while
numerous little islands above the mill added still more to
the charm of the landscape.

In another direction a tall hedge enclosed a park belonging to an estate called the *Maison Blanche;* then
there were more pastures and fields and coverts.

"Ah! this is lovely!" exclaimed the girl, when she saw the river. "How pretty the water is, my dear! it makes a landscape beautiful instantly. I don't call those horrid ditches by the roadside water. We will come here often to walk, won't we, Honorine?"

"It's rather far from Chelles; however, we shall come here, no doubt."

"I intend to learn to fish, my dear; you must teach me the way."

"But I know no more about it than you do!"

"Never fear," said the peasant; "when you have a stout line, and when you've found out a place where there's fish, it goes all alone; but you'll have to buy a license though."

"What bridge is that ahead of us?"

"That bridge leads to Gournay, then to Noisy-le-Grand, then to Montfermeil, if you choose; but you have to pay to cross; it's a toll, a charge—I don't know what they call it; but it's a sou each. It seems that it cost three hundred thousand francs to build, and they want to get the money back; there's eighty years still that we've got to pay, but after that we can pass for nothing. As I don't like to put out a sou, I don't often cross; I'm waiting till it's free."

"Don't be afraid," said Honorine with a smile; "we will pay for you."

"Oh! it ain't worth while; we haven't got to cross the bridge to get to Guillot's field; it's to our left, on the bank of the river."

" But while we are here, I should be glad to know what there is on the other side of the bridge."

" Bless my soul! there's nothing but Gournay, a small village, a quiet little place that don't make much noise in the world. Bless me! there's only a hundred and twenty-five to a hundred and thirty people, at most, and you can guess it ain't likely to be as lively as Paris! "

" True; and if all the villages roundabout are as small, I understand why we have not met, or even seen, a single living being since we left Chelles. Doesn't it seem strange to you, Agathe, to walk for three-quarters of an hour in the country without meeting anyone? "

" Yes, my dear; but I have been fancying that I was walking on my own property, and that all the land in sight belonged to me."

" Indeed, one might well have that illusion. See: even on the river, although it is very beautiful, there is not a vessel in sight: no steamboats, no barges, no skiffs, no washerwomen, not even a single fisherman on the shore! It's as deserted as the surrounding country! "

" Oh! sometimes there's loads of wood go down the Marne; I've seen 'em! "

" Those must be noteworthy days."

" The trouble is, you see, the Marne's as sly as the devil; it has holes and lots of grass. You have to know it well to risk it in a boat; and better, to bathe in it."

" But I don't object to this solitude, this perfect quiet."

" And then, at Chelles it isn't like this; you meet people there."

" True ; we met as many as three people on our way
to that poor farmer's.—So we do not need to cross the
bridge, you say ? "

" No, madame, there's Guillot's field at our left."

" And the Tower," said Agathe ; " why don't we see
it from here ? "

" Because we're in a hollow ; but it's over yonder, behind Gournay, toward Noisy-le-Grand. You wait till
you see all this six weeks from now ; then the trees
will be green and the shrubs in flower, and it'll be much
brighter than it is now."

" You are right, Père Ledrux."

" Look, there's Guillot's field, and I see Poucette dig-
ging."

Poucette was a tall, strong girl, with the bronzed skin
of those who work in the fields. But her round face
was honest and good-humored, her black eyes met yours
unflinchingly, albeit without the slightest touch of bold-
ness in their expression ; and when she smiled, as she
did very frequently, she showed a double row of teeth
whose whiteness formed a striking contrast to her brown
skin.

A little girl of eleven or twelve, with the head of a boy,
whose hair, cut *à la Titus,* presented the aspect of a hedgehog, was working by Poucette's side ; it was Claudine,
the farmer's oldest child.

The two villagers stopped their work to look at the
two young women who were coming toward them. In
a region where you may walk all day without meeting

a cat, one may be forgiven for suspending work to stare at two stylishly dressed ladies.

"Look! that's Père Ledrux!" suddenly exclaimed Poucette.

"Yes, my girl, and I have brought two ladies who want to speak to you."

"To me, Père Ledrux? Bah! you're joking! We don't know any fine ladies."

"You're going to know some; don't I tell you that madame's come here for you—to take you with her? Well! what do you say to that?"

The young peasant flushed to the hair and seemed dumfounded.

Madame Dalmont walked toward her.

"Mademoiselle," she said, "I am looking for a young girl to enter my service; for my friend and I are coming to live at Chelles."

"These ladies have bought Monsieur Courtivaux's house; you know where it is."

"There are only two of us, my young friend here and myself; so that you will have only us to wait upon, and you will not have very severe mistresses to get along with. Tell me if you think that it will suit you to live with us. We have just seen your aunt, who thinks that you will do well to accept; but she leaves you entirely free to refuse the place if it does not please you."

"And you'll have your board and lodging and washing and they'll give you ten francs a month besides; that's not bad, eh?" said Père Ledrux.

Poucette's face became radiant.

"Oh! certainly the place does suit me!" she cried; "and I don't ask anything better than to take it. In the first place it'll be a relief to my uncle and aunt, who have to support me now; but if I earn money, I can help them in my turn, and that will make me very happy."

"I see that you are an excellent girl, my child; and if, as I hope, you serve me faithfully, I promise to increase your wages later."

"You are very kind, madame; I'll do my best. But, you see, I don't know many things, and if I've got to cook, I'm afraid I am not very clever."

"If you are willing, that is enough; I will show you, and you will soon learn."

"As for the will, madame will see that I have plenty of that."

"Well, then, it's a bargain. You accept, do you not? I may rely on you?"

"Certainly, madame, with great thankfulness!"

At that moment they heard a plaintive sort of groan soon followed by sobs. It was the little girl with the head like a hedgehog, crying like a baby.

"Dear, dear! what's the matter, Claudine?" inquired Poucette, turning toward the child, who replied between her sobs:

"You're going to go away from our house, and I shan't see you any more! I don't want Poucette to go away, I don't!"

This outburst of artless, sincere grief moved the two friends, who tried to pacify the little peasant by saying to her:

"Why, my child, you will still see Poucette; she isn't going to leave Chelles, for we are coming here to live. You can come to see her whenever you have time; we shall never prevent you; on the contrary, we shall be very glad when you come."

"Do you hear, Claudine? these ladies will let you come to see me, and you can help me when I clear up the garden!"

"The garden! oh! that's my business," muttered Ledrux; "you won't have anything to do with taking care of that; you don't know anything about it; a fine mess you'd make of it!"

The little girl looked at the two ladies and sighed. Agathe unfastened a velvet ribbon that she wore about her neck and placed it about the girl's, saying:

"See, this is to console you a little."

Instantly the child smiled through her tears and cried:

"Oh! look, Poucette! the lovely ribbon! see how pretty it is!"

"Yes, you see that these ladies are very kind to you already!"

"Pardi! if you give 'em gewgaws and finery," said the gardener, "you'll soon make friends with 'em."

"So much the better, Père Ledrux; that is what we want. I am sure that this child cares more for the bit of ribbon than for rabbits."

"Am I to go with you right away, madame?" said Poucette, dropping her spade.

"No, my child, not yet; we are going back to Paris for a few days. But when we return to Chelles for good, you must come to us at once."

"Shall you return soon, madame?"

"As soon as possible; I think that in a week we shall have done all that we have to do in Paris. But meanwhile I will give you your earnest money."

Honorine had taken from her pocket a dainty purse, and was about to open it, when an enormous dog suddenly appeared in the middle of the field and bounded toward Poucette, glancing with a most impertinent expression at all the other persons present.

"Look out! look out! that's the dog from the Tower!" cried Père Ledrux, retreating several steps.

"Yes, it's Ami," said Poucette; "oh! I ain't afraid of him, nor Claudine either; he knows us well and he ain't a bit ugly! Don't be afraid, mesdames, he won't hurt you."

The two friends gazed curiously at the dog, of whom they had already heard. Ami was of the Newfoundland breed, but seemed to have a trace of shepherd blood. His eyes indicated a degree of intelligence which many people deny to the Newfoundland, which, they claim, is good for nothing but to fish up a drowned man or save people from falling over a precipice, which, in our judgment, would be a sufficient proof of intelligence.—But in addition to these qualities, the dog from the Tower possessed all those of all other breeds; moreover, nature seemed to have endowed him with the gift of divination; for he would divine a given person's sentiments for his master, and his instinct never deceived him. He knew better than his master himself who were his friends and who his enemies. That extraordinary perspicacity—of which men are rarely possessed—proved that prodigies of intelligence may be found among dogs of the Newfoundland breed...

Generally speaking, there is no rule without an exception. Some people claim that men with low foreheads are deficient in wits, while a high forehead is the appanage of genius. We have known some very intellectual low foreheads, and some high ones behind which there was nothing but dense stupidity.

Ami was white, except for a few brown spots on his back, and one on top of his head. His tail ended in a large plume; his muzzle was broad, his ears of medium size, and his black eyes gleamed with extraordinary fire; they seemed to long to speak. He understood perfectly whatever was said to him and did whatever his master ordered, much better than most servants. Such was the dog that suddenly appeared in Guillot's field.

His appearance was so unexpected that Madame Dalmont, who was opening her purse at the moment, was unable to restrain a movement of alarm, and in that movement she dropped a two-franc piece from her purse. She had not discovered the loss when Ami picked the coin up with his teeth and placed it at her feet, as if to say:

"Take your money, which I have picked up for you."

"Oh! the beautiful dog!" cried Agathe; "see, dear, he picks up the coin you dropped and returns it to you!"

"That's so, on my word!" said Ledrux. "I tell you, everybody wouldn't be as honest as he is! But, I say, as the dog's here, the master can't be far off."

"No, no, Monsieur Paul isn't far away," said Poucette; "I see him coming over there toward the mill."

"The owner of the Tower? Oh! where is he? show him to us!" cried the two friends almost at once.

"I don't see but what you're almost as curious as Madame Droguet!" chuckled the gardener. "But never you fear; you'll see my gentleman, and near to at that, for he'll certainly pass here on his way home."

"Do you think he will pass by here?"

"Yes, madame," said Poucette; "Monsieur Paul is going across the bridge and home by way of Gournay. If he wasn't coming this way, his dog would have left us before this, sure."

The two friends looked toward the mill and saw a man wearing a cap with a long vizor and dressed in hunting costume, with a gun over his shoulder, walking rapidly along the bank of the river.

"I thought that hunting was prohibited now," said Honorine.

"Yes, madame," said Poucette; "but he don't hunt; he carries his gun as he would a cane. Nobody says anything to him for that, because he's well known all about here now, and everybody knows he ain't a poacher."

" He don't always carry his gun," said little Claudine.
" Day before yesterday I met him by the Maison Rouge,
and he didn't have anything in his hand but a stick."

" He's coming nearer; you can see his face now."

" None too well," said Agathe; " for my part, my
dear, I can see nothing but his beard. Great heaven!
what a beard! it's enough to frighten one!"

" Ami, there's your master; go after him.—Why, that's
funny! he don't pay any attention to me; he seems to
be all taken up with mamzelle!"

Ami, in fact, kept his eyes fixed on Agathe; he walked
all about her as if to examine her on all sides, then returned to his place in front of her and gazed at her anew.

" Good dog! I have a good mind to pat you!" said
Agathe; " for it seems as if you were inviting me to, and
as if you would like it; but I don't quite dare to risk it, I
might mistake your intentions."

" Oh! there's no danger, mamzelle," said Poucette;
" it's plain enough that you've won Ami's heart! If
he didn't like you, he'd growl so that you couldn't make
a mistake; you can tell right away when he's in a bad
humor.—Why, look! he's rubbing his head against you
now! that's funny; I never saw him so friendly with
anyone!"

" Perhaps mamzelle has something to eat about her,"
said the gardener slyly.

" No, Père Ledrux, I have nothing about me!" retorted Agathe; " and you slander this dog by suggesting
that gluttony has anything to do with the friendly

feeling he shows me.—Come, Ami, come; let me pat you; I am very glad to have made your acquaintance, for hereafter I shall know that I needn't be afraid of you."

As she spoke the girl patted the dog, who made no objection and wagged his tail in token of satisfaction.

Meanwhile his master approached, walking very fast and looking straight before him. But when he arrived at Guillot's field, he glanced aside and saw his dog surrounded by five persons; whereupon he immediately called him in a loud voice:

" Here, Ami, here! come at once!"

The noble beast, obedient to his master's voice, turned his back on the little group; but as he trotted away he turned several times and looked back at Agathe.

His master had reached the bridge and was almost across, when the dog stopped in the middle, turned toward Agathe and began to bark loudly, as if to send her a last adieu.

" That's funny! that's funny!" exclaimed Poucette; " that the dog from the Tower should take such a liking to mamzelle right off."

" Dear me! we shall miss the train!" said Honorine; " it goes at four o'clock; doesn't it, Père Ledrux?"

" Yes, madame, but it ain't that yet."

" But we have to go back to the station, and it's some distance. Here, my child, take these three francs; it's your earnest money."

" Oh! madame is too kind! Look, Claudine, she gave me three francs!"

Little Claudine was engrossed by the velvet ribbon that had been placed about her neck.

"Now let us go, Agathe.—Good-bye, Poucette; we shall see you soon."

"I will be ready when madame comes."

"Very good; au revoir."

"Good-bye, Claudine."

The little hedgehog-headed one smiled, but could not find a word to say in reply; her ribbon absorbed all her faculties.

The two friends hurried off to the station; and as the gardener left them he said:

"Now it's all settled, I may as well take the rabbits away; that will relieve you just so much."

"Yes, yes, Père Ledrux, take the rabbits."

"As for the hens—why, you can see about them later."

"I have already said that we would keep the hens."

"I know; but if you should ever change your mind—however, it will be time enough then."

Honorine and Agathe took the train, the former still thinking of the savage aspect of the owner of the Tower; the other recalling with pleasure Ami's caresses.

XXI

AN ASSIGNATION IN A COUPÉ

After an absence of several days, Freluchon returned home one morning.

He came from Rouen alone, having left the young Pompadour there, making eyes at the *jeune premier* of the Grand Theatre; as Freluchon was beginning to weary of his conquest and was on the lookout for an opportunity to break with her, he did not fail to seize that one. After a tremendous outburst of jealousy, on leaving the theatre where the *jeune premier* had made a great hit in *An Odd Bet*, a vaudeville from the *Variétés*, Freluchon had abandoned his faithless fair and taken the train for Paris.

When he entered the courtyard of his house, he cried:

" How dear to every noble heart one's native land !
With rapture I once more behold this blest abode !"

His concierge interrupted him in the middle of his declamation to say:

" Monsieur, your friend Monsieur Edmond Didier has been here almost every day to ask for you."

" Indeed! dear Edmond! Is he in such haste to see me?"

" And then another one of your friends, Monsieur Chamoureau, whose clothes you have kept since Mi-Carême,
and who is very angry with you. He often comes twice
a day to know if you have returned."

" What's that? Chamoureau angry! Oh, well! he'll
calm down! Why, one would think he hadn't any other
clothes to put on—a man with a real estate office!—Poor
Chamoureau! I would have liked to find him still dressed
as a Spaniard; I should have enjoyed that! But, to console him, I'll give him a stick of sugar-candy that I
brought from Rouen, where they cost more than they do
in Paris; to be sure, they're made in Rouen."

Freluchon had not been at home an hour, when his
doorbell rang violently; he went to open the door, saying to himself:

" That's Chamoureau, I'll bet; if he's still out of
temper I'll talk to him about Eléonore and make him
weep."

But it was not the business agent, it was Edmond who
entered his friend's apartment.

" Well, you have returned at last! " he said; " that's
fortunate! I have been longing for you; I wanted to
see you! "

Freluchon planted himself in front of Edmond, who
had thrown himself on a couch, and gazed at him with a
look of amazement, as he replied:

" This eager desire to see me flatters as much as it
surprises me! not that I doubt your friendship, but between young men friendship never goes so far as ennui

because of absence; we have too much to distract our thoughts. Something has gone wrong in your love-affairs. Amélia has indulged in some new escapade!"

"As if Amélia had anything to do with it! I haven't seen her for a week."

"Have you had a row?"

"Oh, no! I think no more about her than if I had never known her."

"Ah! that is better, and I congratulate you. But if you have ceased to think of her, I'll stake Chamoureau's coat against twenty-five sous that it's because you are thinking of somebody else!"

"Yes, yes! I am thinking of somebody else! but this time—Ah! Freluchon, this is no mere caprice, no amourette; it isn't one of those passions to which desire alone gives birth; ah, no! I feel that I am truly in love, in love for the first time; and this love bears no resemblance to the others! If you knew how it changes one, how timid, humble, respectful one becomes! how little it takes to make one happy! how a trifle causes one to feel the keenest, sweetest sensation! But I can't make you understand all that; no, it's impossible. To form a conception of love, you must be in love yourself; without that, you cannot comprehend the happiness and the torments it causes."

"Sapristi! here's a kettle of fish! What, can it be you, Edmond, that fickle, heedless youth, who have got caught in this fashion! And who is the lady with the camellias, or with the white carnations, who——"

"Ah! Freluchon, you are all wrong; there is no question here of one of those great coquettes or of those fashionable courtesans who take delight in making numerous conquests and to whom all men do homage. No, it is not a woman of the world—*monde*—or of the demi-monde; it is a carefully reared, virtuous girl, and pretty —ah! as pretty as the most beautiful of the angels!"

"Oho! that makes a difference! Where did you find this jewel?"

"At Chamoureau's."

"What! Chamoureau has documents of that soit in his office, and has never shown them to me! that surprises me very much."

"For heaven's sake, Freluchon, stop your joking a minute, and listen to me!"

"Speak; I am like a mute of the harem."

Edmond told his friend how he had made Agathe's acquaintance and by what means he had been able to make himself useful to Madame Dalmont. Freluchon listened attentively and without interrupting him; when the lovelorn youth had finished, he said:

"Well, it's all up with you, I understand that. This young lady is charming, I have no doubt; she possesses all the talents, all the virtues; I am convinced of that. But what do you expect to do now?"

"I haven't any idea, and that is why I was consumed with anxiety to see you. In the first place, I felt that I must talk about my love, relieve my heart; for it was suffocating me. Then I wanted to ask your advice."

"I'll give you some advice that I'll bet you won't follow."

"Why not? Speak."

"As the girl in question is respectable and virtuous, of course you do not expect to make her your mistress?"

"Oh! perish the thought! it has never once come into my mind."

"In that case, my dear fellow, as it would be rank madness for you to think of marrying before you have some position in the world, a fortune, or at the very least some employment which will take the place of a fortune, you must cease to think of the young lady, and you must never see her again."

"Not think of her! not see her! Ah! tell me rather to cease to live!"

"You see that I was right when I said that you wouldn't follow my advice. It was hardly worth while to ask me for it."

"It would be madness, you say, for me to think of marrying.—No, it would not be madness, if I had a fortune or at least a suitable position to offer that fascinating girl; for I should be so happy with her! But, as you have too well said, I have neither! That sixty thousand francs that my uncle left me, I have spent more than half of now, in amusing myself; and what I have left isn't enough to justify me in offering myself as a husband to any woman."

"That depends. Is your young woman rich?"

" No; at least, I think not. The two ladies are going into the country in order to live economically; and the charming Agathe, who is an orphan, has no friend or protector but this Madame Dalmont, who is a widow of .very modest means."

" Forget this young woman, my friend; forget her at once; that is the best thing that you can possibly do."

" No, I cannot, I will not forget her!"

" Sapristi! then don't ask me for advice!"

" My friend, when I have given those ladies time to get settled in their country house, I shall go to Chelles, and I shall call on them; they have invited me to do so."

" Do what you please."

" You will come with me."

" What for? Do you mean to present me to them? But suppose I should fall in love with your damsel?"

" No, I shall not present you. I am not intimate enough with them yet to take the liberty to introduce anyone; but you will wait for me somewhere in the neighborhood, we will pass a few days there——"

" Ah! what a captivating plan! That is to say, you propose to keep me on a strict diet, while you utter heart-rending sighs!—No, thanks!"

" If you refuse, I will take Chamoureau. Poor Chamoureau! he will understand my torments, for he too is in love."

" Really! There seems to be an epidemic of it just now."

" But by the way—I haven't told you.—Gad! it's a
most amusing thing! You would never guess whom he's
in love with."

" His concierge? "

" No; but that magnificent conquest he made at the.
Opéra ball, and refused to open his mouth about."

" I remember his mysterious air, his reticence, his
hints when we talked about his charmer."

" Well, that charmer is Thélénie, the superb, the brilliant Sainte-Suzanne! "

" The deuce! your ex-mistress? "

" The same."

" And you say that Chamoureau has made the conquest of that elegant creature, who adored you, who
continued to run after you? "

" And who runs after me still, alas! "

" Then Chamoureau is an idiot. The woman probably
wanted to talk with him because she knew that he knew
you, and because she hoped to obtain from him information concerning your conduct. That is not hard to
guess."

" I believe that you are right, especially as she expressly forbade him to mention her name to us. He
seems, however, to have little success in his amours; he
is constantly groaning and complaining. The poor fellow is really in love with Thélénie, who treats him, he
says, with extreme cruelty."

" I am glad of it; that will teach him to stop lamenting
Eléonore! The beautiful brunette is making a fool of

him, there's no doubt about that; and you say she is still running after you?"

"Mon Dieu! yes; and I avoid her. See, here's a letter that was handed me just now when I left the house; it's from her, I know, I am familiar enough with her writing, but I haven't even broken the seal. What's the use? I'll just throw it into the fire."

And Edmond was on the point of tossing into the flames a letter that he took from his pocket, when Freluchon caught his arm.

"What! you propose to destroy this missive without finding out what is inside?"

"My dear fellow, I know beforehand what is inside: reproaches, complaints, followed by entreaties and burning words! And all this to lead up to the statement that she expects me to call because she absolutely must speak to me."

"She must have a very impassioned style, that woman. Will you let me read her letter?"

"You are at liberty to do so, if you care to."

"It won't annoy you?"

"How foolish you are! Thélénie is not a married woman, so that one is obliged to respect her secrets; furthermore, she makes no mystery of her sentiments toward me."

"Oh, no, indeed! the only mystery she makes is in the matter of her feeling for Chamoureau. Let's see your Ariadne's epistle."

Freluchon broke the seal of the letter and read:

" Ungrateful Edmond:

" Do you mean to kill me with grief? have you no
pity for my suffering? is there no longer in your heart
a single spark of that fire which you once swore burned
there for me?

" I cannot believe it; I love you too dearly to be forgotten thus! You have ceased to see that flower-maker,
Amélia, I know; you could not love such a woman long.
I forgive you that whim, I promise, I swear to you that I
will never mention it. Let the past be nothing more than
a dream.

" Come back, dear Edmond, come back to her who cannot exist apart from you, and to whom you have made
known a sentiment that will end only with her life.

" This evening, at nine o'clock, I shall drive in a coupé
on the Champs-Elysées. My carriage will stop in front
of the Jardin d'Hiver, on the other side of the road. Open
your left hand twice to my coachman, and he will open
the door.

" You will come; I insist—no, but I entreat you.

" THÉLÉNIE."

" Well," said Edmond, " did I not guess right: reproaches, entreaties, oceans of love, and a rendezvous?"

" To which you will not go?"

" Most assuredly not; for I should be very sorry to
renew a liaison which had lost all charm for me, even
before I knew Agathe! All the more so, now.—What
are you thinking about?"

" I am thinking of the unlucky Chamoureau, whom this fair lady is making a fool of. As you don't mean to go to this rendezvous, we must send him in your place."

" The deuce! do you mean it? "

"Indeed I do! It bores you to receive passionate notes from this Thélénie every hour in the day, does it not? "

" Ah, yes! it bores me terribly, and I would give anything in the world to induce her to leave me in peace."

" Well! this is the best possible way to put an end to the persecutions of your Hermione. When you have sent Chamoureau to her in your place, I'll answer for it that she won't make any more assignations with you.— And then suppose it should result in making the poor fellow happy, in making him the happy vanquisher of the woman he adores—where would be the harm? Will you let me go ahead? "

" I have no objection, on the condition that you go to Chelles with me."

" You still hold to that plan, do you? What on earth shall I do there? "

" Eat *matelotes* at Gournay. They are very famous."

" That argument persuades me. I have never been able to resist a *matelote*.—I hear the bell; I'll bet it's Chamoureau."

" Bless my soul! I remember now that he forbade me to tell you of his love for Thélénie."

" He'll be very glad that I know about it, in a little while."

This time it was in fact Chamoureau who entered Freluchon's room.

"So this fellow has come back at last!" he cried. "*Tandem!—denique!*—Do you know, Freluchon, that your treatment of me has been rather too unceremonious?"

"Good-morning, Chamoureau; embrace me!"

"To go away without returning my new black coat and trousers! You have no idea what that cost me!"

"Embrace your friend!"

"Let me alone.—The trousers were·new, too."

"Do you suppose that I have worn your clothes, I should like to know? do you think that I put on your coat and trousers to go to Rouen?"

"Faith! I don't know."

"I should look very nice in them, as I'm five inches shorter than you! See, there are your clothes, on that chair; I give you my word that they haven't been to Rouen."

The agent carefully examined his coat and trousers, muttering:

"To think that I have two of each now! it was hardly worth while!"

"What! have you bought another black coat?"

"I had to."

"Have you had occasion to take part in some grand function—a wedding, or a funeral?"

"I had occasion—I had occasion to be dressed handsomely."

" Chamoureau, you have secrets from your best friend; that is not right. I've brought you a stick of sugar-candy from Rouen."

" Don't talk to me about candy, Freluchon, I beg you. You remind me of Mi-Carême night, which I would like to efface from my memory ! "

" Why, I was under the impression that you made a magnificent conquest that night; you told us so, at all events."

" Yes, that's so; I did meet a fascinating woman, and she gave me permission to call on her; but I've been no more fortunate for that. Four times now within five days I have been to see her, in the hope of finding her less cruel; but I am always told that she isn't in. I begin to think that she doesn't propose to receive me again."

" The trouble is that you didn't go about it right, my poor fellow. You were probably too prudent, too timid. There are women who prefer to have the appearance of yielding only to violence."

" You see, my trousers split; that embarrassed me the first time I called on her."

" You ought to have worn an apron; then it wouldn't have made any difference about your trousers."

" Freluchon, your constant jesting with a man so miserable as I am is barbarous; for my love for that woman gives me neither truce nor rest."

" The deuce ! and the memory of the adored Eléonore ? have we left that under the shed ? "

Chamoureau took his coat and trousers and was about to depart without a word; but Freluchon stopped him.

" Where are you going? "

" I am going away."

" You run off because I speak of Eléonore! *Quantum mutatus ab illo!*—Come, stay; I won't mention her again; and if, instead of that, I should make you the fortunate vanquisher of the superb Sainte-Suzanne——"

" What! Sainte-Suzanne? You know—he knows— Monsieur Edmond, did you tell him? "

" No, no! Edmond hasn't told me anything; I learned of your intrigue at Rouen; news of that sort is despatched at once by the railroads."

" I don't understand."

" That makes no difference; it's enough for you to know that your friend is at work for you, and that, knowing that you sighed for a cruel beauty, he said to himself:

" ' Chamoureau must be made happy! '

" And I have manoeuvred so well and pulled the wires so skilfully with the fair Thélénie, that I have changed her views completely with respect to you! The result is that she gives you an assignation for nine o'clock this evening, on the Champs-Elysées. She will be in a coupé opposite the Jardin d'Hiver."

" It can't be possible! No, I know you, Freluchon— you're playing a joke on me! "

" I give you my word of honor—and you know that I don't give it lightly—that the charming person with whom you are in love will be in a coupé, opposite the Jardin d'Hiver, at nine o'clock this evening; and that the coachman will open the carriage door, if you open your left hand twice in front of him.—Do you believe me, now?"

"Dear Freluchon! embrace me!"

"I knew it would be so: he is the one who wants to embrace me now. Oh! these men! Someone has said: 'Woman changes oft, and foolish is the man,' et cetera; one might as fitly say: 'Man changes oft, and an ass is the man who trusts him!'—I am rewriting François I; but there have been those who have ventured to rewrite Racine; and frankly I think that he was a greater poet than François."

"In heaven's name, Freluchon, repeat what you just told me! This evening, at nine o'clock, I shall find Thélénie in a coupé on the Champs-Elysées?"

"Yes, in front of the Jardin d'Hiver, on the other side of the avenue."

"And, to induce the coachman to open the door, I am to shake my fist at him?"

"Sapristi! if that's the way you hear! you are to open your left hand twice, before his face."

"Ah! very good! I will open my left hand twice. But, what the devil!——"

"Well, what difficulty is there about that?"

"When I have opened my left hand once, how am I to open it again?"

"Why, you idiot, you must close it again, of course!"

"Ah, yes! to be sure; I won't open it again till I have closed it. It is love that unsettles my mind. And I shall find Thélénie, she will be waiting for me, and she will not spurn my homage!"

"Damnation! my dear fellow, when a lady gives you an assignation at night, in a carriage, that doesn't indicate an intention to be very severe; and if you don't come out of the affair the victor, it will be your own fault."

"You are right. This time I will be a Don Juan, a Richelieu! I will hurl myself into the coupé like a bomb! The rest will take care of itself."

"Bravo! I recognize you now."

"My dearest wish is gratified."

"You must tell us to-morrow how it goes off. That is all I ask for my reward."

"I'll tell you everything; I will conceal nothing from my friends henceforth. Dear Freluchon! dear Edmond! —But what's the matter with Monsieur Edmond? he doesn't say anything."

"Don't you know that he is in love, like you?"

"Oho! with whom, pray?"

"A young person—who lives with a lady who bought a country house at Chelles."

"The deuce! Mademoiselle Agathe!"

Edmond emerged from his reverie, crying:

"Agathe! who mentioned her name?—Have you seen those ladies again, Chamoureau? have you been to their house?"

"I? not once. What would you have me go there for, now? Madame Dalmont insisted on paying me my fee on the spot, and the transaction is concluded."

"She's a widow, isn't she, Chamoureau?"

"Yes, she's a widow."

"And she hasn't a large fortune?"

"No; she told me herself that her means were small, and that she was going into the country to live as a matter of taste and for economy's sake."

"And Agathe—that lovely girl?"

"Mademoiselle Agathe is an orphan, and has no other friend or protector than the lady with whom she lives. That's all I know about them.—But, pardon me, my friends, it's three o'clock already; allow me to take my leave. I will take my clothes away; I'll wear them to-night; these trousers, anyhow, are not too tight for me."

"What! you are going to carry that bundle?"

"I shall take a cab. Your hand, Freluchon. Now I am yours, in life and in death!—Au revoir, messieurs, until to-morrow."

Chamoureau returned home. The day, although far advanced, seemed mortally long to him. He set about curling his hair, perfuming himself, in short, trying to make himself most seductive.

He went out at five o'clock, to dine; but joy took away his appetite. When caused by love, joy sometimes produces that effect.

While he toyed aimlessly with a beefsteak, he said to himself:

"How strange women are in their whims! This one refuses to receive me at her house, and waits for me at night, in a carriage, on the Champs-Elysées! Still, she may have reasons for being afraid to receive me at home. Who knows that she isn't afraid of that Monsieur Beauregard, who used to be her lover, as he says? perhaps it isn't true; there are so many men who brag of triumphs they never obtained! It matters little to me, after all! if she shares my flame, am I not too fortunate?"

Chamoureau left the restaurant and entered a café, called for all the newspapers, did not read one, looked at his watch every instant, and finally exclaimed:

"At last, it is dark! Ah! how impatiently I have been waiting for this!"

But it was early in April, and it grew dark rather early. It was only seven o'clock. However, our widower left the café, saying to himself:

"I'll walk slowly to the Champs-Elysées; that will take up time. It's a little cold, but it's fine. Besides, I don't propose to be late; a gallant man should always arrive first at the rendezvous."

Although he walked very slowly from Boulevard Montmartre, it was not yet eight o'clock when he reached the rond-point on the Champs-Elysées. But it was absolutely dark. Our lover consulted his watch, heaved a deep sigh, and paced to and fro in front of the entrance to the Jardin d'Hiver.

He had been walking there for three-quarters of an hour, passing many carriages; but not one of them was

standing at the place designated. At last, about a quarter
to nine, a cab coming from the Barrière de l'Etoile stopped
in front of the entrance. Chamoureau instantly drew
near and walked around it; the curtains were lowered,
which fact convinced him that his inamorata was inside.

He hastened toward the driver, who had remained on
his box, and putting his left hand close to the lantern,
opened it twice.

The man stared at him in amazement, but said finally:

"I am engaged; I have a fare."

"I know that you have a fare; but it's that fare who
expects me; don't you see this sign?"

And he opened his left hand again.

"You offer me ten francs, I can see that plain enough,"
said the cabman; "that's all right, and if I wasn't taken,
I'd say at once: 'Get in, bourgeois'; but I can't do it."

"Bless me! how stupid the man is! Can she have forgotten to tell him what signs I was to make?"

And again Chamoureau opened his left hand for the
benefit of the driver, who shook his head, saying:

"You might offer me twenty francs—I tell you I've
got somebody in my carriage!"

"And I tell you again that I am well aware of it; and
I repeat that that somebody expects me."

"If you're expected, get in; it's all one to me."

Chamoureau asked nothing better; he threw the door
open violently, entered the vehicle, and found himself
in the presence of a lady and gentleman, to whom his
advent was evidently most unwelcome, for the gentleman

took him by the shoulders and threw him out of
the cab, giving him no time to put his foot on the step,
and crying:

"Who is this insolent villain who dares to enter a carriage that is occupied? Did anyone ever hear of such
audacity! Driver, why did you let this man enter? Were
you asleep?"

"Mon Dieu! he made a lot of signs and told me he
was the one you were waiting for."

"I beg pardon, a thousand pardons, monsieur! I
made a mistake, an error, I see it now; I am waiting
for a carriage with a lady, and I thought——"

"You're an idiot, nothing less; and if I were not with
a lady, I would treat you as you deserve."

Chamoureau bowed to the gentleman and walked
hastily away in order not to hear any more.

"I made a mistake," he said to himself; "I saw well
enough that I had made a mistake. I can understand
that man's indignation; I was entirely in the wrong. It
was my impatience that caused it; for it isn't nine o'clock
yet, and the appointment is for nine. I ought to have
known that I was mistaken: it wasn't even a coupé, but
a cab, and an old one at that! The superb Sainte-
Suzanne would not ride in such a miserable vehicle! I
am too effervescent! I must be calm and watch.—Poor
man! how I did disturb him!"

The agent walked some distance toward the barrier;
but at last he heard the clocks strike nine, and he at once
retraced his steps. As he drew near the place appointed,

he saw that the cab was no longer in front of the Jardin d'Hiver; but on the other side of the avenue a coupé had drawn up.

Chamoureau walked toward the coupé in a state of agitation that caused him to stumble at every step. When he was within a few feet, he stopped, in order to examine the carriage closely. It was a very stylish equipage; the driver was not on his box, but was standing by his horses and seemed to be scrutinizing the people who passed.

"This time I am on the right track," thought Chamoureau. And he walked resolutely toward the coachman, and made the signal agreed upon.

The coachman replied by a slight nod and lost no time in opening the carriage door. Our lover instantly jumped in, head first, and the door closed behind him.

It was in fact Thélénie, awaiting Edmond at the place she had designated; but as he had long since ceased to come to the rendezvous she appointed, now, having heard the clock strike nine without bringing her unfaithful lover, she had given up all hope of seeing him, when the door opened and a man rushed in like a bomb.

Thélénie did not doubt for an instant that it was Edmond, for her coachman had received his orders; he was to open the door only at the preconcerted signal. The darkness inside the carriage made it impossible for her to distinguish the man's features. She threw herself into Chamoureau's arms and kissed him tenderly, exclaiming:

"Here you are at last! You have come! You have listened to my voice! You are restored to me! Ah! this time it is forever, isn't it? you won't leave me any more?"

And Chamoureau, transported by the kisses that were lavished upon him, had the ill luck to answer:

"Why, fascinating creature, I have never intended to leave you, I have always offered you the most tender love, the most passionate, the most——"

He had not time to finish his sentence; a cry of rage issued from Thélénie, she roughly pushed him away, and in an instant had raised the curtains and opened the door.

"It isn't Edmond!" she shrieked; "oh! the villain! —Who are you, monsieur? who are you? who gave you permission to enter my carriage?"

Our widower, who had no idea of the meaning of that sudden change in the lady's mood, faltered:

"I am—but you know perfectly well—Chamoureau— whom you expected—at least, that is what Freluchon told me.—I am that adorer——"

But Thélénie had already had time to identify the business agent, and she pointed to the open door, saying in a voice that trembled with wrath:

"Get out, monsieur, get out at once, and say to those who sent you here that this jest will cost them dear. As for you, never let me see your face again."

"But, madame, I don't understand; I swear to you that I really believed——"

" Go!—or I will call my coachman!"

Thélénie's eyes flashed fire and their expression at that moment was so menacing that Chamoureau backed out of the carriage in deadly terror. He was no sooner on the ground than the coachman drove away.

" My hat! my hat! I have left my hat in your carriage!" cried Chamoureau, running after the coupé.

A window was lowered and the hat thrown out into the avenue. At that moment a calèche passed at a rapid pace; our widower was obliged to jump aside in a hurry, and one wheel of the calèche passed over the ill-fated hat. Chamoureau stooped and picked up the shapeless mass, swearing in very emphatic fashion. Then he returned to the sidewalk, trying to restore some shape to his hat, and not noticing two young men, arm-in-arm, a few steps away, who were nearly convulsed with laughter.

XXII

AN INHERITANCE

That same evening, after he had been home to get another hat, because the first one was entirely ruined, Chamoureau bent his steps toward Freluchon's. He was beside himself with rage and could hardly speak.

" I am going to Fre—Fre—Freluchon's," he stuttered to the concierge.

But Freluchon was not at home; he had gone with Edmond to the Champs-Elysées, at the time appointed by Thélénie, and there the two young men, concealed in the shadow, had witnessed part of the adventure, and had divined the rest when they saw Chamoureau tumbling out of the coupé very soon after he had entered. They laughed like maniacs when they saw the unlucky agent running after his hat. Then they returned to the centre of Paris.

"You say Freluchon isn't in?" stammered Chamoureau, when the concierge stopped him on his way upstairs. "Well, then I will come again to-morrow morning; tell him to wait for me! tell him that I forbid him to go out until he has seen me! and that he hasn't heard the last of this! You understand: he hasn't heard the last of this!"

The concierge heard doubtless; but he did not seem at all impressed by the way in which Chamoureau emphasized his words, and the latter went away, muttering:

"I have been victimized by Freluchon's jests too long; this thing has got to come to an end!"

The next morning, at seven o'clock, Chamoureau entered Freluchon's bedroom; his friend was still in bed and shouted when he saw him:

"May the devil take you for coming to wake me at this hour; I was sleeping like one of the blessed,—the blessed, you know, sleep splendidly;—you come too early!"

"I am glad to see, Freluchon, that you have followed the orders I gave your concierge—and waited for me."

"You! give orders to my concierge! that is delightful, on my word!"

"No joking; I didn't come here to joke. I am perfectly serious.—What! you are lying down again?"

"Yes, I am still sleepy; but that makes no difference, say on."

"Freluchon, your conduct is shameful! You laid a trap for me; you made a fool of me—of me, your intimate friend, formerly the husband of that Eléonore in whom you were so deeply interested! You send me to an assignation which was not for me. Alas! it was not I who was expected; I found that out only too soon!— If you had caused me to play that scene with a woman who was perfectly indifferent to me, I would be the first to laugh at it; but you know that I love Madame Sainte-Suzanne, that I adore her, that I would give the whole world to be on good terms with her, and you expose me to her wrath—what do I say?—to her fury!—When she saw that I was not the person she was waiting for, she was a tigress, a lioness; she drove me from her presence, and forbade me ever to show my face before her again! —Ah! it is that that distresses me above everything! forbidden to see her again! and this is your work. What have you to say in answer?—Come, what can you say to justify yourself?—He doesn't answer! May God forgive me if he isn't snoring! he's gone to sleep again!"

Chamoureau seized Freluchon's arm and shook it violently; whereupon the little man opened his eyes and cried:

"Go on! I am listening!"

"No, you were asleep; but I propose that you shall listen to me. I am going to begin over again what I have just said, and I shall keep on that way till night if you don't listen."

"In that case, I prefer to have done with it at once."

Freluchon rubbed his eyes and Chamoureau began his speech anew; when he had finished, the little man sat up in bed.

"And you have the audacity," he cried, "to come here and complain! Imbecile! I do what I can to make you happy, and you are not content! So much for obliging ungrateful curs! this is how they reward you!"

"What do you say? to make me happy by——"

"By sending you to the arms of the woman you adore, yes, monsieur; you weren't the man she expected; no, of course you weren't, since Edmond was. But I didn't tell you, because I knew that timid as you are, you wouldn't dare to go to that rendezvous if you had known that you were to take another man's place."

"No, most certainly I wouldn't have gone."

"Well! wasn't it very hard on you to go to meet a lovely woman, at night, in a carriage? A woman whom you adore, who is cruel to you—I arrange for you to have a nocturnal tête-à-tête with her, and you complain! But tell me, my poor fellow, how you behaved during that tête-à-tête, that you were sent about your business in such a hurry?"

"Why, I was no sooner inside the carriage, and the door closed—it was too dark to see anything—when the lady threw herself into my arms, calling me the most loving names and giving me the most burning kisses."

"My word! and still he complains!"

"I was enchanted, transported! but when she said: 'You won't leave me any more; this time it is forever!' I replied: 'Why, I never had any intention of leaving you, for I adore you.'"

"Ah! there spoke my blockhead! instead of keeping quiet, of making the most of the mistake—in short, of being happy! My chatterbox spoils everything by jabbering like a magpie! Why, you wretch, if you hadn't breathed a word, you would be at this moment the conqueror of the haughty Thélénie!"

"You should say, that if it had gone any further, she'd have killed me when she found that she'd been deceived, as she was so enraged by the few kisses she gave me!"

"She wouldn't have killed you; women don't kill men for that sort of offence."

"What about Lucretia?"

"What in the devil has Lucretia to do with it; what connection is there between Thélénie and Tarquin's wife? —I say, on the contrary, that she wouldn't have driven you away, because, when a thing is done, why, it's done! She'd have scolded you at first, but then she'd have forgiven you because she couldn't do anything else."

"Is it possible? Do you really think she would have forgiven me, Freluchon?—Oh! unlucky wretch that I am! why did I speak? why did I let her hear my voice? He is right; it began so well! *Nox erat! Ardebat Alexim!* Oh! I am in despair to think that I spoke!"

"And when one has done one's utmost to make one's friend happy, to gratify his most ardent desires, monsieur appears in a rage, he complains, he almost threatens one with his wrath!"

"I was wrong, Freluchon; forgive me, my dear fellow. I realize now that I was wrong. But what can you expect? all these things upset me—these alternations of joy and sorrow; I no longer know where I am; I can't seem to see.—Come, my dear fellow; you have forgiven me— what do you advise now?"

"What do I advise? Oh! now, my poor friend, your case is ruined, totally ruined, the best thing that you can do is not to think of this woman any more, to forget her entirely!"

Chamoureau rushed about the room, crying:

"But I can't do it! it's impossible! every time that she maltreats me and spurns me, I am more in love than ever! Forget that magnificent woman!—for she is magnificent; and in her anger, when she glared at me like a panther that contemplates devouring you, she was superb! I have never seen anything so fine as those eyes when she said to me: 'I will be revenged; say to your friends that this jest will cost them dear!'"

"Ah! she said that, did she?"

" Yes; so you and Monsieur Edmond are duly warned."

" Oh! we have no fear of that woman's vengeance! "

" If I were in your place, I should dread it; she's one of the women who don't look as if they weren't up to snuff, as the plebeians say! "

" Forget her, Chamoureau; that's all I have to say to you."

" Forget her! why, it's more impossible than ever, now that I have tasted her kisses! now that I know her way of kissing!—Ah! my friend! I had never been kissed like that, even by Eléonore! "

" I can believe that! Your wife knew that it was you she was kissing, while this woman took you for another."

" That isn't it at all! it's because Eléonore wasn't passionate, loving, maddening, like the lovely Thélénie."

" Aha! you propose to cry down your wife now, do you? That's very pretty! We are becoming ungrateful! Chamoureau, you make me blush! I shall not be surprised to hear you say in a day or two: ' How glad I am that I'm a widower! ' "

" That isn't what I meant."

" No, but that is your thought!—Look you, I am speaking seriously now, so be reasonable; your love for this woman is absolutely devoid of sense."

" Adieu, Freluchon! "

" Come some day and dine with me; we'll go to the *Folies-Nouvelles,* a charming little theatre, where one always sees some very light-hearted females; you will very soon find someone to divert your thoughts."

" Adieu, Freluchon! "

Chamoureau would not hear of any distractions.

He hurried away from his friend's rooms, went home, shut himself in his office, paid no heed to his char-woman, who told him that several clients had come to inquire for him, neglected all the business that had been entrusted to him, and when the persons who had em-ployed him came to find out how their affairs were pro-gressing, he stared at them with a dazed expression and replied:

" What? what is it? what do you want? "

" That little matter of mine, monsieur—what condi-tion is it in? "

" What's that?—what matter? I don't know anything about it."

" What! you don't know anything about it! Do you mean to say that you haven't attended to it? "

" Apparently not."

" In that case, monsieur, if you don't propose to attend to it, I will employ another agent."

" As you please; it's all the same to me."

" Indeed! it's all the same to you, is it? Then give me my papers, instantly! "

Chamoureau gave up the papers, the clients went away in a rage, and the office gradually became deserted. Cha-moureau passed the day seated at his desk, with his head resting on his hands.

" My master certainly's got a screw loose," said Ma-dame Monin to the concierge; " he's been cracked ever

since the night he dressed as a Spaniard. The man's
going crazy; I don't dare to buy charcoal for him, I'm
afraid of finding him suffocated to death some fine
morning."

A fortnight had passed since our widower had become
as despondent as Werther, when Madame Monin brought
him a letter one morning. Chamoureau took the letter
with an indifferent air, broke the seal, still thinking of
Thélénie, and read without at first paying much attention to what he was reading.

But soon his face changed, became animated; he
rubbed his eyes to assure himself that he read the letter
aright, then read it again, this time with the utmost care.
A cry of joy escaped from his lips and he slapped his
thighs, saying:

" Is it possible! I am not mistaken! Rich! rich!
twenty thousand francs a year—left me by that cousin—
my godfather—for he was my godfather, but I have
never heard a word from him. And he leaves me his
fortune, his whole fortune! and he had saved, in America, property worth twenty thousand francs a year!—
I must read the notary's letter again; I am still afraid
that I read it wrong, that I have made a mistake! "

Chamoureau had made no mistake: a distant relation,
who had been his godfather, and whose name he had
never heard mentioned since the day he was baptized, had
made his fortune in America, and had never married.
Suddenly a longing to see his native country once more
had come to him; he had turned his fortune into cash

and had sailed for France. On landing at Havre, he was taken violently ill; he had barely time to send for a notary, and as he did not know what to do with the fortune he had brought back with him, he remembered that he had a godson and made that godson his sole legatee.

Such was the information which a notary of Paris, who had been communicated with by a confrère at Havre, had transmitted to Chamoureau, requesting him to call at his office as soon as possible, provided with all the documents necessary to establish his identity.

Having read once more the letter that announced this unexpected, unhoped-for good fortune, which instantly changed his whole future, Chamoureau ran to his bedroom to dress to go out; and he jumped and danced and sang and did a thousand foolish things, so that his servant, seeing him waltzing about the room as he put on his suspenders, stopped short, terrified beyond words.

" What in the world's the matter with you, monsieur? " she cried; " here you are dancing, waltzing all by yourself! "

" The matter, Madame Monin, the matter! Ah! you see before you the happiest of men!

> " Wealth, in this world
> Thou dost all for me! "

" Mon Dieu! monsieur, you were so dismal this morning! you looked like an undertaker's mute! "

" But now I am rich, Mère Monin, very rich! I have inherited twenty thousand francs a year! This letter tells me of it."

"Good God! is it possible, monsieur? An inheritance you didn't expect?"

"No more than I expect to be elected to the Academy. —Rich! wealthy! Now I shall no longer be despised; my homage will no longer be spurned; that adored woman will be mine!

"What a new life for me! ah! blessed change! My grief has passed away like summer clouds."

My hat—my handkerchief—my gloves—I have all that I require. Ah! my certificates of birth and of baptism and marriage. No, I don't need the last; it's of no consequence. Now I'm off."

"Monsieur has not drunk his coffee."

"Drink it, Madame Monin, drink it; it is no more than fair that you should partake of my good fortune."

Chamoureau called on the notary, who confirmed what he had written and advised him to go at once to Havre, in order to obtain immediate possession of the fortune which was held at his disposal there.

That same day, our legatee took the express train for Havre. There he exhibited to the notary all the documents which proved that he was the Sigismond Chamoureau to whom Monsieur Eustache-Hector Chamoureau, his cousin and godfather, had bequeathed all his property.

Two days later the former business agent was back in Paris, armed with the well-filled wallet which his godfather had bequeathed to him. It had all come so suddenly and been done so quickly that, when he was in his own rooms once more, Chamoureau wondered if he were not the plaything of a dream, and if he had really become rich. But the rotund wallet was in his hands; he could feel and count the bank-notes, the government obligations, and several drafts accepted by the richest bankers in Paris. Thereupon he said to himself:

"No, I am not dreaming; I am really in possession of a very respectable fortune; therefore I may aspire to the woman whom I idolize. I must not delay; my fate must be decided at once."

He seated himself at his desk and wrote:

"Madame:

"It is no longer a humble real estate agent who lays his heart and his hand at your feet; my position has changed. An inheritance which I was far from expecting, but of which I have just come into possession, gives me an income of twenty thousand francs, in addition to twenty-five hundred which I already had.—I do not refer to my business, which I have abandoned.—I am therefore possessed of twenty-two thousand five hundred francs a year. This fortune I place at your disposal, soliciting anew the title of your husband, which I should be proud to bear.

"If I have offended you, forgive me; I was absolutely innocent in the affair of the Champs-Elysées, where I went confident of my good fortune, and no less deceived than yourself. But since I have known you, my love for you has never diminished; on the contrary, it has grown greater and greater every day. I will not ask any questions concerning the past, and I shall always have the blindest confidence with respect to the present and the future. I await your reply."

Having signed this letter, Chamoureau went out and gave it to a messenger in whom he had confidence.

" Ten francs for you," he said, " if you bring me an answer. If she says that she will write, insist, implore her to give you a line on the spot. I will wait for you in this café, where I shall absorb much chartreuse, to give me patience and courage."

Since the adventure on the Champs-Elysées, the fair Thélénie's humor was uniformly morose; sometimes she passed whole days absorbed in her thoughts. Her friend Héloïse's society had not the power to divert her, and when that young woman said to her:

" Do you mean to pass your whole life regretting that little fellow? "

Thélénie would reply:

" I no longer regret him, I no longer love him; I hate him now ! But I shall not be satisfied until I have had my revenge."

Chamoureau's messenger found Thélénie in this frame of mind. She read the letter which was brought to her, and to which she was told that an answer was expected. She read it a second time more carefully, then handed it to Mademoiselle Héloïse, saying:

" Here, read this proposal that is made to me."

Mademoiselle Héloïse punctured her perusal of the letter with many " ohs ! " and " ahs ! " and when she had read it through she exclaimed:

" Mon Dieu! why, this is magnificent!—twenty-two thousand five hundred francs a year! it's superb! And a man who will ask no questions concerning the past and will have blind confidence in the future! Why, that's a model husband! Is it possible that you can refuse all that? "

" I find it difficult to believe that it's true; I suppose it's another miserable joke on the part of those who played that detestable trick on me before. As for this Chamoureau, he is a downright idiot, who is quite capable of seconding the schemes of those men because he doesn't suspect them."

" But if it should be true! a splendid fortune, my dear ! "

Thélénie rang for her maid.

" Who brought this letter, Mélie? "

" A messenger, madame."

" Is he still here? "

" Yes, madame, he absolutely insists on having an answer."

" Let him come in."

The messenger was ushered into the presence of the ladies. Thélénie examined him for some seconds, then asked him:

" Who gave you this letter? "

" Monsieur Chamoureau, madame."

" You know him, then? "

" Yes, madame, he often employs me. He keeps a real estate office; I know him well."

" Was he alone when he handed you this letter? "

" Yes, madame, he came to my stand for me; he was all alone."

" What did he say to you? "

" He said—Well! he seems to be very anxious to have a written answer from madame, for he promised me ten francs if I'd bring him just a line."

" Very well; you shall earn your ten francs."

Thélénie took her writing-case and wrote:

" I will receive you at my apartment this evening. But bring the proofs of what you tell me, or you won't leave my house with both your ears."

She handed the note to the messenger, who left the house with a radiant face. He had no sooner gone than the door opened again and Monsieur Beauregard entered the apartment, unannounced. At sight of him, Thélénie turned pale; then she motioned to her friend, saying:

" Go into the salon while I talk with monsieur."

Mademoiselle Héloïse rose and left the room, muttering:

" Well, well! I wonder if this is a brother, too! at all events, he isn't of the same type as the other! "

XXIII

CHAMOUREAU TAKES THE PLUNGE
HEADFOREMOST

Beauregard threw himself upon a chair, facing Thélénie. When Mademoiselle Héloïse had left them alone,
they gazed at each other for some time without speaking;
but one could read on their faces that the same thought
was not in the minds of both.

The beautiful courtesan pressed her lips together in
a convulsive fashion, her eyes avoided her companion's
and wandered about the room, and she opened and closed
her hands with a sort of nervous contraction of the mus-
cles that indicated an impatience which she could hardly
control.

Beauregard, on the contrary, seemed perfectly calm
and placid; he amused himself watching the woman before him, and the ironical expression of his eyes might
have created the impression that he took a secret pleasure
in the annoyance which his presence caused her.

"May I be permitted to know to what I owe the honor
of seeing you, monsieur?" said Thélénie, breaking the
silence at last.

"Ah! so you assume, madame, that I must have some
special reason for coming to see you? Why should you

not think that I am impelled solely by the desire to do homage to your beauty?"

"Because I know that my beauty has long been entirely indifferent to you; we have got beyond the complimentary stage!"

"Which may be interpreted to mean that we no longer tell each other falsehoods, may it not?"

"I don't interpret it so! When you told me that you thought me pretty, that I pleased you, I was pretty enough to justify me in believing that you meant it."

"Yes, we men sometimes tell the truth; I am convinced that, as a general rule, we lie less than women."

"Do you think so? it is quite possible! Did you come here to work out that problem?"

"No, indeed; it would take too long; I should prefer the labors of Hercules. Restrain your impatience, madame, I am coming to the purpose of my visit. The liaison which once existed between us two was not without result, as you know."

Thélénie turned paler and pressed her lips together more tightly; but she kept silent and waited.

"In short, to speak plainly, you had a child, whose paternity you chose to attribute to me; in fact, I do not deny it, as the step which I am taking at this moment sufficiently proves. Yes, we had a few months of ardent passion, of exalted sentiments! we even went so far as to live away from the world for some time, in a chalet, surrounded by goats and cheese. It was superb, but it didn't last long; things that are carried to excess never do last.—Briefly, you returned to Paris, and I had gone to Italy for a little trip, I believe, when you wrote me that you had given birth to a son—for it was a boy, was it not, madame?"

"Yes, monsieur, it was a boy; and you didn't even answer my letter."

"Because I was very much occupied then; but when I returned to Paris, nine months later, I lost no time in calling upon you; I had some difficulty in finding you; I had even more in obtaining an audience. You were so surrounded by adorers, courtiers, slaves! You had them in all ranks of life—bankers, Hungarian counts, speculators!—Oh! I must do you the justice to say that you have always had a very marked penchant for finance! —and you no longer cared to receive a visit from me."

"It was my turn, monsieur, to be very much occupied."

"My reign had gone by; I do not presume to make any complaint on that score, madame!"

"And you are wise, for you have no right to; didn't you leave me first—to go to Italy?"

"Possibly; it may be that I had reasons for leaving you. But let us not recriminate; that matter is not in question now. When I saw you again, my first remark was to ask you where my son was; and you replied that he died three months after his birth."

"I certainly did, monsieur; and as it was true, I could make no other answer."

"At first, I was satisfied with that answer; and I left you; but later, other ideas occurred to me, and I called on you again. I found the same difficulty in speaking to you, for you seemed to shun me, and to display the greatest persistency in avoiding my presence."

" Why should I have desired it, monsieur? For a long time we had ceased to have anything to say to each other."

" Pardon me, madame; I had certain questions to ask you concerning the particulars of the child's death; and those questions seemed to annoy you exceedingly, for only with the very greatest difficulty did I succeed in obtaining the answers I desired."

" There are subjects which it is painful to revive; that was one of them; it could not fail to renew my grief."

" Oh! as for your grief, madame, you will pardon me if I refuse to believe in it. I think that maternal love does not fill a very large place in your heart."

" Why do you think that, monsieur? "

" Because, if it were otherwise, you would have been the first to talk to me about our son, to give me a thousand and one details of his birth and death. Whereas, on the contrary, your answers on those subjects were so short and sharp that it was easy to see that you were in a hurry to put an end to the interview."

" Did you expect me to give you very many details of the life of a child that lived three months? "

" A mother would have found them."

" I was not a mother, then? "

" No, not in the full acceptation of the word. However, after making me repeat my questions many times,

you told me that you had entrusted your child to a nurse
who lived at Saint-Denis. I asked you the woman's
name,—you had forgotten it; but I was so persistent
that you finally remembered the name: it was Madame
Mathieu, the wife of a farm hand. I asked you her address. Oh! then you jumped from your seat in your
wrath, as if I had asked you where you had hidden a
treasure! Again your memory was at fault. You finally
told me that the woman lived near the church on the
square, and that that was all you knew."

"Well, what then?"

"Then I went to Saint-Denis myself; I asked for
Madame Mathieu, wife of a farm hand; nobody knew
such a person. I visited all the houses near the church,
and it was impossible for me to discover that nurse. I
found two women named Mathieu at Saint-Denis, but
one was eighty years old, the other sixty-six; so that
neither of them could be the one I was looking for—
quite uselessly, for you had lied to me."

"I beg you, monsieur, to choose your expressions more
carefully."

"I have no need to be considerate toward you, madame,
for I know you and I know what you are, what you are
worth.—A melancholy knowledge, for which I have paid
very dear!"

"What do you mean by that, monsieur? It seems to
me that you never ruined yourself for me."

"Thank God! I left that pleasure to others; but you
know very well what I mean.—To resume, madame, you

lied when you gave me the address at Saint-Denis of a nurse who never existed."

"I told you all that I knew, monsieur; it was not my fault if the woman had left the place where she once lived."

"Peasants don't move about like lorettes, and if they do happen to change their place of abode, everyone knows everyone else so well in a village, that it is easy to find them."

"Saint-Denis is not a village, monsieur, it's a town."

"Once more, madame, I am convinced that you lied in everything that you told me on the subject of that child."

"Why should I have lied to you, monsieur?"

"Because you did not wish to be a mother; because you had never manifested anything but regret at being one; because you were capable of sending the poor little fellow to the Foundling Hospital."

"That is a shocking thing for you to say to me, monsieur!"

"Very well! I do not propose that my son shall be brought up by charity; I want to take the child with me; I want to love him, and I want him to love me. Those sentiments in my mouth surprise you, do they not, madame? But it is all true. I have never had any great confidence in love or friendship, but there must be such a thing as filial love, for I feel the love of a father.— Moreover, for some time past I have suffered from ennui; I am weary of the pleasures one procures with money; it

seems to me that if I had that child with me, it would occupy my mind, it would make a different man of me. My
youth is at an end; I have carried everything to excess;
but paternal love will afford me enjoyment of a new
kind. You will say perhaps that I have waited rather
long before having these ideas, and it is true; but each
day carries away with it some illusion, my passions are
dying out; I feel that I must have something to attach
me to life.—Come, Thélénie, be honest for once. Tell
me what you did with that child, who still lives, perhaps.
Yes, I have a presentiment that he is alive. He must
be seven years and a half old now. Tell me where he is,
and don't be afraid; he will never ask you for anything,
you will never have to spend a sou for him; more than
that, I shall not tell him who his mother is, he will not
know you! It seems to me that you can ask nothing
more. Tell me, where is the child? I have a cab below,
I will go and get him."

"I have told you, monsieur, all that I can tell you
on the subject of your son; it is useless for you to ask
me anything more."

"You have told me a parcel of infamous lies!" cried
Beauregard, whose eyes assumed a threatening expression; and he sprang to his feet, pushing his chair back
with such violence that he overturned it. Having made
the circuit of the room two or three times, he con-
fronted Thélénie once more, and demanded with renewed
emphasis:

"What have you done with my son?"

"I tell you again, monsieur, that he died at the age of three months."

"Where?"

"At the nurse's."

"Then find that nurse for me, let me see her, speak to her, find out where the child was buried."

"I can only tell you again what I have already told you about the woman: she lived at Saint-Denis. It isn't my fault if she has left her house—and the neighborhood too, very likely. I could not answer for such things."

"But when a child dies, no matter how young it may be, there is always a certificate of death; that certificate the nurse should have sent you with a minute of the expenses for the child's burial, for which she was entitled to be reimbursed; such things as that, nurses never forget to do. Well! show me that certificate."

"I lost it when I moved."

"Ah! you are a villain, capable of anything!—Poor Duronceray! who lost his head because I took his mistress from him. Gad! he has no idea how much he owes me! But men never look beyond the present; they never foresee the future."

Beauregard paced the floor for some time longer; it was evident that he was trying to restrain his anger, to recover his tranquillity; but when his eyes rested on Thélénie, he turned them away as if he had seen a serpent. She, on the other hand, seemed to enjoy the torments she inflicted on her former lover; it was her turn now to watch him with a sarcastic expression, affecting a calmness that she was far from feeling.

Some minutes passed thus, Thélénie contenting herself with picking up the chair Beauregard had overturned.

At last he halted in front of her once more, saying:

"Your mind is made up—you refuse to tell me anything more?"

"Because I have nothing more to tell you."

"Very good! now mark well what I say to you: I shall seek for that child, and if I succeed in finding him, I shall teach him to hate and despise the woman who has tried to deprive him of his father's affection! You seem to defy me. You make a great mistake; for I am your enemy now, and I shall act accordingly whenever I find an opportunity. I had forgiven your inconstancy, your conduct, which has been decidedly scandalous at times. One may be vicious without being really wicked; but now I see that everything about you is perverse—mind as well as heart. Your nature is complete!"

"It seems that yours consists now in making impertinent remarks; but I care little for them."

"Beware if you find me in your path! and as for that unhappy child, if I succeed in finding him, rest assured that, though you are in the midst of the most brilliant festivity, be it ball or reception, he will appear and present his respects to you. Adieu!"

Beauregard abruptly left the room after these last words, and Thélénie, who had turned pale at his concluding threat, soon recovered herself.

" Do what you please," she muttered, " you won't find your son! that would require a combination of chances, —so extraordinary—no, it is impossible! So I will simply forget Monsieur Beauregard, who will leave me in peace hereafter, I trust. The idea of that man—a ne'er-do-well, a confirmed rake, a man who believes in nothing and has passed his life making fun of every-thing—taking it into his head to feel a father's love for a little boy that he never saw, that he doesn't know! It is amusing, on my word!—I am very glad to avenge my-self on this Beauregard; he was the cause of my missing a fine fortune; for Duronceray would have married me, I am sure; he loved me so passionately. Oh! I made a great fool of myself!—But I must forget the past and think only of this new and brilliant position which is offered me."

Thélénie recalled Mademoiselle Héloïse, who, in ac-cordance with her habit, had not failed to listen at the door; that fact, however, did not prevent her from asking :

" What did that big bouncer, with his pretentious air, want of you? He always looks as if he were going to laugh in your face. I knew him by his yellow skin; he's the fellow who stalked into our box at the Opéra ball."

" Yes, that's the man."

" Was that man ever your lover? "

" Yes, unfortunately."

" Why unfortunately? "

"Because at that time I was adored, idolized by an extremely rich man, who would certainly have married me, if I had been true to him, or if he had not discovered that I was deceiving him."

"It would seem that you weren't so shrewd in those days as you are now; you wouldn't allow yourself to be caught to-day!"

"Mon Dieu! who can tell what may happen? the most adroit are taken by surprise sometimes. But let us dine at once. I can hardly wait for this evening, to find out if this Chamoureau has told me the truth. Twenty-two thousand five hundred francs a year—that's not bad."

"I should say so! I haven't even the odd hundreds!"

"With the ten thousand francs I have, it would make a fortune; I could go everywhere, be received everywhere!"

"You would become a very *comme il faut* person!"

The two friends dined in haste. Thélénie ate little; she was too preoccupied to have any appetite.

But Mademoiselle Héloïse did not lose a mouthful; and while her companion formed projects for the future, she confined herself to signifying her approval by an occasional monosyllable, never a complete sentence; at table she maintained a laconism which she did not lay aside until coffee was served.

Thélénie left the table to attend to her toilet. Although she was certain of pleasing the man whom she expected, she desired to augment the power of her charms; she

was familiar with all the expedients of the most con-
summate coquetry; she selected the colors which blended
best with the brilliancy of her eyes and her glossy hair;
in a word, she strove to make herself irresistible.

"Do you mean to turn the poor man's head altogether?" cried Mademoiselle Héloïse, as she swallowed
her second glass of *crême de vanille*.

"Oh! I know that that is already done; but as this is a
matter of great importance, I want to confirm my power;
for, as you may imagine, I shall impose conditions."

"Trust you for that!"

At eight o'clock the bell rang, and the maid announced
that Monsieur Chamoureau desired to know if he might
see madame.

Thélénie at once dismissed her friend, saying:

"Come to-morrow morning, and you shall know the
result of the interview."

Mademoiselle Héloïse would have preferred to step
into an adjoining room, in order to listen at the door;
but as she was accustomed to obey without comment, she
took her leave.

A moment later the former business agent was ushered
into the presence of Madame Sainte-Suzanne, who
awaited him, half reclining on a couch, in a pose calculated to deprive her adorer of what reason he still
possessed.

Chamoureau had put on the clothes he had recovered
from Freluchon, but he had paid less attention to his
dress than usual. The moment a man feels conscious

of being rich, he gives little heed to a multitude of trivial details which he formerly magnified into matters of moment. The fact is that wealth instantly imparts a self-possession, an assurance, which sometimes reaches the point of fatuity; and a man is no longer afraid of being unfashionable, when he can say to himself:

"Everyone knows that I have the means to do just as I please."

Chamoureau, then, appeared before Madame Sainte-Suzanne with less than his usual timidity; but when he saw how lovely, how fascinating she was, he became so perturbed that he instantly forgot the sentence he had prepared, and could only stammer:

"Madame—it is I who—I had the honor to write you —still more in love—more enamored—and—how are you?"

"Very well, monsieur, thank you. Won't you sit here beside me?"

Chamoureau made one leap to the couch, and dropped upon it with so much *abandon* that he broke one of the springs. But he reflected that he was rich and could venture to break many springs, even those of the steel skirts which ladies wear nowadays.

"Madame," he said, turning amorously toward Thélénie, "I believe that I must begin by apologizing for my share in that adventure—in the coupé on the Champs-Elysées. I assure you that I was far from suspecting— Freluchon and Edmond Didier had assured me——"

"Enough, Monsieur Chamoureau; I beg you not to refer to that affair again. I am convinced that you were not to blame, but those two gentlemen whom you have just named, they acted like vile blackguards, like true bar-room loafers; it doesn't surprise me on their part, and in a moment I will tell you my intentions with regard to them. Let us come now to your own affairs. Is it true that you have inherited money, monsieur?"

"Perfectly true, madame; twenty thousand francs a year."

"Why, that is a very pretty little fortune! Do you know, monsieur, that this is like a dream, like a tale from the *Thousand and One Nights,* or the conclusion of a comedy! A legacy which you did not expect, which fell upon you suddenly, from the clouds!"

"Good fortune almost always comes like that; when you are looking for it, it keeps you waiting!"

"True; indeed, there are some people who wait for it all their lives."

"Here is the wallet which contains my fortune; be good enough to examine it, madame, to make sure that I have not deceived you."

"Oh! I believe you, monsieur."

Nevertheless, although she said: "I believe you," the fair Thélénie closely scrutinized the wallet, which Chamoureau had placed in her lap. She examined the notes of the Treasury and of the Caisse d'Escompte, the drafts and the bank-notes; then she returned the wallet to Chamoureau, saying:

"Yes, you are rich; there are more than four hundred thousand francs there. What do you propose to do with this fortune?"

"Did I not write you that I offered it to you, with my hand?"

"Yes, you did write me that; so the offer is serious, is it?"

"Is it serious! as serious as is my love for you, which has become a passion that I cannot control."

"Do you know that you are a very dangerous man? that it's hard to resist you?"

Chamoureau's face became radiant; his eyes dilated like a cat's; his nostrils swelled; he seized a hand, which was not withdrawn, and kissed it again and again, puffing like a man who has ascended seven flights of stairs without stopping.

When Thélénie considered that her visitor had kissed her hand sufficiently, she withdrew it, saying in her sweetest voice—for she had inflections for all occasions:

"Be good, and let us talk seriously.—I am going to tell you what conditions I should impose if I consented to become your wife."

"Oh! I agree to them all beforehand."

"Let us not go so fast; I wish you to reflect before accepting; marriage is a chain which cannot be broken, in France; so one should not submit to it heedlessly.— Listen: I believe you to be a sensible man, of orderly habits; but as you may become a gambler, a spendthrift, a rake——"

"Oh! madame!"

"A man who is none of those things, may become one or the other! In a word, I wish to have the sole right to keep the key to the cash-box, to handle our fortune. You know that I myself have ten thousand francs a year."

"Yes, charming creature; but if you had nothing——"

"Let me speak. I desire that, when you marry me, you will certify that I have brought you property to the amount of four hundred thousand francs——"

"Certainly; twice that, if you choose."

"You will leave to me the management of our fortune. It will not diminish, never fear."

"I trust implicitly in you."

"I will give you two hundred francs a month for your clothes and your private expenses; I should say that that was enough, eh?"

"It is more than I need! I shan't spend it."

"You will not have to worry about the housekeeping; that will be my business and mine alone."

"That will be all the better."

"Do you agree to all these conditions?"

"With the greatest pleasure."

"It is well. But there is something else: I do not propose that the man whose wife I am, whose name I bear, shall continue to entertain the slightest relations with those persons who have insulted me, and whom I justly regard as my enemies. You must understand me? you must break off all relations with Messieurs Edmond Didier and Freluchon."

"That is understood. Indeed, I shall regret them very little; I will break with them forever!"

"Unless, however, as the result of events which cannot be foreseen, I myself authorize you to see them again."

"Of course, if you authorize me, I must obey you."

"Nor do I want you to speak to a certain Monsieur Beauregard, whom you have met here, I believe?"

"Ah, yes! a gentleman with a bilious complexion!"

"He is a detestable fellow; he paid court to me long ago, and as I refused to listen to him, he spreads all sorts of slanders and falsehoods about me!"

"I guessed as much, *belle dame;* I said to myself: 'This man abuses Madame de Sainte-Suzanne too much not to have been rigorously treated by her.'—I won't talk with him any more, and if he should try to talk to me, I'll turn my back on him at once."

"Very good; you are submissive. Look you, I believe you will be an excellent husband."

"With you, who would not be? no man could fail to be!"

"By the way, there is one thing more; it is a weakness, a puerile fancy, but I am set upon it nevertheless."

"Speak; I am here to obey."

"I don't like your name—Chamoureau; no, I don't like it at all!"

"The devil! that's rather embarrassing; I can't unbaptize myself."

"No, but listen: you were born somewhere."

" There's not the slightest doubt of that."

" Where were you born? "

" At Belleville."

" Belleville—very well; from this moment you are Chamoureau de Belleville, and you will not sign your name in any other way. Furthermore, you will be careful to use only the last name with any new acquaintances you may make; in that way, before long your name of Chamoureau will be entirely forgotten and you will be Monsieur de Belleville! "

" Pardieu! that's very nice! you have a mind as big as yourself! Monsieur de Belleville—that's an altogether coquettish name, and it pleases me beyond words.— Then you consent to become Madame de Belleville? "

" I must, since you promise to agree to everything I have stipulated."

" And to everything you may order in future; I swear it at your feet! "

And Chamoureau, rising from the couch, threw himself at Thélénie's feet, took her hand and kissed it with rapture, and even tried to take her knees; but his haughty conquest checked him, saying, with an air which had a faint suggestion of dignity:

" Monsieur! remember that I am to be your wife! and respect me until I no longer have the right to deny you anything."

" That is true! " cried Chamoureau, rising from the floor; " I am a villain! a blackguard! you did well to call me to order! I will lose no time about taking all the necessary steps, in order to enter into possession at the earliest possible moment of the charms which overthrow my reason."

"Do so; I approve your purpose and you have my consent; I will not conceal from you now that I desire the marriage to take place at once."

"Ah! dear love! you overwhelm me! I'm beside myself! You share my impatience! Oh! permit me to——"

"Well, monsieur?"

"Fichtre! I was going to put my foot in it again! Your hair is so lovely—you are so alluring!—Upon my word, I believe that I shall do well to go, for I can't answer for myself."

"Go; to-morrow I will look about for an apartment suited to our future position; you will trust me, I suppose?"

"In everything, and blindly. Whatever you do will be approved."

"Au revoir then, my dear De Belleville."

"De Belleville! really I am mad over that name. Au revoir, my goddess!"

Chamoureau kissed once more the hand that was offered him; then took his leave, as light as a feather, saying to himself:

"She loves me, she adores me, for she wants to be married at once! Oh! I'll not let the grass grow under my feet.—The devil! is it only three months since Eléonore died? I certainly am an idiot! it's an endless time since I became a widower!"

While her newly-rich adorer went away in raptures, Thélénie, alone once more, said to herself:

"A new name—an apartment in a distant quarter—a new position in society! Madame Sainte-Suzanne will be lost to sight, and she will hear no more of the Croques and the Beauregards. But she will be careful not to lose sight of those upon whom she is determined to be revenged!"

XXIV

VISITORS

Honorine and Agathe were installed in the little house at Chelles, and Poucette was with her new mistresses. The first days were devoted to arranging the furniture, deciding where to put the various things, making the necessary changes, and attending to the innumerable petty details which follow every change of abode, and which are of much more importance when one takes possession of a house one has purchased. During those early days the two friends hardly had time to walk in their garden or to glance at the landscape.

While they were occupied thus, assisted by Poucette, who did her best to give satisfaction and had already won the regard of her mistresses; while they arranged, placed and displaced furniture, and set the music and the books in order, the spring progressed. It was the middle of May, the time when the country is so lovely, when it is embellished every day by some new flower or leaf; and when at last Honorine and Agathe were able to sit at their windows and to go down to inspect their garden and stroll along the paths, they exclaimed with surprise and delight at the change which a few weeks had wrought in the face of nature.

Agathe would pause in admiration before a linden or an ash tree, crying:

"Ah! my dear! how lovely the trees are! I never saw this one before!"

"You did see it," Honorine would reply with a smile, "but you didn't notice it because it had no leaves."

"Do you think so? it may be true; and the garden too seems to me a hundred times lovelier than when we first came to see the house."

"For the very same reason."

"It certainly does make a great difference! What a pity it is, when you live in the country, that it isn't summer all the time!"

"If it were, we shouldn't have the pleasure of seeing the leaves grow, of seeing all nature come to life anew. Believe me, my dear girl, God has done well everything that He has done, and we are ungrateful when we murmur against the order He has established."

Père Ledrux came twice a week to look after the garden; that was quite as often as was necessary to keep the paths clean and to care for a small kitchen garden;

as for the flowers, Agathe had taken it upon herself to
tend them, and she did it very well, although the gardener
declared that she knew nothing about it.

In short, the two women were enchanted with their
new life; ennui had not once made its way into their
abode, for they always found something to do which
occupied their time; as a general rule, ennui visits only
the slothful.

One morning, when Père Ledrux came to work at
Madame Dalmont's, the peasant, after watching the hens
for a long time, as usual, to see if they did not fight—
their failure to do so always seemed to surprise him—
went into the house, bowed to Honorine, who was breakfasting with Agathe, and said to her:

"I say, pardon, excuse me if I tell you this; but it's
only so that you may know it, and then you can do as
you choose; it's none of my business; I just came to tell
you because sometimes folks are glad to know what
other folks say about 'em."

"What's that, Père Ledrux? do you mean that people are talking about us?" said Honorine, who, no less
than her friend, had felt strongly inclined to laugh at
the gardener's long preamble.

"Bless me! that they are! You can see for yourself,
it's no more'n natural; in a little place like this the
folks as is rich don't have anything else to do but ask
what the other folks do. So then, you and your friend,
when you came here to Chelles to live, you bought Monsieur Courtivaux's house, and you paid cash for it. Now,

you understand, new people—fine ladies from Paris coming here to live—why that's a big event in the neighborhood."

"Very good, Père Ledrux; we are an event, I understand that. What next?"

"Why, they says like this at Madame Droguet's: 'Let's see if they come to call on us, these newcomers.'—Excuse me, but as you ain't been here long, they call you the newcomers."

"That doesn't offend us at all. Go on."

"Monsieur Droguet says: 'They're young women, they must dance; we must invite 'em to come here.'—But it seems that Madame Droguet answered: 'We'll invite 'em, if they come to call first; because the latest arrivals ought to make the first call on the people who live in a town, and it ain't for us to begin by going to see them.'"

"That is true; Madame Droguet is quite right."

"Then there's Monsieur le Docteur Antoine Beaubichon, who says: 'I have the pleasure of knowing these ladies already, and they're very agreeable. As a bachelor and as a medical man I mean to go to call on 'em very soon. I'll let them get settled; we mustn't be in too much of a hurry.'—And after that Monsieur Luminot, he says: 'I'm a widower, and I'm going to call on these ladies; they say they're pretty, and I like pretty women.' —Then there's the Jarnouillards, and they says: 'But we must find out first if they're rich, and what their money's in.'—I tell you all this just as they said it, you understand."

"Yes, Père Ledrux, and there's no harm in it. Is that all?"

"No; for, you see, as you've been in Chelles more'n two weeks, and you haven't called on anyone yet, and nobody ever meets you anywhere, because you don't go to walk—why, folks are beginning to say:

"'Those ladies must be female bears; they don't go to see anybody! they don't go out! They're good mates for the owner of the Tower; all they need is a dog!'— That's what folks say, and I only repeat it so that you may know it; because it's none of my business, after all."

"Thanks, Père Ledrux; I am not sorry to know what people say about us. It is at Madame Droguet's, I presume, that public opinion is formed?"

"It must be there! That's where all the bigwigs meet."

"I admit that the conjectures of the 'bigwigs' will have very little influence on our mode of life. We care little for society, but we are not desirous either to be looked upon as bears; and Agathe is old enough not to avoid society. When the opportunity presents itself to make Madame Droguet's acquaintance, we shall not let it pass; but there is no hurry, is there, Agathe?"

"Oh, no! my dear; and so far as I am concerned, when we have time to walk, it will be much more agreeable to go in the direction of the Tower, than to that lady's house who hides in the bushes to spy upon people. The acquaintance of that beautiful dog, who manifested such a liking for me, is the acquaintance I am most anxious to cultivate."

During the day which followed this conversation, Poucette came to Honorine to say that Monsieur Luminot desired to pay his respects, as one of her neighbors.

" Show Monsieur Luminot in," said Honorine.

" Neighborliness is about to commence," murmured Agathe; " I have an idea that this man is a bore! "

" My dear girl, we are not in the world solely to enjoy ourselves; we need no other proof than all the trials that are imposed on us."

Monsieur Luminot, former wine merchant, was a tall, stout man, with a red face; an excellent type of those rustic buffoons, who deem themselves very clever because they make a great deal of noise wherever they are, and are always the first to laugh at what they themselves say; a device which very rarely fails to arouse the laughter of those who listen, especially as those who listen to such fellows are generally entitled to be numbered among Panurge's sheep.

Monsieur Luminot had arrayed himself in a white cravat, and a dress coat in which he was almost as constrained as Chamoureau in his new trousers; in the country a dress coat is but rarely donned; it is kept in reserve for grand and ceremonious assemblages, so that it serves for a long while. Monsieur Luminot had possessed his for four years, and it was still quite presentable. During that time, however, its owner had considerably increased his bulk, so that the coat, which had originally fitted him very well, had become much too small; nevertheless, he persisted in wearing it.

"I must wear it out," he would say; "it's very good still. I can't have another coat made while this looks like a new one."

"Good-morning, mesdames, how do you do? Allow me to congratulate myself on the pleasure of making your acquaintance."

"Pray be seated, monsieur," said Honorine, offering a chair to her visitor, who entered the room with a radiant expression and approached her as if he proposed to begin by embracing her.

"With pleasure, *belle dame;* I don't like to remain standing, one has enough of that in the street. Ha! ha! ha! that is a *mot!* you will excuse me, I know; I make many *mots!* I am an inveterate joker. Ha! ha! ha! As the ballad says: 'We must laugh, we must drink to hospitality.'—I believe it's in *Le Déserteur,* but I am not quite sure."

"Does monsieur live in the neighborhood?"

"Yes, *belle dame,* within two steps—two and a bit.— Luminot, proprietor of vineyards. Always in the vines. Ha! ha! ha! Pray don't think that I am always tipsy though; it's another *mot!* In Paris I sold wines at wholesale—excuse this *detail.** Ha! ha! Well, how do you like our countryside, *belle dame?* I say *belle dame,* because I presume that this is your daughter—*demoiselle.*"

"Ah! it would be funny if I were her daughter!" exclaimed Agathe; "in that case I should have a mother only ten years older than I!"

---

* In French, *détail* means *retail* as well as *detail.*

"Oh! a thousand pardons! I am a reckless fellow," rejoined the former wine merchant; "I made a mistake; I had not looked carefully at mademoiselle; I see now that you are her aunt."

"You are not a sorcerer to-day, monsieur, you do not guess right. Agathe is simply my friend; but I love her like a daughter and a sister at once."

"Very good, I understand; she's your cousin *à la mode de Bretagne.*—We are both happy and proud to have in our village two roses from the Capital—I might say a rose and a bud. Ha! ha! you catch my thought? Still another *mot!* What the devil can you expect; when one has sold spirits, one must retain a little; I didn't sell everything, and it was not in vain that I was in wines.* Ha! ha! ha! I beg your pardon; I can't help it.—Oh! oh! oh!"

The portly buffoon, amazed that the ladies did not laugh also, grew calmer, and tried to be more sedate.

"You ladies have not told me whether you are pleased with this region."

"We were waiting until you had ceased laughing, monsieur.—Yes, this region pleases us exceedingly, and the surrounding country seemed lovely to us."

"Have you seen our promenade, the Poncelet?"

"No, monsieur; is it in the village?"

"It's on the square; a charming, delightful promenade; you would think that you were on the Champs-Elysées in Paris, barring the size."

---

* Ce n'est pas en *vain* que j'étais dans le *vin.*

"We haven't seen it yet."

"I venture to think that the society here will please .you also. We have a little nucleus* of agreeable and clever people—not large, but large enough; you shall be one of us, you shall be our almond—Ha! ha!—but not bitter.—Ha! ha! ha!—joker that I am; I am the life of the whole neighborhood.—We generally meet at Madame Droguet's—a good house, well kept up; they live very well indeed; we play cards, and sometimes dance; Droguet is mad over dancing. I myself used to be rather a fine dancer once. I could do my little *entrechat*—in the good old way, I assure you! But I've put on a good deal of flesh, so that I am not so light of foot as I was. However, I can still hold my own in a quadrille! You ladies should be fond of dancing?"

"Not I, monsieur; but Agathe is very fond of it."

"In that case, madame, you will play cards with Madame Droguet. Do you know bézique?"

"No, monsieur."

"Why, you surprise me! that refined, intellectual game, which has caused a revolution in Paris!"

"I do not care for cards, monsieur."

"Then you can talk with Madame Jarnouillard, a woman of much intellect—although it doesn't appear. We also have Madame Remplumé, her husband and her daughter—very *comme il faut* people! Mademoiselle is very good-looking, although slightly humpbacked; but

---

* *Noyau*, meaning also *stone*—of a peach or nut.

when she is facing you, it is less apparent; still it has
kept her from being married; men don't take to the
hump! Ha! ha!'"

After a moment or two, Monsieur Luminot, discom-
fited to find that he was laughing all by himself and that
his jests did not make the ladies gasp with merriment,
rose to go, saying:

"Pardon me, ladies, for disturbing you in your household duties; I do not desire to intrude. I leave you,
hoping that you will permit me to cultivate your delectable
acquaintance."

"Whenever it is agreeable to you, monsieur," said
Honorine, rising to show her visitor to the door.

"Those women are very good-looking," he said to himself as he went away, "but they don't seem to be very
cheerful."

"Mon Dieu! what a foolish man!" cried Agathe,
when Monsieur Luminot had gone. "If that's a fair
specimen of the society of the place, we shall do well to
deprive ourselves of it."

"My dear girl, we must not be too severe; everything
is relative. It may be that this gentleman is very agreeable in the circle that he frequents; we are not yet accustomed to his language, but perhaps we shall end by
laughing at it with the rest."

"Let us hope that we shall never reach that point."

"However, I am fully persuaded that he did not
consider us agreeable, because we failed to laugh at what
he said."

Not five minutes after the former dealer in wines had taken his leave, Poucette announced that Monsieur Jarnouillard desired to know if he could see the ladies.

"This is our day for callers," said Honorine; "let us see Monsieur Jarnouillard; he is married, and he comes first, which surprises me; he must be anxious to know us.—Show the gentleman in."

The newcomer was a man of some fifty years, very thin, very ugly, and very slovenly in his dress, although it was plain that he had tried to make himself clean for his visit to his neighbors. He wore a cravat that was almost white, and a shirt collar almost black; a long *redingote,* which fell to his heels, and might at need be used as a dressing-gown; shoes half blacked; and a broad-brimmed straw hat like those worn by women who work in the fields.

Monsieur Jarnouillard had a long, pointed nose, a square, protruding chin, prominent cheek-bones, tawny, furtive eyes, thin, compressed lips and an earth-colored complexion, like one who deems any sort of ablution superfluous.

All this formed an ensemble which did not prepossess one in his favor.

He bowed almost to the floor as he entered the room, as if he were executing a Turkish salaam. But even while he saluted the two young women before him, his eyes found time to make the circuit of the room in which they received him, to scrutinize each article of furniture, and perhaps to estimate its value.

" Mesdames, pray permit me to pay my respects," said
Monsieur Jarnouillard in a clear, metallic voice, pro-
nouncing every syllable distinctly. " Jarnouillard, land-
owner and annuitant; it is several years since I retired
from business and came to this place to live, with my
wife. She will come to pay her respects to you; she
did not come with me to-day because we have a stew
for dinner and she had to stay at home to watch it; we
have no servant, my wife does everything; it amuses her
and distracts her thoughts. I have asked her several
times: ' Do you want a maid? if so, take one.'—But she
replies: ' Indeed I will not! to have everything stolen! '
—It is true that servants are a vile lot; one is very
lucky when one can do without them."

" Since it suits yourself and your wife, monsieur, you
are very sensible to adopt that course; one should always
follow one's own tastes, and not worry about what people may say."

" You are perfectly right, madame, you speak very
wisely. I think that you will like this neighborhood, although there are very few people to associate with."

" We did not come here for the society, monsieur."

" You have bought this house of Courtivaux's, it isn't
large, but it's large enough if there are only you two."

" And one servant, monsieur; we are not afraid of
being robbed, you see."

" Everyone must do as he or she pleases. You have
taken into your service that tall Poucette girl, niece of
Guillot the farmer; poor people—very destitute! "

"An additional reason, monsieur, why we should be happy because we are able to employ someone belonging to them."

"Yes, when they know how to serve; but I doubt very much whether that tall girl knows how to do anything; where can she have learned?"

"She will learn with us, monsieur, and I congratulate myself every day on having taken her into my service, for she is exceedingly zealous, willing and intelligent."

Monsieur Jarnouillard simply bowed, while he inspected once more everything within his range of vision. Then he resumed:

"Madame is a widow?"

"Yes, monsieur."

"Without children?"

"Alas! yes, monsieur! I had a son, but I lost him!"

"The old fool!" muttered Agathe; "to revive my dear love's sorrow with his questions! What an inquisitive man!"

"We haven't any children either, my wife and I, and we congratulate ourselves on it every day! it's just so much less turmoil and trouble!"

"And I, monsieur, do not pass a day without regretting the son whom I lost; to my mind, it is so much less of happiness and of the purest love!"

Monsieur Jarnouillard bowed again; then he continued:

"You didn't pay a high price for this house—that is, if you bought it for fifteen thousand francs cash, as I understand."

"Twenty thousand, monsieur, and I do not consider it dear."

"Pardon me—the garden is small, and it yields nothing; you haven't enough rooms to let——"

"It has never been my intention, monsieur, to try to let rooms to strangers. My house is quite large enough for my friend and myself, and that is enough."

"Oh! that makes a difference. You have furnished it very nicely; it was furnished already, but you have added various things; this couch was Monsieur Courtivaux's, but that étagère wasn't here, or these easy-chairs —Oh, yes! they did belong to Monsieur Courtivaux, but those two pictures weren't his."

"I should say, monsieur, that you had taken an inventory of the property. You must know how many trees there are in the garden?"

"Not exactly, but very nearly; and wretched trees, too—worth nothing! oh! miserable trees!"

"Monsieur doesn't know much about trees, I judge," exclaimed Agathe angrily. "We have the finest lindens it is possible to imagine!"

"Oh! excuse me, mademoiselle, but I consider no trees good that do not bear good fruit and in large quantity. The linden bears nothing—oh, yes! they do make an infusion of the leaves, but you can buy a great quantity for two sous! As a general rule, the land hereabout is poor; it's very stony."

"That being so, why did you come here to live, monsieur?"

"Oh! as a matter of business, you know. I still do a little something. When I can accommodate people, I never refuse, although it's very dangerous, they are all so tricky!—There's a piano which certainly was not here in Monsieur Courtivaux's time. Are you ladies fond of music?"

"Very, monsieur."

"It's very nice for people who have nothing to do. My wife used to play the guitar a little, but I put a stop to it; she broke too many strings; and then, when a woman wants to look after her housekeeping, she must give up music. I said to her: 'My dear love, you must choose: if you keep on playing the guitar, your dishes will be badly washed.'—She realized the force of that reasoning, and the instrument was sold."

"That does credit to your good wife, monsieur, but everybody hasn't so pronounced a fondness for washing dishes; my friend and I are not conscious of a vocation for that—are we, Agathe?"

The pretty blonde smiled at her friend, and Monsieur Jarnouillard regarded Agathe for some moments.

"Is mademoiselle related to you?"

"No, monsieur, she is my friend."

"Ah! I see—her parents placed her in your care?"

The two ladies, who were beginning to be annoyed by their visitor's questions, thought fit not to answer; but their silence did not deter him.

"Is mademoiselle an orphan?—I beg pardon, I ask that because, as a general rule, it is well to be informed.

For example, mademoiselle is naturally in the matrimonial market; well, when one knows the antecedents, the social position, the means, one may be able to propose a suitable match, and——"

"If I ever marry, monsieur," said Agathe, "it will be according to my own taste, and not by the interposition of strangers."

"We can't tell, mademoiselle, there's no knowing. I have arranged several marriages; they didn't turn out well, it is true, but one can never answer for results.—Really, you are very comfortable here, it is quite elegant. Let us see the other rooms."

And the gentleman rose and was about to walk into an adjoining room; but Honorine closed the door, observing somewhat curtly:

"Pardon me, monsieur, but that room is not arranged yet, and no one can go in."

"Oh! that makes a difference; some other time then. I must go home, for I am afraid my wife has forgotten to skim her stew."

"That would be surprising on the part of a person who washes dishes so well."

"Mesdames, I renew my compliments; enchanted to have made your acquaintance. My wife will come to see you soon; we do not often entertain, because our house is very small, but we are pleased to accept invitations. We are not ceremonious people, who keep a strict account of calls, like Madame Droguet for example; she is terrible for that! We do not insist at all that people shall come to see us, but when we are invited to dinner, we can be relied upon to come.—Mesdames, I have the honor."

Honorine escorted the visitor to the door, and bowed, but did not utter a word. As soon as he had disappeared, Agathe cried:

"Oh! what a horrid man! so inquisitive and presuming! He has a bad word for everything."

"You see, Agathe, that, as compared with Monsieur Jarnouillard, we are driven to regret Monsieur Luminot!"

"That is so; he may be a fool, but he hasn't such a nasty, sneering way. Mon Dieu! if Madame Jarnouillard is like her husband, she must be perfectly ghastly!"

"There was no need of his being so emphatic about not insisting that people should call on him; he need have no fear—we shall never set foot inside his door."

A quarter of an hour after Monsieur Jarnouillard's departure, Poucette appeared once more, with a smile on her face, saying:

"Now it's Monsieur le Docteur Antoine Beaubichon, who asks permission to salute the ladies."

"Evidently they have passed the word along," said Honorine; "but this time, at all events, we know whom we have to deal with; show in monsieur le docteur."

XXV

THE LOST CHILD

The short, stout, puffy little man, who gasped for breath when he had climbed a flight of stairs or walked a little faster than usual, appeared in his turn, and saluted the two ladies as old acquaintances.

"It is I, madame, come to pay my respects—that is to say, if I don't disturb you; if my presence at this moment is inopportune, pray tell me, and I will go at once."

"No, monsieur le docteur, your presence is not inopportune; on the contrary, we hope that it will make up to us in some measure for the visit we have just received."

"Ah! have you had visitors from Paris?"

"Not from Paris, but from the neighborhood: first, Monsieur Luminot; he seemed to us to be very jovial, although his jests are not always in the best taste; but after him there came a certain Monsieur Jarnouillard. —Really, we could very well have done without his visit! Everything about the man is disagreeable,—his face, his dress, his language; and his curiosity is beyond words!"

"Oh! as to that, mesdames, it's a common failing in small places; there are few people here, and everyone wants to know what his neighbor is doing. I won't deny that I myself am reasonably curious; it's a disease that

grows on one here.—Well, here you are among us; are
you still satisfied with your purchase?"

"More than ever, doctor; and our house pleases us
so much that we never leave it."

"Haven't you seen our square yet, the Poncelet promenade?"

"No, but it seems that it is very pretty, for we have
already heard of it."

"Why, yes; it's a square worthy of a large city.—
And then you mustn't judge our society by Monsieur
Jarnouillard; we have some very pleasant people—large
landowners; to be sure, they stay at home and rarely
come to our houses.—Have you been to walk in the direction of the Tower yet?"

"Not yet; but we already know the owner of the place,
doctor."

"Really? you know him?"

"That is to say, we met him and his dog on the bank
of the Marne, on our way to Poucette's uncle's field."

"Well, what do you think of the man? Hasn't he
something savage in his expression?"

"Why, no; he has the look of a man who doesn't
care for society, and who doesn't shave; but, as he
walked by very rapidly, I couldn't examine him closely."

"But I," said Agathe, "won the heart of his beautiful dog. He looked at me and caressed me. His master
had to call him, to induce him to leave me."

"You astonish me, for he's a rascal who seldom caresses strangers. However, I must admit that this Ami—

that is his name, you know—is really endowed with extraordinary intelligence. Only three days ago he saved a
child who was drowning."

"Oh! the good dog! how grateful the child's parents
must be to him!"

"Parents?—the little fellow who was drowning hasn't
any; it was the lost child."

"The lost child! Mon Dieu! what does that mean?"

"The peasants have given that name to the little fellow, because no one, not even his nurse, knows to whom
he belongs. It's a mysterious story."

"Tell us about it, doctor; you always have interesting
things to tell, and we enjoy them ever so much."

"You see—the local disease, curiosity, is taking hold
of you!"

"That's very possible; but tell us about the lost child."

"First of all, I must tell you, mesdames, that about
four years ago the widow Tourniquoi won a prize in a
lottery. I don't know just what lottery it was, but that
makes no difference to our story—the important point is
that the widow Tourniquoi, who was not rich, and who
had two children to bring up, won, I believe, about twenty
thousand francs. To a peasant that is a large fortune!
Thereupon this woman, who has an excellent heart,
wrote to a sister of hers at Morfontaine, near Ermenon-
ville; this sister was a widow also, and was not fortunate; so Madame Tourniquoi wrote to her to come to
her; to leave Morfontaine, where she had no regular
work, and come to live with her.

" Naturally the poor sister asked nothing better than to join her sister who was wealthy, or, at least, in comfortable circumstances. So she arrived at Chelles one fine day with a little boy about three years and a half old.

" ' Hallo! ' said Madame Tourniquoi to Jacqueline—that is her sister's name—' I thought you didn't have any children, that you lost your only one when he was only a year old. But never mind, you and your son are welcome.'

" ' This little fellow isn't mine,' replied Jacqueline, ' it's a foster-child that was placed in my charge, and left on my hands. I'll tell you how it happened. I was nursing my boy, who was four months old, and as we weren't rich, I said to my husband, who was alive then: " I'm going to Paris, to enter my name at the nurses' bureau, and then I'll wait for a child to nurse."—He agreed, so I started for Paris. When I got there, I asked a lady who was passing, what way I should go to get to the nurses' bureau. The lady, who was dressed very simply, examined me for some time, then she says:

" ' " You mean to go to the nurses' bureau and enter your name and get a child to nurse? "

" ' " Yes, madame," I says, " I've come to Paris just for that."

" ' " Where do you come from? "

" ' " I live at Morfontaine, ten leagues from Paris."

" ' " Well! your lucky star put you in my path, for if you are looking for a child to nurse, I am looking for a nurse—for a very rich lady who lay in three days ago

of a fine little boy who's as good as a charm. She
meant at first to bring him up on the bottle, but she's
changed her mind, and I'll take you to her; so you
don't need to enter your name at the nurses' bureau,
which is very lucky for you, because in this way you'll
save a lot of expenses."

" ' I listened to the lady with joy in my heart; I was
delighted to find what I wanted just as soon as I got
out of the stage, and I was glad, too, to get the child of
a rich person, because they always pay better. So I told
the lady that I asked nothing better than to go with her;
then she took me to a big square where there was lots
of carriages, told me to get into one of them with her,
said something quietly to the driver, and we started.

" ' I don't know anything about Paris, and I don't know
where they took me. At last the carriage stopped; we
were in a narrow, dirty street, and I says to myself: " It's
a funny thing that rich people in Paris should live in
such nasty streets ! " But the lady says to me:

" ' " We're going in at the rear of the house, because
the noise of the carriage can't be heard so distinctly and
it don't bother madame la baronne so much."

" ' " Good," says I to myself, " the child's mother's a
baroness—that's fine."

" ' We went into a house, not a very handsome one,
and up a dark staircase; then my companion took me
into quite a handsome, well-furnished room. She told
me to sit down and left me, to find out whether her
baroness was ready to see me.

" ' I waited quite a long time; at last she came back after me and took me into another room, where I saw a handsome lady stretched on a beautiful couch with a pile of cushions under her. Oh! she was terrible pretty, that lady was! she was dark, and her long black hair was combed smooth and fell over her shoulders on both sides. And her eyes! oh! what eyes! they were big and black, and I never saw such bright eyes, but they weren't soft. By the lady's side, in a dainty little cradle, was the little three days old boy; he was strong and healthy, I tell you, although he'd never had anything but the bottle. But when I offered him the breast at a sign from his mother—my word! you should have seen how the little rascal bit at it!

" ' While the child was nursing, the handsome lady seemed to be doing a lot of thinking. At last she says to me:

" ' " I see that this child will be in good hands with you, and I place him in your care. How much do you want a month?"

" ' I made bold to ask for thirty francs; I didn't expect to get it, but the lady agreed right off; she took a purse from under a cushion and took out a hundred and fifty francs in gold, and gave it to me.

" ' " Here," she says, " here's five months in advance, and a supply of clothes which you are to take away with the child and the cradle. You will go back at once; the cab that brought you here is waiting below, and will take you to the stage office. I want you to leave Paris

at once, because the air is bad here, and my child's health
will suffer if he's kept here any longer."

" ' I asked nothing better than to go right home, so I
says:

" ' " Yes, madame, I'll take the child and go; but first
tell me the little one's name."

" ' " Emile."

" ' " And madame's name?—for I must know that,
so that I can let her know how her son gets along."

" ' The lady frowned, then replied:

" ' " I am the Baronne de Mortagne. Here is my address on this paper; take it."

" ' I took the paper and put it away carefully in my
pocket; then I says:

" ' " Now, if madame la baronne wants to write down
my address, I'll give it to her."

" ' The lady took a little book from a table—there was
white paper and a pencil in it—and wrote down my name
and address in full: Jacqueline Treillard, wife of Pierre
Treillard, day laborer, Morfontaine. Then they gave me
a good glass of wine and a cake, and when I had eaten,
the person who had brought me there took the bundle of
clothes and says:

" ' " Now take the cradle with the child in it, and let's
be off; I'll go to the stage office with you."

" ' Before I took the child away, I lifted him in
my arms and offered him to his mother, because I supposed she'd want to kiss him, and that she'd cry when
it came to parting with him; but the beautiful lady

didn't seem to feel it much; she just barely put her lips to the child's forehead, then handed him right back to me, saying:

" ' " Take him away, and above all things don't amuse yourself by bringing him to Paris to show him to me; I don't like to have children carried round the country. I shall come to see you when I am able; here's twenty francs more for your journey."

" ' " Faith! " thinks I to myself, " if this lady isn't very fond of children, I can't deny that she's mighty generous."

" ' I got into the cab again with the lady who carried the bundle; we got safely to the stage office; I engaged a seat for four o'clock; and my companion was kind enough to keep me company; she didn't leave me till she saw me on board the stage that took me back to Morfontaine.

" ' Well, when I got home, you can imagine my man Pierre's surprise to see me back so soon. When he learned what had happened, he was as pleased as I was. Bless me! a hundred and fifty francs in advance, and twenty francs for the journey that cost just seven francs ten sous! That was a windfall! I looked at the address they'd given me; but as I don't know how to read very well, I couldn't make it out, it was written so small. Pierre could read even less than I could; so I showed it to the schoolmaster. It said:

" ' " Madame la Baronne de Mortagne, at her hôtel, Rue de Grenelle, Faubourg Saint-Germain."

" ' " The deuce ! " I says to myself ; " it seems that I've been in Faubourg Saint-Germain ! " '

" ' Well, there was the child in our family, and he grew like a mushroom. Two months passed by, and I didn't hear anything from his mother.

" ' " She doesn't have time to come," I says to myself ; " I must let her know how her boy's coming on."

" ' I had monsieur the schoolmaster write a letter, and I put it in the post, but I didn't get a word in reply. My man and I agreed that the lady knew her child was well, and that was enough for her ; apparently she didn't have time to come to see him.

" ' Two months more passed, and I sent another letter —no answer any more than to the first. Then I says to myself : " There's a mother that don't show much affection for her son ! but when the five months are almost gone, she'll have to let us hear from her when she sends me my money. Perhaps she'll come and bring it with her ; yes, that's probably what she's waiting for."

" ' But the fifth month passed and no one came, and she didn't send any money. I had a third letter written, in which I asked for money. I didn't get any answer any more than to the other two, and it began to look queer to us. But about that time I lost my poor husband, and then, a month after, I lost my son ! All the misfortunes fell on me at once, and I forgot all about little Emile's mother.

" ' At last, when my grief began to get calmed down a little, I says to myself : " That lady must be sick, that

I don't hear from her. I think I'll go to her house in Paris with her son; it's eight months now that I've had him; she owes me for three months and I need the money; besides she'll see that her son's in good health."

" ' I got the schoolmaster to read me the address again.; then I put it in my pocket and started. When I got to Paris, I inquired the way to Rue de Grenelle, Faubourg Saint-Germain; someone showed me the way and I found the street. It was a fine, broad street, not at all like the one I went to before, when they took me to my foster-child's mother. But I remembered being told that we went in at the rear of the house, and I says to myself: ".This must be the front this time, for sure."

" ' I asked for the Baronne de Mortagne's house, and the answer I got was: " I don't know her." I went farther along; the same answer. I kept on and on—and it's a terrible long street—but no one knew the Baronne de Mortagne; and I had gone the whole length of the street, asking on both sides. Then I asked for the street that ran at the rear of the houses, thinking that I might perhaps find my way better there; but they laughed in my face and told me that the houses didn't have any rear.

" ' Well! I understood then, my dear sister, that I had been taken in by a bad mother who just wanted to get rid of her baby, and to fix things so that she'd never hear of him again. I might have gone and told my story to the magistrate, who'd have ordered the child taken to La Pitié; but I didn't want to, I was attached to little Emile, and, poor as I was I kept him. Besides, I thought that perhaps his mother would regret it some day and come to look for her son. But it's nearly four years now that I've had the child, and in all that time I've never heard a word from the so-called baroness, who had such big black eyes. As for the boy, here he is; he's got a pretty face and eyes almost as black as his mother's; but when you come to his disposition, well! I can't say he's a very good boy; he's wilful and obstinate, and a little liar, and it's his great delight to torment other children. But he's so young! with time, that will take care of itself.'

"That, mesdames, is the story that Jacqueline told her sister, the widow Tourniquoi; I have tried to tell it to you just as she told it. You know now why little Emile is called hereabout the lost child, for of course the worthy nurse had no reason to make a mystery of the affair; and it was not long before everybody knew that the little fellow she brought with her had been abandoned by his mother, and that no one knew who his parents were."

"Thanks a thousand times for your good-nature, monsieur le docteur. And this Jacqueline, the excellent woman who took care of the child, is she still living?"

"Yes, she isn't very old; she still lives with her sister, the widow Tourniquoi. As for the little boy, who is nearly eight years old, I suppose, he shows himself far from worthy of what she has done for him; he is quite the worst little rapscallion in the neighborhood. His pleasure consists in doing mischief: if windows are broken, fruit stolen, branches broken from trees, animals hurt by stones thrown at them, you may be certain before-hand that little Emile is the one who has done it. So that he is not loved hereabout, except by poor Jacqueline, who always tries to excuse her foster-son's misdeeds by saying that time will take care of it. And time is taking care of it, but not as she means to be understood : it is grow-ing worse instead of better."

LIST OF ILLUSTRATIONS

PAUL AND HIS DOG

VOLUME I